DIVISION

DIVISION

THE PROPHECIES OF EAVDAMOS
BOOK ONE

BROOKE LESNIAK

Paperback ISBN: 979-8-9916239-0-2

Ebook ISBN: 979-8-9916239-1-9

*To Mama, for always believing I could accomplish my dreams,
though you never got to see them flourish.*

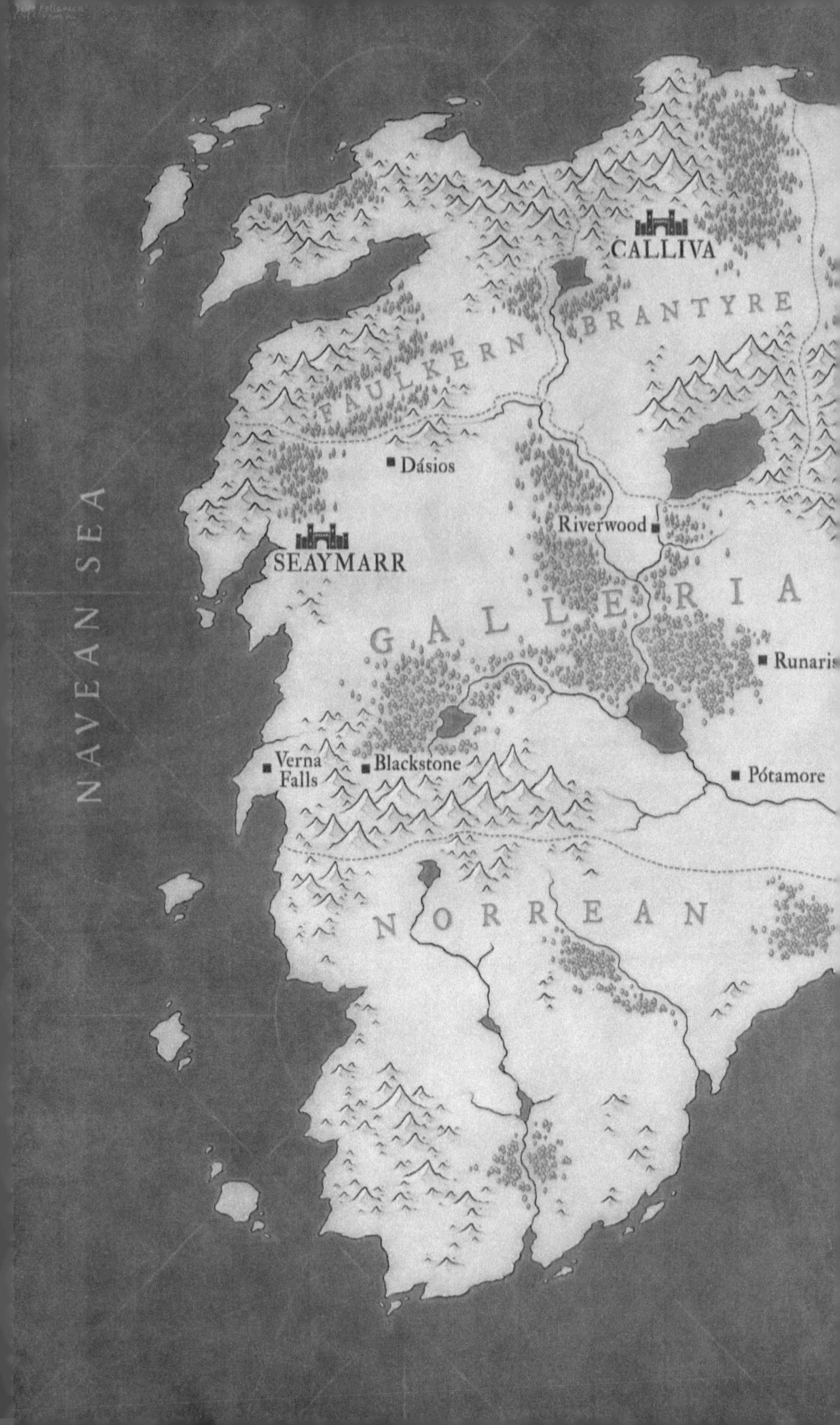

NAVEAN SEA
CALLIVA
FAULKERN
BRANTYRE
Dásios
Riverwood
SEAYMARR
GALLERIA
Runaris
Verna Falls
Blackstone
Pótamore
NORREAN

PÁGOUS SEA
ANITAL SEA
KOVDORAN
ISDELLE
Lividia
Tourrenfield
South King's Road
Elmdale
ESRAIA
Mésis
TALBANE
Ekrewell
EISRAEVA SEA

CHAPTER I
RYKER

The clash of steel shattered the silence in the hour before dawn. Across Mésis City, a light dusting of snow remained as winter slowly lost its hold, surrendering to the warmer breeze brought in from the Southern Ocean. The God of Nature stirred in anticipation of the warmer months while trees and bushes bloomed for spring.

Yet an icy chill lingered in the early morning hours. Sweat beaded Ryker's brow and slid down his back, his haggard breaths fogging before him. His heart thundered in his chest as he circled the barracks training field until his opponent's back was to the outer wall. Adjusting the sword in his sweaty palms, Ryker lunged again, and another clash of steel tore through the air.

"What was that?" demanded Ryker.

"A block," Keanon replied, smirking.

"It was the sloppiest swordsmanship I've ever seen."

"It worked, didn't it?"

Ryker shook his head, unable to suppress his laugh at the mirth in his sparring partner's eyes. "How are you ever going to survive out there without me?"

"With my better looks and charm."

Ryker sighed as he assessed Keanon. It was like looking in a mirror, their reflections one and the same: tall, broad-shouldered, with a head of dark wavy hair. They both possessed the square jaw and angled nose of their father, yet their dark brown eyes were distinctly their mother's. The only difference was Ryker kept his wavy bangs, his hair ending at the nape of his neck, while Keanon wore it thicker and to his shoulders.

Keanon, his brother. His twin. Born minutes apart, the pair were as inseparable as they were identical.

Ryker refocused and charged toward his brother with another string of blows, who deflected and parried. They continued circling the dusty field, with no one else awake to watch them spar. Every time their swords clashed, the force sent tremors rippling down Ryker's arms. The dull training sword was heftier than his own and grew heavier as their heated battle progressed.

Keanon lowered his sword, too, his steps slowing. Careful to contain his excitement, Ryker calculated his brother's next move. As predicted when Ryker attacked, Keanon performed an easy parry, which Ryker followed with the last of his strength, quickening his swings as he pushed his brother back with each strike.

Keanon stumbled; Ryker swung. It should have been the finishing blow, but at the last second, he noticed his brother's cheeky grin. Too late to stop, Ryker swung high. Keanon ducked and charged forward, using his shoulder to plow into Ryker's stomach and send him to the ground. The sword flew from Ryker's hand but before he could move to retrieve it, Keanon's sword was at his chest, pinning him in place.

"You need to step up your game there, *Captain*."

Despite the defeat, a grin stretched across Ryker's face upon hearing his new title. "Next time will be different," he promised, taking Keanon's proffered hand. Ryker dusted himself off as his brother retrieved his weapon for him. The brothers returned the swords to the weapons rack and left the training yard as the barracks awakened.

The gate's chains creaked and rattled as the doors to the city opened. Carriers flew through the opened doors toward the general's sleeping quarters, each one with a rolled-up parchment curled in its claw. One rushed past Ryker, close enough for him to note its rich navy feathers and the silvery spots across its beak—a bird from the royal court in Talbane. It had traveled a long distance, all the way from the eastern edge near the Anital Sea. It flew straight through the window to the general's quarters while all the others flew into the carrier cage beside the general's building to deposit their letters and receive food before heading back to where they came.

The blacksmiths were situated well behind the carriers' cage so as not to bother the birds with their smoke. Most soldiers poured out of the sleeping quarters at the far-left corner of the barracks and made straight for the dining hall. Ryker moved to join them when Keanon grabbed his arm, stopping him.

"Before we eat, I have something to show you in the stables."

The delicious aromas of roasting ham and freshly baked bread wafted from the dining hall, beckoning them, and after strenuous sparring, Ryker's stomach growled, protesting the delay. Keanon smirked, and Ryker shoved him.

"Fine, but make it quick."

He followed Keanon toward the stables across the way from the training field and dining hall. His brother stood tall as he moved, his face locked straight ahead. Ryker narrowed his eyes.

"What are you hiding?"

His brother ignored the question as they stepped inside. Over the past few days, Keanon had been acting off—grinning and teasing Ryker more often than usual. Ever since Ryker had been promoted to captain, it seemed Keanon was determined to ensure the title didn't go to his head.

With a shake of his head, Ryker followed, greeted with the smell of fresh hay, grain, and manure. While it was not entirely unpleasant, it did not compare to the scent of breakfast being served across the way. They passed the stalls mostly filled with horses, yet a few contained eldeer who shifted around as they awoke for their morning meals. Eldeer were graceful, taller, and slimmer than horses, commonly found in brown or black. White ones, however, were exceptionally rare. He'd only ever seen pictures of them in books. While both males and females had antlers, the females' were much larger, protruding to the sides with a subtle curve. Ryker had contemplated getting one for himself, but they were expensive, and though he'd been saving, he'd held off on making the purchase. Maybe with his recent promotion, he could consider it.

They weaved past young stable boys and girls, who ran around them with buckets of food and water. Guiding the young ones were three older stable hands, offering help when needed. A smaller girl, whom he recalled as the stable head's youngest daughter—maybe seven or eight years of age—stumbled in front of Ryker, spilling water across the stone floor. Ryker bent down and offered her a hand, smiling.

"Here."

Uncertainty brimmed in her big brown eyes as she stared up at him. Tentatively, she took his hand, and he helped her to her feet, handing the water bucket back to her. "You're doing a great job, just try not to fill the bucket so high next time, alright?"

She beamed from the compliment and gave a vigorous nod. "Okay."

Excited, she ran back to fill her bucket more carefully.

Still grinning, Ryker caught up with Keanon, who had stopped at a stall towards the back, leaning nonchalantly on one of the doors. He didn't fool Ryker. Keanon tapped his crossed arm with his finger and kept his face averted.

"What is it I'm here to see?"

No longer able to suppress his grin, Keanon met Ryker's eyes and gestured into the stall. "Look in there."

Ryker's mouth fell open at the beautiful animal inside. It was a female lykos—a magnificent creature resembling the wild wolves in the forests of the south. Her long nose angled up, sniffing the air, and her pointed ears perked upon hearing their voices. The animal's large front paws hid razor-sharp claws—ideal for hunting prey, and her hind legs ended in hooves, like horses or eldeer, filled with solid muscle to aid her sprinting at great speeds. Her fur was golden, except for the black socks that stretched to her knees on all four legs. The end of her bushy tail appeared dipped in black, matching the mask on her face. Dark eyes studied him, like she was gauging what kind of person Ryker was. She tipped her head to the side and tilted her ears, waiting and watching the mysterious people outside her stall.

Lykos were the mounts of seekers, an elite group of soldiers who used these animals to hunt lowlifes and runaways. Their keen sense of smell helped them track a person from miles away. If Ryker hadn't followed in his father's footsteps to become a general, he would have become a seeker just to own such an amazing mount.

"What's a seeker doing in the barracks?" Ryker tore his eyes from the incredible animal, noting the knowing smile on his brother's face.

"There are no seekers here," Keanon said. "But I have a

seeker friend, and his lykos had pups a year ago. I know how much you've talked about wanting one. You don't know how long I've been hiding this secret."

Words escaped Ryker, who opened and closed his mouth, trying to respond. Nothing came out. All coherent thoughts escaped him. The first thing he latched onto was: *she was for him?* Meeting the creature's watchful gaze again, he noted her youth. Ryker assumed she was a year old—the age when lykos were released from their parents and trainers to bond with a rider. Her head tilted the other way as she narrowed her eyes on him. She was young, healthy, and perfect.

"How—" he stammered. "But—"

Keanon laughed at Ryker's pitiful attempt at words but answered his questions as though he'd spoken them. "Soldiers can have lykos too. They must be of high enough rank, which you now are, and they must purchase their own." His brother's laughter faded as he said, "I knew you would make it."

A lump formed in Ryker's throat as he embraced his brother. How Keanon had managed to keep this a secret for a whole year was beyond him, but he supposed it was a testament to the skills Keanon had acquired, becoming one of the greatest spies ever trained. Finally, Ryker managed to speak. "Thank you."

The brothers spent some more time with Ryker's new lykos, who proved to be a bundle of energy. He decided on the name Artis before leaving to grab breakfast before the dining hall cleaned up. As they sat at a lone table—most of the soldiers having filed out for the day or dawdling before training—a young boy, who he recognized as their general's assistant, approached the table.

"General Moreland would like to see you both right away." The youth stood tall and confident, even as he spoke to the two more seasoned soldiers. Freckles sprinkled across his pale face, and his bright blue eyes held onto Ryker's.

Ryker couldn't fight the grin at the young man's assertiveness before soaking in the kid's words. He glanced at his brother over their still steaming, untouched food before they both sprang into action, shoving as much of the potatoes, ham, and greens into their mouths as they could muster. Grabbing a roll each, they left the rest to follow the boy. The barracks were alive with activity as the loud clash of swords resonated from the training field, loud conversation, and shouting blasting from all directions. They followed the boy to where the carriers had flown and now preened along the roof of the captain's quarters —all except the navy, silver-speckled one from the royal court.

Ignoring the birds, the boy politely knocked at the general's door but did not wait for a reply before opening it. Inside, General Moreland sat at his desk, where letters and maps were splayed out before him. Behind him, two large bookshelves covered the entire wall of his study, while specialty weapons lined the adjacent wall. He greeted them as they entered, and though his grin was concealed behind his full face of sandy brown hair, his dark eyes crinkled at the edges as the twins stepped inside.

"Thank you, Leo." He nodded at his young charge, who then retreated out the door. "Boys, come in, take a seat." The general moved around his desk and leaned on the edge as they fell into the two chairs facing him.

"What's going on?" Keanon asked, leaning forward in his seat.

"We have just sent the letters to the other kingdoms, and the emperor suspects King Alystaire will be difficult to sway." Ryker's stomach clenched. He hadn't known what to think when he'd first heard the news that their former king, King Asher, had been blessed by the gods—beyond that of any king before him—to reign over all seven kingdoms of Eavdamos together, with Emperor Asher, the sole ruler. But the gods had spoken, so Ryker would do his best to serve his new Empire with everything he had.

General Moreland crossed his arms and inclined his head toward Keanon. "I have suggested we get ahead of things and send you to Galleria. I believe you will receive instructions from Talbane soon."

Keanon nodded and sat back, his expression set and difficult to read. Ryker could catch what most others could not, such as the subtle downturn to his brother's mouth or the way his finger tapped against his leg. His narrowed eyes focused on something in the distance. This would be Keanon's first huge assignment, sending him away for months.

Ryker glanced away from Keanon when General Moreland addressed him. "You're going to need to push your new troops hard in training. As captain now, you must be sure everyone is prepared for what is to come."

"Of course, Sir."

General Moreland smiled, and despite the seriousness of their conversation, Ryker couldn't deny how he swelled with pride at the general's approval. General Moreland had been close friends with the twins' father for years and had helped train them from the time they were small. Since their father's health began to deteriorate a little over a year ago, General Moreland had taken it upon himself to be there for the brothers, offering comfort and support while pushing them to keep moving forward, as their father would have wanted.

"Do you really believe we will go to war?" Keanon interjected. The general sighed.

"I do."

The men were quiet for a few minutes as they digested the news. War. Even as a trained soldier, the idea filled Ryker with dread. He would lose good men and women, no matter how well he trained them. It would be a rough season ahead.

General Moreland rose and broke the silence. "I have received your request, Keanon, and considering you will be sent away soon, I will allow you two to go and see him today." The general rested a hand on Keanon's shoulder. "This may be your last chance, so make it count."

General Moreland dismissed them, and they wasted no time vacating the barracks. Since Artis would need more time to bond with Ryker before riding, the twins took their horses. The brothers ignored the bustling Mésis marketplace and streets as they made their way out of the city gates. The air was warm, with the telltale signs of spring as the sun beat directly over-head. Outside the gates, the land opened onto wide grassy plains dotted with small farmhouses. Farmers worked outside, planting crops in preparation for the warmer season. Wagons bounced over the uneven road as travelers and farmers jour-neyed in or out of the city. Ryker and Keanon trotted toward the tree line in the distance, smiling at those they passed. When they reached a fork in the road, their horses' steps slowed until they walked side by side, turning off the main road onto a more secluded dirt path into the woods.

"Do you think he is any better?" Keanon broke the tense silence between them.

Melancholy settled on Ryker as they rode past the familiar moss-covered boulders and fallen trees. Woodland critters offered a warm welcome, and the scent of new plant life offered a nostalgic, bitter comfort.

"He didn't wake up at all last time we were here." Ryker fought down the shriveled bit of hope that tried to take root from his brother's question.

"I know." Keanon brushed a hand through his hair and frowned. "General Moreland said these menders were the best the Empire could offer."

"Of course, he sent us the best," Ryker countered. "But that doesn't mean they can perform miracles. They are keeping him from feeling any pain, and for that, I am grateful to them."

"Damn it, Ryker. I know that!" Keanon snapped, yanking his horse to a halt.

Ryker stopped his mount, surprised by his brother's outburst.

Keanon took a steady breath. "Sorry, I just…" He let his words die with a subtle shake of his head.

Ryker placed his hand on Keanon's shoulder, who gave him a half-hearted smile before they continued down the dirt path that slowly turned to gravel as the woods thinned and a quaint two-story home came into view. Ryker's bittersweet emotions swelled at the sight of the shaded front porch with its carved white pillars. A small bench settled under a lone tree in the front yard to the left, the wood worn from use and the elements. Vines budded along the well-crafted stone walls of the home, stretching up the sides and covering two of the first-floor windows.

Tethering their horses to the posts by the front porch, they made their way up the steps and walked through the large, wood-paneled door. Once inside, Ryker felt sucked back in time. As a young boy, he would run through these halls, usually chasing—or being chased—by Keanon. The staff would often admonish them for tracking mud along the carpets or knocking down decorations in their haste. No matter what, their father had the staff's back, just like their mother had in their first home, forcing the boys to clean whatever mess they'd caused. As they grew up, the brothers learned to keep their chaotic energy outside, and after their mother passed and they moved away from Talbane, the boys became more serious in their training and played much less.

A few maids scuttled about to keep the house in order, even though the only occupant wouldn't notice if it went to disarray.

Ryker followed his brother up the creaky wooden staircase and down the hall, their boots clicking on the wooden floors and echoing along the corridor. Growing up, he hadn't noticed the contrast to the home they lived in before when their mother was alive. That one had been adorned with banners, rugs, curtains, flowers—everything that made a house a home. This one was mostly empty. Their father had spent little time decorating, and now it was desolate.

Menders came in and out of the door at the end of the hall, and Ryker's heart squeezed as they drew near. A mender offered a sad smile to the brothers before opening the door for them. Sweat beaded along Ryker's forehead, his throat squeezing as his traitorous heart still clung to a smidge of hope. His hopes were crushed as he stepped inside, a mix of medical herbs and decay pervading the room. He pushed back the bile that rose in his throat. A lone figure lay in the four-poster bed, his slight figure swallowed in the thick mattress. Tears burned as he took the withered man's hand.

The man had the same squared jaw and angled nose as his sons, but had lost most of his once dark hair. His cheeks had hollowed, and his eyes were sunken and shallow. General Leeam Kessler, once tall and strong—a formidable presence, now lay shriveled and skeletal in the bed. A tear slid down Ryker's cheek as he brought his father's pale, wrinkled hand to his lips and kissed it.

Keanon came up beside him and smoothed the covers over their father before sitting in one of the nearby chairs. From his seat, he muttered, "Hi, father." Tears brimmed in his eyes, and he coughed to keep them at bay. "I... uhh..." His voice trailed off again. This time he clamped his jaw shut and lowered his head.

Ryker gently squeezed his father's hand and spoke softly, "I hope you're feeling better today."

There was no response.

His heart throbbed in his chest, but he was determined to keep going on the off chance their father could hear them. Ryker wanted him to know they visited him whenever they could. He wished he could talk to his father about recent events. Everything had changed since the last time he'd been conscious, though Ryker knew he would be proud of how hard the brothers had worked to serve their people. Their father's greatest goal had been to serve and protect them too.

Keanon cursed and wiped the tears from his face, leaving the room. Ryker took the moment alone with his father to share the news. "I've been promoted." His voice hitched, and he swallowed the lump forming in his throat. Would his father ever be alert enough to hear these words? Would Ryker ever hear his father's voice again?

"I'm the youngest captain in our army, even younger than you were when you became a captain. I'll be the next General Kessler." His jaw quivered; he took a moment before continuing. "I'll make you proud, father." There was still no response, and a sob shook his shoulders. "I miss you. General Moreland has helped, but it's not—" His father jolted, his hand spasming inside of Ryker's as he spluttered nonsensical noises.

"Help!" Ryker's shout ricocheted off the walls. Several menders burst through the door in seconds, with Keanon on their heels.

"What happened?" His brother demanded.

He shook his head. "I don't know."

"They are muscle spasms." A mender reassured them, wiping the sweat from their father's brow. Another mender eased a cup of medicine to his lips, and after a few moments, their father lay still again, his breathing settling. The same mender, with graying brown hair and a face beginning to wrinkle, smiled with compassion. "There, the medicine has eased the tension in his muscles. He'll rest soundly now." He retreated from the room, and the other menders followed suit.

Keanon clenched his jaw, his hands clasped tight by his sides; his red-rimmed eyes remained fixed on their father. Would their father pass before Keanon was sent away? Ryker squeezed his father's hand in farewell before following the menders out the door so Keanon could have a moment alone.

Sitting on the cool wood floor outside the room, Ryker fiddled with the chain around his neck where his father's old compass resided. He clicked it open and watched the dial spin as it continued to point north, even as he twisted his hand. On the back of the compass were his father's initials—*L.K.* Ryker's mother had gifted it to his father for his birthday not long before she passed. Right as his father began to get ill, he passed it on to Ryker.

"Every soldier needs one of these. Even one that has studied the lay of the land as much as you have. There may come a time when your knowledge fails you, and when that time comes, you'll need something to guide you home again." His father grinned, even as his eyes glittered with tears as he passed the compass to his son. His dark hair had just begun to gray and thin; the fatigue from his illness was barely evident then. Ryker turned it over and popped the lid. The arrow spun for a moment until pointing northeast.

"Thank you," was all he had said.

The door opened, tethering Ryker back to the present. Keanon stepped out, not much more composed than when he'd gone in, and together, they retreated from the house and back to the easy distraction of training and preparing for what was to come. The brothers were much more melancholic than they had been that morning as they approached The Battleaxe, their favorite bar. It was always crowded at that time of night. Serving ladies weaved around tables, sloshing ale as they meandered through the crowded pub. Boisterous conversation and laughter rolled around them, but the camaraderie couldn't penetrate the sorrow lingering over the twins.

Ryker swished the last remnants of his third cup of ale, wishing he could join in the chaos and lose himself to drink. Yet, as a captain with more responsibility, he cut himself off so he wouldn't regret it the following morning.

Deep in their drinks, a particularly raucous group of patrons burst out into cheers. One lifted his mug, his drawled-out speech punctuated with hiccups. "Long—live Emperrrorr Asherrrr!" The whole table raised their cups to toast, with Ryker offering a half-hearted lift of his mug. The rest of their conversation was lost to the rambling of the dining room.

"What do you think about all that?" Keanon asked, his brows pinched as he tapped the side of his mug.

"About what?"

"Emperor Asher. The seven kingdoms coming together as one." Keanon stared intently into his ale, as if all the answers to his questions could be found at the bottom of his cup.

Ryker frowned. There wasn't much for him to question. Ryker wasn't a priest with insight into the gods' plans, so who was he to question it? "I haven't given it much thought, to be honest. It is a lot to take in, but the priests know the gods' plans better than I ever could."

"Yeah," his brother sighed. "I guess so." After a few moments of silence that seemed to eat away at his brother, Keanon added, "General Moreland didn't seem to think the other kingdoms would respond well."

"I know." Ryker lowered his gaze to the dark liquid in his own cup. "We will have separate jobs to do soon."

"Yeah." Though Keanon's eyes were sullen, his lips quirked. "Who's going to whoop you when I'm gone?"

Ryker glared but couldn't fight the grin, tipping his mug

toward Keanon's. "I'll be sure to beat you when you return." His brother's smile reached his eyes as he clanked his cup to Ryker's. They dropped all conversation about the impending war, their father's failing health, and their future separation. At that moment, Ryker enjoyed the evening with his favorite person, pretending the world was still a normal one.

VIVIAN

The throne room was abuzz with nervous conversation as everyone waited for the letter to be opened that had arrived early that morning. Vivian had noted the embossed seal of a red sun setting between two hills—King Asher of Esraia's new emblem. Since his coronation a decade ago, Brantyre had little correspondence with the southern king. In fact, they had very little correspondence with any of the southern kingdoms. Vivian's curiosity was piqued, and she was sorely disappointed when her father had not invited her to attend the meeting. She shouldn't have been surprised, but it still hurt.

Refusing to be left out of the know, Princess Vivian watched her father's court from her hideaway on the balcony above. It was difficult to make out faces from where she lay on the floor, her nose pressed against the railing. She'd had a moment of regret, knowing her head maid, Marienn, would be upset as her velvet dress of violet and lavender gathered dust from the floor.

A long, spruce table was set in the middle of the throne room for the council meeting. The dark wood was a sharp contrast to the polished marble floors and ornate pillars stretching up to hold the balcony on which she hid. Sitting on the raised dais were three thrones for her parents and her sister, Aida, the chosen heir. They were of polished dark wood with chilver swans carved into the front legs of each chair.

Chilver swans were the largest swans throughout Eavdamos, and the largest bird to thrive in the cold Brantyre mountains. The real bird was covered in tiny, thick black feathers that shimmered, reminiscent of the elegance of royalty. On the thrones, their heads were bent as though they bowed to whoever sat in the chair, their long necks stretching down while their wings fanned out on either side. Each wooden feather was detailed with gold, and when the sun cast rays through the windows, the wings glittered. The thrones were empty, though, as Vivian's parents chose to sit with their advisors at the table.

Beside her father, King Nicholias, sat her mother, Queen Renea, elegantly dressed in a deep blue dress crafted of the same velvet as Vivian's. The bodice was embroidered with white pearls, and the skirt flowed down, hugging her tall, slim frame and perfectly complementing her dark complexion. Her mother's black hair was pulled up in a braided crown like Vivian's was that morning, but while her mother's hair was long, beautiful, and tame, Vivian's was always a struggle to manage. In addition to her braided hair, her crown sat atop her head, crested with blue and white gems. Her mother's small facial features gave her a gentle appearance, though her dark eyes held an air of strength that demanded respect. Vivian wished she looked more like her mother but inherited her father's wider nose and bigger forehead, which she, fortunately, hid behind her hair.

On her father's left was a near spitting image of the queen and Vivian's younger sister, Aida. A simple, silver tiara rested upon her head as a symbol that she was the gods' chosen heir.

She wore a pale blue dress in a similar style to their mother's, which shimmered against her dark skin. Aida was regal and elegant like their mother, with identical dark curls often left down to perfectly frame her face. Since her sister was born, it had been obvious she would be the one the gods would favor to rule. Vivian laid her head in her hands.

Many times, she had told herself she did not wish to rule the kingdom. She didn't want the same expectations and pressures her sister had, but in situations like this, where she had to watch from above while her sister sat with the advisors below, Vivian could not deny her twinge of envy. Why did she have to crinkle and ruin her dress to hear about important matters of the kingdom she loved and lived in?

In attendance at the table were her parents' advisors, the head scribe, the two generals of Calliva, and the royal high priestess Sasha on Aida's left. Sasha's pale eyes were a stark contrast to her dark skin, and she wore the traditional dark blue robes with silver trim for the high priests of Brantyre. She rested one wrinkled hand on her simple black cane.

Her father frowned, his face worn as he studied the envelope in his hand. Everyone quieted as her father opened the letter and began to read it aloud.

"Greetings, King Nicholias of Brantyre. I hope you and your kingdom are well." The letter began with normal pleasantries from one kingdom to another, yet as her father continued, the room broke into chaos. "The gods have revealed a new prophecy to our priests. It is a vision to unite all of Eavdamos into one Empire with me, Emperor Asher, as its sole ruler."

The volume rose to an indecipherable level as her parents' strong masks dropped to matching wide-eyed and slack-jawed expressions. Aida covered her mouth with a hand, her dark eyes filled with panic. Vivian's stomach dropped as the letter's implications settled over her. With King Asher now the ruler of all of Eavdamos, what would that mean for her family? A shiver raced down Vivian's spine as she thought about what happened to royal families who lost the gods' favor. In order to ensure the new ruler's successful rise to power, the old family would be executed. The priests would lead the people to find and kill all those related to the old royal family, removing all possibilities of an uprising.

Vivian curled a stray hair around her finger, her mind racing. Why was this the first time they were hearing about this? Was this a formal letter of their coming execution?

"Enough!"

The crystalline, clear voice of the queen silenced the room and Vivian's raging thoughts. Her mother had regained her composure and stood before the council. Her mouth was set in a grim line, but there was no other indication of what she was feeling as everyone sat back in their seats. King Nicholias inclined his head in appreciation and continued with the letter.

The more her father read, the faster Vivian spun the lock around her finger.

"The priests believe this prophecy has come to unite us. As such, I welcome your family to step into this new relationship with me to govern over the land Natura has granted you and help me lead the united people of the Ashera Empire into a new future."

Vivian struggled to comprehend what this would mean. Would the priesthood of Brantyre still receive visions for the next in line, who would then act as a governor, not ruler? It meant her family would be safe, but what kind of authority would they have if Emperor Asher took charge? Vivian couldn't wrap her head around it. Why wouldn't their priests see this vision, too? What expectations and responsibilities would they have over the people of Brantyre?

Vivian flinched at the sudden sharp pinch from her scalp,

frowning at the strands of hair curled around her finger. She clasped her hands together under her chin and redirected her attention to the commotion below.

"Who does this king think he is to stake a claim over all of us?" General Johan smacked a fist on the table.

"If this *is* the gods' will, it has nothing to do with him." Colette, one of her father's advisors, straightened in her seat and tapped her slim finger on the table.

"Why would the gods choose a man who's barely ruled a decade?" said Kenric, her father's closest advisor. While he was much calmer than the others, his face betrayed him. His mouth curved into a deep frown, and the way he brushed his fingers through his beard gave away his concern. His son, Tristain, was betrothed to Princess Aida, and their wedding was set to take place in a few months' time at the upcoming Winter's Light Festival.

"He doesn't even have an heir," Kenric mumbled so lowly that Vivian almost missed it.

"He *was* the old ruler's advisor before they passed. The gods may have prepared him for this task from the beginning." The head scribe, Tiberius, pointed out.

"I didn't ask for a history lesson!" General Johan was on his feet now.

"That is enough." Her father interrupted. General Johan plopped back in his seat, crossing his arms. "I appreciate your concerns, General Johan and Kenric." He turned to Priestess Sasha beside him. "But I would like to know what your thoughts on this matter are."

"Hmm." The old woman leaned forward on her cane, her pale eyes distant as though lost in a vision. "I have not received any premonitions about this prophecy. I will consult with the others to see if they have, and I will be sure to reach out to King Asher's High Priest to see if he can offer more clarity."

King Nicholias nodded. "We will wait until you get better insight and see how the other kingdoms react before making any decisions." With that said, he waved a hand of dismissal, and everyone dispersed from the throne room, all the faces passing below either pinched with worry or rage.

How would the other kingdoms react? King Therrowin of Faulkern was stubborn and proud, especially of his kingdom and his only son and heir, Prince Bastien. Though Queen Claudelle of Kovdoran and King Henrik of Isdelle were stubborn rulers, as all northern kings and queens tended to be, their kingdoms suffered internal problems. Vivian had overheard rumors that their crop season had spoiled, and they struggled with famine and the uprisings that followed as a result. The two kingdoms had sought her parents for as much aid as they could give, and as Brantyre had been blessed with a plentiful season, her parents had been generous, sending good portions of their harvest to Kovdoran and Isdelle. However, their harvest could only spread so far, and no matter their aid, the other two kingdoms continued to struggle.

What were they going to do? Emperor Asher had said the Empire would share everything produced throughout the lands. Would that be enough enticement for the proud king and queen to surrender their kingdom?

As for the southern kingdoms, King Alystaire of Galleria and King Gideon of Norrean, Vivian wasn't as familiar with them. She'd not traveled south since she was a little girl and she'd not heard much about them in recent years.

Voices below regained her attention. Her parents were the last ones in the throne room. All the advisors, High Priestess Sasha, and her sister Aida, had cleared out. Her father held his queen tight in his arms, resting his head atop hers. He murmured something in her ear, and her stiff frame relaxed into him. She wrapped her arms around his waist and whispered something back.

Vivian's face flushed at her parents' tender moment. They did not often display affection in public, but she could not deny the love her parents shared; it warmed her heart. It was something she hoped she could achieve with whoever she ended up with. Even though her marriage would be arranged, her parents had been arranged too, and they were lovely together.

However, it was time for her to escape before she was caught. With silent movements, Vivian slid back on her stomach until she could no longer see her parents; she rose onto her hands and knees and crawled the rest of the way. She frowned at the poor state of her dress, knowing she would have to change.

At the door, she slowly turned the knob and pushed it open on quiet hinges. It closed with a soft click. The single door to the balcony exited into a long hall with smooth wooden floors and long, plush blue rugs with silver embroidery stretching along the hall. The wall across was covered in tall windows, allowing in lots of sunlight, and offering a beautiful view of the Calliva mountains.

"Eeepp!"

Vivian squealed when something poked her shoulder from behind. Her stomach dropped to her toes, and she spun to face the humorous glint in her sister's eyes. Heart easing back to a normal rhythm, Vivian glared at Aida's smirk. Though Aida was younger, she was taller than Vivian, and it irked her to have to look up to meet her sister's gaze.

With her arms crossed and brows raised, her sister said, "I knew you wouldn't be able to help yourself, Vi."

Unable to deny the truth, Vivian asked, "What do you think Father will do?"

All mischief drained from Aida's face as she lowered her

gaze to the floor. "Honestly... I'm afraid." She wrapped her arms tighter around herself as if to shield from what was to come. "Becoming queen is what I've been raised for my entire life."

At that moment, Aida was Vivian's little sister again, like she was before she was chosen. Vivian remembered the day well. Not long after their younger brother Glenn was born, High Priestess Sasha called the family together. Vivian had been twelve, and Aida ten. They'd stood side by side before the priests while their mother held Glenn beside them. The priests blessed each sibling before High Priestess Sasha stepped forward with a simple silver tiara. She gave a prayer of praise before placing it on Aida's head.

Her mother's raised brows were the only indication of her surprise, but Vivian had always known. As soon as the priests began to pray, Vivian stepped back. Something in her heart told her she had not been chosen.

Vivian holed up in her room while Aida had been whisked away to the temple. Later that evening, Aida returned, and the two lay together in Vivian's bed. Vivian had combed through Aida's hair, struggling to comprehend the responsibility now placed upon her, while Vivian processed not being chosen. They fell asleep together, and since then, Aida always came to Vivian when her obligations and responsibilities became overwhelming.

Aida protested halfheartedly about Vivian's dusty dress as she pulled her into her arms. Her sister rested her head on her shoulder and held on tight.

"I'm sure Father will figure this out." Vivian said as much to reassure herself as her sister.

Aida nodded against Vivian's shoulder and then pulled away. The transformation only took a few moments. Gone was Aida's visible fear and uncertainty and in its place was a mask of calm serenity—a mask their parents had worn all their life. Aida learned to master it over the years, while Vivian, despite her efforts, was always given away by her eyes.

Quick footfalls approached from around the corner. Vivian's eyes widened as she took in the poor state of her dress, and the tiniest of smiles broke the facade on her sister's face. She indicated to the wall behind Vivian, where a thick tapestry hung to the floor—a depiction of Natura, the God of Nature, raising up the mountains of Brantyre. It wasn't ideal, but as the footfalls grew louder, Vivian rushed behind it, pressing flat against the cold stone. The last thing she wanted was to be caught snooping around the throne room after a meeting she'd not been invited to. Aida stayed in the hall to distract whoever it was.

"There you are!"

At the sound of the young, masculine voice, Vivian relaxed and left her hiding place. Their younger brother, Glenn, stood beside Aida and flashed Vivian a sly grin as she came out from behind the tapestry. His dark, curly hair was almost as unruly as Vivian's, but he kept his shorter so it wouldn't get out of hand; he was all limbs with long arms and legs. Vivian often teased that it would take him his whole life to grow into them, but he was almost as tall as she was at just eleven years old. At the rate he was growing, he would soon be taller than their father.

"Tristain was looking for you." He motioned to Aida, whose eyes flicked away at the mention of her betrothed, her hands fidgeting at her sides. Glenn was oblivious to her sudden shift in mood.

It wasn't that Aida disliked Tristain. He had grown up alongside the royal children and was close friends with all of them; Glenn had become the older boy's shadow since he could walk. Yet when the betrothal was announced a year ago, Aida had revealed her mixed emotions to Vivian about marrying such a close friend.

"Well then," Aida straightened and inclined her head back to where Glenn had come. "Let's not keep him waiting." The two made their way down the hall, and once they had rounded a corner, Vivian made a dash for her rooms.

Vivian pulled her cloak tighter against the chill as she sat on a bench in the upper gardens of the palace, overlooking the surrounding mountains and Calliva City below. Vivian longed for the summer months that drew near. Brantyre only had two months a year that promised small relief from the relenting cold. Snow still covered every surface as far as she could see, but the surrounding bushes began to bud. It had been two weeks since they had received the letter from Emperor Asher, and her parents still had little clarity on what they were to do.

"Ah, there you are, my dear."

Vivian jumped at the intrusion.

High Priestess Sasha stepped up beside her, using her cloak to brush snow off the bench before sitting. Vivian began to nod in respect, but Sasha shooed the gesture away. "Don't waste your good manners on me." With open arms, the elderly woman smiled. "Come here."

Without hesitation, Vivian let the priestess embrace her. Sasha took Vivian's hand when she pulled away. For a moment, the old woman studied her with a serious expression. Vivian squirmed under her gaze.

"What is it?"

The priestess squeezed her hand. "I've had a new vision." Sasha's pale eyes captured Vivian's. "This one has you in it, my dear."

Her heart stuttered as the words struck her. Priestess Sasha had never had a vision about Vivian. Why was she having one now, with everything else going on? What could the gods possibly want with her? Too many questions raced through her head. Unable to respond, she sat with her mouth agape.

"There are a lot of changes happening right now and lots of conflict and hardships ahead." The priestess appeared distant, as though recalling the vision right there. "It will take a great deal of faith and courage for everyone involved to do what is right, and amidst everything, I see you."

Vivian's stomach dropped, a chill rippling down her spine. She'd only heard one other prophecy spoken before: when her sister was chosen. Aida had told Vivian the priests' visions were often vague and indirect, but this was her first time experiencing it for herself. "What…" Her voice was faint, and she had to swallow the lump in her throat. "What does that mean?"

"You will have a role to play in these tumultuous events to come." Sasha placed her other hand on Vivian's cheek, offering a sympathetic smile. "This role will be one you were not prepared to take, and the choices you make will impact the future of Eavdamos."

Vivian's heart constricted, her breathing shallowing. She wasn't the heir, so what could the gods possibly have planned? How could her choices impact the kingdoms more than the Empire's prophecy already had?

She laid her head in her hands and took deliberate, slow breaths as she tried to comprehend the weight of the prophecy crashing over her. The priestess laid a reassuring hand on her shoulder and said nothing until Vivian calmed. When she trusted her voice, she asked, "What about Aida or my father? Surely they have more say in the current events than I do."

"Their jobs *are* important, and their paths have yet to be decided. Our priests are split on whether we should believe this new prophecy or not." The old woman sighed and shook her head. "Prophecies aren't always clear. It is the gods' way of entrusting us with this little piece of information, for us to lean on their guidance, and our understanding of their will and our hearts."

Vivian frowned. "If they aren't clear, how do you know who the chosen heir will be?"

Sasha chuckled and reiterated, "I said they aren't *always* clear. The chosen heir is the one time a prophecy is always certain and easy to understand." Her shoulders sagged, and she appeared worn and tired. "At least that was the case before the priests of Esraia had the one about Emperor Asher."

"When will the priests come to a consensus about this?"

"Ahh, dearie." Sasha gazed out over the gardens before facing Vivian again. "I'm afraid the gods have been silent on this matter. It seems they are leaving this to us to interpret and decide."

"But surely—"

Another voice cut in before Vivian could finish.

"Priestess Sasha!" A palace guard jogged over, wide-eyed. "The king needs to see you right away."

As Sasha rose to go with him, Vivian followed suit and called after the retreating guard. "What's going on?"

The guard's expression was grave as he answered. "The Empire has declared war on Galleria."

CHAPTER 3
FREYA

Creaking followed Freya's movements as she shifted on the branch. Sweat slid down her back, and the sticky air made her hood and cloak cling uncomfortably to her body. She notched an arrow in her bow as the first line of soldiers appeared through the tree line. With a soft, heart-slowing breath, Freya waited as they drew closer. A gentle, warm breeze blew across her face, and the branch beneath her swayed precariously. She teetered before steadying her balance, her boots clinging firmly to the rough bark while the leafy branches concealed her from the soldiers below. In the tree next to hers, the branches bowed, revealing another hidden archer for a brief moment before the wind settled, hiding them once again.

About fifty soldiers continued their march down the South King's Road toward the tree where Freya perched, all dressed in pale gray tunics with the emblem of a setting sun between two mountains etched on their chest, indicating their allegiance to the Empire. South King's Road was the unowned strip of land that ran between Galleria and the Empire, stretching all the way from the northern kingdoms to the Southern Ocean. Once, the road was used by merchants and civilians traveling between kingdoms, but now it is primarily used by the Empire to transport their armies and supplies along the border.

The group guided three horse-drawn wagons that clattered over the bumpy road. Freya studied them. From that height, it was unclear what sort of cargo they were shipping, but that mattered little. Galleria's army grew every day, recruiting soldiers quicker than the blacksmiths could forge their weapons. After the Empire's first invasion, all the people from towns and cities nearest to the border sought refuge further west. Now the overpopulation was causing a short supply of everything: food, clothes, horses, and medicine. She forced her hands to relax, tensed from the bubbling anger rising inside her whenever she thought of how her people had suffered.

Singling one man out from the mass, Freya followed his every step as the troop marched closer still. Finally, they paraded directly below where she hid, and she released her arrow. Six soldiers gasped and fell to the dirt, arrows protruding from their throats. Before the rest of them had time to fully process what had happened, she nocked another arrow and six more fell.

Chaos ensued as the soldiers shouted commands, trying to form ranks against the open fire. Some managed to take cover behind the wagons, but Freya took down four that tried to rush into the trees, their swords drawn. Aiming low, she hit a soldier's foot from where he hid behind the wagon, who cried out and stumbled. When his body hit the ground, she sent another arrow to ensure he stayed there.

When only a few soldiers remained behind the wagons, Freya dropped silently to the ground. Peeking around the tree for any trace of movement, she nocked an arrow and waited. Bodies littered the open path. The horses hitched to the wagons tossed their heads nervously, but remained in position. Even in the spaces beneath the wagons, there were no signs of anyone. Everything was still.

Freya raised her hand and five cloaked figures emerged from behind the trees. Bow at the ready, she inched onto the path, her steps noiseless as she glided across the dirt. One of the cloaked figures by the rear wagon let their arrow fly, and the soldier hiding behind it gasped and fell.

When she neared the first wagon, her heart leapt in her throat as someone sprang out from behind, swinging his sword. He lunged, but an arrow plunged into his neck before she could even raise her bow, and the man collapsed at her feet. The last remaining soldiers were dispatched quickly as the six hooded figures surrounded them.

Freya tucked her bow over her shoulder and pulled off her hood, shaking away a few strands of copper hairs that had escaped her braid. The breeze caressed her sweaty face, offering momentary relief from the heat. With one hand on the hilt of her sword, she approached the bay mares pulling the first wagon and used a soft voice to soothe them.

"That went well," drawled a deep voice behind her.

Freya glanced over her shoulder, smiling as her friend Lanzo pulled off his hood, releasing hundreds of long, tiny braids down his back. He came to stand beside Freya and helped calm the other mare.

"This was too easy," Harper piped up, climbing into the back of the first wagon. Freya chuckled at Harper's complaint. Looking at Harper's small frame and round, innocent-looking face, anyone would think she was simply overconfident. Freya knew better. Harper called out, "We've handled larger troops, Cliff."

"The Empire's caught onto our efforts, Harp. I've had to be more careful to weed out any misinformation so we don't end up in chains." Cliff strode from the wagon at the back and crossed his arms. With sandy brown hair, green eyes, and a lean but well-muscled frame, Cliff had become somewhat of a heart-throb back home, particularly among the women of the court. His past as a troublemaker, as he tagged along with Freya and Harper, only heightened the women's interest, much to his dismay.

"Don't get all worked up, man." Lanzo teased as he wrapped his massive arm over Cliff's leaner and taller build. Lanzo was unfazed, even when Cliff rolled his eyes. "Harp's just upset I took out more than she did."

"You stole that last one!" Harper poked her head out, pointing an accusing finger at Lanzo, who burst out laughing. Freya couldn't suppress her grin either, and Harper huffed, ducking back inside the wagon. Lanzo was the first person Freya had ever known to beat Harper at anything. Though he was only better than Harper in archery, it still ate at her. Freya grew up with Harper as her sparring partner, and even she had not become as skilled.

"It's mostly weapons this time." A blonde head popped out from the second wagon—Laia. She jumped out, twirling a blade in her hands.

Cliff pushed away from Lanzo to stand beside her. "What's the verdict on these?"

"Some of these are Gallerion blades, so those are really good quality. The rest aren't bad either." Raised by her uncle, the master blacksmith of Galleria, Laia had a strong eye for well-crafted weapons.

"There are arrows here. We can replenish our stocks before sending the rest to Seaymarr." Harper added.

"We'll take it to Potámore," Freya said, pushing more flyaway hairs from her face. "General Ariss can take his pick and then send the rest to my father."

Freya's father, King Alystaire of Galleria. She ignored the

twinge in her heart at the mere thought of him and her home. Freya had been the one to beg her father to let her and a team fight out on the field, so she refused to feel homesick.

They were a long way from where she grew up in Seaymarr, the capital of Galleria on the far west coast. Her palace home overlooked the Navean Sea, where the salty ocean breeze greeted her every morning as the waves crashed along the rocky beaches below. Though the lush forests and wide-open plains stretching along Galleria's eastern side held an admiral beauty, nothing could beat her favorite sight of the sun setting over the ocean, casting the sea and sky in an array of reds, oranges, pinks, and purples.

But she'd had to leave. Six weeks ago, news reached her family of the Empire's invasion and the devastation that followed. Freya knew she had to do something. Sitting at home in the palace while the people suffered was not something she could live with. She wasn't the heir to the throne like her brother, Damian, nor a master strategist like her sister, Kiarra, but she could fight. Fighting out on the field, picking off the Empire's soldiers bit by bit, and taking resources to provide for the people was where she was the most helpful. After promising her father that she wouldn't cross the border into the Empire's territory and would always defer to Cliff if he feared a job was too dangerous, her father finally granted her permission.

Turning to the two men, Freya directed, "Go make yourselves useful by helping Archer deal with the bodies so we can get out of here before any Imperial patrols show up." With her head, she indicated toward the final member of her team—Archer. Archer had joined them over two weeks ago and had proved an integral part of the team with his superior skills and knowledge in healing and mending. He said nothing as Freya directed the other two men to help him, though he nodded at the princess, barely concealing his smile beneath his full, dark beard.

With a groan from Lanzo and a roll of the eyes from Cliff, they did as instructed. Within the hour, the road was clear, and they drove the horses into Galleria.

As THE SUN neared its descent behind the tree line in the distance, Freya's team approached the gates of Potámore. It was a smaller city surrounded by fields and forests, where the Potámea River cut the fields in two. Glowflies blinked in and out across the field, and a pleasant chittering of small insects resounded among the tall grasses accompanying the flowing water. Horse hooves clopped over the stone bridge above the rushing water, the lull making Freya's eyes grow heavy. She shifted in her seat to try to clear her head.

"Princess." A guard outside the gates bowed low as they drew near, his face illuminated in the warm glow of the sconces on either side of the entrance. "Another shipment for us?"

"Mostly weapons this time, but there's some mender's supplies in the last wagon." Freya hopped down to pass the reins to the guards.

"This is perfect timing, Princess. We just got in some more recruits, so these will go a long way in arming everyone." The guard's relief and gratitude filled Freya with contentment, but also worry.

"More recruits, huh?" Freya sighed. While she was incredibly grateful and proud of her people for standing up to support her family and home, she hated the number of men and women leaving behind their families and how many youths gave up their childhoods for swords. Not wanting the soldiers to see the turmoil on her face, Freya turned away, leaving them to collect the wagons.

"Princess!"

Freya halted at the sudden intrusion before she could suggest her team go into the city for the night. She whirled toward the gates, where a young man—maybe a year or two older than her nineteen years—strode toward her. He had dark hair that hung around his face in waves and dark eyes to match, which sized her up as he drew closer. He stopped a few paces away and bowed, meeting her gaze as he straightened. Freya tried to ignore how her stomach fluttered at the slight quirk of his lips. For several moments, they just stood like that. Staring. It felt as though this stranger saw through her eyes and into the very core of her being, and the longer she looked into his, the harder her heart pounded.

Crossing her arms to keep her heart inside her body, Freya asked, "Did you need something?" She was proud of the strength in her voice.

He bowed low again and said, "Princess, my name is Keanon."

"And?" She raised a brow, though he didn't seem put off by the snark in her tone.

"And I wish to join your team."

That gave her pause. What did he know about her team? While they weren't keeping their movements a secret from the people, they weren't spreading the word either. Archer had discovered them by chance after Cliff took a well-aimed hit from an imperial soldier; quick to note Archer's exemplary mending skills, Freya requested he joined the group.

Otherwise, her team had to be careful not to let their plans get into the wrong hands. Beneath the shelter of the night, they would drop supplies off to the generals in the cities and let them distribute what they brought. Keanon must have witnessed the current drop-off, but did he know what they had done to acquire the goods? Freya stepped closer, tipping her head to maintain eye contact. She tried to ignore how the easiness of his expression made her stomach flutter. The torchlight danced in his dark eyes, confidence glimmering in their depths; there was something more about him—something she couldn't quite put her finger on.

With a sardonic smile, she replied, "We aren't looking for another member."

"I'm sure you could use an extra bow," he shot back. His brazen smile that set her heart to racing again. Strapped to his shoulder was a bow and quiver of arrows. The wood was worn but of good quality, and a sword was sheathed on his hip.

"Why not join the army if you want to help?"

"I saw how you helped just now, and how you are providing for my town and family. I want to be a part of that." His expression sobered into one of sincerity, but she couldn't shake the feeling something was off about him. His nearness wasn't helping, and yet she couldn't stop staring into his eyes. The fluttering in her stomach refused to cease.

Nothing was stopping her from saying no—her team didn't *need* another member—yet the word refused to leave her lips. Dragging her eyes away from his, Freya faced her team with a raised brow.

Cliff studied Keanon with the same suspicions as Freya had been. Laia whispered something to Harper, who grinned maniacally.

"I'm alright with whatever you decide." Lanzo was the first to answer Freya's unspoken question, his face unreadable as he glanced between her and Keanon.

Freya gave Cliff another hard look, who gestured to the trees with an incline of his head. Stomach still growling, and her body fatigued from hunkering in that tree all day, Freya huffed, "Give me a moment," before following Cliff a few paces away.

"I got a weird feeling about him." Cliff started the moment they were out of earshot.

"Yeah, I do too." She leaned against a tree and pinched the bridge of her nose. "But I also have a strange inclination to tell him yes."

Cliff frowned, raking his fingers through his hair. "If he isn't trustworthy, having him around could put us at risk." Cliff leaned back on his heels as he considered the situation, his arms crossed. "But if he comes with us, we could keep him from causing harm elsewhere as long as we keep our guards up."

Freya couldn't fight the grin at the conspiratorial look on Cliff's face. "Are you suggesting we bring a potential spy into our midst for the sole purpose of keeping him from being able to spy on anyone else?"

"If I make it clear I don't trust him, he's going to be desperate to prove himself, which means he will have to give us something tangible." Cliff's grin grew. "The 'ole give and take of the spy trade."

"As long as we play our cards right, we can avoid any setups he tries to make for us and use his inside knowledge to our advantage." Freya's mind raced with the possibilities but also the danger they could put themselves in.

Cliff nodded, his face set in contemplation. "With him coming along, it means we won't be able to use the tunnels for some time."

Freya gave a careful sideways glance, but Keanon was too far to have heard. If this new guy was a spy, the last thing they wanted to do was to lead him to the tunnel system running beneath the entire Kingdom of Galleria. From Galleria's northern borders with Faulkern and Brantyre, or to the castle in Seaymarr on the west coast, one could travel to any point in the kingdom underground. How the tunnels came to be had long been forgotten, but it was believed they were carved before the seven kingdoms were formed, and it was this system Freya and her friends used to keep undetected—even their own people knew nothing of it. The knowledge of their existence was limited to the royals, spies, priests, and generals.

Keeping the tunnels a secret allowed Galleria's spies to use the system freely and also protected the people since the underground system could be dangerous. The floors, walls, and ceiling were made of cool stone, with many underpasses leading to dead ends. Anyone without knowledge or a map of the underground maze would never find their way back out.

When Freya was only ten, she discovered them by accident while hiding from her tutor. She'd found a door in a dark, unused corridor of the castle, where inside was an old storage room and a hatch hidden behind the shelves. When she'd pried it open, a staircase appeared, descending into darkness. Curiosity won quickly, and Freya had rushed blindly down the stairs, her wide-eyed wonder soon turning to fear as each turn of the tunnels looked the same. When she tried to retrace her steps, she could not remember the way she had come. In a panic, she'd rushed and took a dizzying number of turns, and only when she hit a dead end for the fifth time did she collapse with exhaustion.

Curled in a ball on the stone floor, Freya had cried herself to sleep until, by a miracle of the gods', her father found her. Tears trailed down his face as he scooped her into his arms, and she cried with great relief. He'd squeezed Freya tighter than ever before, his soft sobs making her cry harder as she clung to him the whole way home.

As traumatic as the experience was for her, Freya was determined not to let the tunnels best her. Knowing she wouldn't give up and terrified she would get lost again, her father relented and allowed her to study the maps of the tunnel system. He regretted his decision later when she and her friends used this knowledge on several occasions to sneak out of the palace. Once, they even made it all the way south to Blackstone to visit Laia. Her father had been forced to place guards around the hallways that offered access to the tunnels, instructing them not to let Freya or her friends pass for any reason.

Cliff shrugged. "We'll just have to travel like normal for a time. I'll be extra vigilant when I gather information. If we can prove he is a spy, we'll get him arrested, but on the off chance he isn't, we gain a new member which *will* help us take on larger troops, as everyone so eloquently pointed out this morning." Cliff smirked at Freya, who glared back at him, though the stupid grin on her face ruined her feigned anger.

It would be a shame to lose the underground for a time, but Cliff made valid points. Since they were close to the border, they were less likely to run into many people.

"Let's do it."

RYKER

"Come on, lad, you can do better than that." Ryker corrected as he refrained from using another duel-ending blow. He stood across from General Moreland's young assistant, Leo; the boy panted, his sandy hair soaked in sweat. The sky lightened as the night guards trudged past, relieved of their shifts. They headed back to the soldiers' quarters for a well-earned sleep.

Since Keanon had left over a month ago, Ryker had taken to his new position with fervor. Training new recruits had become his favorite part of the day. Leo had also come to Ryker, wanting to learn to fight. Ryker was surprised, but the young lad explained that General Moreland was too busy with war strategies to teach him. It was true; the general was under more stress recently, so Ryker had agreed to help. The only time Leo had to train was in the early hours before General Moreland needed him and before Ryker had to focus on his troops. However, if the boy was ever to be taken near a battlefield in the future, Ryker would ensure Leo could defend himself.

Twisting his blade in his sweaty palms, Ryker charged with easy-to-block swings, which Leo met each time. "Good. Excellent." At Ryker's praise, the boy's face lit up. "Now faster." Ryker quickened his pace, using the same stream of blows. Leo matched each one. "Yes, that's it! Now it's your turn. Give me all you've got."

Leo responded to his command and went on the offensive. His form was much improved from when he'd first started, but he was still a bit clunky when shifting from one parry to another. Ryker focused on dodging and blocking so Leo could practice. While his moves were predictable, the blows were getting stronger as the boy grew more adept at wielding a blade. Leo had proven himself a quick study, and after a few more parries—when Ryker could tell the boy was almost spent —he called it. "Alright, that's enough for the day."

Leo almost dropped the sword, but Ryker pretended not to notice. "The fires in the dining hall are lit, you should have just enough time to freshen up and grab food before General Moreland summons you." Ryker was about to take Leo's training sword for him but didn't want to wound the kid's pride as the boy half dragged the blade back to the racks. As Ryker followed behind to return his sword, he was surprised to find General Moreland at the edge of the training field.

"Don't worry, Leo." General Moreland raised a hand when the boy's face fell, exhaustion written in his eyes. "I'm here to speak with Ryker. You go ahead and have a quick rest after breakfast."

The boy didn't hesitate to hurry away. Ryker stalled after returning his training sword. "What's wrong?"

"I have something I need to discuss with you." He gestured with his head to the general's quarters. "Would you come with me." Though phrased as a question, the command was not lost on Ryker. Wordlessly, Ryker followed the general back through the barracks towards the sleeping quarters along the back wall. It seemed General Moreland's mind was preoccupied, so Ryker chose to remain quiet as the two made their way down the dirt path between buildings, receiving quick nods of recognition from the passing soldiers. Ryker was pleased with himself as he recognized the faces of his trainees.

General Moreland took Ryker to his personal quarters, and once the door closed, he wasted no time. "I have a task for you." General Moreland signaled Ryker to sit before picking up several parchments from his desk. "Emperor Asher doesn't want to drag this war out any longer than necessary. I have been in correspondence with the other generals, and we believe we have discovered the best way to end things quickly." As he spoke, General Moreland handed the papers to Ryker, whose interest piqued at the carefully designed maps on each page. Ryker scanned each one briefly before turning back to the general.

"This is where you come in." General Moreland smiled, though his eyes were serious. "We want to go after Blackstone, and I need you to find the best route for our armies to take."

Ryker's jaw went slack at the revelation. Upon further inspection, he realized each map detailed the southern regions of Galleria. They showed the grassy plains of the southeast, where the South King's Road connected the Empire to Galleria, the mountainous border of the far southern kingdom of Norrean and Galleria, and the far western edge where Blackstone City nestled into the Blackstone Mountains with the Navean Sea on the other side. The last map showed both borders of Galleria and the Empire, where, in the south, the city of Ekrewell was circled. The general had scrawled words at the bottom. Their army would gather at the southern city before marching through Galleria.

Glancing back up, Ryker asked, "How are we going to take the city?" Blackstone City was the most formidable of all Galleria's cities—of all Eavdamos, in fact. Its walls were crafted from the very stone the city got its name from. The dark, gleaming stone was near indestructible, and though all the kingdoms searched their mines for the precious material, only Galleria had a vast amount within the Blackstone Mountains. Their blacksmiths had mastered welding it, so much so that they built the city's walls almost entirely from the dark stone.

"Our plans for taking the city are in the works." General Moreland pointed at the maps in Ryker's hands. "But what I need you to focus on is getting us there."

Nodding, Ryker took his leave and went to work with ardor. He felt guilty for delegating most of the training to his lieutenant but knew he had to focus. Ryker placed his father's compass on the desk beside his papers and opened it. The dial spun before settling, facing east. While the compass was of little use, it did provide him comfort; it was as if his father stood beside him as they poured over the maps together.

Only when Leo popped into his office did Ryker pull away to train. He didn't want to neglect the boy, and it was good for Ryker to clear his head and keep his limbs loose after sitting for hours at his desk.

"Is what you are doing hard?" asked Leo.

Ryker paused, smiling at the question. While Galleria was one of the kingdoms Ryker had studied most growing up— since it directly bordered old Esraia—finding a safe route for an entire army was quite an undertaking. "Most of Galleria's southern border in that neutral strip of land is mountainous, and those mountains only get bigger and more treacherous the farther west we travel. Finding a safe and relatively fast route through those mountains without taking us straight into any of their southern cities is not as simple as I first thought."

Leo frowned, scrunching his brow. "Do we have to travel on the southern border, then? Why not go through the grassy plains or forests further north?"

"Ahh," Ryker's smile grew wider at the boy's predictable decision-making. "You see, the farther north we go, we risk marching past the likes of Potámore City—not to mention river crossings are no picnic for large armies. Our destination is in those mountains, so we will have to enter them eventually, and considering the vast number of soldiers, no route will be perfect." Rolling his blade in his hand, Ryker prepared to charge. "I just have to find the one that will work best."

CHAPTER 5
FREYA

"I'm starving," Harper groaned, sprawled across her pallet.

"You started cooking before the sun went down. How is it still not done?" Laia probed, peeking over the edge of the pot, which simmered above the open fire.

"You get back." Lanzo shooed Laia away from his stew before whirling on Harper. "Do you want good food or scraps only worth feeding to dogs?"

"At least I wouldn't be hungry anymore," Freya joined in with a mischievous grin.

"You're a princess!" Lanzo pointed his ladle at Freya in mock indignation. "Of all people, *you* should be the one demanding quality food."

Freya gave an exaggerated eye roll and leaned back against the tree, while Laia plopped beside her, legs crossed. Harper groaned again. While Archer simply ignored their antics, the small upturn to his bearded lips the only indicator he was listening at all as he sorted through his bag of mending supplies.

"Sooo," Laia drawled with a teasing glint in her eyes. "How

was your training session with Keanon this morning?" She kept her voice low so the rest of the team wouldn't overhear.

At the mention of Keanon, Freya's heart skipped, and she averted her gaze in the hopes Laia wouldn't notice. It had been a month since Keanon had joined her team, and he'd been working hard to prove himself a loyal member. He followed orders without complaint and had proven to be a capable sleuth like Cliff, which gave Cliff the perfect opportunity to gauge Keanon's true motives. Though everything Keanon did seemed honest and showed he was hardworking, Freya couldn't shake her earliest feelings that something was off about him.

With Freya's doubts unwavering, she'd decided to spend more time conversing and training with him to see if he'd let something slip. Yet nothing he did heightened her suspicions. Freya's mind wandered back to their moment that morning where she'd sparred with Keanon, who was indeed quite the capable fighter. She attempted to probe him: "Who trained you to fight?"

"My father was a soldier," Keanon answered with an easy smile, parrying her next swing. "He trained me and my brother since we were young."

"Your father's a soldier?" She paused.

Keanon shrugged. "He was never of a rank high enough for you to know his name. He never needed to be the one in charge so long as he served and protected his people."

"Sounds like someone worthy of a position."

"Perhaps." Keanon lowered his eyes. "If he was still here, I'd tell him of your high regards."

Her stomach clenched as realization struck her. He'd said his father *was* a soldier. She wanted to kick herself for being too absorbed in her probing to have missed it. Freya lowered her sword. "Oh, I'm sorry."

"Don't worry about it." Keanon shook his head and gave her a sad smile. "That's why I'm here with you. I want to help people just like he did."

A slow warmth rose from Freya's stomach into her face as his gaze held hers with such intensity. When he smiled, her heart skipped. Then, he charged. Freya's mouth fell open as her sword flew from her hands. Keanon pinned her where she stood, pointing the tip of his blade at her chest.

He smirked. "Never assume the battle is won until your opponent is dead. It's a common mistake my brother makes, which is why I always win."

When he lowered his sword, Freya crossed her arms over her pounding heart, unable to keep up with the speed of her flitting emotions, from remorse and shock to frustration; she could hardly process them. She stood as Keanon retrieved her sword for her and paused inches away. Her insides swirled once again. Keanon stared down at her as he held her sword up between them, and with sweaty palms, she grasped the hilt, her fingers brushing against his. He didn't let go. Instead, Keanon tilted his head, giving her a half smile that made her insides hotter than a blazing summer's day.

What was wrong with her? She should pull away. If her instincts about him were right, he wasn't trustworthy. But she found herself taunting him in a low voice, "You won't always win." The way his expression intensified yet softened all at once made her breath catch.

"But I will." His voice matched hers, low and airy against her cheek, his gaze flicking down to her mouth. It was suddenly much harder to breathe as he leaned forward, their faces a breath apart.

Rustling sounded in the trees, and with a jolt, Freya stepped back, ignoring the disappointment in her heart reflected in Keanon's eyes.

"Freya? Are you in there?" Laia's voice broke Freya from the memory.

Shaking her head to clear her thoughts, she grumbled, "Sorry..."

Laia smirked, and Freya shoved her, trying—and failing—to hide the warmth creeping into her face.

"From your prolonged silence, I've gathered the training was very good," Laia teased.

"Stop, that's not—it's not like that," stammered Freya, but Laia laughed, unconvinced. When Freya sighed, the girls sobered. "I'm still not convinced he's on our side."

Laia nodded. "I know, which just makes Cliff worry about you all the more. He saw how you two were looking at each other in the woods this morning. It put him in quite the tizzy, I'll tell you that."

Freya brushed her thumb over her knuckles and stared up at the stars peeking through the branches overhead. "What do I do?"

"Honestly," Laia leaned back on her hands, glancing up at the sky too. "I know you don't think he is who he says, and knowing you, you're probably right." Before Freya could say anything, Laia continued. "*But* I also feel this sense of peace about him. I get the feeling that he's good—that he wants to do good. You might just be the person he needs to help him figure out what that is."

Before Freya could come up with a response, Cliff and Keanon waltzed into camp. Her heart skipped a beat as Keanon's dark eyes found hers, his face illuminated in the warm glow of the fire.

"Empire's got a shipment of goods going out in about a week," said Cliff as he plopped onto a log by the fire.

"It's headed for Ekrewell City on the southern border," Keanon added; he sat cross-legged on the ground beside Freya, who refused to meet Laia's gaze burning into the side of her face. Keanon's knee was so close it almost brushed her leg, and the heat seeming to radiate from his nearness made it difficult to focus on the conversation.

"I'm surprised they are using the South King's Road again," Laia pondered. "I started to think they had wised up about that."

"From what I gathered, this will be a larger haul than we've done before. They think they'll be safer in larger numbers." Cliff leaned forward, draping his arms across his lap.

"They've been sending quite a few shipments south these past few weeks," Harper mused, finally sitting up from her pallet to join the conversation.

"If we go past Potámore to collect this shipment, I'll be sure to speak with General Ariss on his thoughts about the Empire's movements," said Cliff.

"We'll make it a point to stop by Potámore." Freya stood to gain some distance between herself and Keanon, trying to think clearly under the guise of getting food. Lanzo had just ladled the first spoonful of stew into a bowl, and Freya's stomach rumbled at the smell of the rich, meaty aroma.

"I see you're the first in line, Princess." Lanzo raised a brow and flashed a smug smile, handing her the bowl. "You know my cooking is worth the wait."

"I know I'm hungry." She grinned, snatching it before he could pull away. Lowering herself onto her pallet just outside the firelight, Freya barely suppressed a sigh as the first mouthful hit her tongue. The broth was perfectly seasoned, brimming with soft carrots and potatoes and huge chunks of beef that melted in her mouth. Warm broth dribbled down her chin, and she quickly wiped it on her sleeve as Keanon came to sit by her. The rest of her friends gathered around the fire, chatting amiably between themselves and leaving her alone with

Keanon. Cliff gave Freya a quick side eye before Laia leaned in, whispering something in his ear that kept him in place.

Keanon didn't immediately dig in after sitting; instead, he studied Freya with a peculiar expression. She squirmed under his intense gaze, and tried to focus on her food, which proved rather difficult while his eyes bored into the top of her head.

Finally, he broke the tense silence. "Can I ask you something?"

Freya raised her eyes back to his quizzically. Something about his tone set her on edge. Her heart skittered as she nodded.

"Where do you think this prophecy from the Empire came from?" His brow furrowed, as if contemplating his own question. "Do you think they misinterpreted something?"

Freya's worries about him spiked, but his question surprisingly seemed genuine, and as she thought about it, she had to admit she wondered about this prophecy, too. Laia's comment about Keanon's goodness encouraged her to answer as honestly as she could. "A misinterpretation makes the most sense. If they had taken the time to further discuss our concerns when my father refused their proposal, we might have gained a clearer answer. Our priests haven't had the same opportunity as theirs to hear or try to interpret the prophecy for themselves, so all we have to go on is how confident our priests are that my brother is meant to rule as king, not some *governor*."

Keanon said nothing, his expression unreadable. He took another bite of his stew. Lanzo would be crushed if he witnessed the little attention Keanon gave to his meal, so it was good that his back was turned as he conversed animatedly with the others. He was sharing a story Freya had heard about his homeland up north.

"Has this whole thing been bothering you too?" Freya refocused on Keanon, who remained silent. When he raised a brow, she added, "This prophecy changes so much about everything. All it's done is cause division amongst our once peaceful king-doms." Freya frowned, placing her empty bowl on the ground beside her.

"I'm sure the priests would say the gods don't always explain everything," Keanon murmured. "They would say that they offer guidance and give us glimpses into their plans with the prophecies but leave it to us to work out their will together."

Freya's mouth pulled up slightly. "That does sound like something a priest would say."

His mouth pulled into a straight line, and he raked a hand through his hair. "That's not what our priests are saying, though."

"No… It's not."

A WEEK LATER, Freya's team was once again situated over the South King's Road, waiting for the Empire's troops. Freya was poised on a large branch, her legs beginning to cramp. The first signs of movement in the distance caught her eye, and ignoring the tightness in her calves, she watched as the Imperial troops marched toward where she hid. There were roughly sixty soldiers. She frowned. This troop wasn't as large as she had expected, based on what Cliff had told her. Something seemed off. Freya pushed aside her confusion. There was little she could do about it now, so she grabbed an arrow from her quiver and settled it on the bowstring as they drew closer. Taking aim at a singular soldier amongst the mass, she took a steady breath and waited.

When they marched directly beneath her, she let loose. Seven arrows hit their marks, and the soldiers went down. Her team was swift and precise as they quickly took down all the Imperial soldiers.

After several silent heartbeats—once she was certain most of the soldiers were dead—Freya hopped down from the tree and stretched out the kinks in her back and legs. On her right and left, Laia and Keanon hopped down from their positions, too, but waited for Freya's signal to approach. Freya raised a hand, nocking her bow while treading lightly onto the open road. She searched for any movement behind the wagons or amongst the dead bodies while tiptoeing closer.

Nothing moved.

Long seconds passed, and finally, her team relaxed. All hands remained on their weapons as they descended to inspect the goods.

"I thought you said this was going to be a big haul?" Harper voiced Freya's own concerns.

Cliff crossed his arms, furrowing his brow. "It sounded like it was going to be a big one when I overheard the soldiers talking."

"I got the same impression." Keanon came to Cliff's defense, scanning the four wagons. He crossed his arms, tapping a rhythm on his forearm with his finger. Freya glanced between his finger and his face, her heart filling with trepidation.

"Perhaps they were going to make it larger but split the shipment in two because of us." Laia offered, sounding unconvinced.

"That's plausible, but we thought they were making this shipment larger so they would be safer in numbers," said Lanzo. He hadn't yet lowered his bow, an arrow nocked and ready.

"Everyone back up." Cliff ordered with a particularly hard look at Freya. "Let me take a look."

Freya did as was instructed as everyone backed up to the

tree line. All of them pulled their bows out, watching as Cliff made his way to the first wagon.

As he prepared to pull back the drawn curtains, a glint in Freya's eye made her squint. Tilting her head to stare into the woods beyond, a bush swayed, but there was no wind. That was all Freya needed.

"Cliff, lookout!"

Cliff leapt back as the flaps of the wagon flew open. Soldiers poured from the four wagons—at least five or six in each—followed by an onslaught of soldiers rushing at them through the trees. Lanzo was the first to shoot down the soldier closest to Cliff, giving him time to sprint away. The massive swarm of Imperial gray flooding onto the road made Freya's heart sink.

"Fall back!" Freya shouted as her team helped cover Cliff on his retreat to the border. Lanzo and Archer were flanked on either side of Freya as the Imperial soldiers fired back. Their aim was perfect, knocking down as many archers as possible while Freya helped Laia and Harper cover for Cliff as he neared the tree line, the hidden soldiers from the wagons right behind him.

Lanzo nudged her as the army drew closer. "Go!"

There was no room left to argue. Freya turned to flee with her team on her tail. As she rushed through the trees, her hood flew from her head, her copper hair like a beacon against the green foliage. Panic set in as the Imperial soldiers pushed past the border into Galleria, rushing in their pursuit. Potámore was the only city close to the border that was still occupied, but it was too far to sprint there with a whole army on their tail. Freya's mind raced for some direction to take her team. There was only one way she could think for everyone to escape, but they hadn't used the tunnels since Keanon joined. An entrance to the tunnels wasn't too far—if they could get there, her team would disappear.

With a quick glance, Freya's heart sank when she couldn't

catch a glimpse of any of her friends. Shouts rang out in the distance, and the metallic clang of swords ignited fear in her heart. She changed course toward the sound when an arrow whizzed past her into a nearby tree. She ducked as it splintered in the air.

Slicing pain shot through Freya's calf, and her leg buckled beneath her, sending her sprawling. She caught herself before her face smacked against a large tree root, but blood spurted from her leg where an arrow had skimmed it. She hissed at the stinging pain as she tried to rise onto her hands and knees.

"Don't move!" a deep voice barked behind her. Freya froze and glanced over her shoulder to see seven soldiers standing in a semi-circle; two had arrows aimed at her head, and the rest had their swords ready.

"Stand up slowly." The same voice commanded. "Hands out where I can see them."

Biting her tongue, Freya did as she was told. She scanned the trees: desperate for any way out of this. There were still no signs of her friends, though the continued sounds of fighting rang out in the distance. Could she duck behind a tree before the archers released their arrows?

"Go get her." Footsteps crunched over sticks and leaves as the soldier approached from behind. Then there was a gasp, followed by a thud and a clash of swords.

"Keanon? What are you doing?" The soldier in charge cried out. Freya used the distraction to rise to her feet, ignoring the shooting pain in her leg. Pulling her sword from its sheath, she turned, flinching at the pain in her calf as she struggled to put weight on it. It felt like it was on fire as hot blood drenched her dark trousers. Gritting her teeth through the pain, Freya sliced through the soldier that came at her.

After taking out the second archer, Keanon rushed to her side, standing with his back against hers. More soldiers trickled through the woods toward them, yet Keanon's support allowed her to balance most of her weight on one leg as she fought. In the distance, other fights rang out throughout the woods, accompanied by her friend's voices. The last soldier attempted to flee, but Keanon pulled out his bow and shot him down.

Heart hammering, Freya turned to Keanon, whose mouth was pressed in a tight, straight line, his brows furrowed.

"How did they know your name?"

"Not now." He grabbed her hand as another group of soldiers rushed toward them.

Throwing up his hood, Keanon pulled Freya into the trees. Pain shot up her leg, and she almost stumbled if not for his hand, keeping her on her feet. Cursing under his breath, Keanon lifted Freya into his arms, ignored her protests, and ran.

All Freya could do was wrap her arms around his neck to keep from falling, even as warring thoughts raced through her head. They knew his name. She should push out of his arms and run, but instead, she clung tighter as an arrow shot past Keanon's head.

"Why don't you guys use mounts?" Keanon gasped as he pressed forward. If the situation had been different, Freya would have laughed, but she was still struggling with a solution to get them out of there.

"How much farther into Galleria are they going to chase us? Where's everyone else?" Freya peeked over his shoulder.

"They'll be fine," was Keanon's curt reply. She clung tighter as he ducked behind another tree, then carefully slid down a hill toward a small outcropping. Keanon leaned against the dirt wall, holding Freya close as tiny pebbles rained down on their heads from the disturbance. Freya slowed her breathing as best she could despite her racing heart thumping in her chest. Boots pounded on the ground above them, growing closer.

"Where did she go?" said a woman's voice above where they

hid. Freya placed a hand over her mouth, and Keanon's grip around her tightened.

"We can't go much farther. This was supposed to be an easy capture—a guarantee." A man's voice. The man's boots crunched on the ground as he spoke, and more dirt fell over Freya's and Keanon's heads.

"We're going to have to figure something else out. We're getting drawn in too deep. There could be patrols anywhere," said another masculine voice—this one older. At least three voices sounded above them, but the number of footfalls suggested there were six in total. On a normal day, that wasn't too many for Freya and Keanon to take on themselves, but cornered as they were, and with more searching the woods, she kept quiet.

"Damn it, he was sure this would work." The woman's voice spoke again.

"We'll get another chance," spoke the senior voice. "For now, we retreat. We don't need any more needless bloodshed for an unsuccessful mission."

Their footfalls retreated the way they came, but still, she remained silent. Keanon's face was pinched as he cradled her, and she was now aware of just how close his face was to hers. In fact, she was aware of everything—how strong his arms felt wrapped around her body, and how her hands rested on his shoulder and chest. Freya's stomach flipped and her insides grew warm. When his dark eyes lowered to meet hers, her breath caught.

Then she remembered what the soldiers had said, and she pushed away.

"Here." Keanon gently lowered her onto the ground and pulled out his packs. "Let me look at this. I may not be Archer, but I can try to help a little."

"They knew your name." Freya was glad for the strength in her voice despite the turmoil coiling around her insides.

"I think you've always known there was something off with me." As Keanon spoke, he pulled away the torn cloth of her trousers and began to pour water from his flask onto her wound.

Freya hissed. The cool water stung, and she squeezed her hands so tight they turned white. While the arrow had only skimmed her leg, the sharp point had torn through layers of skin. The blood wouldn't stop. With a pinched expression, Keanon ripped some loose cloth from his packs and wrapped it above her knee. "This will hurt." Without giving her a moment to respond, he tied the cloth tight, and she clenched her jaw as the bottom half of her leg immediately tingled from the pressure.

"I'm sorry, but we have to stop the bleeding." After cutting away the rest of her tattered pants, Keanon wrapped another bandage around the injury, his fingers gentle as he made sure to cover the whole thing. When he was done, he sat beside Freya, his eyes encapsulating hers. She couldn't blink or turn away, and her heart raced as he shifted closer.

With a ghost of a smile, he whispered, "Before I explain everything, I need to do this first."

And then his lips closed on hers. Freya stiffened as he kissed her softly. She should stop him. He wasn't who he said he was, and today proved it, but her heart and body refused to listen to reason. When he brushed his fingers across the side of her face, Freya relaxed into him and deepened the kiss, her insides swirling with warmth. She gripped his tunic for support as he brushed his fingers into her hair.

When Keanon pulled away, they were both breathless. He rested his forehead against hers, his dark eyes burning. "You're right. I'm from the Empire." He only gave Freya a second to absorb the news before continuing. "I was sent here to gather information and plant doubt in the people so they might rebel against you, but when I ran into your team, my objective changed." Keanon brushed his thumb along Freya's jaw. "The Empire wanted me to help them capture you." Freya's heart thrummed faster from his confession. Deep passion brewed in his eyes that made her insides burn more intensely despite his words. The longing in his voice gripped her as she waited for him to continue.

"You were also right about another thing," he admitted. "This prophecy has been bothering me long before I met you. I asked many priests and scribes back home about the prophecy, and though their explanations were all solid, I couldn't come to terms with the drastic changes." Keanon shook his head. The hand resting on her cheek tensed. "I tried to ignore it and follow orders, but being with you—and seeing how strongly your people have chosen to rally behind your family—has made my doubts impossible to ignore. Something must have been misconstrued somewhere along the way."

"So, what are you going to do?" Freya was proud when her voice, though airy, came out strong and unshaken.

"Freya!" Cliff shouted her name in the distance, and Keanon lowered his hand from her face. She missed his touch immediately, though he grabbed her hands instead.

"We're over here! Archer will want to take a look at her, but I've got her stable for now. Is everyone else alright?" Keanon shouted back, still staring down at Freya with warmth in his gaze.

"Everyone will be!" Laia shouted from the same direction.

Lowering his voice so only she could hear, Keanon answered her question. "I'm going to help you. There's one thing I have to do at home, but when I return, I won't be going back to the Empire."

Freya's mind reeled at the constant twists in their conversation, and her gut clenched at the idea of him returning home after everything he'd revealed.

"What? Why would you go back?"

"I have to see my brother at least once." His voice was impassioned. "When I return, we can figure out what's going on with this prophecy together." Though he tried to reassure her, it didn't work. Freya shook her head vehemently. Something about the whole plan didn't sit right with her. Could he still be working against her? Was this all a ruse?

"Surely we can get a hold of your brother in a less dangerous way." She tried again, but he shook his head.

"He's my brother. I care about him too much not to try." Keanon's words didn't ease her worries, and her emotions must have shown on her face because he added, "Don't worry, this is what I've been trained for." He gave her a sly grin. "I told you I always win."

CHAPTER 6
VIVIAN

It had been three months since Brantyre received word of the war between Galleria and the Empire, and news continued to flood in from all over Eavdamos. When Galleria declined, it only took a week for the Empire to declare war on anyone opposing Emperor Asher's claim. While Kovdoran and Isdelle joined the Ashera Empire, King Therrowin stood behind King Alystaire in refusing Emperor Asher's rule. Word was that Faulkern was sending troops south to aid Galleria. King Therrowin had asked her father to come, too, and although they had good standings with Faulkern, her father had yet to make a decision. Their whole kingdom was divided on which choice was right.

How did no one know what to do, and why were the gods so silent when everyone was falling into war and chaos? What could Vivian possibly do to help?

Brantyre had just entered their warm season, where the sun took longer to set, and its warmth eased the chilling mountain air. Vivian's wardrobe shifted from thick velvet dresses and long coats to lighter satins with long sleeves. This was her favorite time of year, but on this beautiful day, she was stuck inside. She sprawled across the plush, pale blue couch in her sister's sitting room, the large fireplace opposite cold and barren. This was the only time of year it was left off during the day. Large windows invited all the warm light from outside, and Aida, ever the princess, sat straight in the chair beside the couch. By her sister's glazed expression, Vivian knew her mind was elsewhere.

"Oh, this pattern is beautiful." Her mother exclaimed, cross-legged on the floor. Her flowing green dress billowed around her as she held up a swatch of fabric for Aida's wedding dress. Even in such an unqueenly position, her mother still appeared regal, but while she had mastered the royal mask, her eyes appeared more tired than normal.

The pattern her mother held was of fine white satin embroidered with ice-blue lace snowflakes, creating the image of snowfall. It would be wonderful for Aida's wedding dress. Strewn about the room and across every surface were hundreds of patterns and materials for her dress. As was tradition, the silks, furs, and linens were all in shades of pale blue or white, like the ice and snow that would reclaim the mountains on the eve of the wedding, which was set to take place at the end of the summer. Though there were a few outliers in deep shades of green and dark blue for Vivian and her mother's dresses, the focus was on the bride's.

When neither of the sisters responded to their mother, she sighed and set the piece aside. "Alright, come here, you two." Rising to her feet, she nudged Vivian's legs off the couch and patted the spot between them for Aida to sit. "I know it's not easy right now," said their mother, picking up Aida's hands. Vivian ignored the twinge in her stomach. "Things are a lot more complicated than when I married your father, and I remember how hard that was for the both of us."

"But you love Father," said Aida, mirroring Vivian's confusion.

"I do. Of course, I do." She reassured them. "It is hard to explain, but like you with Tristain, your father and I grew up close friends." Their mother's smile of nostalgia then turned serious as she continued. "Though I believe I always loved him, I had been *betrothed* to him. When the choice is taken from you, it makes you wonder if you truly love someone or if your heart thinks it's in love because it knows no different." At the horrified expressions on both Aida's and Vivian's faces, their mother chuckled. "Don't fret now. I've come to understand, without a doubt, I would choose your father all over again, arranged marriage or not."

Their relief was short-lived as Aida slumped, staring at her hands in her lap. "It's not my feelings for Tristain I'm worried about... it's this prophecy. Am I not good enough to be queen?" A lone tear escaped and slid down her cheek. "I don't know who I am anymore."

"You are royalty, Princess Aida." Their mother brushed Aida's hair behind her ear, wiping away the tear streak with her thumb. Vivian placed her hand on her sister's arm. "*You* are chosen by the gods to watch over this land and guide the people, and you are my daughter, so loved and cherished, no matter what the future may hold."

Guilt washed over Vivian as a stabbing pain pierced her heart. With everything going on, Aida needed their mother's love and attention. It was not a time to be selfish and wish her mother would turn to her and say the same. However, the reminder did little to dim Vivian's desire as the hurt and guilt swarmed inside her.

As though she heard Vivian's inner turmoil, her mother glanced at her. "Don't you worry, your father and I will have everything figured out long before Aida will have to decide anything." But Vivian's worries had not been mollified. While she was concerned for her sister, Vivian could not shake Sasha's warnings. What about *her* future?

While Aida had been assuaged enough to participate in the preparations for her wedding, Vivian remained distant until someone knocked on the door.

"Your Highness." The servant bowed as he entered. "His Majesty has requested you and Princess Aida's presence in the throne room."

"Of course. We will be right down," replied her mother with a nod of dismissal. The servant left as her mother placed the fabric swatch on the table. "Well, I guess we will have to continue this later."

Vivian remained where she sat on the couch and watched with that familiar ache as her mother and sister departed from the room. After they left, she took the opportunity to escape to the terrace gardens, her favorite place on the palace grounds, and where she'd received her prophecy from Priestess Sasha. The gardens were now in full bloom, and though the breeze was still crisp, the sun was warm and invigorating. Vivian inhaled the sweet mountain air. She loved when the snow melted, and the hills were covered in wildflowers. The beautiful array of purples, pinks, blues, and yellows made the mountains look like a painting. These flowers were resilient in the harsh climate and bloomed immediately at the start of summer; they only had a few months before the snow covered them again.

The gardens were filled with many planter boxes and garden plots with well-trimmed bushes and flowers. A simple stone path carved a way through the shrubbery, and Vivian meandered through the garden beneath the vine arches forming a canopy above, and over to the bench, where she could peer across the mountains and Calliva City.

Placing her hands on the sun-warmed stones of the garden

wall, Vivian took in Brantyre's splendor. Even when everything else was falling apart, the beauty of Natura's creation always remained. If only Ductu, the god who was supposed to offer wisdom and guidance, would be more direct in his guidance. She shook her head at the awful thought and sighed.

"Hey, Vi." She jumped at Aida's voice, who stood rigidly behind her. The sun glittered on the silver tiara tucked atop her black curls. Her mask had slipped a bit, and her frown had deepened, frustration glinting in her eyes. Vivian gestured to the bench, and the two sat.

"Another letter from the Empire?" She'd seen a carrier arrive that morning. At her sister's nod, she frowned. Three letters seemed excessive, but she supposed her father's continued silence made them anxious for an answer.

"It was similar to the last one." Aida's voice was wooden. "They reminded us that it is the gods' will for us to unite, and Galleria is proof of what they will do if we refuse them." Vivian clasped her hands tightly in her lap, her gaze far off in the distance.

"As soon as we make our decision, we will be forced into war." Vivian hung her head, large curls spilling into her vision; she twirled one around her finger.

"That is what Father is afraid of, too. He doesn't want to send our troops to war, but we won't have a choice, not once we decide whether to accept this prophecy or not."

"How do we know what to do when our priests aren't in agreement?" Vivian huffed. *Why can't the gods be just a little clearer?*

"I know." Aida brushed her hair out of her face and stared at the canopy above their heads. "We got a letter from Galleria as well."

"Oh?"

"They're asking for help to fight against what they say is a misguided prophecy. They warn that if we don't decide what to do soon, we may not have a choice at all. If Galleria falls, so will Faulkern. Brantyre's army would not be able to stand up to that force on its own."

Vivian's twirling halted, her heart sinking at her sister's words. Although the far southern kingdom of Norrean had been silent on their allegiance, there was little chance the two kingdoms could take on the entire Empire if Galleria failed.

"What do you think Father will do?"

Aida shook her head. "I'm not sure… but Galleria also mentioned they would be willing to make a generous offer to our kingdom if we came to their aid."

"Did they say what that offer is?"

"Not yet. They are sending an ambassador to discuss it in person. He should arrive in the next few days."

Vivian's brow furrowed, and she spun her hair again. "Their deal won't matter if the priests confirm the prophecy is true, though."

Her sister shrugged. "If we don't get any clear indication from the gods, and our priests don't come to a consensus, Father may make his choice based on who gives Brantyre the best offer."

CHAPTER 7
RYKER

The sun beat down on Ryker's face, but the rushing wind offered sweet relief from the intense heat. Ryker leaned low on Artis's back as she raced down the dirt road away from the city, racing past farms and fields as they flew off the main track onto the dirt path in the woods.

Keanon's letter arrived four days ago, and Ryker had barely been able to focus on anything since. He'd spent all morning trying to scan over the maps he'd drawn for General Moreland while his mind wandered to thoughts of his brother. Keanon's note had been brief, but Ryker found himself repeating it over and over in his head.

Meet me in four days at the elm by midday.

Though there was no sign-off, it was clearly Keanon's handwriting, and he knew of only one elm his brother could be referring to. Since Ryker's promotion, and his ownership of a lykos, he was offered more freedom to ride out of the city than most other soldiers. Lykos required more exercise than the common horse or eldeer, so no one questioned Ryker when he rode out of the barracks before midday. All his trainees were getting in line for their midday meal, so Ryker had time before needing to head back.

His heart raced at the thought of seeing his brother again after three months apart. While he was excited to see Keanon, he frowned at the risk his brother was taking by leaving, potentially compromising his position. If Keanon was caught by Princess Freya, he would lose any credibility he had gained with her or her team, but Ryker trusted Keanon knew what he was doing, though he couldn't help but wonder why they kept failing to capture the princess. If Keanon was so confident in his position to leave it, why were they still unsuccessful? General Moreland had struggled to keep his composure when their most recent trap had failed. It had been a solid plan, yet they had returned empty-handed.

Their lack of results worried Ryker, but he hoped by talking with Keanon in person, they could come up with a better solution together.

All his thoughts ceased when his family home came into view at the end of the road, and he slowed Artis to a light trot. Her back hooves clipped on the gravelly path leading up to the house as he skirted the side and entered the backyard, pulling Artis to a halt.

At the bottom of the grassy hill beneath a large elm tree, his brother knelt before a stone pillar. Ryker fought the tears burning in his eyes and throat and instinctively reached for his father's compass hanging from his neck. About a week after Keanon left on assignment, their father had succumbed to his illness. Burying their father by himself had been one of the hardest things for Ryker to do. General Moreland had helped immensely, purchasing the stone, and bringing soldiers together to dig the grave, but more than anything, Ryker had wanted Keanon to be there.

On silent feet, Ryker descended the hill slowly to give his brother as much alone time as possible. Seeming to sense the solemn atmosphere, Artis remained quiet by his side as they approached. A lone horse nibbled on the grass nearby—clearly Keanon's mount—and it whickered upon noticing Ryker and Artis, drawing Keanon's attention. His watery eyes met Ryker's.

"Hey." It was the only word Ryker could think to say, but it was filled with all the sorrow and joy mingling inside him. It was such a strange and powerful combination, forcing tears into his eyes.

"Hey." Keanon offered a wobbly smile.

Several moments ticked by as the brothers stood there. For the first time, they shared the loss of their father in silence. A light breeze blew across Ryker's face, cooling the sweat beading on his forehead.

Finally, Keanon spoke. "It's good to see you."

"It's been too long," Ryker agreed. As though their words broke some invisible hold keeping them in place, Ryker bridged the distance and wrapped his arms around Keanon's shoulders. Suddenly, Ryker was whole again.

"How have you been?" Keanon asked as he pulled away. Artis took the opportunity to butt her large head into Keanon's chest, who complied with her demand and scratched behind her ears. She leaned into his touch.

"Artis, go free," Ryker commanded, and Artis immediately bounded across the grassy fields. While she exerted her boundless energy, Ryker returned his attention to his brother. "I should be asking you that question." He smiled, though obliged nonetheless. "Mostly, I've been training the new recruits, but I was given an interesting task by General Moreland that I just recently completed." He couldn't fight the proud grin lighting up his face as he relayed the job to plan their army's route through Galleria.

"Wow, that's huge, man." Keanon smiled, tapping his index finger rhythmically against his leg, but as his brow furrowed, Ryker knew his next question. "We're going after Blackstone?"

"Yeah, I know." Ryker shook his head. "General Moreland hasn't shared the plans for the city yet. He wanted me to focus on getting us there first, and I think I've come up with several paths that will work. Whatever the plan is, one of them should do."

"Knowing your talent for geography, I'm sure you've got something solid." While Keanon's praise filled Ryker with great pride, his brother's agitated finger-tapping continued.

Worried, Ryker prodded, "Alright, now talk. How is everything really going with you?"

Keanon brushed a hand through his hair. "I'm alright, really. The princess and her right-hand man were both very suspicious of me from the get-go. Trying to build that trust has been quite tedious."

"But you're here," Ryker pointed out, "so you've built enough trust to sneak away without causing suspicions."

"I believe I have finally gained her trust." Keanon's face was unreadable as his tapping continued.

Ryker frowned. "Something's bothering you. You can't hide things from me."

"I managed to keep Artis a secret," Keanon countered. When he said her name, Artis paused her prancing to glance in their direction. Her tongue lolled as she tilted her head before bounding around the wrought-iron fence at the edge of the field and into the trees. She hadn't had a good hunt in some time, so he let her go. She wouldn't go far; Ryker knew a quick whistle would have her rushing back.

Keanon brushed a hand through his hair and sighed. "Do you remember the question I asked you in The Battleaxe before this all started?"

Ryker's mind raced through past conversations, trying to remember the night in question. They had spent many nights in The Battleaxe before Keanon left. It was near impossible to pinpoint the exact conversation he referred to.

When Ryker shook his head, Keanon pinched the bridge of his nose. "Yeah, I figured." Keanon scratched the back of his head and took a deep breath. "I'd asked you what you thought about the prophecy."

Clarity struck Ryker, and his shoulders tensed. "I believe I told you at the time that the priests know better than I ever could."

His answer didn't appease Keanon like it had last time. "Yes, I remember that being your answer."

A tight feeling of dread filled Ryker. "So, why are you asking again? Nothing has changed since then. I imagine the priests took their time considering the gods' intentions before sharing such a huge prophecy with Emperor Asher."

At the emperor's name, Keanon glanced away. "You've never once wondered if there was a chance they misunderstood the vision?"

Confusion and horror seized Ryker at his brother's audacity. "No, Keanon, that's blasphemy." What was happening? These were not the kinds of questions and concerns an Imperial spy should have.

"It's not blasphemy to question things, Ryker." Keanon's voice grew agitated. "It's how you expand your own understanding of how the gods work. They speak to more people than just the priests, you know."

"Are you saying the gods have sent you a vision? Ductu has told you specifically that this prophecy isn't true?" snapped Ryker.

"Come on, now. You know that's not what I'm saying. I never said the prophecy wasn't true. I merely wondered if it had been misinterpreted." Keanon's growing frustration only heightened Ryker's fears.

"Why are you saying this? Where is this all coming from?"

"Can't you just—" Keanon began pacing, shaking his head. "I wish you would—"

"Just what, Keanon? Just believe the worst in our priests? In our emperor? In everything we have believed in and trained to protect?" Ryker clenched his fists as he threw accusations at his brother. "Where is this coming from?"

"They fight for *them*." Keanon's face was pinched as he spun to face Ryker. His eyes flashed with such intensity that Ryker stepped back. "The people, the soldiers—even the priests of Galleria fight for the royal family." Keanon's voice rose the more he spoke. "How many royal families in history that lost their rights to rule kept the loyalty of their entire kingdom intact? Especially when they resisted the new authority?" He raised a hand before Ryker could answer. "Being the one who studied more of our history, I'll tell you! Not a single one of them."

"That doesn't mean anything now!" Ryker snapped, "This is something that has never happened before, so of course the priests of other kingdoms could resist, but the priests of Kovdoran and Isdelle accepted the changes."

Keanon's jaw tightened, and he shook his head. "I had hoped you would have at least considered things."

"Is this why you still haven't captured the princess?" Ryker shot back. There was a flash of something unreadable in his brother's face, so subtle that most people would assume they'd imagined it. But Keanon's finger was tapping, and a feeling was building inside Ryker—a feeling he couldn't explain. His brother didn't have to say anything because Ryker already knew the answer.

"I have to go." Keanon turned and grabbed the reins of his horse.

"Wait!" Ryker called out as Keanon mounted. His heart hammered at the sadness yet firm determination in his brother's eyes. "You're not... You're not going to do anything rash, are you?"

Keanon shook his head. "I don't do anything rash, Ryker. I pray someday you will be the same. Maybe you'll think about what I've said someday, and I'll see you then."

With that blow to Ryker's heart, Keanon bounded away. For several long seconds, Ryker stood rooted to the spot, numb as the retreating back of his brother disappeared behind the house. What had happened to him? Was the princess using him? Had she weaseled her way into Keanon's head and manipulated him against his own people? One terrifying thought uprooted Ryker from where he stood.

Keanon was in trouble.

Heart beating from his chest, Ryker let out a loud whistle and began running up the hill toward the house. By the time he reached the back of the building, Artis bounded up beside him. He launched onto her back before racing down the dirt path, onto the main road, through the gates of the city, and into the barracks. With every stride she made, that one thought overpowered all others. Keanon was in trouble.

The sun had lowered in the sky, and shadows from the trees and buildings stretched larger with each passing minute. Ryker's panic continued to build. It wouldn't be long before his brother crossed the border, and they had to get to him before then.

Ryker rushed past soldiers milling through the barracks. He leaped off Artis's back and burst into General Moreland's office, whose eyes widened at the intrusion. He immediately rose to his feet, his hand on the hilt of his sword.

"What's wrong?" The general demanded as Ryker gasped, catching his breath.

"It's my brother, Sir." Ryker panted. "I think he's been compromised."

General Moreland was around his desk in seconds. "How do you know? What have you learned?"

In broken half-truths, Ryker told him about his brother's letter, the meeting with him, and how his brother seemed off. "There was something about him. He isn't himself, Sir, and something about the way he spoke... I think he's in trouble."

"Has he gone back?"

"He was riding back, but he's probably still in Ashera. A seeker would be able to catch him."

General Moreland nodded. "There's no time to waste then."

Ryker shadowed General Moreland's every move as he got to work. Following the general's orders, the seekers rode out. Lykos' howls erupted into the quiet of the late afternoon. All the while, the pang in Ryker's heart and the hollow feeling in his stomach grew. Would they get to his brother in time? He took a few brief moments to return Artis to her stall before finding General Moreland again.

"Why didn't you tell me when you got your brother's letter?" General Moreland asked, breaking the tense silence.

Ryker flinched. "I'm sorry, Sir." There had been nothing in Keanon's letter suggesting it be kept a secret, but something about the way the carrier had flown straight to his quarters— and the lack of signature—made it feel like a secretive affair. "I guess I was so excited to see him, but I should have told you."

"Yes, I agree." General Moreland placed a hand on Ryker's shoulder. "But I am glad you have come to me now."

"Where is he?"

Ryker cringed, his hands automatically clenching by his sides at the sound of that clipped, aggravating voice. Vaan appeared behind General Moreland, his dark eyes flashing as he glared at Ryker.

"What do you want?" Ryker snapped.

"I was informed we had a possible loss of assets and that your brother may be compromised," sneered Vaan, practically swooning at the revelation. "It's my job to clean up this mess, find out what's happened to him, and what the princess has learned about his true identity and allegiance."

Ryker's blood boiled, and he had to bite his tongue before he said something unsavory in front of the general. Since they had started their training together, Vaan's great disdain for the twins was clear. Nothing Keanon or Ryker said or did to try to befriend Vaan worked, and the brothers could not figure out why he hated them so. When it was clear they wouldn't change his mind, the twins made it a point to avoid him as much as they could. Somehow, the arrogant, slimy man had worked his way up to a high-value position with the emperor. Though Ryker wasn't exactly sure what Vaan did, he seemed to have his hand in almost everything.

The sun had set behind the walls of the city, the sky melting into shades of red and pink, casting shadows across the barracks. Shouts rang out from the gates, and a howl ripped through the air. A sinking feeling filled Ryker as he watched the seekers burst through the gates, where Keanon sat on the back of one of the lykos, with his hands bound like a criminal.

From across the barracks, Keanon's eyes locked with Ryker's. After their argument, Ryker expected rage, fury, even disappointment. He was completely unprepared for the grim acceptance and compassion in his brother's eyes, who gave him a sad smile.

Ryker's heart seemed to tear in half as he watched the seekers lead Keanon to where Ryker stood beside General Moreland and Vaan.

"I'm sorry, Keanon. We'll sort this out," General Moreland said when Keanon stopped in front of them.

Almost skipping forward, Vaan stepped in front of the general. "Bring him this way." Before anyone could move, more shouts rang out from the gates.

"We need help!"

"Someone get the menders!"

Everyone's eyes went wide as they all rushed toward the gates. General Moreland pushed to the front. "What's going on?"

"It's bad, Sir." The soldier at the gate replied, her face pinched with worry. On the ground behind her, a lone soldier had collapsed on his side. An arrow protruded from his shoulder, blood coating his clothes. His breathing was shallow, his face a sickly pallor.

"What happened to you?" General Moreland bent down.

The soldier blinked, his eyes pale and laced with pain. "A... a... mbush... fail..."

Ryker's jaw went slack.

"Were you part of the latest ambush for the princess?" asked General Moreland, his voice urgent but gentle.

The young soldier nodded.

"What happened to you?" Vaan barreled to the front and bent low beside the general.

"Be... trayed..." The soldier gasped, his voice losing strength. "K... Keanon... shot..." The soldier passed out before he could say more. The blood rushed from Ryker's face as the injured soldier's words sank in.

"Move out of the way," a deep commanding voice of the lead mender pushed through the growing crowd. "This man needs attention, not an interrogation." With that, the menders carefully lifted the limp body and carried him to the mender's ward.

"This makes things infinitely more interesting." Vaan smirked as he turned back to where Keanon stood with his hands still tied and seekers surrounding him. Keanon's jaw was tense, refusing to back down from Vaan's gleeful gaze.

"We are going to have a wonderful conversation now." Vaan didn't seem fazed by Keanon's indifference as he led the seekers toward the back of the barracks.

"Stay here, Ryker." General Moreland ordered, following Vaan to his quarters to interrogate his brother.

Unable to do anything, Ryker collapsed to the ground by the front gates, struck by fear and pain. What had he done? What was going to happen to Keanon?

The sky blackened, and the stars came out; soldiers lit the torches along the walls as Ryker remained on the ground, unblinking, his vision blurry, and his eyes dry.

"You think he'll be okay?"

A sudden voice jolted Ryker from his stupor, and he blinked. Leo stood a few steps away, his expression forlorn. The boy came and sat on the ground before him.

"I... don't know." The words fell from Ryker's mouth and left him hollow.

"I'm sure he'll be fine," Leo said, trying to reassure Ryker. "You've told me so many good things about him." Ryker forced a faint smile, and the two sat in tense silence.

Finally, after the night guards took over their shift, the doors to the general's quarters opened, and both Ryker and Leo stood. General Moreland stepped out first, his expression unreadable as he made his way over to Ryker. Vaan followed behind, the slimiest grin on his face. Keanon was brought out next with a seeker close behind him, holding onto his arm.

"I'm sorry, Ryker." General Moreland began, his stoic facade breaking as he spoke. "It's worse than you thought."

"What do you mean?" Trepidation made Ryker's voice faint and he peeked over the general's shoulder to where Vaan led the seeker behind the barracks with Keanon in tow. "Where are they going?"

"I've had to place your brother under arrest for treason." Tears glinted in General Moreland's eyes as he placed a hand on Ryker's shoulder. "He's been sentenced to death."

Unimaginable agony pierced Ryker's heart, and if it weren't for the general's hold on his arm, he would have collapsed. He was only half aware of the general holding him up as, along with Leo, they guided him back to his quarters. His feet moved mechanically as his mind refused to acknowledge reality.

This wasn't real.

This couldn't be real.

CHAPTER 8
VIVIAN

Several days later, just as Aida had predicted, the advisor from Galleria arrived to discuss their kingdom's offer. Vivian stood at the top of the grand marble staircase. In the foyer, where the polished white steps descended in a curve, the grand double doors opened, allowing the southern entourage inside. She rested a hand atop the black iron railing as the Gallerion advisor bowed low before her parents. He introduced himself as Quintin Scanlon. Despite being the king's advisor, he wore a simple sea green hood, black trousers, and boots with no embellishing jewels or embroidery. His dusty brown hair was speckled with gray, and the skin around his green eyes crinkled as he spoke.

Her parents directed him to the double doors to the left of the staircase leading to the throne room. Quintin prepared to follow but stalled as his eyes fell on Vivian at the top of the stairs.

"Is this your eldest?"

"Yes, this is Princess Vivian," answered her father, though his brows creased as Quintin studied her.

"Would it be possible for her to join us today?" he asked,

turning back to face the king with an open and hopeful expression.

Vivian's grip on the railing tightened. Why did he want her to attend? Throughout the years, no one had specifically requested her attendance in the meeting, not since Aida was chosen. Excitement and dread warred inside her as Priestess Sasha's prophecy flashed in her mind.

Her father did not let anything show on his face as he considered the advisor's request. After a few painfully long moments, he agreed, and indicated for Vivian to follow. Her heart soared as excitement won, but she tried to disguise it as she descended the stairs. If the prophecy was going to be fulfilled, she was glad it was happening now. She was losing her mind in the waiting.

The long table had been arranged in the center of the room for the meeting, and a servant finished situating another chair as they filed inside. Only High Priestess Sasha was present at the table with them. Her father and mother sat at the head of the table, with Aida on their right and Sasha on their left. Vivian hesitated. She'd never sat at this table before. Aida saved her by indicating the spot beside her, and Vivian fought the urge to run to it.

She clasped her hands tightly in her lap, her fingers itching to spin a curl of hair that was styled around her face. *Of all days to wear it down*, she thought. So focused on stilling her hands, Vivian missed the pleasantries as the meeting got underway. She reminded herself to pay attention. There was a smaller attendance for this meeting, and she suspected her parents had kept it minimal to hear and consider Galleria's offer without external opinions first.

"I understand the gods' visions aren't always clear. Many times, I have consulted with my king over a prophecy he was given that didn't explicitly tell him what to do. Together, we prayed and sought Ductu to guide our steps." Quintin paused, meeting the eyes of everyone present. When they landed on Vivian's, he held a beat longer. She squeezed her hands tighter until he looked away. "This kind of prophecy is reminiscent of one we receive regarding the chosen heir. If that is the case, I would expect all our priests—yours and ours—would be given this vision as well."

Vivian fought a neutral expression as she considered his words. It was something she'd questioned, too. Why hadn't the gods sent the vision to everyone? Like an heir taking the throne after their parents, it would have made the transition smoother if everyone was reassured the gods' will was being fulfilled.

"You are asking the gods to clarify their will?" Sasha raised a brow and leaned forward, resting her wrinkled hands atop her cane.

Good luck with that. Vivian glanced around, hoping her thoughts hadn't reflected on her face, but no one was paying her any attention.

"Our priests prayed; we all did when we received the message about the prophecy. I was there when King Alystaire discussed it with the priests and asked if he was supposed to surrender his crown. The only vision our priests saw was of Prince Damian sitting on the *throne* after his father." The emphasis on the word throne was not missed by anyone. Beside her, Aida shifted in her seat and wrung her hands under the table, her expression neutral.

"Hmm..." Sasha rubbed her chin thoughtfully, but said nothing.

Quintin took in everyone's silence and continued. "I realize this is complicated. Never before have our kingdoms been so divided on a matter of the gods." His admission revealed how worn he was from the ordeal, his green eyes faded and tired. He shook his head. "I won't press this decision from you at this moment. I know how hard this all is, but I do worry Tempus will force a choice upon you soon enough." He straightened in his seat and changed the topic to the matter at hand. "My hope is that what I have come to offer might aid you in coming to a decision sooner. King Alystaire is willing to make an offer with Brantyre that will help both our kingdoms prosper.

"First, we would like to make it easier for our kingdoms to trade. We wish to offer a similar plan that we've made with Faulkern. There's a nice section of land—a day's journey west of Riverwood—where we would like to develop a new town that Brantyre would have dual ownership of. This would offer a place for both kingdoms' people to reside and use for business and easier trade."

Vivian was impressed by such an amazing opportunity. She hadn't realized how closely Galleria and Faulkern were allied, but to have access to Galleria's warmer climate and farmlands would be amazing for their people.

"We would also like to offer a discounted rate within this new town for the purchase of blackstone tools and weapons for Brantyre." Vivian's eyes widened at that. None of the people in their kingdom used blackstone tools, except a select few generals and personal guards with swords crafted from it. Galleria had kept the prices of the precious material high, making it incredibly difficult for any of the other kingdoms to accumulate much of it.

If this was how King Alystaire treated kingdoms he was closely allied with, she wondered why they hadn't befriended them before. Why had her parents not put in more effort to strengthen their relationships with any of the southern kingdoms? Brantyre's only connections were their northern neighbors, and for the first time, Vivian wondered why.

"There is one last thing we would like to offer, Your Majesty," Quintin continued, but when he glanced around the room again, his eyes resting on Vivian, her heart slowed. "We understand your youngest daughter..." He nodded respectfully at her sister. "Princess Aida is your heir. We would like to arrange a way to unite our kingdoms in a strong bond that would last for generations." Vivian forgot to breathe at the look in his eyes; her body went rigid as a sense of knowing filled her. "We would like to arrange the marriage between your eldest, Princess Vivian, and our crown prince, Damian."

Unaware of her turmoil, Quintin redirected his attention to her parents. Her world turned upside down as the words crashed over her. Sasha said she would have a part to play. Now she realized she was to marry Prince Damian and become a queen. There had been arranged marriages between the kingdoms' royal families before, but it was rare, and she'd never heard of it involving a chosen heir like Prince Damian. Once the gods had chosen Aida, Vivian had accepted she would never be queen.

She clenched her fists, battling with the sudden need for space. When she opened her eyes, they fell on the High Priestess, who leaned forward on her cane, eyes narrowed and focused as she considered the news. It wasn't Sasha's fault. There was no way the older woman could have known what the gods had planned, but resentment still seeped into Vivian's heart.

Her father rested his chin on his clasped hands, only a hint of shock registering in his dark eyes as Galleria's offer settled over him. It was clear he was interested in the prospect of having another daughter being crowned queen. Empathy softened her mother's face when her eyes met Vivian's; she flashed her daughter a sad smile.

Tears welled in Vivian's throat, and she blinked several times to keep them at bay. She stared at the pale-yellow flowers trailing down the side of her blue skirt, while her heart hammered in her chest. She focused on her breathing to stay calm and keep from bolting out of the room.

A few more things were said between the advisor and her father, but she was no longer paying attention. She was relieved when everyone rose. Vivian forced a blank expression as Quintin was guided away to a room for the evening, but when he was gone, she ran. Someone called after her, but she wasn't listening. She burst through a side door of the throne room and darted up the winding staircase leading to the hall with the royal chambers. The need for air enveloped her. Straight across the staircase was a large double door that she burst through into her favorite terrace garden. Mountain air caressed her flustered, warm skin, and she breathed deeply, letting it fill her.

Vivian soaked up the beauty of her home, and the mountains she loved so much that it hurt to think of leaving it behind, but the stirring in her heart was as clear as the blue skies above. This was going to happen just as the gods had decreed it would.

She sat on one of the benches and pulled her knees to her chest. It wasn't very princessy—or queenly, for that matter—but she didn't care. Wrapping her arms around her legs, Vivian laid her head on her knees and let the first tear fall.

There was a click on the stone path as footsteps approached and she scrambled to sit upright, wiping her face.

"Don't worry about formalities, dear."

She cringed at Priestess Sasha's voice. The priestess was the last person Vivian wanted to talk to. Sasha came and sat on the bench beside her. It wasn't her fault. The prophecy would be fulfilled regardless of if Sasha had told her or not. Vivian rested her head back on her knees, facing away from the High Priestess.

"You are fretting about something that hasn't been decided yet."

"But it has been decided." Vivian didn't turn as another tear trailed down her cheek. "This is exactly like what you said, right? The gods were going to use me for something I wasn't prepared for." When the priestess didn't respond, she continued. "I knew I wouldn't be married for love, but I'd always thought my father would choose one of his advisors' sons like he'd done with Aida. Me and Aida always talked about how she wanted to make me one of her advisors when she was queen, so I could stay here in the palace and marry someone I at least knew."

"Look at me." Sasha waited until Vivian caved and turned to her. The older woman's pale eyes bore into her own as she spoke. "We do not know this is what the gods meant when they sent me that vision." She placed a reassuring hand on Vivian's shoulder. "I won't lie to you, dear. This does sound promising from what I saw, but I cannot say for certain if this is the path you are meant to take." Her faded gray eyes were kind as she added, "If this is the gods' will for you, they will guide you as they do for every king or queen."

"I've never felt led by the gods, though," Vivian countered half-heartedly. She wasn't sure how the gods guided anyone. Besides the priesthood with their visions, how should she know what they would do to lead her?

Sasha chuckled. "There are many people that don't realize how they are led by the gods unless they are paying attention. Rich or poor, royalty or not, Natura is always bringing new life; Tempus takes every spirit of those who pass on, and Ductu guides all that need him." She patted Vivian's shoulder and gave her a reassuring smile. "For your whole life, the gods have been just as invested in you as they have been to Aida."

It hadn't felt like the gods cared much about her life until now. No one paid her as much attention as they did Aida, and although she understood it was because of Aida's responsibility and title, Vivian knew she could have done more as a princess of Brantyre if she'd been allowed. She had a lot to offer. Oftentimes, she helped prepare Aida for meetings, who would offer Vivian's advice as her own—advice their father loved.

"I still wish I knew Prince Damian."

"Hmm…" A smile reached Sasha's eyes as she snickered. "If you'd been listening to the advisor, you would have heard that Prince Damian plans to visit us himself."

"What?" Vivian dropped her legs and turned to face the priestess. "He is?" When Sasha nodded, her stomach fluttered and thoughts flooded her. What was he like? What did he look like?

Sasha pulled herself to her feet with her cane but gave Vivian one more word of encouragement. "Have patience, dear. Everything will come to pass at the right time."

She listened to the click of Sasha's cane as the priestess left her to take in the sight of the glorious mountains once more. There were only a few short weeks left before the peaks would be covered in snow again. Would this be the last time she got to see them like this?

Two sets of feet drew toward her, and she braced for whoever could be seeking her out now.

"Vi?"

Her stomach churned at her mother's voice, and it dropped when both of her parents stood before her. Her mother's face was tight, her mouth turned in a strained smile of comfort, though her father didn't fight his frown, his eyes worn and tense. This was the most their masks had broken in front of Vivian, which unnerved her. After a moment of stretched-out silence, her mother sat beside her on the bench. Her father remained standing.

"I want you to understand we will not rush you into anything." Her father faltered before continuing. "While this might be a great opportunity for Brantyre, we still have other things to consider."

Other things? Was she one of those things? Even if she was, nothing her parents said or did would change the certainty she had in her heart that she was leaving.

Her mother took her hand in hers like she had done for Aida several days ago. "*I* want you to have a say in this decision." Her voice was firm, and though her father's frown deepened, he didn't argue.

But her mother would not be shaken. "Your thoughts and opinions will be taken into account as strongly as your father's and I's."

Clearing his throat to gain their attention, her father said, "An ambassador from the Empire is set to arrive any day now. With the prince's visit and the ambassador, we should be able to receive some clarity about this prophecy and draw closer to a decision for Brantyre."

Vivian nodded her understanding. Why she still hesitated to share Sasha's prophecy with her parents, she didn't know, but she kept quiet. Something inside her made her hold her tongue, and with a final squeeze of her hands, her mother rose and disappeared with her father toward the palace.

With a long sigh, Vivian returned her gaze to the splendor of the mountains, while the rhythm of her beating heart resounded with an assurance that this place would not be her home for much longer.

CHAPTER 9
FREYA

"Keanon!"

Freya's anguished cry pierced the air as soldiers dragged her away, kicking and flailing. They held her tight while her body shook uncontrollably, her eyes never wavering from Keanon's lifeless form on the ground, and the man responsible standing over him with blood pooling at his feet. Freya's heart crumbled with every breath she took.

A surge of boiling rage overtook her, and she swung her elbow back at one of the men holding her, connecting with his chin. He cried out and released her as blood dribbled from his mouth, and with her hand now free, she punched the other soldier in the nose, and it cracked. As soon as his hold slackened, Freya sprinted back toward Keanon, seeing nothing but him.

She'd not managed to get far when the tip of a sword forced her to a sudden halt. Fists clenched and heart stuttering, Freya came face to face with an imperial general. She cast her eyes between him and Keanon's body only a few feet away.

"Don't challenge me, princess. You are of use to us alive," the general gestured behind him, and she chanced a glance to where Laia was held between two soldiers, one of whom held a blade against her throat. A trickle of blood stained her neck as he pressed it deeper. "But she's not."

Freya's moment of hesitation was enough for more soldiers to surround and grab her, giving her no choice but to obey. Rage abandoned her, and she did not resist as they pulled her away. More soldiers appeared, blocking her view of Keanon's body. The further from Keanon she went, the greater the numbing fog consumed her. She was vaguely aware of her surroundings as they reached the prison she'd broken Keanon out of moments ago.

The soldiers led her underground and stripped her of everything—weapons, packs, clothes—then replaced it with plain, tattered rags like those Keanon had worn. Even her boots were removed, leaving her barefoot on the cold, filthy stone floor. They clamped chains around her wrists, and she flinched at the cold metal digging into her skin before they shoved her in front of Laia. The fog around Freya's mind kept her from processing anything but her direct surroundings. A few stray sconces flickered with just enough light to guide her next steps on the uneven ground as they led the pair down a long, dark corridor.

They opened one of the cells at the end of the hall and forced them both inside, chaining their ankles to the far wall. The door clanged shut with a finality that sent Freya to her knees. Fat tears slid down her cheeks as she choked on her sobs, desperate for air. Keanon's tender, pained expression was clear in her mind as he'd lain in her arms, his body jerking as he desperately tried to gulp more air as blood filled his throat. Through her tears, there was a ghost of his warm, rough hand brushing against her cheek as his voice whispered from The After, *"I love you, Freya."*

Pulling her knees close, she rocked on the cold stone floor, her wails echoing down the halls. Laia's distressed voice called out to her, but her pleas couldn't penetrate Freya's anguish. In the back of her mind, Laia placed a hand on her shoulder and shook her, but Freya couldn't find a way out of the darkness to respond.

Instead, she curled on the floor and cried until she was a husk of herself. When she finally peeled her crusted eyes open, it was impossible to tell the passage of time without windows. The darkness was almost complete except for the faint torchlight emanating through a small grate at the bottom of the iron door.

They sat in the same cell they'd broken Keanon out of that morning. Was it just that morning? Her heart stuttered as she continued to study their surroundings. The cell was damp, and the air was cooler underground. The summer sun couldn't penetrate the underground stone box they were in, and the rags she wore offered little reprieve from the chill seeping into her skin.

Pushing away the mass of hair plastered to the wetness on her cheeks, Freya leaned on her arm as she attempted to organize her thoughts into something useful. The walk to their cell was hazy, but Keanon's had been the one at the furthest end of the hall. She struggled to recall where the guards had taken her belongings, but they would need those to get out.

Freya's frustration mounted as she wrestled with her addled brain, piecing more details about the prison together. There were two other cells along the hallway, but they were empty, meaning the only prisoners were Freya and Laia. The guards had stationed themselves at the outside door when they snuck in to get Keanon. Straining her ear now, she assumed they must be up top, as there were no noises on the other side of the door. They were down there alone.

Gentle fingers stroked Freya's back. She glanced up at Laia, who stared blankly into the darkness, keeping her hand pressed against Freya's back as if to say, *I'm here. You are not alone.* Shadows warred in Laia's dark eyes, and tears stained her pale cheeks. A small stain of blood remained on her neck from the soldier's sword.

Freya stretched and winced at her body's resistance after being curled tight for so long. The chains rattled and banged against her ankles, and Laia jumped at the sound, the agony in her dark eyes urging Freya closer. She took Laia's hand, and they snuggled together as the cool air seeped in and made them shiver.

As they lay there, Freya remembered the day she first met Laia. Five years ago, she accompanied her uncle to deliver specialty weapons to the king. Freya had been peeking into the throne room from the servants' stairwell with Harper and Cliff when the master blacksmith and his niece came into view. Laia appeared to be a sweet city girl, her big brown eyes wide in awe at the grandeur of the palace. Freya and Harper had both been excited about the beautifully crafted blackstone weapons, but Cliff had a hard time taking his eyes off the girl. At that moment, Freya and Harper made it their mission to befriend Laia, much to Cliff's embarrassment. It had proved an easy task; the girls were quickly won over by Laia's impeccable eye for well-crafted blades.

Heart hurting, Freya spoke through her raw, aching throat. "We have to get out of here."

"We'll figure something out," Laia said, squeezing her hand.

Freya coughed, then declared into the dark, "I'm going to fix this." It was almost a relief to push aside her pain while her mind worked to find a plan. Though guilt threatened to wash over her, her aching heart could wait. They needed to get out of there.

Laia shivered and shook her head against Freya's shoulder.

"There's nothing *you* have to fix. I sent a note to Cliff after we left. They'll come for us."

Freya winced at the thought of the team hearing about what she'd done. Cliff would be so panicked, but this wasn't his fault, nor was it his responsibility to keep her safe despite her father bestowing him that task. Thinking of Cliff's agony filled Freya with more guilt than she could bear.

What made it worse was knowing she had failed. She should have known better—should have planned better. Instead, she'd let her heart direct her head and put a lot at risk. Her father had enough problems in this war without her muddying the waters further.

They both jumped when a bang ricocheted off the walls and rattled dirt from the ceiling. Footsteps descended the stone steps, growing louder as they drew near. Freya was on her feet when the person stopped outside their door. She bunched her hands into fists, but the cell didn't open. Instead, the grate at the bottom of the iron door screeched, and a single tray slid through the opening. On top was a piece of bread, a hunk of moldy cheese, and two small cups of water.

What a grand affair.

Even the unappetizing food made her stomach growl. How long had it been since her last meal? At least the meager bread wasn't moldy, and she tore the rock-hard roll in half. Tiny flakes crumbled to the floor like dust, making her long for Lanzo's freshly baked bread. Never again would she criticize his need for good food while on the road. The first bite turned to tasteless shavings on her tongue, and Freya coughed up crumbs, her eyes watering. She lunged for the small cup.

Laia wisely dipped her half of the roll into the water. She still frowned as she popped it in her mouth, but soggy bread was better than choking on it. Freya peeled off the fuzzy, green bits from the cheese and put those back on the tray. There wasn't much left, but at least it tasted fine. When the two returned their cups to the tray, Freya knocked on the grate, and whoever was on the other side opened it and dragged the tray back through the opening with their boot, tipping over the empty cups as it scratched along the stone floor. The person retreated the way they had come, and when the door banged closed above, Freya relaxed.

Laia shivered, and soon after, chills raced up Freya's body.

"Come on," said Freya, offering her friend a hand. "We don't know how long we will be here, but we can't sit idle."

The cold, damp floor seeped into Freya's bare feet, but she ignored it and paced the width of the cell as far as her chains allowed. Laia followed her example. After some paces, they managed to warm up, but she didn't want to overdo it. She itched to practice some combat, but worried their chains would cause unnecessary harm.

It didn't take long until exhaustion caught up to her and she collapsed beside Laia. The pair agreed to take turns resting in case someone should come down the stairs. Sleep proved elusive, though. Whenever Freya closed her eyes, her subconscious tortured her by replaying Keanon's death. Laia didn't fare much better, her chains rattling as she tossed and turned.

Time passed with no change. None of the soldiers spoke to them, or even opened the door, and the only way to gauge the passing of time was through the food pushed through the grate three times a day. Otherwise, it was dark and quiet. After their meals, they would pace the cell to keep warm and fit in the miserable darkness, and all the while, Freya's frustration mounted as a solemn fear took root.

There was no way to escape this hell.

RYKER

Ryker stared blankly at the waist-high, stone pillar. Moss grew up the sides and covered the words on the bottom, and though the rest was faded and hard to read, he'd long ago memorized them. *Hailey Kessler, beloved woman of the faith and guide to the lost. Loving wife and mother. Tempus called her home too soon.* Ryker's mother passed away when her father was the advisor to the previous king when he and his brother were six. His memory of his mother was limited, but he could still envision the way her smile lit up her face and how her dark eyes glittered when she laughed. Even though it was traditional for priestesses to pull their hair up, she'd always preferred to keep her long auburn hair down. His most cherished memory was of her and his father slow dancing in the foyer, which they often did when they thought the twins had gone to bed, but once his mother had caught him peeking from the top of the stairs and winked at him before being twirled away.

When his father had stepped down as advisor after King Asher was crowned and was sent west to Mésis City, he'd ripped up the original stone for his wife's grave and brought her with him, where she had been reburied in their new backyard under the singular, massive elm at the back of the sprawling grassy field. Sunlight sprinkled through the wide branches and kept the tombstone well-shaded. Now, two more stones accompanied his mother's. Ryker couldn't bring himself to acknowledge either of them yet. Squeezing his eyes closed, he tried to shut out the pain of reliving the last time he was here as he'd walked down the hill to find his brother on his knees. Ryker clutched the compass around his neck, wishing desperately for a scrap of his father's wisdom.

From the corner of his eye, he saw the empty hole in front of the newest stone. One of the last maids remaining at the house had offered to dig it for him—her last kind gesture before moving to serve a new family. She was one of the few people who had been willing to help him since Keanon had died in dishonor. General Moreland was the sole reason Ryker had been permitted to bring Keanon home to lay him beside their parents. Everyone said he did not deserve to be remembered, but how could Ryker ever forget him?

A bitter, nostalgic smile played on his lips as his mind betrayed him with images of his father and brother in this yard. They would train in the fields for hours with a variety of weapons, though their father urged them to value their studies too. *"A sword is a last resort, son. The greatest soldier is one that uses their head in the hopes they don't have to use their weapon."*

While Ryker had found a love for maps and studying the geography of Eavdamos, Keanon had delved deep into the histories and scriptures like their mother and had a knack for stealth and deception. Even when Father fell ill, he still worked with them on their studies, sitting in a chair while the boys sparred, offering tips on their technique. Then he struggled to get out of bed, and the twins worked twice as hard to make him comfortable.

A whine behind him saved him from the past and brought him into the nightmare that was his present. Artis stomped her back hoof and shifted awkwardly from the wagon she was attached to. She tolerated it better than most lykos would, which was fortunate because Ryker struggled to acknowledge what lay inside. Sweat slid down his back and beaded his face, but he was in no rush to do what he was there to do.

Instead, he forced himself to look at the second grave beside his mother's. The words on this one were still pristine. Grasses grew around the base, like the stone was settling comfortably into the ground, but the plants had yet to take over. Ryker's hand shook as he traced the first word with his finger. *Leeam Kessler, proud general of the old kingdom, and advisor of kings. Devoted husband and father. Tempus took him in his prime.* He placed a palm across the words, and a flash of his brother doing the same invaded his mind.

"I'm sorry, Father." His voice cracked, and his heart stuttered in his chest. How the blood still flowed through his body, he wasn't sure. "I'm sorry. I couldn't keep him safe." The world grew blurry as he gulped in air. "I, uhh—I messed up. Forgive me."

Ryker squeezed his eyelids against the welling tears and leaned his forehead against his father's stone. A soft breeze blew across his back, offering temporary relief from the blistering heat, like a reassuring touch that he wasn't alone. But when he opened his eyes, he was. Now, he always would be.

With lead-filled boots, he rose to his feet and trudged to the back of the wagon. His brain was numb as he lifted the limp form over his shoulder, refusing to take in any details of the person he carried to the empty hole. A large, simple wooden box was already inside, and he grunted as he lowered his charge to the ground. The thud when the form hit the dirt made him wince, even though they couldn't feel it.

Trepidation made his hands grow clammy as he lowered himself into the box. Immediately, the space was too tight. Dirt filled his nostrils, and the shadow from the tree was amplified by the four walls around him. Clenching his jaw against the panic wanting to take root, Ryker lifted the figure from the grass and gently laid it inside the box.

Face to face, he was no longer able to ignore his brother. Keanon's eyes were closed, which he was grateful for, but it appeared like he was sleeping. Ryker's fingers itched to shake his shoulder, as if his brother would wake and smack him for the disturbance. But Keanon wasn't asleep, and the gaping hole in Ryker's heart deepened as he laid his brother's sword on his chest and positioned his hands to clasp the hilt.

The ground still loomed over Ryker, but his hands hesitated on the lid of the box. Keanon's face misted as Ryker's unblinking eyes burned. He blinked to clear his vision, and in one solid motion, he lowered the lid and pulled himself out of the grave. Grabbing the shovel, his body was mechanical as he filled the hole with soil. Each shovelful of dirt pounded a rhythm that tore away pieces of his heart.

His hands were slick on the shovel's handle, and he often paused to wipe them on his clothes, sweat dripping from his nose and down his neck.

Thump. Thump.

Scoop, swing, dump.

The monotony of his task distracted his brain for a few blissful moments, but then he was done, and the shovel slid from his grasp. Shadows grew deeper as the sun descended below the tree line in the distance, and the wind picked up, caressing his face. Sweet relief from the sweltering summer heat.

This was the time when someone should say something, but no one was there to help him. No words would come. All he could do was read what he'd asked the man to carve on the stone. "Keanon Kessler, expert spy, and wonderful—" Ryker's voice caught, but he pushed on. "Wonderful son and brother. May Tempus guide him home." He voiced the last line as a prayer. Since his brother turned on the gods, he prayed they would still accept him into The After.

The sky shifted from blue to vivid reds and yellows as the breeze grew stronger, blowing in clouds over the treetops. Stars blinked into the sky, and pale silver illuminated his surroundings. He should go. His task was done, and General Moreland had wanted him back by nightfall.

A hand on his shoulder made him jump, and Ryker whirled to find General Moreland standing behind him with a sad smile.

"I'm sorry." The general's voice was soft, but his grip on Ryker's shoulder was firm.

Ryker lowered his gaze back to his brother's tombstone. General Moreland's presence offered a sliver of comfort. He'd worried the general agreed with everyone else, yet here he was.

Glowflies flickered at the edges of the trees, floating above the grassy field. The darkness deepened as clouds hid the stars from view.

"I wish things could have been different," General Moreland said. "He was a good man."

Ryker's hands clenched as he stepped away from the general, whose hand fell from Ryker's shoulder. "Then why did you sentence him to death?"

General Moreland didn't flinch, his steady gaze meeting Ryker's as he countered, "Why did you come to me when there was a chance Keanon was going to betray us?"

"I wanted you to help me stop him!" he snapped. "I wanted you to *save* him!"

"His position was more than compromised, Ryker. From the moment you came to me, you must have known the possibility of this outcome." The general's voice was firm, though he remained somehow calm.

Ryker gritted his teeth over the scream building in his lungs. He'd feared for Keanon's life. He'd known his brother would be arrested and possibly disgraced, but his brother's life had mattered more than those outcomes.

General Moreland crossed his arms and pressed again. "What would you have done in my place? If it had been any other person—when there was proof he had betrayed us—what would you have done?"

"It wasn't just any other person." Ryker's stomach churned with each question the general asked. He knew the rules as well as General Moreland did. Ryker knew the consequences for treason, but he'd still turned Keanon in. His heart throbbed as he tried to push away the implication.

"What about when he was escaping? You found him just as I did and helped stop his escape."

Ryker flinched and lowered his gaze to the ground. He desperately pushed back the memory of that day. It hadn't happened the way General Moreland thought. Ryker's heart raced as he pictured that final moment of bitter hope when he spotted Keanon escaping the barracks with two hooded figures. At that moment, Ryker couldn't do it again. Knowing the outcome would be his brother's life, Ryker couldn't do it. While Keanon's choices could lead to his death, Ryker wouldn't betray his brother a second time. But it hadn't been up to him, as just then, General Moreland appeared.

"Do you really believe my heart wasn't crushed when you told me about Keanon?" General Moreland's heartfelt voice brought Ryker out of the painful memory. "Hearing what he'd decided, and knowing what I would have to do, killed something inside me just as much as I know it did you." He placed his hands firmly on Ryker's shoulders, his face forlorn. "When the day comes and you become general, I can only pray you will never be faced with a decision like this one."

Ryker slumped. "What do I do now?"

The general didn't hesitate. "You fight. You train your troops so Galleria can't take any more good soldiers away from us."

Something ignited in Ryker that tamped down his grief as the general's words sank in, offering him something to cling to. Light illuminated the dark sky in the distance, and the elm overhead began to sway as the wind picked up. A single raindrop caressed Ryker's cheek, followed by more.

"Come on, we should get back," said General Moreland.

With a final glance back at the three tombstones under the elm, he said goodbye to his family, then headed over to Artis, who licked his face in solace. Climbing into the wagon, they headed back up the field and circled the house, where General Moreland's eldeer waited. Its rich brown coat blended well in the darkness; its frame illuminated only by the glow of the torch hanging from his wagon. Its ears twitched expectantly as they approached, but General Moreland surprised Ryker when he tied his mount to the wagon and climbed back inside beside Ryker. They rode down the wooded path as the occasional drop grew into a constant mist.

If it weren't for the torch hanging from the wagon, it would be impossible to see in the complete darkness of the woods. Branches rustled as the wind blew through them; another distant flash offered a small glimpse at the forest before darkening again. Even when the wagon tumbled onto the main road, it was dark and empty. At this late hour, only those up to no good would lurk among the shadows, but Ryker and General Moreland's dark tunics and the swords at their hips indicated their positions as high-ranking soldiers. It was enough to ward off any lowlifes looking for trouble. Seekers had been busier in the past few weeks since more soldiers were sent away. There were less to patrol the cities. Rogues were getting bolder, but not enough to take on two Imperial soldiers. The mist turned to a steady rain that rolled off Ryker's face and plastered the clothes to his body. Without the canopy above, the warm rain hit them in full force as they blundered along the road. Ryker savored how it washed away the sticky sweat from his skin.

As the city gates drew closer, General Moreland offered some hope. "We will win this war, Ryker. We've come to possess some new weaponry that could bring about King Alystaire's downfall by the end of the summer."

"Really?" Ryker leaned forward in his seat, but his anticipation was squashed when General Moreland didn't elaborate.

"Yes, so don't lose hope now." The general gave him a pat on the back. "Let's win this for Keanon."

Ryker led Artis up to the gates of Mésis City. The torches on either side of the wall flickered against the darkness. They both nodded to the night watch in greeting as they trudged through the gates.

"What about the princess?" Ryker spat, bitter hatred roiling in his gut.

Raindrops dripped off General Moreland's beard and hair as he straightened and crossed his arms. "She, along with her companion, will be taken to Talbane. Emperor Asher wants her in a more secure location where she can be used as an asset against her father."

"Who is in charge of her transfer?"

General Moreland didn't immediately answer as they were greeted at the gates to the barracks and rolled the wagon inside. He sighed. "Ryker..."

"Would you let me lead?"

Ryker stopped Artis in front of the stables as General Moreland turned to face him fully, his expression sympathetic. "I would love to let you do this, but I know the kind of pain and anger that sits inside you right now. Emotion like that can make a man do things even when they know they should not."

Ryker could not deny how his blood boiled every moment he thought of the princess. It sat like burning coals in his gut, knowing she still had breath when his brother did not. Even now, Ryker's hands itched to grab his sword, fly down the stairs to her cell, and end it, but he steadied his gaze on the general. "I will not harm her; I won't allow anyone else to harm her. I swear it." He spoke with a conviction that he prayed met General Moreland's approval. This was something he *needed* to do. He needed to prove he could handle this.

General Moreland pinched the bridge of his nose and sighed again, still uncertain.

"You can't seriously be considering this, General." A new voice broke in, and the sound of it immediately grated on Ryker's nerves. Ryker bunched his fists as the speaker stepped into the light of the torch, casting eerie shadows across his face. Vaan was the only person Ryker knew that would sulk out in the rain at this hour, eavesdropping on other people's conversations.

"I thought you left earlier this evening." General Moreland hopped down from the wagon and crossed his arms as Vaan approached.

Ryker followed the general's lead and stood beside him. The glow from the torch reflected eerily in Vaan's dark eyes.

Vaan ignored General Moreland's comment and continued his rant. "You can't possibly let *him,* of all people, be responsible for someone so valuable. As the one tasked with her interrogation, it would be natural for me to handle these matters myself."

The general frowned and narrowed his eyes. "I am well aware of her value, and I also understand the emperor has requested your return as swiftly as possible, which is why I assumed you would have left earlier."

"I had planned too, but I needed to make sure the princess's entourage was in order. Besides, I received a carrier earlier. Seems there's been a change in plans. My trip to Talbane has been delayed until tomorrow."

Ryker's curiosity piqued, but Vaan wouldn't elaborate further, so he didn't bother asking.

"Well then, I think it wise you get a full night's rest and focus on your own task sent by His Excellency. Ryker is more than capable of stepping up."

"Oh, yeah?" Vaan crossed his arms to match the general's stance. "After the mess that happened with his brother? How sure of him are you because you would have said the same things about Keanon a week ago."

Ryker lunged, but General Moreland grabbed his shoulder before his fist could connect with the smug bastard's face.

"Enough!" The general's voice thundered with enough rage and command that even Vaan stepped back. Vaan's eyes widened as he realized he'd pushed too far.

General Moreland drew close to Vaan's face and growled, "I will not hear you speak ill of the dead or dishonor Ryker. Get out of my sight. Rest assured, Ryker will be delivering your prisoner as soon as he is able."

Vaan's jaw clenched as he shook with barely suppressed fury, yet there was a small glint of fear in his eyes. He whirled around and retreated toward the sleeping quarters. He may be special to the emperor, but General Moreland still outranked him.

Ryker sagged in relief from this small victory. He had a chance to prove to everyone that he was not his brother. It was clear now more than ever that they had never been so different.

CHAPTER II
FREYA

Freya grew restless as the days in the cell blurred into a monotonous routine, and the longer they sat with no signs of change, Laia tried and failed to hide her mounting despair. Finally, on the fourth day of captivity, something changed. The door above swung open for their second meal of the day. Boots thundered down the stairs, and Freya's stomach growled in anticipation for the pitiful meal awaiting her. When the tray slid through the grate, her heart skipped. On top of the tray was a small piece of paper, which she picked up with shaking hands, squinting to make out the neat scrawl in the dark.

Your Highness,

I have been in correspondence with Cliff. A plan is in the works to get you out. The Empire intends to move you and your friend to a more secure prison in Talbane in a few days' time. The barracks is in lockdown until the transfer, so we won't be able to get you out until then. I'll keep in contact with Cliff and work out a place on your journey for your team to intervene. I apologize that I am unable to give you anything more to eat this evening. Slide this missive back under the door with the tray when you finish reading.

May the Gods bless you,
Long live King Alystaire

THE SECOND SHE FINISHED READING, Freya snatched the food off the tray and handed it to Laia. Not wanting to waste any more time, she chugged her water, and Laia followed her example, quickly returning their cups to the tray along with the note. She knocked, and the grate opened. There was a crackling noise as the letter was burned, and the stranger retreated down the hall and up the stairs like all the other soldiers had. Freya absently nibbled on the stale bread Laia placed in her hand and waited for the doors above to clang shut again, her stomach in knots.

Barely audible, Freya relayed the missive, watching the tension in Laia's shoulders ease, a spark of hope returning to her eyes.

What she assumed was early the next morning—as they had yet to receive their paltry breakfast—the door above burst open, slamming against the wall with such force it rattled their iron cell door, and dirt crumbled off the ceiling. Several sets of footsteps descended the stairs, and she shared a weary glance with Laia. Were they being transferred already? Dread and anticipation settled in the pit of her stomach as the stomping drew near.

Keys jingled outside their door. Freya rose to her feet and clenched her fists alongside Laia, who stood beside her, face grim yet determined. There was a click, and the cell door creaked open. Three imperial soldiers stood in the doorway. The one in the center wore a dark gray uniform with a single red stripe down his left arm, singling him out as a soldier with a station than those on either side of him, dressed in plain, pale gray. He looked to be a few years older than her; his sharp features were unnervingly perfect. When his dark eyes settled on her, she shuddered. His smile seemed to suck all the warmth out of Freya's body, and her fists tightened until her knuckles turned white.

The young man stepped forward. "It is so wonderful to make your acquaintance, *Your Highness*." His formality turned callous when he addressed her by title, but he breezed past as though there was no change. "My name is Vaan, and I used to work closely with Keanon before he passed."

Keanon's name on this man's lips felt wrong and Freya's jaw clenched as she bit down on several choice words. His presence made her skin crawl, and she hated how this Imperial scum affected her.

He placed a hand to his heart, feigning hurt when she glared at him. He shook his head. "Come now, what's with the cold shoulder? I lost him too." His eyes narrowed as he added, "You should be a bit more considerate of others' losses, Your Highness."

Something about his tone made her doubt very much that he cared a lick about Keanon or his recent passing. He was trying to rile her up, and she would not give him the satisfaction.

Her continued silence seemed to finally dissolve Vaan's facade. Sneering, he stepped closer until he loomed over Freya, his hot breath fanning her face. "I was told to be gentle with you." He spoke with a softness that didn't match his cruel words. "You are meant to remain *presentable* for Emperor Asher." He tilted his head toward Laia beside her without breaking eye contact. "Of course, I was not instructed to be careful with her." His eyes sparkled as he made his threat, and Freya had to fight every muscle in her face not to turn around. Her jaw twitched, and vision blurred, but she refused to break first.

With a sigh, Vaan leaned back on his heels and stared at his fingernails. It didn't feel like a victory to her. His callous demeanor and threat against Laia's life wouldn't allow her this small triumph.

With a lackluster shrug, he sighed. "Unfortunately, I was asked to keep things cordial until we get you both back to Talbane, but I decided I'd give you the opportunity to have an open discussion with me before we leave." He paused to recapture her gaze. "Should you choose to open up now, your stay with us will be far less painful, but if you stay quiet, I can promise your friend over there will be screaming for death in a month's time."

She believed him. The way his eyes glittered with malice and anticipation, she knew he would follow through on his word should they make it to Talbane.

However, he didn't ask any questions as silence stretched between them. He continued watching her closely, and with each passing second, it grew harder to hide the discomfort settling inside her stomach like lead as his beady eyes bored into her. Finally, he rose, cracking his neck with a gleeful twinkle in his eyes.

"I'll give you to the end of the day to show your compliance. I do hope for your pretty friend's sake you will make the right choice." Vaan turned and strode out of their cell with his guards trailing behind him. He slammed the door shut and darkness swallowed the two friends once more.

The silence lingered as the soldiers retreated. Freya ground her teeth as she sat back to ease the pressure on her wrists. Of course, Vaan had not left her with questions to ponder; by the way his face lit up, he knew she wouldn't cooperate. But he didn't know there were plans in motion to keep her from making it to Talbane.

Freya's stomach clenched when the doors clanged open a few hours later. She hated her reaction to the possibility of Vaan returning, but she decided to spit in his face if he got too close.

When the grate opened, Freya's muscles eased, and a thrill of excitement filled her when their food was accompanied by another piece of paper. Freya divided the food quickly, and they both drained their cups. This time, she held the letter between them so they could both read it.

Your Highness,

Things are moving faster than I anticipated, but don't worry. They plan to move you and your friend tomorrow. I have given Cliff all the information he needs. It has been my honor to aid in your escape, Princess.

May the Gods bless you and give you swift victory over our enemies.

FREYA REPLACED the paper with the cups and nibbled on her crumbly bread as the tray disappeared through the hole in the door. The note was burned, and the person retreated without another word. Freya wished she knew who was on the other side, but it was safer for them this way. When this war was over, she would have to seek them out and reward them for the great risk they had taken.

Once the door clanged shut, and they were sure no one remained below, Laia whispered, "So, we leave tomorrow, then?"

Freya nodded, her anticipation building. "Yeah. Now we just wait for the morning."

CHAPTER 12

VIVIAN

"Vi, slow down!"

Tristain's shout was nearly lost in the rush of wind enveloping Vivian and pulling loose curls from her braid. She ignored him and let her leophinx, Talon, hurtle through the trees as fast as he could, holding tight to his gray-speckled fur. The air was crisp as Brantyre awaited the return of the biting cold, but for now, the intense sun held it back a while longer. Still, Vivian wore her thick, black riding pants, a soft tunic, and a velvet cloak to fight against the mountain chill. Finally, she halted at the base of a sheer cliff, waiting for everyone else. Up ahead, the path became rocky and uneven as it wrapped around the steep rock face on one side. On the other side was an open drop to the trees below, offering a clear view of the castle and Calliva City. The homes and shops were built from stone with strong timber roofs, and the castle was much the same—a rough and rugged kind of beauty nestled within the cliffs.

"I thought we were riding together," Glenn huffed as he pulled his pale white leophinx to a stop. He'd named her Ice, an homage to her pale blue eyes. Leophinx had thick, soft fur that ranged from white to darker gray. Their coat was dappled with black spots, useful for blending with the snow and rocks. They had large manes around their necks for extra warmth, a bushy tail, and wide paws, padded to distribute their weight over soft snow, and their claws were perfect to latch onto the mountainous terrain.

"Sorry." Vivian smiled sheepishly.

"If you'd wanted a race, you should have asked," Tristain smirked as he rode Night, his dark gray—almost black—leophinx beside hers. Tristain, her sister's betrothed, had his father's looks, with a strong jaw and easy smile that lit up his face. His dark, wavy hair tumbled across his forehead and matched the warmth of his eyes.

"But this way, I can't lose." Vivian shoved his shoulder when he got close enough, and he threw his head back, laughing.

"She just doesn't want to lose to Callia and me," Aida added. Vivian stuck her tongue out at her while Callia settled beside Ice, her identical sister, and licked Glenn's hand so he would scratch her ear. Glenn had a soft spot for the two creatures that were born three years ago. Though the royal children were responsible for their own leophinx, Vivian and Aida knew how much Glenn loved Callia and Ice, so they allowed him to pamper both.

Watching her siblings banter made Vivian's heart hurt. She wouldn't be with them for much longer. Prince Damian was on his way, and if her father agreed to Galleria's terms, she feared she would be leaving with him. Everyone had changed since learning about Galleria's proposal. Glenn found more time to spend with Vivian, and Tristain spent as much time with her as he could when he was not preparing for the wedding or his upcoming responsibilities as future king. Aida had been quieter like she was already pulling away. Vivian missed their closeness.

"Vi!"

She jolted back to the present when Aida shouted her name. Her sister's expression was difficult to read, her emotions concealed, while Vivian had given hers away. "Sorry, I was distracted."

Glenn tilted his head, frowning. "Are you alright?"

"Yeah, I'm fine." She gave him an encouraging smile, though he didn't look convinced. He'd been more perceptive of her in the past few days, and she'd struggled to keep their conversations light and happy. She wanted these last moments with her family to be ones she could look back on; she was about to suggest a race up the cliff when Tristain called out, "Is that what I think it is?"

They all squinted to where Tristian pointed. Through the trees, on the main road leading to the city gates, was movement. A large white and red banner blinked in and out of view between the trees, and Vivian's stomach dropped. The Empire's ambassador was here.

Without another word, the four of them flew back the way they came. Talon leaped over rocks and twisted around tall pines as they raced toward the city. No wagons or travelers took this route as it was too winding and steep, with no direct connection to the towns or cities. Hunters occasionally used this path through the woods, but it was not well maintained like the main roads. Tristain had gone hunting down this path with his father a couple of times and had shown it to the royal children; the route had quickly becoming a favorite of theirs, offering the best views of the mountainside.

Aida and Glenn popped in and out of sight as they dodged and weaved in front of Vivian, Tristain keeping close behind them. He was always careful to keep a close eye on the royal children—Aida even more so—whenever they were out together. Usually, there wasn't much reason to worry about their safety since not many people were dumb enough to go against the gods' wishes, and the Leanders were well-loved by their people.

Through the trees, the walls of the city drew closer, and they skidded to a stop before the gates as Aida addressed the guards. "Has the ambassador arrived yet?"

"Not yet, Yer' Highness." The woman at the gate bowed as she answered. The four of them sagged in relief.

"We saw them approaching in the trees. They will be here soon," said Aida, springing into action. Vivian followed her sister through the gate as the soldiers rushed to prepare for their visitors.

Inside, the city was extra busy as the people prepared for the upcoming Winter Lights Festival. Everyone busied themselves with their daily jobs, as well as preparing decorations, food, and activities for a week full of feasting and fun. Vivian followed Aida with Tristain and Glenn on her heels through the crowded markets until slowing at another gate dividing the city from the palace. They trotted along the stone path into the palace courtyard and over to the stables to drop off their mounts.

"You two go ahead. Glenn and I will take care of all these guys." Tristain squeezed Aida's shoulder, who gave him a faint smile.

Vivian rushed across the courtyard with Aida, reaching the palace doors as the guards announced the ambassador's arrival. Wide-eyed, the sisters glanced at their simple riding attire. They flew into the foyer, up the stairs, and burst into Aida's rooms. The two rushed through dressing Aida in her lovely, pine green dress with golden trim and flowers on the bodice. Vivian struggled with the clasps in her haste but managed to get them fastened then they dashed across the hall.

When they entered Vivian's room, she tripped on the plush rugs, stumbling over to the couch before losing her balance and falling onto the cushions. Her cloak bunched around her legs until she was a mess of fabric, so when she tried to stand, she rolled onto the floor.

Laughter burst behind her, and she glared at Aida, who was doubled over in hysterics. Vivian laughed then, and soon, Aida joined her on the ground, tears flowing from their eyes. When her stomach and face hurt from laughter, the sisters stopped. Aida helped detangle Vivian from her cloak, her face sobering as she helped Vivian into her bright yellow dress that complemented the flowers on Aida's.

"I don't want you to leave," Aida whispered to Vivian's back.

Vivian's heart constricted. She was glad Aida couldn't see the sorrow on her face. Attempting to keep her voice light, she replied, "Mother and Father haven't decided to take Galleria's offer yet."

"Yeah…" Aida sounded unconvinced, her fingers stalling on the final button of Vivian's dress.

Vivian twirled a loose curl from her braid. "And now we have to see what the emperor wants from us."

"As if he hasn't already asked for enough." The bite in Aida's voice surprised Vivian, who turned to face her sister. Aida's face was pained, her eyes distant and arms rigid at her sides.

Vivian grabbed her sister's arms until their eyes locked. "We can do this."

Aida sagged, and Vivian pulled her into her arms. They held each other tight until a call rang out down the hall, announcing the ambassador entering the palace.

The sisters checked each other over to ensure they were both presentable before walking much more calmly back the way they had come. At the top of the stairs, Vivian had a sense of familiarity as she watched her parents welcome a southerner into their home once again.

The ambassador from the Empire was much younger than the one from Galleria. She appeared to be a few years older than Vivian. Her brows furrowed, surprised the emperor would choose to send such a young woman as ambassador. She had pale southern skin, her cheeks and nose flushed from the chill. Her blonde hair cascaded past her shoulders when she bowed low, introducing herself to Vivian's parents.

"Thank you, Your Majesties, for such a warm welcome. My name is Linette," she said in a strong and clear voice.

"Of course. We appreciate you coming to discuss these matters at hand." Vivian's father nodded, his expression neutral and guarded. He indicated to the double doors behind him. "Shall we?"

Her mother glanced up and gestured for both girls to follow as she and their father led Linette into the throne room. Together, they descended the stairs, and, for the second time, Vivian sat at the long table. As with Galleria's ambassador, Priestess Sasha was the only one of her father's court present besides the royal family.

Once everyone was seated, her father steepled his hands, leaning forward with his elbows propped on the table. "Enlighten us on what this prophecy is all about."

"Of course. My Lord understands this is quite difficult for everyone. It is a lot of change so suddenly, and in light of Galleria's refusal, it has made it more challenging for you to make a choice with this added strain."

"Or perhaps your declaration of war against them has made our decision more strained." Vivian's mother's voice was sweet as honey, yet the undertone made Vivian's stomach clench. Vivian glanced hesitantly at Aida, whose expression was unreadable, her mask firmly in place. Yet, beneath the table, she clasped her hands tightly in her lap.

Linette caught the queen's tone too, and she frowned. "I can assure you, Emperor Asher never wanted to go to war, but he seeks to follow the gods' will. Isn't that what we all want?" Linette let the question linger uncomfortably before moving on. "He understood that such a drastic change would have repercussions. His greatest fear when he prepared to send the messages to the royal families was an absolute refusal."

"The balance of fulfilling such a prophecy and keeping everyone happy would be difficult," added Priestess Sasha, her demeanor much calmer than Vivian's mother.

The ambassador's smile returned. "Yes. My Lord has such a heavy burden, but he's proven he will to do whatever it takes to make this happen." Her dark eyes grew somber as she added, "Even going to war." Linette's eyes met Vivian's for a moment, and her stomach churned as the ambassador continued. "To ease Emperor Asher's burden and your worries about the welfare of your people, he has a proposal for you."

Vivian's nausea heightened as Linette's dark eyes strayed toward hers; she swallowed hard to keep the bile from rising in her throat, her heart screaming for Linette to stop.

"Since your youngest daughter is to be your successor, My Lord wishes to take your eldest, Princess Vivian, as his bride and the first Empress of Ashera."

Vivian's heart pounded in her ears, blocking out anything else spoken between her parents and the ambassador. She squeezed her hands so tightly that her nails dug half-moons into her palms. Her heart had believed Galleria's proposal was what the gods had meant when they sent Sasha her vision. Was it possible *this* was what the gods truly wanted? For Vivian to become an Empress? A position with so much power she would rule over her parents? The mere thought made her insides churn. How could Vivian ever be capable of becoming an Empress? She was not half the perfect royal her parents were.

Warring thoughts and emotions battled in Vivian's mind as she struggled to comprehend the peace she'd come to accept with marrying Prince Damian. But if the gods had sent this prophecy to combine the people under Emperor Asher, surely this was what Brantyre was meant to do... Was she meant to solidify the start of a new era and bring about the end to this war so the kingdoms could move forward as one? But if this was what she was meant to do, why had she been so confident about Galleria's proposal? Even Sasha had told her nothing had been decided yet.

"Thank you again, Your Highness, for such a warm reception and for taking this decision seriously." Linette's silky, smooth voice broke Vivian from her thoughts. "Emperor Asher understands your hesitation and appreciates you leaning on your priests' wisdom before making a decision." As Linette finished speaking, everyone rose to their feet.

Vivian winced as she pried her nails from her palms, noting the blood caked beneath them. Her chest was tight, and it grew increasingly difficult to breathe like it had after Galleria's proposal.

"Surely you will stay the night at least?" asked Vivian's mother. "Even in the summer, these mountains get bitterly cold when the sun goes down." Her mother's words sounded far off in the distance as Vivian kept her gaze lowered, not trusting her expression as she focused on filling her lungs with air.

"I must regretfully decline such a gracious offer, Your Highness." Linette's voice was rueful. "My Lord requested I return to Ashera with great haste, so I must begin my journey home at once while there is still light."

"Very well," responded Vivian's father. "We look forward to

hearing from Emperor Asher soon." His voice faltered on the emperor's title.

Linette bowed to Vivian's parents again before she was escorted back out of the palace. Vivian stared a hole into the back of her blonde head, a throbbing pain building in her chest the more she tried to breathe. When the door closed, Vivian turned to her parents with barely contained panic and excused herself with a curtsy. Her father opened his mouth to stop her, but her mother must have noticed the anxiety in Vivian's eyes, placing a hand on her husband's shoulder and nodding for Vivian to go. Vivian didn't even glance toward the priestess or her sister as she walked briskly toward the side door she'd used the last time she received such news.

This time, she sought solace in her own rooms and collapsed on the bed, the pain in her chest continuing to pulsate. She curled into a ball. What did the gods want from her? What was she meant to do? She wanted to scream and shout at the gods for their sick games, but she just lay there until sorrow overwhelmed her, and she slept.

CHAPTER 13
FREYA

Chains rattled along the stone floor as Freya wrestled with sleep again. Whenever her eyes closed, she saw Keanon's tear-stricken face, which forced them open. When it was Laia's turn to rest, Freya would sit facing the door, still weary to keep watch in case anyone came down the stairs. If the spy were to show up while they were both asleep, they could miss important information or risk the spy getting caught. Since Vaan had barged down the stairs, they'd only received one meal that day, which she could only guess was around midday. Hours passed at an agonizing rate as the girls tried to get some rest so they could be ready for the day ahead. It seemed Laia fared no better at resting as she tossed and turned beside Freya.

The air thickened with the mounting pressure as the night dragged on. If they failed tomorrow, Laia would suffer, and Freya's father would be forced to make sacrifices Galleria could not afford, and it crushed Freya to know her father would. He'd surrender his crown to get her back if he had to. But would he save her before she broke?

Freya shuddered as she pictured the torture Laia may have to endure at Vaan's hand. Would Freya be capable of holding her tongue while her friend screamed, or would she spill all of Galleria's secrets? Her eyes welled, and her teeth clenched. She would not let that happen.

Unable to sit idle, Freya paced along the short leash of her chains. Bolts of pain shot up her legs each time her feet smacked the stone surface, but she ignored it. All her determination to escape and protect Laia meant nothing while she was tied to these chains. She had to pray her team could do this.

The door above banged against the wall, and dirt crumbled off the cracks in the ceiling. Freya froze, and Laia stood beside her, face steely as footfalls descended the steps. She placed a hand on Freya's arm, allowing Freya to relax enough to pry her nails from her palms.

When the door swung open, she was relieved when Vaan was not among the soldiers.

"Stand still," ordered the oldest among them. His dark eyes bored into them as his soldiers descended into the cell, undoing the chains holding them to the wall. To her dismay, they attached her ankle chains to Laia's, a pitiful link between them. Walking was going to be a nightmare.

Laia rested a hand on Freya's shoulder to keep balanced as they prepared to move, but the old man swung his fist into Laia's gut. She bent over, choking and holding her stomach, tears flooding her eyes.

"I didn't say you should move yet," he snapped.

Freya's blood boiled; she lunged to break his already crooked nose but didn't make it half a step before another soldier yanked her arm behind her back. She winced from the sharp pain in her shoulder as the old soldier sneered, looming over her.

"I wouldn't do that again if I were you."

"Or what?" Freya spat. "You can't harm your *prized* prisoner."

Though his eyes narrowed, he made no move to strike her. She was about to spit in his face to further challenge his words when a gentle but firm hand on her arm stalled her. Freya glanced at Laia, her face imploring. It was enough to sway Freya's head, who swallowed the rest of her anger, and relaxed so the soldier would release her. Rage simmered under the surface, but Cliff needed them to cooperate if they were to escape. Once the soldier released her, she rolled her aching shoulder, waiting for the old man to give the order to proceed.

The eyes of the senior soldier never left the two prisoners. "Guards on the ready." Immediately, his soldiers surrounded them: four on either side of the girls, two behind them, and the old soldier taking the lead.

"We are going to move ahead nice and steady." The senior guard leaned low to meet Freya's eyes. "I don't want to see a single toe move out of line, understand?"

She glared back, but the soldier must have taken her silence as agreement as they started forward. The first few steps were agonizing as the two struggled to find their rhythm with the chains attached to their ankles. Irons clamped tight around Freya's skin, and she had to bite down on her cries as blood slid from beneath her bindings. Laia managed to adjust her stride to be even with Freya's, so their progress was quicker and less painful.

When they reached the bottom of the stairs, Freya's legs shook, the bottoms of her feet wet and sticky. Tentatively, she lifted her foot for the first step, cringing as the chains shifted against her torn skin. Her heart lurched as Laia collided with her shoulder, and the stairs loomed closer to her face. Freya sidestepped and grabbed Laia; miraculously, they regained their balance before toppling to the ground.

Swords were drawn and pointed at them from all directions. The old soldier in front turned his beady eyes on them. "Was that a toe?"

"She tripped," Freya ground out, releasing Laia. *From your stupid chains.* She kept the last part to herself, but her glare said it for her. Time ticked. Sweat slid down her back, followed by chills as the cool air connected with her damp body through the rags. The soldier's cold eyes watched her, unmoving, but they both knew he could not do anything. He'd probably already done more than he was supposed to when he punched Laia.

"I suggest she not do it again." He nodded, and the swords returned to their sheaths. Their trek up the stairs continued.

Every step had to be smooth and precise so Laia could match each one. Freya's head pounded from squinting in the dark, sweat streaming down her back and face. They almost tripped a few more times, tearing more skin as the chains twisted and banged around their ankles, but the soldiers did not draw their swords again. The consistent pooling of blood at her feet made each step more precarious as they threatened to slide along the smooth stones. Though Laia's were likely just as bad, she didn't slip again.

Freya gasped in relief when they made it to the top and the soldier shoved open the door. Blinding light greeted them, and she slammed her eyes shut, keeping the tears from streaming down her face. Red streaks crisscrossed on the back of her eyelids, the pounding in her head intensifying. After six days underground, the fierce rays of sunlight were unbearable. Strong hands grabbed Freya's arm, yanking her up the last step.

Warm dirt and grass replaced the cool stones beneath her feet, and her toes prickled as feeling returned to them. Hot air encompassed her and beat down from above. Even the soft wind that blew across her face was warm. Tingles raced up her arms and legs as the underground chill that had seeped into her bones was replaced by heat in seconds.

A hard shove coaxed her forward, and Freya blinked rapidly, trying to adjust to the harsh light. Everything was too vibrant: the grass was too green, and the sky too blue. All the surfaces seemed to reflect the sun's rays, and the throb behind her eyes turned to pounding as she forced them to stay open so she didn't trip and pull them both to the ground.

Dirt clung to the sticky blood on her feet, leaving a trail of red footprints in the grass behind her. When the world finally came into focus, her stomach churned. Every few feet, soldiers stood at the ready with their hands on the hilts of their weapons. On the walls of Mésis City, countless archers were positioned back-to-back. One focused on the procession, and the other watched the fields for anyone who might approach. It struck Freya then how much danger Galleria's spy was in. The risk they took corresponding with Cliff could have easily blown their cover, considering the Empire's many precautions.

At the far side of the barracks by the gates, their ride awaited them. The metal cage was like the underground prison cell, except smaller. It was constructed of solid iron with three tiny, barred windows on either wall and the back door. As they drew near, her stomach turned at being forced back into the dark. Freya reminded herself it wouldn't be as long this time, but it did little to ease the rising nausea.

To distract herself, she studied the massive creature pulling the wagon and was surprised to see it was an oxose. The creature was larger than the cart he was attached to. He had one monstrous bowl-shaped antler protruding from the center of his forehead, extending well past his small ears and dulling at several points. As if his antler wouldn't be enough to kill a man, he also had six smaller tusks, three on either side of his face that ended in sharp, blade-like points. Oxose migrated in large herds throughout Galleria and the Empire's territories; some even traveled into the northern kingdoms, and overtime, they'd become herding animals for their meat and fur. Though mostly docile, they could have unpredictable temperaments and were intimidating to stand beside.

She ignored the beast, who seemed calm. Studying the soldiers in the procession, it appeared much larger than those her team normally took on. There were at least ninety soldiers, twenty of them being archers. She sent out a silent prayer to the gods for her friends' protection.

"Hurry things along! I want us on our way in the next five minutes."

Emotions struck Freya like a blow, almost sending her to her knees. The deep, resonant voice that barked orders rolled over her like a wave, and her heart raced, slowed, and dropped all at once. Her face betrayed her and locked eyes with Captain Ryker Kessler's, his deep dark eyes a perfect match for Keanon's. Except there was no familiar warmth to them—only venom. Freya's heart ached, struck by the memories his familiar face ignited. Bubbling rage flushed her features. Ryker's jaw clenched so tight she was surprised his teeth didn't crack. It was cruel for someone so heartless to share the face of the person she'd loved.

Sensing her actions before she made them, Laia grabbed her arm. Freya had to tamp the urge to shake her off. She would not lash out at her friend over this sad excuse of a human but she refused to back down from his malicious gaze. She felt a moment of satisfaction when he turned away first.

"Throw them in the back!" Captain Kessler shouted over his shoulder as he walked away.

The soldiers took his command literally, lifting them both off the ground and tossing them inside the wagon. Freya crashed to the floor and winced as all four chains squeezed around her wrists and ankles. Laia landed beside her, yanking Freya sideways, who bit down a scream as the irons smacked against her ankles. Blood trickled along her wrists and stained her fingers red.

"You alright?" Laia's words were strained and punctuated by the door to their cage banging shut behind them.

"I'm fine." Freya awkwardly pushed to her hands and knees, and the pair worked together, shifting until they sat side by side against the iron wall. Freya's legs were longer than the width of the wagon, forcing her to bend them.

A low bellow from the oxose rattled the cage, then the entire wagon lurched forward.

"How are you feeling?" asked Laia.

Freya hesitated. Her throbbing ankles had been a good distraction from her warring emotions upon seeing Captain Kessler's face.

"I'm worried. I'm hurt. I'm angry." There was no word to express the truth of what was going through her heart and mind, but she knew Laia would understand. She laid her head on Freya's shoulder.

"I miss him too. He always knew what to say."

Tears welled, and Freya failed to suppress them as they slid down her cheeks. "Because he was trying to convince us he was on our side the whole time."

Laia chuckled at that, bringing a wobbly smile to Freya's face.

"Maybe, but he was good, like I told you. Even in his deceit, he had good intentions." Laia paused. "I wish he was still here."

Laia's wish left Freya's heart hollow. She couldn't rely on wishes or hopes. Keanon was gone and wasn't coming back.

Silence lingered between them as they pondered their own pain and worries. While sunlight peeked between the iron bars, the lull of the cart and the warmth from the summer day made Freya's eyes grow heavy. She drifted in and out of sleep as the day dragged on, and the light outside faded.

Hours later, at sunset, Laia whispered, "I wonder how much further we have."

"It can't be much longer." Freya's legs were cramped from the full day's travel, and she tried to straighten them further, but they hit the wall. Standing wasn't an option either, not with their ankles bound together or with the rocking of the wagon. "If we get too far, we will have a nightmare of a time trying to sneak out of the Empire." Mésis City was almost a day's journey on horseback from The South King's Road and Galleria. Inside their cage, Freya had no way of knowing what direction they'd taken to head toward Talbane, which was all the way on the east side of the Empire.

Laia nodded against her shoulder. "Cliff would try to find somewhere close enough to the border so we could run it, but it also has to be far enough from the barracks, I suppose."

"I just hope it's soon," Freya mumbled, trying to rub the stiffness from her legs.

As if on cue, the cage abruptly stopped, nearly knocking them over. The oxose gave a pain-filled cry, and then a crash that shook the cage so hard she thought it would crumble. Soldiers shouted in confusion and fear while excitement sparked in Laia's eyes as the pair struggled to their feet.

After a few more moments, the beautiful sound of clinking keys captured their attention. The cage door swung open, and Cliff leapt inside, his expression grim.

"We need to hurry." He rushed over and worked to undo their chains. "They managed to send a carrier back to Mésis. Reinforcements will be on their way soon."

Though the news was troublesome, it couldn't dampen the feeling of home washing over Freya from the sound of his voice. When her chains fell away, she busied her hands and brushed her fingers over her wrists to refrain from wrapping her arms around him. The skin was purple, and there was a jagged cut all the way around.

Cliff continued his debriefing as he unlocked Laia. "We've stashed some horses northwest of here. When you reach them, ride hard northwest and you'll reach Runaris before midnight. The carrier will reach Mésis long before we make it." Sweat beaded his face as he stood. He pierced Freya with his deep green eyes. "I'm not sure if we will make it before they send seekers after us."

Laia smirked. "We will just have to run fast."

He fought the smile playing on his face; ignoring her remark, he handed Laia her short sword and set of throwing knives. "Here."

She grabbed a knife and threw it past Cliff, where it sunk into the throat of a soldier about to jump through the open door. Cliff could no longer fight the grin as he handed Freya her long sword and said, "Let's get you two home."

Together, they rushed out of the cage and into the fight. Cliff barreled through the first set of soldiers outside the door, allowing Freya seconds to take in their surroundings. Archer's large, burly frame was easy to spot in the midst, and a glimpse of Harper's blonde hair told her she wasn't far behind him. An arrow plunged into another soldier before he could attack Harper from behind—Lanzo. He covered them, hidden between the trees, hugging the side of the path.

A soldier charged toward Freya, pulling her into the fight. Leaves and dirt crunched beneath her toes as she blocked his first swing and ducked the next. Her cramped limbs protested their sudden use, so she kept on the defensive, trying to loosen up. Sidestepping the soldier's next strike, she brought the pommel of her sword down on top of his hands. There was a loud pop, and he dropped his sword with a scream Freya cut short with a sword to his gut.

Laia was in her own fight and lodged a throwing knife into a soldier's thigh, who fell on all fours before Freya finished him off. Her arms throbbed, but she made quick work of the next few soldiers. Then, a familiar face caught her eyes.

Ryker Kessler.

The rest of the battlefield disappeared as she charged toward him. Hatred fueled each step, and when their swords clashed, it was like the battle ensued outside of herself. Her mind seemed to detach from the action, watching her body move of its own volition. Each rage-filled swing pushed him back a step off the path and into the trees.

"Freya, stop!" Her sword froze, suspended midair from a blow that would have knocked Ryker to the ground. *"He's my brother."*

A sudden, deep love—one that did not belong to her—replaced her hatred for the man she faced.

Gritting her teeth, she shouted back at the voice in her head, *"Your brother that betrayed you!"*

"He's lost, but I love him too much not to try to help."

Her sword lowered at the familiar words inside her head, and Ryker seized the opportunity.

"Block!"

She responded to Keanon's command and managed to block Ryker's blade before it sliced off her arm. As she refocused, her heart was now split, and her swings more careful. She blocked and dodged, taking in the surrounding woods while formulating a plan. She smiled as she recalled something Keanon had told her about his brother.

After days in confinement, she played into the idea her

strength was fading. She slowed her swings and lowered her sword, which was beginning to grow heavier as the fight continued. With each of his blows, she let him push her back and lose ground. She almost grinned at the victorious glint in Ryker's face as she pressed her back against a tree.

"Never assume the battle is won until your opponent is dead. It's a common mistake my brother makes. It's why I always win."

To finish her performance, she let the tip of her sword hit the dirt, and he lifted his to impale her against the trunk. At the last possible second, she rolled along the tree. A *thunk* followed as his sword hit its mark and lodged in the bark. Before he could remove his sword, Freya swung her blade and forced him to let go. His foot snagged on a tree root when he backed up, and the moment he landed, she held the tip of her sword at his throat.

Her heart hammered as Ryker's dark eyes widened. Killing him should be so easy; pressing into the sensitive skin on his neck would be effortless, but Keanon's cries inside her head tore at her resolve. Hot tears burned in her eyes, and Ryker's face swam across her blurred vision. Her arms ached from keeping the sword steady, and she gave a strangled curse as her limbs refused to obey her. *Fine, Keanon! You win.* She swung the pommel of her sword and smacked the side of Ryker's head, who slumped in the dirt. His chest still rose and fell.

"Freya!"

Cliff shouted from the other side of the path. The night had taken over. The bodies of Imperial soldiers littered the ground. Laia was the last to follow the rest of the team into the trees. Freya let out one last curse for Keanon's interference and left Ryker on the ground to race after her friends.

Cliff waited until Freya was beside him, keeping pace with her as they sprinted behind the others. Her team were like ghosts in their black cloaks, blending into the night, but the tattered white rags worn by Freya and Laia punctuated the darkness, glowing beneath the moonlight. It was good that stealth wasn't what they needed.

Dried leaves and sticks crunched underfoot, prickling against her skin, but Freya ignored it. Pushing forward, her legs strained with each step, and her throat burned for a drink. Strays of hair stuck to her face and whipped in the breeze. She longed for her hair ties.

Freya's hopes rose as their horses came into view. There were two left, tied to a low branch with ropes. No saddles or reigns, but that was no problem for her. Yet her joy was short-lived when a howl pierced the night. A chill rippled down her spine as more cries accompanied the first. Seekers. The Empire had sent seekers after them, and safety was still too far. Their lykos would eat up the ground between them, even on horseback.

"I'm here, Freya." Archer appeared from the dark and ran beside her as another low howl indicated the seekers were gaining on them. Archer's presence eased Freya's nerves. There was something about his wild appearance, coupled with his soft demeanor, that always had that effect on her. His presence assured Freya that she and her friends would be alright.

Together, they skidded to a stop by the horses. Freya untied one of the mounts, but Archer didn't. His face was grim as the seekers drew closer. "They will not get you again," he said, turning back the way they had come and pulling out his bow. With his hood on and his dark hair and beard concealing his pale face, he almost disappeared into the darkness.

"What are you doing?"

"Go! I can hold them off so you can reach Runaris." Archer's voice was firm, but Freya shook her head.

"Not a chance, you idiot!" She dropped the ropes and lifted her sword, though her arms protested when she tried to raise it. "I'm not leaving you behind."

His eyes never wavered on hers. "Yes, you are." Then he glanced over her shoulder. "Cliff, get her out of here."

Cliff's arms wrapped around Freya's waist, lifting her onto his horse before galloping away. Freya's sword fell from her hands as she twisted and flailed in a futile attempt to resist.

"NO! Stop!" She dug her fingers into Cliff's arm to try to pry herself free, but his grip only tightened, and his horse picked up speed. "We can't leave him, Cliff!"

Shouts rang out from the seekers, along with barks and growls from the approaching beasts. Freya gave up struggling, and tears burned her eyes as the trees flew past. Cliff didn't put her down until the woods thinned and the busted gates of Runaris appeared. Once inside, he set her on the cobbled streets. Pebbles bit into the soles of her feet, and she shifted until they settled on a smooth surface.

"Go on ahead." Cliff gave her reassuring smile and began to turn the horse back around. "You didn't really think I'd leave him, right?"

Freya's smile wobbled as he galloped back into the trees. She refrained from calling after him. They were right. Galleria's people didn't need her risking their safety any more than she already had. Her heart squeezed as he disappeared, flinching at another howl in the distance.

"You two better come back," she whispered, and as she turned away, a single sob escaped her lips.

Runaris was a painful reminder of how much she had risked by following her heart. Before ducking into the city's barracks, she forced herself to take in the desolation. Doors to once quaint storefronts were bashed in, and shattered glass coated the streets. Vendor's carts were scattered among piles of rubble, and all the buildings were crumbling and charred black.

News about the Empire's attack had reached Seaymarr while her family had breakfast. Spring had finally taken over winter, and the tall windows overlooking the Navean Sea were opened to allow in the crisp sea breeze. Yet the peaceful day did little to ease the strain lingering around the royal family. A tension had stuck ever since her father had sent his response to Emperor Asher. They hadn't anticipated the retaliation to follow.

A courtier had burst through the doors to the dining hall with a message from General Sanders from Runaris. Freya's hand froze, a spoonful of honeyed oats poised by her opened mouth. Imperial soldiers had swarmed the city so fast they hadn't had time to prepare their defenses. The first wave had snuck through the trees, and although General Sanders had done his best to protect the citizens once the assault started, the reinforcements from neighboring towns came too late. General Sanders surrendered the city and fled with his remaining troops, guiding the citizens to safety.

Around her now, blood stained the cobbles and walls where soldiers had failed to hold the gates. Freya's first steps into the barracks made her freeze. The Empire's fleet had focused on the soldiers first, allowing the civilians time to flee, but the state of the barracks sat in her heart like lead. Weapons and shields lay scattered across the ground where brave men and women had fallen, blood seeping into the dirt. Only three buildings still stood; the rest had turned to ash.

One such building was the general's quarters at the back, built of stone. Harper stood by the door, scanning the dark. Her long blonde hair was pulled in a bun atop her head, the battle having tugged several strands loose about her face. She attempted to tuck a stray hair behind her ear, but the evening breeze blew it back.

"The boys holding them off?" Harper inquired as Freya drew near.

"Yes." It was all she could say as another howl pierced the

night. If any of her friends died tonight, she would never forgive herself.

"Alright, get in there." Harper opened the door to the general's quarters and beckoned with her head for Freya to enter, who raised a quizzical brow. Harper gestured to the broadsword slung over her back. The sword was almost as long as she was tall, though it was much lighter than its imposing size would suggest, enabling her to handle it with great precision and speed. Two years ago, Laia had crafted the weapon with some help from her uncle for Harper's birthday—it was her favorite blade.

Her friend smirked, nudging Freya toward the door. "No way those two get to have all the fun." Harper jogged back toward the gates, her horse on her heels. Over her shoulder, she yelled, "We'll get those mutts off track and meet you by the Potámea tunnels."

Freya's feet remained rooted in place as another of her friends raced away, risking their lives for her safety. If she could renounce her title—the value she possessed simply for being born—she would do it if it meant she could fight alongside her friends and aid in their escape. For them, she would give up her royalty.

When the dark swallowed Harper, Freya turned and entered the general's quarters. Papers scattered the floors, and books were torn apart; the desk had been tipped over and shoved to one side, blocking the door to the bedroom. On the back wall, a built-in-bookshelf stood, though some of the shelves had splintered and all the books removed. Squatting by the bookshelf, Freya felt around the underside of the bottom shelf until her fingers bumped over a slight groove in the wood. There was a click when she pressed on it, and she grunted, pushing on the shelves until it groaned, scraping along the ground. Her arms shook from the effort.

The wall finally opened to reveal a staircase descending into darkness. With a final breath of the warm night air, Freya closed the wall, listening for it to click into place. She rushed to the bottom of the staircase, following the light of a single torch illuminating the cave at the bottom where Lanzo and Laia waited. Her heart hurt, but they'd done it. They were free.

RYKER

"**I**diot!"

The blow that followed caught Ryker off guard. He doubled over, pain exploding in his head as his vision narrowed and blurred. The side of his head was black and blue from his fight with the princess, and the throbbing headache bloomed anew.

Ryker had no idea how Vaan had turned up and found him on this route. He'd spent hours studying paths from Mésis City to Talbane, formulating a journey that was both swift and unpredictable to avoid potential rescue from Galleria. As soon as the general gave him the responsibility, he'd planned the route a day later, barely eating or sleeping as he poured over maps. None of the soldiers had known the planned route; even when General Moreland checked on his progress, he hid the maps away, wanting no room for error. Yet, somewhere, he'd slipped. Someone had gotten a hold of his route, and the princess was gone.

Now Vaan towered over him, his fists clenched. Moonlight illuminated bodies littering the ground and glinted off the open door to the prisoner's cage. Lykos whimpered and growled as they returned from their hunts empty-handed. Some of the beasts dragged limp, bleeding bodies of other lykos and their fallen riders on pallets. Artis let out a low growl from where she lay in the dirt. She'd been one of Galleria's first targets, knocked out with a single arrow tipped with some sort of sleeping draft, instantly taking her out of the fight. The wound was small and after a little tending, she would heal fine. If she was on her feet, Vaan would not be so bold as to be in Ryker's face.

"Do you realize what you've done?" Vaan continued his tirade. "We don't know if *your brother* shared any sensitive information with her." He got right in Ryker's face, his voice low and menacing. "That is two people you have gotten rid of before they could be questioned. Are you trying to hide something from us?"

Blinding rage filled Ryker at the accusation, and he lunged. Vaan ducked, but Ryker was faster, kicking Vaan in the back and knocking him to the ground. He kicked Vaan in the stomach, who cursed and rolled away before Ryker could do it again. Vaan launched to his feet, but the pounding of hooves halted them both.

The pale glow from the moon was enough to reveal General Moreland and his troops heading toward them. He rode up beside them and dismounted, his face a mask of barely contained rage.

"What happened?" His barked command shook Ryker to his core. He forced himself to face the general.

"What happened is your precious *protégé* lost one of our best assets!" Vaan redirected his anger toward General Moreland, flailing his arms as he shouted, "I told you to leave the princess to me, but of course not! You clearly can't help them. They're just as useless as—"

"Enough!"

General Moreland cut Vaan off with so much venom in his

voice that even Ryker recoiled. But this time, Vaan wasn't intimidated. A wicked grin crept up his face. The expression was unsettling, but General Moreland didn't seem fazed.

"Weren't you supposed to return to Talbane?" The general spat at Vaan.

Ryker wondered that too. They were five days away from Talbane—two or three for a single rider if Vaan took a more direct route. Why was he out here?

Vaan didn't flinch. "I was on my way there when I received a message that my plans had changed once again." Glaring at Ryker, he added, "It appears I have no reason to rush back." Then, he whirled and remounted his eldeer, a leering smile playing at the corners of his mouth before he rode away into the night.

When he had gone, the general aimed all his frustration and anger at Ryker, who fought the urge to crawl into the empty prison cage to hide.

"I will ask again. What happened?" He punctuated each syllable, keeping his anger just below the surface.

Shame made his ears grow hot, and he was suddenly glad for the darkness. "We were ambushed. Archers waited in the trees and took out the oxose and our archers first. When they'd taken out enough of our numbers, they came in and released the prisoners during the fight. We sent the message to you, but we were too far for you to arrive before they were gone."

"How did they know when and where to ambush you?"

"I don't know, Sir."

"How is it you still stand while all of your troops have perished?"

"I..." Ryker opened and closed his mouth several times, but the words died in his throat. The princess's face flashed in his mind as she'd pinned him to the ground, her bright blue eyes a whirlwind of fury, pain, and another emotion he couldn't name.

The wind had blown her copper hair around her pale, dirty face, the worn, white rags billowing just below her knees as she stood barefoot in the leaves. So unlike the princess she was. He swallowed involuntarily as though the cool steel was still against his neck.

"I don't know, Sir."

"Ryker…" General Moreland brushed a hand over his face and shook his head. "What would you have me do here?" He spread his arms wide, motioning to the surrounding bodies and the seekers who pretended not to listen as they dealt with their dead. "In front of all these people that have witnessed your failure, what am I supposed to do? And Vaan has these opinions of you." He raised a hand before Ryker could add anything. "Opinions I do not share, mind you, but he has a lot of influence with the other soldiers, and the emperor values him greatly, so his word holds a lot of weight with the others. And now, with all these strikes against you, people are going to talk, and I fear your ability to lead your soldiers will suffer."

Ryker's lungs deflated. The strangest sensation seized him, as if his feet were rooted in place, forcing him to stay and listen to the general's every word. It felt like the ground was disappearing, like he was falling, wondering when he would hit the bottom. His mind screamed at him to flee, but the roots in his feet were too deep—too embedded. General Moreland's next words slammed Ryker with a blow that left him winded.

"I can't save you this time." The words were sorrowful as they shattered Ryker's world. "As of this moment, I am revoking your position as captain. You will go report to Captain Lena Bennett in Tourrenfield. She's young, and though she was recently promoted, she shows great promise. Hopefully, you will be able to prove yourself again under her leadership."

General Moreland turned his back and walked away, like slamming a door shut on who Ryker had always wanted to be.

Through some miracle, his legs remained upright as darkness seeped into his mind—hopeless, endless darkness settling within his heart as if returning home.

It hardly registered in the fog of Ryker's mind when one of the seekers rushed over to General Moreland. Their voices were soft, yet their expressions were animated. The general spared one last regretful glance at Ryker before walking away, the seeker in tow.

All Ryker could do was watch as the last shreds of his dreams were ground into dust.

CHAPTER 15

FREYA

The torch cast eerie, dancing shadows along the cave walls. When Lanzo opened his arms wide as Freya touched the last step, she didn't hesitate. His massive frame fully encompassed her as she rushed into his bulky arms, which lifted her off the ground. The warmth of his embrace, mixed with the scent of smoke and pine on his clothes, made her heart constrict. When he placed her down, his smile was gentle.

"You alright?" His deep voice soothed the tightness in her chest. At her nod, he grabbed a large pack and handed it to her. Inside were two sets of clothes for her and Laia, four flasks of water, and a couple of biscuits and jerky.

"We shouldn't stay long." Lanzo gestured to a large boulder behind them before turning his back to give the girls privacy.

She followed Laia behind the boulder, and they divided the clothes. After discarding the old rags for the soft linen shirt and trousers, Freya felt more like herself. To complete the transformation, she donned a pair of sturdy boots and a dark cloak to match the others.

"Cliff decided I couldn't make you a full-course meal,"

Lanzo whined, his back still turned. "But those are the biscuits I made this morning, and I smoked some oxose steaks and cut them into strips for easy travel. Should do ya fine for now."

The biscuits were a little stale but were buttery and doughy in the center, and while the oxose strips were chewy, they burst with a salty flavor that complimented the biscuit perfectly. Compared to the prison bread that turned to dust in her mouth, this was the best biscuit Lanzo had ever made. She would never tell him, though. He'd be distraught to hear his best creation was stale biscuits. Instead, Freya savored every bite, then downed a whole flask to cool her parched throat. She sighed deeply when she finished.

Sipping on her second flask, Freya stepped back into the torchlight. "Harper said to meet them by Potámea."

Lanzo turned and nodded. "We planned for the possibility we would have to split up, and if we did, we would meet back there."

She considered his words with a frown. "How are they going to keep the seekers from tracking me, though? They have my old clothes; the lykos could use them to hunt for me."

"We placed some of your stuff throughout Runaris, and Harper, Cliff, and Archer are all carrying a piece of your clothing so they can split the seekers up." Lanzo folded his arms, his brows pinched with worry. "We even have one of your cloaks hidden in the barracks, so if the seekers do follow your trail there, it should convince them they found a false one."

Glancing at the stairs, she shook her head. "We may want to seal off this entrance to be safe. We can't risk the Empire finding these tunnels." It had been three months since her team had used the tunnels beneath Galleria, and there was no chance they'd risk exposing their existence now after months of hiding them from Keanon.

"If they find this now while the city's deserted, they'd have free access to this entrance," Laia added.

"What if they hear the collapse above?" Lanzo pointed out.

Freya frowned. It was possible that seekers were currently in the city above them and would hear or feel the quake when she collapsed the stairs.

"The city is falling apart, though." Laia leaned on the cave wall, arms crossed. The torch cast shadows over her face as she stared at the staircase. "A building collapsed right as we entered moments ago. It's completely possible for another one to give out."

Lanzo didn't look convinced, and Freya was torn. It would be a shame to lose this access point, as it was one of the closest tunnels to the border, but she couldn't take the chance for it to be discovered. Guilt threatened to pull her under as the realization of her decision to save Keanon by herself was costing them so much. Closing her eyes, she silently prayed Ductu would lead the seekers astray and pulled the torch off the wall.

With a regretful glance at Lanzo, she said, "I can't let them find this intact. If they're around to hear this and come looking, hopefully the rubble will be enough to fool them." She paused under the stairs that were securely held by wooden slats and beams. "Be ready to run." Then, she set fire to the beams and sprinted after her friends.

It took a few moments before the ground shook beneath their feet. Stones crashed behind them, and Freya grabbed the wall to stay upright, ducking as rubble crumbled overhead. When the dust subsided, Freya blinked to find the stairs had collapsed, and large boulders filled the tunnel.

If there were seekers in the area, they would have heard the cave-in, but she knew the general's quarters above had fallen, too, and possibly other buildings nearby. She gave another silent prayer that the gods would conceal the entrance and guide her friends safely to Potámea. It would take a few hours to travel there, and Freya was grateful for the snippets of sleep she'd managed in the wagon, seeing as their journey would take most of the night. The river entrance to the tunnels near Potámore City would require Cliff, Harper, and Archer to swim to reach it and could make the lykos lose their scent. It was risky —as lykos were not easily tricked—but if anyone could pull it off, it was those three.

They traveled in tense silence, Freya's mind reeled. Had concealing the entrance been the best choice, or should she have left it and trusted her friends? Were her friends alright? Would they all come back tonight? Freya's thoughts distracted her from her aching feet and legs.

Gushing water signaled their approach, and they all picked up their weary paces. Around the final bend, the tunnel opened into a larger cave. Water cascaded from the ceiling into a pool on the far side, surrounded by smooth ground for them to rest. Two more tunnels appeared heading in opposite directions: one would lead north, and the other south and west.

Laia hung the torch on the wall mount. Potámea River flowed right over the top of the cave, dumping a constant stream of water through the top into the pool at the back. The moon was bright enough to reflect inside the torrent, offering a cool glow that mixed with the warm light from the torch, illu-minating the space.

Freya refilled her flask with the water in the pool. Despite the summer heat, the pool was cold and reminiscent of a dark abyss. Even with the constant stream of water pouring in from the river, it never overflowed, as if it were endless. If Freya could hold her breath for long enough, would it take her to the other side of the world? A shiver raced through her from the idea of the tight space and frigid water.

"It could be a few hours before the others make it here."

Lanzo laid out two sleeping mats on the flattest surface and glanced between the two girls. "You two should rest. I'll watch for them."

"We slept some in the wagon," Freya objected. "You need rest too. Laia and I are well enough to do rotations." Her legs threatened to give as she stood before him, and though her eyelids grew heavy, she crossed her arms and refused to budge.

"Fine," he smirked. "I'll take first watch."

Laia spluttered on the water she'd been sipping as a laugh burst out of her. Freya couldn't fight the smile as Lanzo tsked and shook his head at Laia, patting her back as she coughed.

She swatted at him with tears in her eyes. "I— I'm fine."

Their back-and-forth could go on for a while, and Freya didn't have the energy to argue with him further. Admitting defeat, she settled on one of the pallets, her body immediately sagging with relief. Lanzo sat on a small, flat boulder beneath the torch and leaned against the wall. He pulled a simple black book from his chest pocket and flipped it open. The letters were too small to read in the dark, but she knew it said, 'Parables of The Wise One' on the cover. Sleep pulled at her, but before she succumbed entirely, Lanzo's deep voice washed across the cave. "May Natura bless you and give you dreamless sleep."

Lanzo's prayer must have been answered because Freya's sleep was deep and uninterrupted by nightmares.

Eyes still closed, she shifted on her pallet despite her body's protest.

"Hold still."

"That hurts!"

"Yeah, I bet it does, and it will continue to hurt unless you let him help you."

Those voices washed over her like a warm embrace, and she could hardly hold back tears. Freya lay still and pretended to sleep so she could listen to more of her friends' antics.

"Here, I can hold her still for ya." Mirth filled Lanzo's voice as his boots clicked across the cave.

"Don't you dare!" That was Harper's voice, much more strained and furious.

"Please, Harper. I'm almost done." Archer's countenance remained calm and soothing, even when dealing with the prickly, irritated warrior.

Harper must not have been mollified by Archer's kind words because Cliff reprimanded her. "Stop being childish and let the man work."

Ouch!

Freya bit back a smile, not wanting to give away she was awake. Cliff's stern, older brother tone had the desired effect on Harper, and moments later, Archer declared he was done. Trying not to give herself away, Freya opened one eye. Harper sat on the far side of the cave, glaring at the surrounding men. Her leg was wrapped in thick bandages from just above her knee to just below it. Archer packed his sewing needle and bandages into his pack, and Lanzo leaned on the wall beside them, grinning.

Harper's sulking evaporated when she spotted Freya. "You're awake!"

Having been caught, Freya gritted her teeth and sat up, her calves and arms burning. Cliff sat on a boulder behind her with Laia close by, her wrists already bandaged.

Archer must have caught her wince of pain because he immediately sat before her with his pack of mender's supplies. "Here, let me see what I can do."

"It's nothing too serious."

He ignored her and picked up her hand to examine the cuts on her wrists. His touch was gentle as he worked, wiping away dirt and applying a balm. It stung a bit, but she wasn't going to put up a fuss like Harper had.

"Check her ankles, too." Cliff directed from where he sat. "They were bleeding when I unchained them."

Freya glared at him, but he was unfazed. Archer pulled off one of her boots before she could protest, and she winced at the amount of blood coating her foot. The chain had dug into the skin and formed several bloody rings around her ankle. When he cleaned it away, purple and blue spots were revealed from where the chain had smashed her skin.

Everyone in the room sat in strained silence as they watched Archer mend Freya's injuries—injuries that screamed of her failure and imprisonment. The air was thick with unspoken questions, and she forced herself to meet Cliff's gaze.

"Why didn't you trust me?" The hurt was plain on his face, and Freya's heart shattered.

He deserved an answer, but she struggled to give him one. When Cliff had learned of Keanon's arrest and looming execution, he'd told the others first. She'd walked in on them discussing it, and all rationality deserted her. Cliff had told everyone before speaking to her.

Why she thought her friends would not have helped save Keanon was beyond her now. Laia proved it when she caught Freya going alone. Nothing Laia said could persuade Freya to wait, and Laia was faced with a tough choice: watch Freya attempt Keanon's rescue by herself or accompany her. In the end, Freya's selfish decision saved no one; it hurt the people she cared about, not only endangering them but her father's kingdom too.

Keanon's loss hit Freya hard, and mixed emotions welled in her throat. The knowledge Freya would not see his smile or soft eyes almost resurfaced the overwhelming agony she'd felt in that cell. Darkness weighed in her mind before she shook the feelings away.

Glancing between her friends' faces, Freya lowered her

head, knowing her torment was clear for all to see. No apology or fancy words could fix what happened. She'd failed everyone, and the person she loved most was gone.

"I'm sorry..." It was all she could say, but it was not enough.

"Freya."

Harper's voice was a soft command, and Freya lifted her tearful gaze to her friend's. Harper limped over and nudged Archer out of the way, who was finishing wrapping Freya's second ankle in bandages. He begrudgingly shuffled over.

"You can be so frustratingly hard-headed, Freya." Harper's brown eyes bored into hers. "But I love you, and I forgive you."

The dam burst inside of Freya, and quiet sobs shook her shoulders. Harper pulled her close and held her tight as a tidal wave of grief washed over Freya. The rest of the group wrapped their arms around her, too. She clung to her friends to keep from drowning in her emotions, allowing their love to wash over her heartache instead.

When they pulled apart, Freya knew she would make it. A piece of her would always be missing—gone with The God of Time in The After. She wasn't sure if Keanon's loss would ever stop hurting, but she could live with it. And she would make sure his sacrifice was not in vain.

There were no dry eyes in the cave when they finally pulled apart. Freya swallowed down her tears. She was ready to push forward now.

A loud grumble broke the peaceful silence.

"I'm hungry," Laia said dryly. The comment made Freya aware of the emptiness in her own stomach, which rumbled a complaint, too.

Cliff smirked. "I can help with that." He pulled out two loaves of bread, a large wedge of cheese, cured ham, and some of the largest plums Freya had seen.

"Oh, this is why you didn't want me to make the food? So,

you could go out and get it yourself." Lanzo feigned irritation as he plopped down beside Harper.

"How else would I get to remain the favorite?" Cliff didn't look up as he distributed the food, though the quirk of his face gave away the grin he was hiding.

"Whose favorite, exactly?" Harper raised a brow, popping a piece of bread in her mouth.

Freya was too hungry to participate and went straight for the plums. She almost teared up again as the sweet juice filled her mouth. The bread was soft and still warm, and she placed a piece of cheese and ham inside before taking a large, blissful bite.

Cliff ignored Harper's jab. "When I was sure it was safe to resurface, I went to Potámore City at first light to grab food. I also met up with General Ariss." All teasing vanished from his demeanor, and everyone grew serious. Turning to meet Freya's gaze, he said, "I sent a message to your father informing him of your safety, but I had one from him waiting for me already."

Freya frowned as he pulled the letter from his pocket, scrawled with her father's simple handwriting. Cliff didn't hand it to her but shared the words aloud.

"He's in Verna. He wants me to take you to him as soon as you are safe."

Freya's heart stuttered. Homesickness hit her harder than before, as did anxiety. After everything that had transpired, she feared standing before him. This had been part of their deal, though; if he let her go, she was to return to him as soon as he requested her to. Freya had promised she wouldn't cross the border, but she had gone all the way to Mésis City in her attempt to save Keanon. She'd promised to defer to Cliff if he felt a job was too dangerous, but she'd gone behind Cliff's back and forced Laia to do the same. She'd put her own life, Laia's life, and the safety of the kingdom at risk by going after Keanon.

"Why is he there?" Laia's question distracted Freya from her turmoil.

"I'm assuming he is preparing for the Empire's army to start their approach across the south," offered Cliff.

"So, they are traversing the south for sure?" Laia scrunched her nose and took another slow bite of cheese. With a mouthful of food, she mumbled, "I guess it makes some sense, seeing as it's the fastest route to Seaymarr, but how do they plan to get past Blackstone?"

There was little chance the Empire's fleet could march right past Galleria's most formidable city. Built within the mountains and crafted from the strongest material in Eavdamos, Blackstone was also home to one of Galleria's largest armies, second only to Seaymarr. If the Empire attempted to get to Seaymarr from the south, they would have to deal with Blackstone first.

"General Ariss believes the Empire plans to lay siege to Blackstone first. If they could take the city, it would almost ensure their victory before marching on to Seaymarr." Cliff leaned back against the rock wall and smiled. "It's a good thing a siege won't work."

"If the Empire lays siege to the city, they'll need our help to bring in supplies so they can outlast the Empire's fleet." Freya tapped a finger on her knee, considering this new information. Frowning, she added, "We need to learn what the city is in most need of, and since my father has summoned me, we may as well get our answers in the West."

Her team agreed and began moving to obey her orders. In moments, they were packed and on their way to Verna.

VIVIAN

A cool breeze brushed against Vivian's face. She stroked Talon's gray mane and stared at the sheer rock face before her. After the advisor from Ashera had left, she'd woken early to sneak out for a morning ride alone. Her mind was still processing what she was supposed to do with two marriage proposals on opposite sides of a war. Yet this decision was not hers to make alone. Her parents and the priests were in deep discussions, trying to uncover the right decision for the kingdom. Nevertheless, her mother made it clear she wanted Vivian to have a part in the process, but which part was she supposed to play?

"Excuse me?"

Her heart leaped into her throat, and she whirled Talon around to where a young man about her age trailed behind her. His pale skin—and his lykos—made it clear he was a southerner. He could have been one of the soldiers escorting the ambassador, but they should be further away by now. His appearance gave little away. He wore old, worn trousers, a thick wool cloak, and sturdy riding boots in boring shades of brown, cream, or black. He had no accessories or emblems to signify where he came from, but she knew lykos were rare for normal soldiers.

Something about him was different, though. His crystal blue eyes entranced her, and he held an air of strength and confidence. He had a full head of copper hair that draped across his forehead, further accentuating the blue of his eyes.

"I apologize if I startled you." He offered her a slight smile, and her insides warmed as she realized she'd been staring.

"Are you lost?"

"I don't think so."

Vivian narrowed her eyes as he studied her, and Talon side-stepped upon sensing her suspicion.

"I'm out here searching for Princess Vivian. I was told she may have run off this way." The glint in his eyes suggested he knew exactly who he spoke to already, and she frowned, her curiosity rising.

"What do you want with me?"

"I suppose introducing myself would help," he said with a slight bow of his head. "It is an honor to meet you, Princess. I am Prince Damian of Galleria."

Vivian's jaw fell open as the information sank in. There stood the crowned prince of Galleria, her potential betrothed. Where was his riding party? Why was he there and not at the palace? As though she'd spoken her thoughts aloud, several more Southerners rode into view through the trees behind Prince Damian. Most were mounted on horseback, their light armor glinting in the sunlight. One also rode a lykos like the prince. She assumed he must be a general by his mount and his older, wiser appearance.

"Mind if I come along?" Prince Damian's voice regained Vivian's attention. When he indicated the cliff face behind her, she raised a brow as his question sank in.

His lykos was young and strong, but it wasn't as lean or

long-limbed as Talon, and she worried about the hoofs on its back legs. Would it be able to scale such a steep incline? It would be unbefitting for her to refuse the prince, but she didn't want to risk his safety.

"Don't worry about Okeanos." Prince Damian assured her, patting the lykos's shoulder. "He's climbed his fair share of cliffs along the coast of Seaymarr."

"Are you sure? Once you start climbing, you cannot stop or slow down."

He nodded and leaned lower on his lykos's back. Vivian would have to trust he knew what he was doing, or her decision on which proposal to accept would be made for her. Talon's tail twitched in anticipation as she redirected him back to face the cliff, holding tight. With a gentle squeeze of her heels, he vaulted up the rock wall using every small outcropping and ledge, digging his claws into the surface to keep his momentum as he ascended to the top.

Vivian had to focus on the climb, not daring to look back to see how the prince fared. It wasn't until Talon launched over the final hurdle to the prairie above that she could see the prince behind her. She sighed in relief as he rode his lykos up beside her, the general not far behind. Talon gave Okeanos a curious sniff, and the lykos licked his face. She was impressed the lykos had managed the climb, but the prince was fortunate it was the warmer season, and the cliffs weren't covered in ice and snow like they were most of the year.

Prince Damian's eyes widened as he took in the view before them. Thousands of vibrant, multicolored wildflowers covered the high mountain plains. Purple and pink were most prom-inent, with some bright blue or yellow speckles. In the center, a small pond reflected the snow-capped mountains and flowers on its flawless surface. The rich, floral fragrance filled the air around them, and Vivian's heartache hit her again.

"It's beautiful," Damian exclaimed. "It rivals the view of the Navean Sea at sunset." Pride filled Vivian at the prince's admiration.

"This is my favorite time of year to come up here." She sensed his eyes on her as she continued staring across the landscape. "The flowers are here for a short time before the hills are covered in snow again."

"How long do they last?"

She met his eyes, captured by his bright blue gaze. "We have a few more weeks before the frost begins."

"That's a shame." Prince Damian freed her by returning to look at the surrounding fields. "I guess it makes the time they are here much more special."

"I suppose so."

They rode silently for some time, their mounts meandering toward the pond. She didn't know what to say. When they eventually stopped at the water's edge, she studied his reflection in the water. Prince Damian's gaze wandered over the mountains and beyond. His shoulders relaxed, and his expression grew distant as the quiet put him at ease. She shifted on Talon's back, unsure of what to do or say. While the silence appeared comfortable to him, it began to eat away at Vivian until she couldn't take it anymore.

"Why did you seek after me? Why not go speak with my father?" It seemed like the safest question among all the others swirling in her head.

Prince Damian cast her a sidelong glance, and it was his turn to be uncomfortable. "Of course, I will speak with your father, but I have not come to seek his hand in marriage." He shifted on his mount dand averted his eyes.

Vivian's stomach flipped from the reminder she could be looking at her future husband. At least he was nice to look at and had a nice confident air about him, too. She sensed it the moment he approached her; it wasn't overwhelming or haughty, but pleasant—comfortable, even. Those thoughts only made her heart stutter more. Then, she remembered the ambassador from Ashera. "You aren't the only one who has asked for my hand in marriage."

His face was grim, but he didn't look surprised by the news.

"I don't know which proposal my father favors."

"Which do you prefer?" he asked.

Once again that bold assuredness in his demeanor as he met her gaze, unwavering. His question was genuine, his face open to her answer. What could she possibly say to that? She'd just met him and had never met the emperor. If she had it her way, she wouldn't accept either proposal. She wasn't a queen or an empress, but none of that mattered. What she wanted didn't matter.

"It's not important which I prefer. All that matters is what the gods' will is for me." She pointed a finger at him, and he raised a brow. "How do I know the right choice is you?"

Prince Damian's face fell. "I know the line is blurry right now. Our priests sought this answer for days after the Empire's letter arrived. After tireless prayer, most still agree they see me as *king* after my father."

"You say the majority... does that mean other priests have considered their visions and believe you are meant to be the governor as the emperor claims? How could you be so certain when there is some contention?" If her words bothered him, he showed no indication; instead, he answered her questions with grace.

"I prayed about this myself when I heard the news. If I was meant to step down, I asked Ductu to make it clear to me."

"I don't think it works like that." Vivian's shoulders slumped as she considered her own prophecy and how lost she was in receiving answers from the gods. Not even Sasha was clear on what Vivian was supposed to do.

"I don't think that's true," he countered with a kind smile. "As I prayed, I could never shove away the heavy burden I felt to lead my kingdom and its people. No matter how hard I tried, I couldn't shake it. While the gods may not send another vision to clarify their will in this matter, I trust they will guide us on the right path if we let them."

His confidence was unwavering, and his words sounded a lot like Sasha's. The commitment he had to his people was admirable, like he'd be willing to surrender his crown if he believed the gods wished it. Vivian wished for the same level of assurance in which choice she was meant to take, even if his conviction did not make him right.

It was apparent he believed the Empire was acting on a misinterpreted vision or a lie—a false prophecy. Such a thing was never heard of in Eavdamos. If it was true, who dared to speak as though they were gods? All the priests in the Empire would have to be committing blasphemy together, which was unheard of. How would Eavdamos face something like that? There were also the other kingdoms to consider—those who agreed to join the Empire. Vivian frowned.

"What does that say about Kovdoran and Isdelle? Were they going against the gods' will when they joined the Empire?"

"I cannot speak for them. However, I recall they reached out to us not long ago in need of our help. Their kingdoms struggled from a poor crop season, and the people were going hungry." This was true, and she had wondered if the kingdoms' conditions would have an impact on their decision too. We tried to work out an agreement to aid them at the time, but we couldn't possibly provide for two kingdoms on top of our own. With their internal struggle of famine consuming them, denying the emperor's claims may have been a risk they could not afford to take. Part of the emperor's promise was to utilize all resources and distribute them throughout the whole Empire. Though I may not agree with King Henrik or Queen Claudelle's decision, I understand the need to do whatever you can for the sake of easing your people's suffering. It's what the chosen ruler is supposed to do. Serve the people as best you can, even at the cost of your wishes and desires."

"But you started a war." Vivian was incredulous. "How can that be what is best for your people?"

He shook his head. "We didn't start this war."

When his face grew weary, guilt hit her. He brushed a hand through his hair. Vivian feared she'd pushed too hard, but she also needed to know such answers if she was to come to a decision on who to side with.

"When we declined the emperor's offer, we left it open for him or one of his priests to come and discuss the prophecy further. Maybe there was something we misunderstood or missed that they could better explain to us in person." His face hardened as he fought to control his voice. "Instead of taking our invitation, they invaded our kingdom, destroyed our cities, and killed innocent families. How does he expect us to have any desire to turn our kingdom over to him after that? A war was never what we wanted, but it was forced upon us. Now we are doing everything we can to win for the sake of our people."

Vivian stayed quiet and considered everything he said. His anger reminded Vivian of her mother's strong reaction when speaking to Ashera's ambassador. When she'd heard the Empire had invaded Galleria, she remembered how her heart had sunk to her toes. Such quick and violent action had left a bitter taste in her mouth, but she had tried to keep her mind open. It wasn't her place to claim the emperor was wrong, but her heart hurt all the same at innocent lives lost.

The Empire's actions were why her father had hesitated so

long in picking a side. Prince Damian's passion was evident and his blue eyes captivating, making her catch her breath. However, she had to remind herself that he could be wrong.

Vivian guided the prince back toward the castle and hoped her parents would gain the clarity she had struggled to find.

At the bottom of the cliff, the prince's company waited, and together, they rode on to the city. General Johan rushed over to meet them as they made their way into the courtyard.

"Welcome to Calliva City, Your Highness." He bowed low as he greeted the prince, who dipped his head in return. The prince was swiftly surrounded, and Vivian took the opportunity to escape. After returning Talon to the stable hands, she slunk into the palace behind the Gallerions. No one paid her any attention as she disappeared down an empty corridor; everyone was too busy introducing themselves to the southern prince.

Vivian needed a few moments to collect her thoughts and was grateful no one called out to stop her. On the right, she passed the tall windows spaced out along the stone wall and then passed a door on the left leading to the palace library. It was tempting to go in and lose herself in a book, but she didn't want to run into any of her tutors or scribes. The door at the end of the hall led to the royal gallery, and Vivian headed straight to it, her riding boots clicking on the smooth, white marble floor.

A familiar sense of reverence washed over her as she stepped between ornate pillars to take in the wall of paintings. Generations of Leanders stretched out before her: all previous rulers of Brantyre. Vivian's heart squeezed. Aida was supposed to be the next one on the wall with Tristain, or at least that was what they had believed until now. Would the paintings remain if Aida became a Governess? Would they take them down and start over with her sister? Would they be removed entirely and replaced with Vivian and the emperor? Hating the direction of her thoughts, Vivian shook them away and focused on each beautiful, dignified face of her family line.

She stopped when she stood before her parents' portrait. Their portrait had been painted not long after they took the throne. Even as a newly crowned young couple, they were regal, elegant, and proud. They fully encompassed how a king and queen should look.

"Your father hated standing still for so long while they painted us."

Vivian jumped.

Her mother stood behind her, smiling at her daughter's surprise. She gestured toward the painting. "We nearly had to finish it in a separate session because of his impatience."

Studying the portrait closer, Vivian was amazed at how the painter had captured a hint of her father's restlessness in his eyes. It was so subtle that only those who knew him would notice. "You can hardly tell. You two look perfect."

"Hmm." Her mother smiled and stepped beside her. "You know we aren't, though, right?"

Vivian scrunched her brows as her mother took her hand. "Though called by the gods we may be, we are still human. Your father and I have made plenty of mistakes in our lives and our reign."

The words hit Vivian's heart and were her undoing. Her shoulders slumped and tears welled in her eyes. "I don't know what to do."

"Vi." Her mother cupped her cheek. "I know none of this is easy. Many voices will try to influence you in the upcoming days, and while I was serious when I said I wanted you to have a say in this, I never meant for you to feel like you were making this decision on your own."

"But what say does anyone have?" Vivian pulled away. "Everyone keeps talking as though it's just a matter of choosing between two marriage proposals, but it's not. The will of the gods and the future of all Eavdamos is on the line, and no one seems to know which path is the right one to take." Hot tears slid down her cheeks, and her mother stepped closer.

"Yes, everyone is seeking the gods' will above all else, and we may not all agree on what that is, which is exactly why I want your voice to be heard." Her mother reached out and took Vivian's hands again. "You have always had a close connection with the gods, Vi. The way your siblings always seek you out first when they have problems—especially Aida—is because of your strong inner voice guiding you to say what they need to hear. It is the gods' influence inside you. I always knew you would be called to something special. On the day Aida was chosen to be heir, I knew they must have another task for you."

Vivian's heart raced as the words struck her. It was almost like what Sasha had said, but her mother had known it long before the High Priestess had her vision. Why hadn't she said anything? Why had she spent so little time helping Vivian while she was growing up? All her life, Vivian had watched from afar as her parents devoted most of their time to helping Aida grow into the queen she was meant to be, so Vivian had done the same. She'd taken on all of Aida's burdens and problems as though they were her own, so much so that Vivian didn't know what to do now that she was the one with the problems.

"I don't know what I feel this time though," Vivian mumbled

"You will." Her mother's smile was encouraging, and she kissed her forehead. With one last squeeze of her hands, her mother released her and returned down the hall.

Though her mother tried reassuring her, Vivian was still lost and uncertain. A flicker of fabric caught the corner of her eye, and when she turned, she met the gaze of her sister, who appeared behind one of the pillars.

She'd been hiding.

Aida's mask had fallen, her face contorted with sorrow. Before Vivian could say anything, Aida bolted.

"Wait!"

Aida ignored her and rushed down the gallery after their mother. Vivian chased after her, but when she burst through the door into the hall, Aida was nowhere in sight. She frowned as she stared down the empty corridor. What had upset Aida so much? Vivian was the last person to be upset with Aida for eavesdropping, so what could have happened to make her sister run?

CHAPTER 17
RYKER

Shrill chirping and croaking filled the evening with song, though Ryker gave it little attention. He stared blankly into the crackling flames before him. Sparks from the fire floated into the sky to join the stars until gravity seized them, bringing them down to earth and diminishing their light as they hit the ground. Ryker was one of those sparks. He'd flown too high and was now nothing more than a speck in the dirt. Absently, he turned his father's compass in his hands, his life feeling like the spinning dial that refused to settle.

A dark muzzle pushed its way into his lap, and Ryker let the compass fall back against his chest so he could stroke Artis's head. She was calm for once and snuggled against him. She was his only companion on this journey—his only companion in life.

Closing his eyes, flashes of metal, blood, and horror greeted him in the dark, forcing them open once more. The weight of his eyelids grew heavier with each night as he fought back the memories. For two days, he'd been on the trail and would reach Tourrenfield on the morrow. Though sleep tempted him, he refused to succumb to it. He could have taken the main road, stopped in the small town of Elmdale, and slept in the Inn, thus arriving in Tourrenfield early the next morning, but he'd chosen the longer route. The road meandered through the Elmwoods, with no towns, villages, or even a hovel nearby. While it was not as used as the main road, it was still well-kept and defined, offering him the solace he desired.

Artis licked his chin, and a ghost of a smile traced his lips as he scratched her ear. She leaned into his hand until she trapped it in his lap, her head too heavy for him to move it.

"What do we do now?" He breathed, his voice raspy. Artis whined and licked his chin again but could not answer him. Deep sorrow and loneliness settled on Ryker's shoulders like a blanket, and not even Artis could help. As the fire dwindled to smoldering coals, darkness and fatigue overtook him.

HE BOLTED UPRIGHT, drenched in sweat and shaking from terror. The sky was beginning to lighten, the stars winking out one by one. Tears stained Ryker's cheeks. Startled by a nightmare, he'd fallen off the log and now winced at the twinge in his back as he pushed himself up. He shook his arms, trying to rid the tingling sensation after sleeping so long with his arms as a pillow.

Artis bounded into the clearing as Ryker got to his feet, prancing around him. Her expectant face filled him with guilt as she showed him the catch wedged in her jaws. She was good at hunting animals without mangling them and would offer the dead creature for Ryker to cook and split between them. Artis loved it when he made the food smokey and crisp, but his stomach churned at the sight of the little paws hanging from her mouth. He shook his head.

"Sorry, girl. Not this time."

Her tail dragged in the dirt as she sulked away to eat her

breakfast alone while he packed up their meager camp. Nothing but a black marring on the ground from the fire showed he'd been there. Artis seemed to have forgiven him as he grabbed her riding gear, sprinting in happy circles around the clearing.

"Heel."

Artis plodded over to stand beside him, her tail wagging so hard her body still wiggled. Her tongue lolled out the side of her mouth as he loaded her up and mounted. The sky was barely light as Artis's long stride ate up the ground. He hoped they'd reach the city before nightfall.

The Elmwoods provided plenty of shade from the intense summer sun, the foliage casting thick, leafy shadows along the trail. The air was sticky and clung to his skin until Artis hit top speed. Wind rushed through his hair and pulled his tunic loose, offering sweet relief.

Ryker had chosen the Elmwoods for the quiet but was beginning to resent the long trek alone, and as the trees flew past, his mind numbed, unlocking the darkness inside him to have free rein of his thoughts.

"Keanon!" The princess' piercing scream filled his ears, and he flinched as though the blood sprayed his face. Red hair blocked his view of his brother bleeding on the ground.

"How do you know she isn't using you? Why would you turn your back on us for this woman?" Ryker had said, his sword clashing with Keanon's. Ryker flinched.

"Because I love her." The unwavering certainty in Keanon's eyes shook Ryker even now.

"You knew his fate was set when he turned his back on us." General Moreland's words made Ryker grit his teeth at the implications. *"I can't save you this time."*

Blue eyes flashed before him as a ghost of cool steel pricked his throat. Hatred, more powerful than he'd ever known, hardened his heart as every horrifying moment in Ryker's existence was because of her. He let the darkness in to bury the pain, replacing it with rage.

As the sun neared the center of the sky, rushing water greeted his ears and grew louder as he guided Artis alongside the River Torr. Soon, the trees thinned, and he pulled to a stop right before they left the coverage of the woods. The last stretch of their journey would be in the endless open fields before him. With the river cutting through the center of the vast plains, it created rich soil for crop fields and lush grasslands for grazing animals. A single path weaved alongside the river on one side while a browning wheat field grew on the other. Small trails of smoke rose in the distance from farmhouses, and beyond, the city walls stretched toward the sky.

The remainder of the journey would be spent in direct sunlight, so he stopped under a shaded tree to allow Artis to drink from the river and rest. Though he'd been raised and trained in Talbane and Mésis for most of his life, he'd been sent to Tourrenfield once. It was well-known for making excellent soldiers and was one of the closest cities to Galleria's border in the west and the late kingdom of Kovdoran in the north. With the ongoing war efforts, General Averill was with his soldiers on the front lines, so the barracks were running under Captain Bennett and her lieutenant's command.

Tourrenfield was a quaint city. The River Torr ran straight through its center, cutting the main street in two. Many bridges spanned the distance to cross from one side to the other. Tall buildings flanked the road, where a variety of shops resided, and stalls with the city's best fruits, vegetables, and cuts of meat filled the market square. When he was seventeen, Ryker had traveled to all the major cities to better understand the map of old Esraia. After moving from Talbane in the east to Mésis in the west, he felt compelled to visit the entire kingdom, a decision his father had supported as long as he took the time to train with the generals while there.

They made their way along the river as the sun lowered in the sky. Over the next hill, the city's gates appeared like a silhouette as the sky darkened behind it. Artis slowed to a stop. Guards' heads peeked at him from the top of the wall, but his simple gray uniform had them turning back with disinterest. His old tunic—the symbol of his status as captain—had been dark gray with a red streak down one sleeve: an outfit demanding respect. They didn't spare him a second glance. The higher the rank, the darker the uniform, until it was all black. Lieutenants had the red streak on the left arm, captains on the right, and generals wore all black. All the Empire's uniforms had the emperor's symbol of a sun setting between two red mountains on the chest.

Only a few stragglers scuttled their way home as the streets grew dark, candlelight glowing within building windows. The grates in the city walls and man-made channel allowed the river to flow through, the lights from the windows reflecting on the water's smooth surface.

Tourrenfield's barracks hugged the city wall, so he didn't have to go far before entering another gate. This time, the soldiers on watch side-eyed him, but Ryker ignored them, keeping his face forward. The barracks were situated like the one back home in Mésis City, with stables by the entrance on his left and the armory on the right beside the tower leading soldiers to the top of the wall. Next to the armory was the training field. Boisterous laughter and the smell of roasted venison emerged from the dining hall beside it. A small mender's building was across from it, and along the back wall were the sleeping quarters.

Ryker rode straight for the center building to report to Captain Bennett first. Some soldiers mingled outside talking, but their chatter grew quiet as he drew near. Smiles fell when they caught sight of him, and when he passed, their fervent whispers followed. Snippets of their conversation hit him like a punch to the gut, words like "traitor" and "demoted" following his path. His grip on Artis's neck tightened as he fought to keep his head high, even as their judgmental glares bore into his back. Artis responded to his tension and drew back her ears, emitting a low growl. None of the soldiers dared to approach but kept whispering as he made his way to the opposite side of the barracks.

Finally, he dismounted in front of the simple wooden building, where a man stepped out from the shadows.

"Ryker Kessler." The man that greeted him appeared to be a couple of years older with soft, bronze skin tone and thick dark hair tied up high on his head. He approached without hesitation, even as Artis dug her claws into the dirt. Ryker patted Artis's side to calm her and accepted the man's proffered hand.

"Lieutenant Kovac." Kovac's handshake was firm as he introduced himself and then gestured to the door behind him. "Captain's waiting for you."

Ryker nodded and stepped past the lieutenant. Captain Lena Bennett sat at her desk, which, besides the built-in shelf of books and maps behind her, was the only piece of furniture in the cramped space. Recalling his quarters back home, Ryker assumed that the closed door to her left would lead to her bedroom and washroom.

The captain leaned back in her seat when he entered. Her raven hair was pulled in a thick, long braid, tucked over one shoulder. General Moreland had said she was young, but Ryker hadn't expected she would be a similar age to him. She was the only other person he'd heard of to attain such a high rank at their age. Captain Bennett studied him with her dark eyes, the lingering silence beginning to unsettle him.

"I expected you earlier," she said, her words clipped. She tilted her head to one side. When he opened his mouth to speak, she lifted a hand and continued. "General Moreland sent a carrier with all I need to know about your arrival and his expectations. You will begin training with Lieutenant Kovac in the morning." Her tone was final, and the dismissal clear as she waved her hand and bent over the papers on her desk.

With little energy to care about her flippancy, Ryker did as he was told. Upon exiting the building, there were no soldiers left milling about except for Lieutenant Kovac. Artis remained where he'd left her, her tail twitching in agitation. When he guided her to the stables, he was surprised when Lieutenant Kovac kept pace with him.

"A captain with a lykos?" Kovac glanced sideways at Ryker, though he sounded more curious than suspicious.

"She was a gift." Though that was all he said on the subject, the lieutenant seemed satisfied with his answer. As they continued in silence, Ryker was unnerved by how closely Lieutenant Kovac studied him, much like the captain had. Due to the circumstances of his arrival, their scrutiny of him was valid —a fact that pained him to his core. He hoped they did not share Vaan's opinions of his loyalty.

He was relieved when Lieutenant Kovac did not follow him inside the stables, but he had a feeling the man would be waiting for him outside. The barn was like all the others he'd seen, with horses and eldeer toward the front, and a couple stalls at the back for lykos. Stalls for lykos were larger and built with iron walls and doors instead of wood; they had a freshwater trough but no place for food. Every meal was delivered to them fresh unless their riders took them out to hunt.

Flashes hit him of his brother fighting a grin as he leaned against a stall door where a younger Artis waited. Ryker's steps faltered. Sorrow stabbed him like a sword to the chest as his body flowed through the motions, his mind numb. He found an empty stall, bombarded by memories of playing and training his brand-new mount with his brother. The stall already had a large bed of hay and a trough full of water, so he removed her riding gear and placed them on the pegs at the back wall. She licked his chin when he'd finished, and he grabbed the sides of her face, resting his forehead against hers. Ryker's body shook, unable to stop, and Artis leaned further into him, offering her comfort and stability to keep him upright. The dial kept spinning in his mind as exhaustion and pain overtook him, making it difficult to grasp onto his earlier rage—rage for the one who'd caused it all.

The rage that kept him moving forward.

CHAPTER 18

FREYA

A yawn escaped Freya's mouth and made her eyes water. After renting horses from Potámore City, they'd left them with a struggling farmer around midday. She'd paid him well to care for them and return them to their owners, being sure to give him a little extra in case they arrived late and the owner tried to raise the rent. The war had not been kind to many Gallerions, so she hoped they'd given him enough coin to provide for his family for a while. They'd re-entered the tunnels, taking the straight, direct route under the mountains. Blackstone City resided on the eastern side of the Blackstone Mountains, while Verna was on the west side by the Navean Sea.

"How are you?" asked Cliff as he came up beside her.

"I'm alright." Freya absently brushed her fingers over the cuts on her wrists. Archer didn't think they would scar, but the ones on her ankles would. "I've missed my father more than I thought I would, and yet..." Freya sighed, glancing at him. "I'm not looking forward to seeing him at the moment."

"Understandable." Cliff flashed her a sideways grin and brushed a hand through his hair. "This is going to be a difficult conversation."

Her stomach rolled again, and she frowned. Freya had hoped the next time she came home, Keanon would be with her. She'd sent letters home after meeting Keanon, suspecting he'd been sent by the Empire. She left out how close they had become in the end, and Freya only hoped her perceptive sister, Kiarra, hadn't read between the lines about her feelings for him. She'd wanted to introduce Keanon to her family in person.

But he was not with her. He would never meet her family.

Cliff slipped an arm over her shoulders and squeezed, pulling Freya back from her aching thoughts. "We're in this together, alright." He smiled genuinely this time, his eyes kind. "Trust us; we're here for you."

She swallowed back tears as they rounded the last turn to what appeared to be a dead-end. The sconce on the wall was unlit, and when she pulled on it, a soft click followed. The boys rushed over to pull the large stone wall, holding it open as the team filed through.

The dark, plain tunnel entered a spacious, well-adorned study; as the door closed behind them, it formed part of the stone wall enclosing the space. On the right stood a large, cramped bookcase filled with old tomes, rolled up maps, and small weaponry. Across from the bookshelf was a sturdy wooden desk with neat stacks of papers, charts, and trinkets, like a beautiful, large seashell, an ornamental dagger, and a piece of polished blackstone.

At the desk sat a roguish but beautiful woman. She was lean but muscular, her tone evident beneath her lightweight armor. Her pale—almost white—blonde hair was cropped and styled to stand like spikes on her head. She leaned forward on her desk; her sharp, blue eyes pierced the motley crew that stepped into her office.

"Welcome back."

Her voice was clipped and aloof, but a slight glimmer of

relief flickered in General Annalice Vance's eyes. As one of the best soldiers in Galleria, she trained all the royal children. She was not affectionate, though, not even to her daughter, who stood beside Freya now but didn't approach. General Vance did give Harper a small nod of acknowledgment, but the two never showed physical affection toward each other—even after months apart.

General Vance would never allow anyone to believe Harper got any special treatment for being her daughter. She wanted to make it clear all of Harper's accomplishments were achieved by rigorous training and dedication. The general was the same with the royal children and wouldn't let them get away with anything just because of their status, though Freya, Cliff, and Harper had been her favorite students growing up, which simply meant she pushed them more than anyone else. General Vance saw greatness in their reckless, mischievous tendencies and made it her mission to push them to become the warriors she knew they could be.

"General," Freya returned the greeting and tried to fight her shame. With her recent failure, she didn't feel like the capable leader General Vance had believed in. It made this homecoming even more painful.

"It's good to see you too, Mother." Harper crossed her arms, matching her mother's tone. It was clear the two were family. They shared the same pale hair, round face, and strong, robust demeanor. Though Harper didn't know who her father was, Freya assumed she had his dark eyes.

"I would have hoped I'd trained you better." General Vance stepped around her desk to stand before them, and Freya fought the sudden urge to shrink back. "To not go waltzing into the enemy's hands without a proper plan or backup." Crossing her arms, she glared at everyone before her eyes landed on Freya. "Perhaps I should take you and your *fine warriors* through some basics again, since clearly none of you learned the lesson the first time."

"Some training sounds good, Ma'am." Lanzo stood tall with a sincere smile, and Harper elbowed him in the stomach.

"Flattery doesn't work on my mother," she hissed.

Lanzo's smile didn't waver as he mumbled through his teeth, "Never hurts."

"Actually, it could," grumbled Cliff, who had tried many times over the years to get out of trouble or training through his charms and wit. General Vance was the only person who didn't fall for it.

The general ignored Lanzo and directed her command to her daughter. "Harper, I will escort Princess Freya to her father. Take everyone else up top to eat and rest."

"Sure thing, Mother." Harper waved for the team to follow, but Freya remained where she stood. Her father... Freya's heart shuttered at the realization she would be seeing him again. After almost five months apart, Freya wanted to sprint to him and throw herself into his arms. But after everything she'd done and been through, she would rather crawl away and hide from his disappointment.

Once the door closed behind her team, General Vance sat on the edge of her desk. Her expression softened as she indicated the spot beside her. When Freya sat, she asked, "What happened?"

For several moments, Freya was quiet. The general waited while she collected herself, but her voice still shook as she admitted, "I messed up."

"Hmm, before or after falling in love?"

Freya's mouth fell open. General Vance must have spoken with Kiarra. Freya's sister was the only person who could perceive Freya's true feelings through letters. General Vance gave a sad smile and took Freya's hand, gently squeezing it.

"Come now. It's painted all over your face, Princess. Kiarra suspected it immediately."

Freya averted her eyes.

General Vance patted her hand one last time before standing. "I won't pry further, but please, in the future, be more careful about who you give your heart to. Friend or enemy, he was a risk no matter what choice he made."

She made it sound simple, as though Freya could have denied the strong pull drawing the two of them together. A flash of Keanon's intense gaze hit her from their training, and all the times he'd leaned in close. No, Freya hadn't been able to fight her feelings as hard as she'd tried; even her friends had known there was something between them. But she wasn't about to argue. Instead, she followed the general into one of the most breathtaking places in Galleria.

Verna barracks was built on the side of a cliff, half of which was inside a cave behind a massive waterfall. The cascade of water roared as it rushed over the side of the cliff and into the Navean Sea. From inside the cave, Freya could not see the ocean past the falls, but as the sun set on the other side, brilliant rays of red and orange glittered on the water, casting warm hues across the cave.

The rock ceiling stretched high above, and along the walls, wooden walkways spiraled to a small opening at the top, adorned with sconces to light the pathways. Smaller caverns connected to the large one and were used as different rooms for the barracks. A natural stone bridge crossed the width of the cave. The general's quarters was a cavern at one end of the bridge.

Generations ago, pirates had landed in Galleria and discovered Verna Falls' hidden cave. They raided the towns above but disappeared into the rocks whenever soldiers tried to hunt them. Seekers traced their scent to the ocean before it was lost, and any ships they sent out couldn't find them off the coast. Pirates plagued them for a year before the heir at the time, Princess Rosaline, used the tunnels beneath the kingdom to discover their hideout. With that knowledge, Rosaline's father was able to overtake the pirates, and when the princess became queen, she turned it into the Verna Falls barracks and housed Galleria's greatest navy fleet. Freya had only been twice before: the first time was for training with General Vance, and the second was when she, Cliff, and Harper snuck away from the palace to visit Laia and brought her to see Verna. The splendor of the barracks filled Freya with wonder every time.

Not many soldiers lingered inside the cave. Most were on the surface for dinner or guarded the cliffs. Freya followed General Vance down the gentle slope to the base of the cave, where they crossed a small bridge over a gentle stream that made its way from the ocean into the mountain. On the opposite wall stood the facade of a building covering one cavern. It was the only structure larger than a simple doorway, built with the same plain, unadorned wood.

General Vance stopped at the door to offer a last remark, her cold demeanor having returned. "I better see you up bright and early."

As the general walked away, Freya remained rooted in place. The door to her family's chambers was worn, and the wood splintered from age and moisture. Freya's heart hammered in her ears as she took hold of the doorknob and pushed.

Inside was a spacious, well-lit space with a stone arch separating two rooms. The entry room had a small hearth for warmth in the winter months, but it was untouched now. Two cushioned chairs faced the hearth, and a wooden table was between them. Through the large arch was a sturdy, wooden table and chairs taking up most of the space in the room. Two of the chairs at the table were occupied, and tears filled her throat.

Kiarra sat at the table, surrounded by stacks of books and parchment. Her long black hair fell down her back and was tucked behind her ears, so as not to get in the way while she read. Her bright blue eyes were scrunched in concentration as she scanned the pages, pausing to take a sip of the tea in her hand. Forever absorbed in her reading as always. Kiarra was unaware the door had even been opened.

At the head of the table sat her father, sitting tall in his chair. His thick, black hair revealed signs of stress as gray streaked throughout it. His crown rested on the table beside him. Green gems glinted in the silver circlet with a polished blackstone rock in the center. Her heart caved when his sea-blue eyes latched onto her, filled with relief.

"Freya?" His deep voice was soft and hit her like a tidal wave.

"Father..."

"Freya!" Kiarra bolted across the room and threw her arms around her sister, almost knocking them both to the ground. "Oh, thank the gods, you're alright."

Freya held her sister tight as tears clogged her throat. When Kiarra pulled back, their father took her place. Freya fell into his arms, tears streaming down her cheeks as she breathed in her father's scent: the salt of the ocean and his favorite black tea. He pressed a soft, hairy kiss on her head, and a sob shook her shoulders. In his arms, she was safe. The world couldn't hurt her—not while he held her in his arms. But then he stepped back, and the world crashed around her.

"Come here." He gestured to the table and summoned food to be delivered before she could say anything.

Moments later, a plate piled with grilled fish, roasted vegetables, and a large slice of steaming bread was placed before her, along with a cup of black tea and a container of sugar. While she ate, her sister and father had another cup of tea.

"Where's Damian?" she asked as she scarfed down the food.

"He has gone to Brantyre to try to solidify an agreement with King Nicholias, in the hopes he will side with us." Kiarra took a sip of her tea before adding, "Now finish your food."

Freya did as she was told and sopped up every bit of juice with the bread. Then, she dumped two large spoonsful of sugar into her tea and sat back, preparing for her family's questions.

"Are you hurt?" was the first one her father asked.

"Not really, the emperor wanted me unharmed. I guess he knew you would be easier to negotiate with if I was in one piece. Or he wanted to preside over my torture himself."

"What happened?"

"Who was Keanon?"

If the two questions weren't packed with painful memories, Freya would almost find humor in her father's directness and how quickly Kiarra got to the heart. Freya took another sip of her tea, stalling. They must have already known what Keanon had meant to her, but she knew they would want to hear her say it, as opposed to hinting at it in a letter.

"You remember my suspicions about Keanon?" At their assurance, Freya continued. "Well, I was right. He was sent from the Empire, and he confessed as much to me."

"Why?" Kiarra's voice was soft but prodding.

A sorrowful smile lifted the corners of Freya's mouth. "Well... um.." As Keanon's loving face flashed in her memory, she struggled to voice the words trapped in her heart. "He told me he was leaving the Empire, but he decided to go back one last time. I asked him not to, but he wanted to talk to his brother. He wanted to try to convince his brother to come with him." Her grip tightened around the cup in her hands as she relived everything.

"And?"

A bitter tear slid down her face. "And his *brother* turned him in."

Her father rested a hand on top of Freya's before her grip cracked the cup. "You decided to go after him." For several moments, they sat while her father brushed his thumb over the back of her hand, skimming over the marks on her wrists.

When she lifted her eyes to his, there was no condemnation. He wiped away her tears and whispered, "I remember how hard it was when I lost your mother."

Freya cried then. Full and hard, and her dad pulled her close. Her mother had died giving birth to Freya, so she'd never met her but had learned about the beloved queen of Galleria through stories. The tapestry in the castle's halls showed Freya that she was the spitting image of her mother, both with long fiery red hair, bright blue eyes, and a heart-shaped face. She used to stare into that beautiful face for hours growing up, picturing a world where she was still here. Whenever she needed someone to talk to, she would find her mother's tapestry, but sometimes when she looked into those smiling blue eyes, a sense of guilt would sink in. The beloved queen had died to give her life, and Freya didn't know if she could properly mourn her, especially as she'd never met her.

When Freya's tears subsided, her head throbbing, and her eyes red and puffy, her father set her on her feet, pushed the stray hairs out of her face, and kissed her head again. "We'll discuss more in the morning. Go get some rest."

Too spent to reply, Freya nodded, and he let her go. She missed his comfort but left the dining table behind. Glancing back, she gave her family a wobbly smile before braving the horrors she knew awaited her when she closed her eyes.

CHAPTER 19

VIVIAN

T he following days after his arrival, Prince Damian kept his word and spent most of his time with her father. They spent hours of the day out in the city or holed up in her father's study, making it difficult for Vivian to find time to talk with him again. She grew increasingly frustrated every time she watched him go behind the closed doors of her father's study. If she was supposed to help decide which proposal to accept, Vivian wished to ask Prince Damian more questions and get to know him better. Her desire to speak with him had absolutely nothing to do with his entrancing blue eyes... nothing at all.

Vivian's only opportunity to see him was at every evening meal, so now she stood in her room, preparing to join her family in the dining hall as she tried on different dresses. She was torn between the bright yellow dress made of fine silk or the deep violet dress with soft pink flowers along the bodice and skirt.

"Wear this one, Princess," said Vivian's eldest maid, lifting the yellow one with a kind smile. "You look stunning in this color."

She nodded her thanks. Marienn helped her dress and

pulled her hair into two long braids. After glancing in the mirror to ensure everything was in place, Vivian made her way downstairs.

The palace bustled as servants put up decorations for the upcoming festival and wedding. They hung garlands along the walls, which would be adorned with wildflowers on the first day of the festival. Rich blues, purples, and pinks would be entwined with the green leaves, pulling in the view of the mountains from outside the tall windows. Crystal sculptures of chilver swans were carefully placed in the center intersections of the hallways, and pale blue and white ribbons twined around the pillars and banisters.

When Vivian entered the dining hall, her parents, sister, and Prince Damian were already seated. Her father sat at the head with her mother on his right and Aida beside her, who fidgeted as Vivian approached. After her sister ran away from the gallery, Vivian tried to seize every opportunity to ask her what had happened, but Aida avoided her. Vivian couldn't ask her at the table—not with Prince Damian present—so she was determined to grab Aida after supper. For now, she would try to have a conversation with the prince, who gave her an awkward smile as she drew near. Before she could sit, the doors burst open behind her.

Glenn and Tristain spilled through the door, chatting and laughing. Tristain wrapped a burly arm around Vivian, pinning her arms at her sides.

"How's it going, Vi?"

"It's going just fine, thank you." She tried to pull out of his grip, but he squeezed tighter. When she glared at him, though, his expression made her pause. While his big, goofy smile was still plastered on, the glint of genuine concern in his eyes gave his question new meaning.

Quietly, she answered again. "I'm alright. Truly. Don't

stress about me." Vivian gave him what she hoped was a reassuring smile; he studied her for a few more moments before nodding, seeming unconvinced. Vivian didn't want Tristain to worry about her so much, especially when his wedding was only three weeks away. Releasing Vivian, Tristain walked over and whispered something to Aida before taking his place across from her. Prince Damian glanced at Vivian and away again when Tristain sat beside him, though his expression was unreadable. Vivian hoped to have some conversation with him throughout the meal.

Try was the best Vivian could do. She wasn't sure why she thought this dinner would be any different from the previous ones. Her father monopolized a lot of the conversation, and the topics were kept to small talk, such as Damian's stay, books, studies, the upcoming festival, and the like. Aida ignored Vivian the entire time, while the prince only glanced her way occasionally throughout the meal, mostly conversing with her father. When he'd first arrived, he'd been so intent on speaking to Vivian before anyone else, and now she got nothing. Though it was unladylike, she was sorely tempted to plop her elbows on the table and shove her head in her hands, exasperated.

As the meal ended, her sister quickly rose to her feet and excused herself. Vivian followed after her sister. After that painfully long meal, Vivian couldn't let Aida get away from her without talking. Once clear of the dining hall, her sister was already halfway down the corridor.

"Aida, wait!" Vivian sprinted after her, but Aida ignored her again. Gritting her teeth, Vivian picked up her pace. She refused to continue suffering in her sister's silence.

Vivian grabbed Aida's arm, but she refused to turn. "What has gotten into you?"

"Nothing you should have to concern yourself about." Aida's voice was hard, and she still would not look at Vivian.

"What do you mean? I'm already concerned about you."

"Well then, you're the only one." Aida whirled, her face pinched with suppressed rage and hurt. The venom in Aida's voice made Vivian backpedal and release her arm. "Mother and Father have completely forgotten about me—everyone has! Everything has been about you and deciding on your proposals. It's no matter that my *wedding* is only a few weeks away or that my whole kingdom is under threat of war, not to mention that my crown—who I am—could be taken from me."

As Aida's words washed over Vivian, years of suppressed anger bubbled to the surface. "I didn't ask for any of this to happen either!" Tears threatened to well in her eyes, her anger growing. The last thing she wanted to do was cry. "Never in my wildest dreams did I think of becoming a queen. Let alone be offered a position so grand as an empress. That position didn't even exist until now." She pressed her palms to her eyes to keep back the tears, and lowering her voice, she continued. "Now you see how my whole life has been led. Gods, Aida, everything has always been centered around you! The chosen heir. Our parents spent so much time raising and training to prepare you for the position, leaving me alone."

Her sister's expression only hardened. "I guess we both know how it feels to have our lives flipped upside down, but my life is in *your* hands." With that, she whirled away, but Vivian didn't run after her.

How could her sister think she held any power over her life? Their parents had more say over the kingdom's matters than she did. Nothing happening was what Vivian wanted. Why couldn't her sister see that?

After a few moments, Vivian crossed her arms and made her way back up the grand staircase, yet movement caught the corner of her eye as she reached the top. She lifted her head to meet the prince's crystal-blue eyes. He tilted his head with a shy smile.

"Might I have a moment of your time?"

Vivian had wanted time to speak with him alone, but now that he stood before her, all her questions fled to the back of her mind. As she nodded, her stomach was in knots, and the two strolled down the corridor. As they walked, Prince Damian brushed a hand through his hair, averting his eyes toward the tall windows. He appeared tense, and she found a loose curl from her braid and spun it around her finger.

Finally, he broke the awkward silence. "I apologize that I have not spoken with you much since my arrival. To be truthful, it has been difficult to find the right words to say."

Vivian raised a brow as he glanced away again. His discomfort was apparent, but she wasn't sure what she could say to make it easier. When they first spoke, he'd been so well-spoken and confident.

Face still averted, he said, "It's difficult being here while knowing what is going on back home. I am desperate to return and help my father, but I know I need to stay here." He finally met her eyes, his expression torn. "I need to be available to you and your parents to answer any questions and appease your concerns, but I have been neglecting you." He gave her a tentative smile. "If we were to marry, I cannot continue to neglect you."

Vivian's stomach flipped at the mention of marriage, and it was her turn to avert her gaze. Seeing his distress, and hearing his reasoning behind his distance, Vivian felt her frustration fade. It had been clear when she first met him how much he hurt for his people, which was an admirable trait for the chosen heir. It also brought her some comfort to see he was as awkward about their potential marriage as she was.

They stopped in front of one of the tall, open windows, and

she was acutely aware of how close they stood. She had to tilt her head to meet his eyes—so blue, yet filled with many fears and sorrows—but also a strength and hope. Hints of stubble gathered along his strong jaw, and the wind blew his copper hair across his forehead. For a few moments, they studied each other, and she worried about her inability to hide her thoughts. Could he see how his nearness affected her? Though his face was kind, she couldn't read any of his emotions.

Finding her voice, she asked, "What's Galleria like?"

"It's much warmer than here." His face lit up with the warmest smile. "This time of year, it can get really hot, but there's nothing like swimming in the sea on a hot summer day."

At the mere mention of swimming, Vivian shivered. The lakes and rivers near Calliva remained frigid all year round, so she never desired to learn how to swim. Not many residents of Brantyre knew how. Vivian didn't interrupt as he continued. "Seaymarr sits where the cliffs meet the Navean Sea. The sight of the endless waves and sky is breathtaking, and when the sun sets on the horizon, and lights it with so much color..." He let the sentence hang.

He returned his attention to her. "It sounds beautiful." It did sound wonderful, and she would love to see it for herself someday. But how would it compare to her mountains of flowers?

"I've heard the Winter's Light Festival is approaching." He changed the topic as they continued their stroll.

"Yes, the festivities will begin in the next few days. On the eve of the first day of celebration, we will witness Natura light up the night sky. On the last day of the festival, we get our first snow, and my sister will be wed."

"Might I accompany you during the festivities?"

Vivian's eyes widened. "You're staying through the festival?"

"Your father has requested I stay, and..." His voice trailed off, the worry and sorrow returning to his face. "I think it's best I accept his request. We can attend the festivities together and become better acquainted."

Vivian's heart hurt at the sorrow he couldn't hide. While she was happy to hear he was staying, she knew it couldn't be easy to be so far from his family when they were at war. If their roles were reversed, Vivian would be beside herself with worry. Every time she'd spoken to the prince, she liked him more. Yet the more she liked him, the harder it would be for her if Brantyre decided to side with the Empire. If they chose to side with the Empire now, she feared the prince and his family would suffer the same fate as the royals who lost the gods' blessing. The emperor would have them executed. Could she handle being responsible for the prince's death?

Before either of them could say more, Glenn bounded around the corner, and Vivian self-consciously took a step back from the prince. "There you are." He ran over to Vivian, panting. "Mother and Father request your presence in their quarters right away."

Vivian's mind raced with what her parents could want from her. Glenn's expression was grim, his eyes wide. Her heart sank. She glanced at Prince Damian, who smiled reassuringly. "Probably not a good idea to keep your parents waiting. I'll see you soon."

She nodded and walked toward her parents' quarters, through the doors to the royal family's rooms, and down to the last room at the end of the hall. The large double door opened to the king and queen's personal rooms, the entryway expanding into a grand sitting room with a plush couch and two chairs before a large marble fireplace. Spread on the floor was a luxurious, deep blue rug embroidered with silver thread. Many tapestries of Brantyre's landscapes hung on the wall.

Her parents sat in the two chairs by the fireplace and asked for her to sit. She sat on the couch, her stomach in knots as she waited for them to speak.

"We have received another message from the emperor." Her father began, and Vivian squeezed her hands together.

Her mother grabbed her father's hand and took over. "He has requested a meeting in old Kovdoran. A week after the first snow, he will meet us in Lividia City on the border."

She caught her breath, her heart hammering in her chest. A summons to meet the emperor?

Her father saved her from having to reply. "Your mother and I have talked about it already. He wishes all three of us, including High Priestess Sasha, to meet with him. It's a bit of a journey for the older woman, but she is determined to make the trip to meet with their high priest, Baralia. However, our departure would be right after the Winter's Light Festival and Aida's wedding so we have decided that I will stay here to attend to matters after the wedding while you and your mother go with Priestess Sasha. General Flynn is preparing a retinue to assure you have safe travels."

"So, we must leave right after Aida's wedding?"

"It was a difficult decision, but we will depart directly after the ceremony," said her mother. "The celebration will be in full swing on our departure, but we want to ensure we get out before the snowfall."

Vivian frowned at that. Everything was happening so fast. Would the emperor expect a decision from them when they met him? This gave her the next few weeks to get to know Prince Damian and ask him questions. After the festival, he likely needed to return to Galleria. Vivian's heart constricted as the pressure mounted on top of her anew. They would need to decide what to do soon, and she was nowhere near closer to her decision.

CHAPTER 20

RYKER

Ryker winced from the blow to the back of his leg and jumped back, almost losing his balance to avoid another hit. While the strike was from the flat of a practice sword, it would add to his growing number of bruises. His opponent was a few years younger than him, his face twisted with an ugly, self-satisfied sneer. The kid was fighting dirty, and everyone knew it, but no one would stand up for the recently demoted captain, rumored to be a traitor. Ryker could easily throw all the kid's sneaky attacks back at him, but he'd learned on the first day of training that he was not allowed to hit any of his opponents—even with the flat of a training sword —or he would suffer consequences from his peers later. After he'd beaten several opponents in training on his first night, the senior soldiers found him in the sleeping quarters and taught him a lesson. They'd warned him to watch his traitorous blood next time, or he would be in the mender's ward for a month. Their threats meant Ryker struggled to find inventive ways to defend himself without hitting his opponent or taking the hit.

He was relieved when Kovac called the fight, and the kid backed off. Rolling his shoulders and neck, Ryker tried to loosen up. It didn't matter who he was placed against; they all did their best to make him suffer without getting penalized for it. Ryker gritted his teeth, limping to return his sword to the barrel while everyone went to the dining hall. Scents of hearty stew and fresh bread wafted in the air, but it did little to waken his meager appetite. The thought of sitting amongst his fellow soldiers, who flashed him judgmental glares while he ate, was even less appealing. To them, he was either the captain who failed and lost them the princess or a traitor who deserved death.

With everyone eating, he would have the soldiers' quarters to himself, so he decided to go to the baths. This was the one time of day he could be alone. Passing through the communal common room of the barracks, Ryker took the left door to the men's bunkroom—a long hall with bunks along the walls—and finally, the bathing room at the end. The room had three large tubs for a full bath and a wall of smaller basins with mirrors for quick scrubs. Coarse hand towels were stacked on a shelf, along with several pitchers; he took one and used the hand pump to fill the tub as much as he could be bothered.

When Ryker pulled off his tunic, he tried to avert his eyes from the dark purple bruising along his torso and his protruding ribs. He hissed as he submerged in the icy water, bumps rising all along his body. He scrubbed off every inch of dirt.

Two weeks. It seemed like a lifetime, but it had only been two weeks since Ryker had been sent there. The dark and loneliness settling in his heart grew more familiar day by day. He dunked his head under the water again, willing the cold to distract from the pain eating him on the inside.

When his fingers and toes were red and lost all feeling, Ryker climbed out and toweled himself off, donning a fresh uniform. Flickers of memories teased him as his weary body moved of its own volition toward his bunk. If he was in bed before the other soldiers arrived, he wouldn't have to worry about anyone bothering him, but the horrors that thrived in the darkness rejoiced as he sat on the edge of the bed. Ryker lay down and threw the blankets over his head. His breathing shuttered as he succumbed to the haunts that plagued him. He deserved this life—he'd created it—and he could not ignore it.

THE NEXT MORNING, he dragged himself from bed. Every inch of him throbbed, and his eyelids were heavy as he remade his bed and tiptoed outside. He had another hour before everyone else got up. Inside the common room, Ryker pulled on his boots and combed his fingers through his hair before stepping outside.

The sconces were still lit, but the sky lightened as the moon continued its descent. There was a soft crunch in the pebbly dirt beside him, and his brain took a few sluggish moments to process he was not alone. With the training still strong in his addled brain, Ryker straightened upon recognizing Captain Bennett. Since he'd arrived, he'd not seen much of her. Her black hair was pulled over one shoulder in a thick braid like the day he met her, and her dark eyes regarded him with little emotion.

"Come with me." She turned on her heels, and he fell into step beside her, limping and struggling to keep up. She made no indication she noticed. He could not fathom why she wanted to speak with him so early, but he said nothing as she led him away from the sleeping quarters, past the dining hall, and toward the front gates. Only the thump of their footsteps along the dirt path interrupted the quiet morning.

She stopped beside the training field and met him with another impassive stare. "Kovac believes it would be best for me to take over your training for a time." Her expression never shifted, even as the cold bite in her voice smacked him like a blow to the gut. His legs barely supported him, and his arms ached at the mere thought of lifting one of those bulky practice swords again. He said nothing.

A part of him was relieved not to be training with the rest of the soldiers anymore, but from Captain Bennett's icy expression, he wasn't sure this would be much better. He could only hope her professionalism would keep her from fighting dirty like the rest of the soldiers.

Trepidation made his empty stomach churn as he stood opposite the captain, who rolled her shoulders and raised her sword. "Alright, let's see what you can do."

Then she charged.

Captain Bennett wielded her sword like it was an extension of her arm, every move fluid and precise. He stumbled back from her steady stream of blows and lifted his blade in time to meet them, despite his arms protesting every time he did. Ryker floundered into her rhythm. Although she was relentless, she kept her attacks fair, and it was a relief not to play mind games. The fog in his mind receded, and he found his limbs loosening up as the fight continued.

"Curious." Captain Bennett eased her onslaught. "Since you and your brother were so close, did you see his betrayal coming?"

"What?" Ryker's voice croaked from disuse, and he fumbled while blocking her next attack.

She was unfazed and came at him with another flurry of blows. "For someone that knew him so well, had he shown any signs?"

Ryker clenched his teeth as he tried to keep up with her. Being twins did not give him divine insight into his brother's mind, despite what everyone seemed to believe.

"I'd seen my brother once after the three months he'd been sent to Galleria. His decision to turn on us was made while he was away. When I did find out, I..." His voice faltered over the confession, and he could not bring himself to finish.

Captain Bennet brushed aside his comments and pressed further. "So, he just told you he was leaving?"

"Basically." Ryker's response was terse, but it was all he could say. He lived these moments enough in his dreams and had little desire to vocalize them. Despite what General Moreland believed, a part of Ryker wished to go back and undo it all.

Pain snapped him back to reality. There was a dull throb in his arm where the captain had smacked it with the flat of her sword. Shifting from foot to foot, she twirled her blade and raised a brow with a slight smile, one that almost seemed encouraging.

Ryker shook his head to clear his thoughts and took on the offensive, but she met him blow for blow. As they danced around the field, sweat beaded along his forehead, even though the sun had yet to ascend. The bruises along his body shifted from a dull ache to shocks of pain as he moved. His arms trembled, and he backed off while Captain Bennett allowed him time to regain his strength as they continued circling the field.

"What happened with the princess?"

He cringed. "I thought General Moreland would have told you."

She waved his comment away. "I've heard plenty of gossip. I want to hear from someone who was there." She watched him intently as he processed how to respond. He'd expected these questions upon his arrival, and had hoped as time went on, she wasn't going to ask.

"The Gallerions had set up an ambush on our route to Talbane. Archers waited in the trees and took out the oxose, pulling the prisoners first." He recalled the oxose's bone chilling cries, Artis crashing to the ground beneath him, and a rage filled face and blue eyes. Shaking off the memory, he continued. "They picked off our soldiers before rushing in to release the princess." Shame warmed his insides, but the heat and exhaustion from the fight hid it from his expression.

"How did they know where to set up an ambush?"

"I don't know..." The answer sat like lead in his stomach. "I picked the route myself. I didn't allow anyone else access, not even General Moreland. Somehow, they got knowledge none of my soldiers had, even though they were on the road with me." It was that fact that left the most bitter taste in his mouth. He'd rarely left his quarters while he determined the route to take, and General Moreland had locked down the barracks while the princess was there. There was someone within Mésis City's barracks leaking information to Galleria. Ryker had no idea who that could be but could only assume General Moreland was aware of the spy and was taking precautions.

"Hmm..." Captain Bennett frowned, considering his story. It did not paint him in a great light, but how could anyone believe he had chosen this kind of torturous life on purpose?

"How is it you lived when the rest of your fleet died?"

Cold blue eyes and cool metal at his throat flashed again, and he almost dropped his sword. Instead, he tightened his grip around the pommel and clenched his jaw. Pushing the words between his teeth, he had to admit, "I don't know."

The captain's face was unreadable as they continued to circle the field. Each step tested his strength, and his knees threatened to buckle beneath him. Ryker's rage at the mention of the princess did not distract him from his pain for long. He could not take another day cooped up in the barracks. "Can I request a day of prayer?"

A slight grin played on Captain Bennett's face as she sighed. "You know I can't deny a man's right to pray, even if I wanted to." Rolling her shoulders and raising her sword once again, her grin widened. "I will, however, expect you to work twice as hard tomorrow."

She charged at him again, but his limbs were slow to respond. He barely raised his weapon in time to block her, dodging, parrying, and stumbling back against her onslaught. It was like the first round had been her warmup, and now she danced in different rhythms, pushing him to his limit. His legs trembled, and his arms burned from lifting the sword. Waves of pain rolled down his body each time their swords clashed until he couldn't do it anymore. Though he still held the sword in his hands, the blade rested against the dirt, and he could bring himself to pick it up. She swung and knocked it from his grasp, pointing her blade at his chest. He didn't dare move, terrified his legs would give out if he did.

With a nod, she stepped back, seemingly satisfied with his effort. "You need to learn to anticipate the unexpected better." She tilted her head and placed one hand on her hip. "Your life has been full of it recently; I should think you would have learned to stop assuming you know more than you do."

Her words struck him in a way that made his skin crawl. It sounded like something his brother would say. Her expression never changed, and he shook off the feeling that she was speaking about more than just the sword fight. With a last, almost reassuring nod, she retrieved his practice sword from where it fell and left him there.

When she disappeared past the dining hall, Ryker tumbled over to a bench on the edge of the field and collapsed onto it. Laying his head in his hands, he took steadying breaths to regain control of his shaking body. The back of his throat burned with each intake, his mouth dry like the Norrean savannah. His fresh uniform from last night was soaked in sweat clung to his body. Even though the sun had yet to rise above the city walls, the air was sticky, and heat continued to rise. The morning was upon them as the barracks awoke. He wanted to be gone before any of the soldiers arrived for morning training, and finally, he forced himself to his feet.

With a free pass to leave for the day, Ryker kept his head down as he exited the gates into the city. None of the guards questioned him as he departed, and he found he could breathe easier as the city expanded before him. Much like Mésis, Tourrenfield was bustling with people: citizens rushed about their business, vendors called out their wares, and children ran underfoot. The only difference was the River Torr. Mixed with the constant lull of the river, the busy sounds offered him familiar comfort.

In the distance, a tall stone spire rose in the sky and loomed over the rooftops. It was the city's temple. Ryker made his way there through the center street along the river, the captain's words ringing in his head as he walked.

Anticipate the unexpected... He was sick of the unexpected. He wanted life to go back to when things made sense—back when Keanon was still around before he'd left for Galleria—before the prophecy had changed everything. The pang in Ryker's chest was overwhelming; he shoved the blasphemous thoughts away. He would try to remind himself of Captain Bennett's advice the next time they sparred.

He dodged some dirty, barefoot children as he crossed over the river to the temple courtyard on the other side. Tall, stone walls surrounded the temple, making it only accessible across the bridge. It was crafted of polished white stone, and four carved, marble pillars adorned the front stoop, leading to a grand double door. As he drew near, he noted the temple didn't have a single crack or blemish anywhere; as thick clouds dulled the sunlight, every surface glittered.

Last time he had been here, the temple stones had been

cracked and marred over the ages. Tourrenfield's temple was one of the oldest, where the first line of kings and queens had received their blessings from the gods to rule. Its rich history and grandeur had been a sight to behold, whereas now it resembled the palace in Talbane.

Beggars sat at the base of the grand staircase, hoping for generosity from those going to pray. Their rags hung limp over their frail bodies, with one beggar appearing no older than seven. Ryker averted his eyes from their hopeful faces and hurried inside. He had nothing to give them.

Inside, the interior was just as opulent. Ryker's boots clicked across the shiny floors, reflecting the chandeliers above. More carved marble pillars held up the dome ceiling, and a marble arch separated the entry from the altar room. On the far wall above the altars, beautiful, multicolored light shimmered through a magnificent stained-glass window, depicting the three gods. The God of Nature was on the left, the God of Time on the right, and the God of Wisdom in the center, bestowing their power and blessing on a single man to rule over Eavdamos. Asher Rowden knelt, accepting the crown they placed atop his head with a map of the seven kingdoms behind them.

Just like the temple, the stained glass was new. It must have been crafted within the five months since Emperor Asher received the prophecy. It sent a chill down Ryker's spine as he stared up at those amber eyes, which glowed as the sun shone through. Unsettled and awed, he walked down the center aisle toward the front altars.

The original stained-glass was of the first king and queen, Barnabas and Miriam Esrine, at the founding of the Kingdom of Esraia. For generations, the Esrine family had ruled, but their line ended with King Darius after the gods bestowed their blessing on the Soryn family instead. But when the Soryns perished with no living heir, the blessing passed to Asher Rowden, and ten years later, the gods made him emperor.

Ryker walked down the center aisle where three altars representing each god stood, glowing in many colors beneath the window.

"Wonderful, isn't it?"

Ryker jumped at the intrusion, and the priest chuckled. "Forgive me; I try not to make it a habit of frightening those who come to pray." His dark hair was plaited in a multitude of small braids. His rich red robes were embroidered with gold accents, indicating he was a high priest. Several gold bands draped around his neck, and a large blue gemstone ring glinted on his finger. The priest arched a brow and smirked, waiting for Ryker to speak.

"Ahh—yeah. The window is beautiful." Ryker averted his eyes from the priest's humored expression. The silence lingered until he finally confessed, "I haven't been inside a temple in some time. A lot has changed."

That was a bit of an understatement. The last time he'd stepped foot in a temple was when his father passed. Before his father passed, he'd only ever gone when made to. The weight of the compass felt more prevalent around Ryker's neck.

"We began to rebuild this temple two years after Asher's coronation. It has taken a long time to bring this place new life, and as we neared completion, we received the prophecy of Asher rising to his place as emperor. Displaying this vital part of the Empire's history was deemed important. Do you not agree?" He offered Ryker a genuine smile but raised his brows in question.

"Uhh, yes—no, sorry." Ryker brushed a hand through his hair. "Maybe I've been away too long."

The priest chuckled again before his face grew serious. "So, what is troubling you so much it's brought you back today?"

"I..." Ryker's mind blanked as he stared at the priest. He looked back at the stained-glass window. How could he hope to explain the events that led him there? He didn't want to talk about his shame and failure again. He struggled to find the words to say, but the priest stood quiet and patient. Finally, he blurted, "Why are the gods changing things?"

The question stunned him.

That wasn't his question. It was Keanon's. It was a question Ryker found himself asking after every unexpected in his life, hoping for a solid answer he could stand on.

"Ahh, young man." The priest rested a reassuring hand on Ryker's shoulder. "Do not fret. You are not the first person to ask that very thing. The new and unknown can be frightening." He smiled sadly and stared at the beautiful window. "For generations, the gods have blessed and guided the seven kingdoms with their wisdom and love. Whenever we have faced adversity, the gods have always been there to help guide those they knew could fix it."

"What do you mean?"

"It's in Esraia's history, soldier. One of the darkest times in our own history was five generations ago when the Esrine family lost the blessing to rule. King Darius's children were furious the gods hadn't chosen one of them. They created allies, assassinated their parents, and hunted down the true chosen heir to the throne.

"The priests of the time were executed if they spoke the truth, and the royal children managed to amass an army to do their bidding. King Lucan had to start his reign in hiding, but the gods were faithful to their chosen ruler. They guided him to priests willing to fight for him and reached out to the only other kingdom at that time to have their royal family blessing passed to a new one. Brantyre.

"The Leanders agreed to help, along with the Gallions, the

first rulers of Galleria before the Calloways. With their help, King Lucan took back his kingdom from Darius's children. To make sure no uprisings could ever happen again, the priesthood executed everyone related to the Esrine family."

Ryker shivered. To have an entire family destroyed because of a few selfish exceptions left a bitter taste in his mouth. He supposed the priests had suffered greatly under Darius's children, the pain of which led them to such drastic actions.

"None of Darius's children were fit to rule the kingdom." The priest continued, seemingly unaware of Ryker's turmoil. "They were selfish, prideful people and proved their inadequacy the moment the gods decided to give the kingdom to another. They sought to take it by force. If we had chosen one of them, they would have started a civil war among themselves as they each vied for the crown. With Ductu's infinite wisdom, they selected a man with a pure, but strong heart that would serve his people—not lord over them. In our kingdom's darkest moments, the gods guided those who could make the difference." The priest faced Ryker, his expression filled with conviction; he placed his hands on Ryker's shoulders. "We may never know the reason behind the changes they make, but we can trust them to guide us, and lead the ones with the power to unite us once again. It is our job to do our best, listen to their calling, and follow."

Ryker had read the story about the rise of King Lucan Soryn when he was young, but he'd not put much thought into why the gods had not chosen one of King Darius's children. He'd been more focused on studying maps or new battle techniques than his historical studies, paying little attention to the passing of the crowns through the generations.

"So, the gods could be doing something new just like they did when choosing King Lucan? And the kings are fighting like Darius's children did before." Ryker said in a bid to understand.

"Change isn't always pleasant." The priest sighed, his eyes sorrowful. The words he spoke next sent chills down Ryker's spine. "The greed of men can lead to the deaths of many innocents, and the more powerful the man, the greater the numbers."

CHAPTER 21
FREYA

Freya savored the warm ocean breeze as she exited the cave, reminding her of Seaymarr. Hairs blew from her braid, but she didn't mind. Stars glittered in the sky and shifted the canvas from indigo to shades of red, yellow, and blue. The Verna cliffs dropped off to the vast Navean Sea below, where carved in the rocks was a trail leading to a massive network of docks stretching deep into the water. Gentle waves lapped at the wooden pillars of the docks, rocking the Gallerion ships tied to port.

Verna was one of Galleria's largest trading port cities. It was established by Queen Roselina to house their warships during their struggle with the pirates, but over time it was developed into a port to trade with Faulkern and Norrean. Few ships had set off since the war started. Walls surrounded the barracks on three sides to separate it from the rest of the city, and the cliff on the final side kept it protected. Verna had a glorious view of the ocean to the west and the Blackstone Mountains to the east. The Dark River trailed from the mountains and got its name from the mountains, too, while the black soil and rocks gave it a darker hue than any other river, its rough current cutting through the rugged terrain leading to the falls that tumbled into the ocean.

Inside the walls of the barracks were the dining hall, a blacksmith, an armory, a training field, and smaller sleeping quarters for any soldiers uncomfortable with sleeping underground.

A clash of steel shattered the peaceful summer morning as two lone figures practiced on the training field. Freya sighed, exasperated, as Harper and her mother exchanged blows. Both wielded broadswords instead of training swords; General Vance didn't believe their use had any value. When new trainees would ask about using a blunt weapon, General Vance would scoff, "Your enemies will never go easy on you, so why should I?"

"That bad?"

Archer joined her at the mouth of the cave.

"You've not trained with General Vance before or you would feel the same way," replied Freya.

He shrugged. "Harper doesn't seem to be suffering much, even with her leg still healing."

"That's because she was cut from the same cloth as her mother," Cliff chimed in, coming to stand beside them. "Trust me, my friend. You are about to experience the workout of your life."

"I wouldn't be surprised if Harp said she was born with a sword in her hand." Lanzo rolled his shoulders and stretched, following behind Cliff.

"Probably a dagger," Laia muttered, rubbing her eyes. Her hair was still a bit disheveled, and she struggled to tame it with her hair ties. With a huge yawn, she added, "Sword would be too big for a baby."

"Hey there, bedhead. Glad to see you made it." Cliff

wrapped his arm over her shoulders, and she glared and shoved him back.

"Come on; we shouldn't keep the general waiting." Laia hurried away to keep everyone from seeing her face redden.

"Real smooth." Lanzo elbowed Cliff, who rubbed the back of his neck and mumbled something incoherent under his breath.

Freya lowered her head to hide her smirk and jogged to catch up to Laia. Linking their arms, Laia huffed. "He's an idiot."

"Yeah," Freya agreed with a chuckle.

ALL THEIR LAUGHTER and teasing disappeared once General Vance was finished with them. Freya's entire team lay sprawled on the ground, their clothes clinging to their bodies, hair drenched, and faces red. All Freya could think about was the dryness in her throat, made worse with each gulp of air. It had been years since she'd experienced such harsh training from General Vance, and she suspected recent events had something to do with the severity. Not only did they repeat the basics and then the advanced techniques twice, but they proceeded to duel with the general one at a time. Every one of Freya's limbs screamed.

General Vance stood over them now, unaffected by the strenuous training she'd given them. She crossed her arms, taking in their exhausted state. "Hmm, could be worse." With that said, she retreated toward the cavern below, but not before calling over her shoulder. "Freya! Your father wants you and Cliff to report to the meeting hall when you are done panting and whimpering."

Cliff couldn't fight the grin, and Harper raised a victorious fist in the air. No one spoke for several more moments.

Lanzo found his voice first. "Well, that went better than expected."

"The highest of praises," said Harper.

"Well, sounds like we have to get going." Cliff managed to push himself to his feet first, coming over to Freya and offering his hand.

"Have fun in your meeting." Lanzo gave them a wide grin, then turned to the rest of the group. "Anyone up for a swim?"

Freya rolled her eyes. As wonderful as the water would feel in the blistering summer heat, Verna's sharp, rocky terrain and strong current didn't make for the safest environment for swimming.

"That is not happening, you oaf. We're not allowed to swim here." Laia was quick to put Lanzo in his place.

"It's not stopped us before," said Harper from her sprawled position on the ground. Lanzo gave her a high five.

Freya laughed as she followed Cliff, leaving Laia to handle those two. But when Archer called out, she paused and turned to him. He took her hand and placed a small vial in it.

"What's this?" She studied the dark liquid and sniffed it. It had no distinct smell to give her any clues as to its contents.

"Something to help you sleep."

Her head shot up. "What—"

"I'm a light sleeper." He shrugged. "I've heard you crying in your sleep and caught you sneaking away in the middle of the night. I wanted to give this to you sooner, but it took me a bit longer to put together than I'd hoped." He offered her a sympathetic smile, and she ducked her head to hide the warmth rising in her face.

She'd tried to hide her heartache from her friends, yet now wondered how many of the others knew she wasn't sleeping. They had a job to do, and they'd already wasted precious time and energy on fixing her mistake. The last thing she wanted was for her friends to worry about her more.

Archer clamped his hand over her shoulder, and she hesitantly met his eyes. "There is no shame in having nightmares, Freya. Not after everything you've been through." Though his voice was gentle, it was clear he disapproved of her shame. To her relief, he didn't push her further. He tapped the vial in her hand. "Just a drop or two in a cup of water or tea before bed, and you should sleep soundly. No nightmares."

"Thank you." Freya gave him a sincere smile, her heart warmed by his kindness. She rushed away and held the bottle close to her chest.

Cliff waited for her by the mouth of the cave. The two of them made their way down the rickety walkway along the cliff walls, lit by torches as they descended further underground. The temperature dropped, offering blissful relief.

About midway down, they crossed a bridge over the cavern below toward one of the façade buildings built into the stone. Freya kept her eyes straight ahead, avoiding the dizzying drop until she made it to the other side and opened the door. Inside was a spacious room with braziers along the walls, lighting a long table in the center, a coarse rug beneath to make the space cozy, and two candelabras in the middle of the table, in which her father sat at the head; her sister was to his right, with General Vance beside her, while the royal High Priest Klaus sat on her father's left.

Klaus donned his traditional deep sea-green robes with golden trim, signifying the high priests of Galleria. Though the trim was fraying on his sleeves, it was wrinkled, with dirt covering the hems. His once-dark hair was almost all gray; his pale face had more lines than she remembered, and his eyes were drawn and weary. Upon her entry, though, his face lit up, and he quickly rose and welcomed her with open arms.

"There she is." His soft, gravelly voice enveloped her with warmth as they embraced. "Welcome home."

"It's good to see you, too." She responded as she pulled away. He indicated the seat beside him, and Cliff sat on Freya's other side as her father began the meeting.

"How well have you kept up with current events?" Freya leaned back in her seat, realizing the question was directed at Cliff.

"General Ariss mentioned their growing army in Ekrewell, and his suspicions they will lay siege to Blackstone."

"Yes." Freya's father nodded. "We have one of our spies inside the city who has told us about the Empire's growing army, but whether it is a siege, we cannot be sure. So, we are preparing for anything from them." Her father frowned as he studied the maps spread out on the table. Markings had been written across the mountains of Blackstone and along a path leading from the Empire's border, which depicted the path her father believed the Empire would take.

"Why not go north past Riverwood? It's not as formidable as Blackstone." Freya scrunched her brows as she followed the northern path, which would be the easier route for Ashera.

Kiarra sat taller as she answered. "I know that might seem like the better route. Everyone knows how near indestructible the walls of Blackstone are, but I believe they have made a smart decision on how best to deal with our kingdom." She pointed along the markings on the map as she spoke. "First problem with going across the north is the Rubywood forest and the Woodland River. Getting a whole army through both is no simple feat and would create an incredible risk if they had to retreat. It is also no secret Faulkern has allied with us, and if the Empire were to go north, they risk being met with two armies, and if we win over Brantyre, they might have to face three. Norrean has remained silent since the emperor's ultimatum, so we don't know who they may side with at this time, but it means the Empire has more security that we will not be receiving help from the south. Unfortunately, they would be correct in thinking so." Kiarra shook her head as her father took over.

"King Therrowin is sailing here with his armies as we speak. We have prepared the port for his ships' arrival and can only hope they will arrive before the Empire attacks. King Nicholias has been less enthusiastic about taking his people to war, which I can understand." He paused and glanced at Klaus, who took over the conversation.

"We have negotiated with them and hope we have offered them a deal great enough to win their support."

"What kind of deal?" Freya's heart thrummed as her father and Klaus exchanged glances.

Klaus smiled. "We have offered to arrange a marriage between Prince Damian and their eldest daughter, Princess Vivian."

Freya's mouth fell open. They were not close to King Nicholias or his family. She only had one memory of meeting them, which was at Brantyre's celebration ball after the gods chose Princess Aida to be the heir. Freya was eight at the time and remembered the awe she'd experienced from the snow-covered mountains and grand castle. She hardly remembered the Leander family. Over the years, she'd heard bits about Aida, the future queen, who was said to be graceful, intelligent, and well-loved by the people of Brantyre. However, Freya knew little about her older sister, who was rumored to be a beauty like her mother. Beauty did not make her worthy of being queen of Galleria, but Freya supposed if her father and Klaus saw this as worthwhile, she would have to accept it. She wondered how her brother felt about the proposal, though he wasn't around to ask.

Kiarra shifted the conversation back to the current problem. "If the Empire managed to take Blackstone, they would have clear passage to Seaymarr and would cut off our access to the blackstone mines, and thus our primary source of weapons. Our chances of winning this war at that point would solely sit with Brantyre's decision, and even then, it will be a long and hard fight if we can't save the city."

"Yeah, but they still have the impossible task of taking the city." Freya waved a dismissive hand. "A siege takes time and numbers. Plus, there's no chance they could hold out with their resources when we can continuously sneak more in."

"That may be true," Kiarra reasoned. "However, from where they are standing, this is a good course of action. With a siege on such a large city like Blackstone, the Empire could expect us to last several months, but with all their resources and numbers from Kovdoran and Isdelle, their odds aren't bad. Even if they are unsuccessful in taking the city, we will still suffer losses. Our people will still go hungry, suffer diseases, and could die in the process of the constant fighting and waiting."

General Vance spoke for the first time, her elbows on the table and hands clasped together. "Our hope is Faulkern will make it here before the Empire arrives, and we can force them to retreat before our city suffers for too long."

"What are we doing while we wait?" asked Cliff.

"We have evacuated as many citizens as our other towns and cities can afford to take in. Anyone too old, young, ill, or raising young have been sent north," answered Freya's father, brushing his hand through his beard. "Just because we can get supplies in during a siege doesn't mean we wish to put our people through that. The evacuation means fewer mouths to feed."

Freya agreed, but the longer the siege lasted, the worse off all the overpopulated towns and cities would be. While removing the people at least kept them away from the crossfire, it did nothing to distribute their kingdom's resources. Galleria's trade with all the kingdoms had shut down since the war began. Both her father and sister had a heaviness about their shoulders. Kiarra was worse off, her young, pretty face drawn, her eyes having lost their gleam for life. Her sister's cunning came at a cost. Though she displayed an incredible sense of strategy, inside was an all-encompassing empathy that drained her heart.

"Would you rather we focus on providing supplies for Blackstone or for the inflated cities up north?" Freya offered.

"You won't be doing either one."

Her heart sank at the harsh tone in her father's voice. He straightened in his seat, the light from the braziers reflecting off his crown. His expression was hardened and brooked no room for argument. "I allowed you to go on several conditions. You were supposed to stay inside our border, not set foot in any Imperial city, and allow Cliff to deem any job too risky. You broke your promises which nearly cost you your life, and that of your team. As of now, we are still unsure if your escape has cost our kingdom its greatest secret. The tunnels you have pointed out are one of our strongest assets for withstanding what's coming. We have a whole spy network out there who are more than capable of keeping up your efforts for all our needs in the coming months."

Freya's chair crashed to the floor as she shot to her feet. "Father, my team is the best at this! We've provided for our people and our troops for months. And we are about to experience the full power of the Empire's army right on our doorstep. You can't possibly keep us home now when this job is so important." Her voice rose, even as she fought to keep it level. She couldn't keep the wobble from her next plea. "I know I messed up, Father, but this is the best way I can help. This is the best way I can move on."

The pressing anxiety of being forced to sit around, wait, and remember made her heart squeeze. She swallowed hard to keep from being sick and kept her trembling hands behind her back so no one would notice.

Her father's face remained impassive despite her begging. He rose, ending any further discussion. "My mind is made up. You will stay here where you are safe."

FREYA CURSED under her breath as she paced the cramped living space her family occupied. Orange light seeped through the small window by the door, making the room glow a bright hue. She was surprised her incessant back and forth hadn't worn a mark on the stone floor. Over the past several hours, Freya had tried to think of a way to change her father's mind. She couldn't stay there. She couldn't sit at home while her team could be out there, offering much-needed relief to her people and soldiers— soldiers who fought for her family. She couldn't live with herself if she did nothing but sit by while others fought and died, and the growing ache in her heart was an ever-present reminder she couldn't handle doing nothing or coexisting with her grief.

Her heart leaped to her throat when she turned to find someone standing in the once-empty doorway. Cliff grinned as he leaned against the doorframe, arms crossed.

"I don't know what you're smirking at. You've been put on house arrest as much as I have."

"So, we're following your father's orders then?"

His question gave her pause. Could they just leave? Was there a possibility they could sneak out of the barracks? If they managed to escape, there would be little her father could do. After all, he couldn't afford to send any of his spies after her. If Freya's team focused on the overpopulated northern towns, she would be far away from him while the other spies focused on helping Blackstone. Cliff raised a questioning brow, a grin still plastered on his face as he waited for her answer.

Freya rubbed her wrist, brushing over the still-healing skin. A shiver raced down her spine as her father's punishment weighed upon her, recalling the sensation of cold irons clamped around her wrists and ankles. Her throat closed, and she couldn't push away the image of Keanon's dark eyes glazing over.

"Hey."

Cliff was across the room in seconds, lightly shaking her shoulders. She met his green eyes, which glittered with calm assurance. "You know I'd follow you anywhere, right? We can commit treason together." He smiled, and she laughed a little as he continued. "Whatever you choose, and wherever you go, I'll be right behind you." With that said, he pulled her into a hug. Freya clung to him tight. Even after everything she'd put him through, his unwavering confidence and loyalty made her heart constrict.

Cliff offered a final encouraging smile before pulling away and turning to leave. As she watched him go, her heart stirred again with the need to do something. She refused to stand by while others were out there fighting and dying for her kingdom.

Before Freya second-guessed herself, she called Cliff back. "Wait!" He stalled in the doorway and turned to her expectantly. "Have everyone ready and in the tunnels by dawn tomorrow before the morning rotation of the guards. And tell Harper to get a dose of the stuff Archer made for me. She'll need to sneak some of it into General Vance's drink tonight."

Cliff raised a brow at her last comment but didn't question

further, nodding as he left. Freya's mind and heart raced from what she'd put in motion, but the intense relief from a promise of freedom eased the tension in her shoulders. There would be repercussions. Cliff knew it, too, but none of it mattered. She and her friends could help, and they were determined to do just that.

THE BLANKETS KNOTTED around Freya's legs from her consistent tossing and turning until she finally shoved them off. Not even the cool cave and the peaceful lull of the waterfall could ease the tension in her gut. Movement outside her room had ceased long after her family retreated to their rooms for the night. Meanwhile, she'd laid in her bed in the darkness, unable to shut her eyes. The medicine Archer had given her remained untouched in her bag. Tonight, she could not risk oversleeping.

Frustrated, Freya got out of bed and rifled through her supplies for the third time. After her conversation with Cliff, she'd snuck into the dining hall and packed away some food to last a few days' journey and filled all her flasks with water. A few pairs of fresh clothes were in there too, along with a new cloak.

After wiping her sweaty palms on the rumpled blanket, she pushed her fingers through the terrible knots in her hair. "Ductu." She frowned, her fingers catching in a large knot. She grabbed the hair comb from her nightstand and got to work. As she fixed her hair, she whispered into the dark. "Please help me and grant me your wisdom. I know I am not your chosen heir, but I pray you will still guide me." She winced as she pulled on a bad knot and braided her hair after detangling it.

"Help me so I can help my brother, the one you have chosen. Guide me so I can uphold your wishes in Galleria. Please." A stream of tears slid down her cheeks as she finished her prayer. She used a tie for her braid and wiped the tears from her face. No grand power seized her, nor did a great vision fill her head. Freya's nerves and worries remained there, but it was accompanied by a strong will to succeed. Whether Ductu heard her prayer, she wasn't sure, but a fresh confidence filled her. She would not fail again.

The cave was filled with the same all-consuming darkness. Clouds had rolled in early that evening, covering the night sky and concealing all light. Her fingers wrapped around the door handle was Freya's only indication of where she stood in the cave. She pictured the cave's layout in her head and, with a quivering breath, released the doorknob. The small stream in the cave's center was her biggest concern as she trudged across the large room. She outstretched her hands before her, feeling for the rail of the bridge. She bumped the first wooden beam with her foot and crossed the tiny stream.

It was like she existed in a mass of blackness and couldn't find a solid surface to grasp onto. Even the incessant pounding of falling water and crashing waves fed into the feeling of complete isolation. The urgency in Freya's heart to go faster warred with her poor awareness of the surroundings. Was the cave always this big?

Relief washed over her as her hands grazed the rock wall on the other side. Hugging the wall, she shuffled up the gentle slope, pressing both hands against it as she climbed, hyperaware of the looming drop only a few steps away. When her hand brushed against wood instead of stone, she wanted to cry out for joy, but her joy was replaced with panic when something grabbed her from behind and spun her around. Heart leaping into her throat, Freya almost grabbed for the dagger at her hip when flickering candlelight revealed her sister's face.

"What are you doing?" Freya hissed as loud as she dared.

Her sister raised a brow, her face inscrutable. Dryly, she said, "I could ask you the same thing." Before Freya could fumble through an explanation, Kiarra held up a hand. "Don't try it. You dragged me into enough trouble growing up for me to know when you are about to break Father's orders."

Freya's excuses left her, and she slumped. She was so close, and her friends were waiting for her in the next room. All she could do was meet her sister's eyes. "I can't stay."

Kiarra's face fell, revealing just how tired she was. "I'm not here to stop you." Freya's eyes widened, but her sister stopped her again and continued more sternly. "I do not believe what you are doing is right. I don't think Father is entirely right, either, but he *is* right that what you did was reckless." Sorrow twisted her features. "I understand why you did it, but it is also the same reason you should stay here. You need to take the time to grieve."

When Freya tried to defend herself, Kiarra silenced her with a scathing look. "Don't you dare try to deny what you are doing by running away." Her voice softened again. "I know you aren't ready to face it yet, which is why I am letting you go. But I trust you will take the time to mourn when you are. He is worth it, Freya. If he meant something to you, he is worth the time it takes for your heart to mend."

The sound of Freya's own screams echoing down a dark corridor filled her mind, and she clenched her jaw. The overwhelming pain in her heart threatened to consume her again, and she struggled to push into the deep recesses of her mind. Freya didn't want to go back there. Her sister was right. She wasn't ready. The heart-shattering pain receded to its consistent throb, her constant companion since losing Keanon.

Upon seeing the agony on Freya's face, Kiarra embraced her, holding her tight. Freya clung to her sister for as long as she could before pulling back. Tears glimmered in their eyes.

"I know this is probably your plan to avoid Father but focus on the northern towns for now. The overpopulation is going to cost our people if we don't provide them with any relief—but please... be more careful." Kiarra turned to go but paused with her back to Freya. "A part of me wonders if Father knows you will run. I mean, he raised you and knows you just as well as I do. But he isn't here to stop you, and I suppose he knows he can't. You're too much like Mother: hard-headed, stubborn, spirited, and filled with a powerful devotion to our people."

Tears welled in Freya's eyes. Kiarra was right. How could her father not know what Freya would do? There was a possibility he was counting on General Vance to block their escape, but he would have done more if he was serious about forcing her to stay. As Kiarra walked away, a wave of guilt washed over Freya, so powerful it almost convinced her to turn back. But she wasn't the heir like her brother, and she wasn't a master strategist like her sister. Leading her small band of friends to fight on the field was where Freya could have the biggest impact in this war, which was the thought that had Freya entering the general's quarters without looking back.

Inside was dark, but Harper had been successful in dosing her mother with the sleeping draft. General Vance was passed out at her desk. Still, Freya tiptoed around the room, careful not to bump into any furniture. She knelt by the bottom shelf of the bookcase for the small groove to release the hatch on the door, and stepping through, she was greeted by all her friends. Freya smiled.

"Alright, let's get to work."

CHAPTER 22

RYKER

Sweat dripped down Ryker's brow, the pommel of his sword slick in his hands. He adjusted his grip seconds before blocking a stream of attacks from Captain Bennett, and when their swords pressed together, he shoved her with all his strength. She stumbled back a few paces, giving him the edge he needed. Ryker pushed forward. Though she met him blow for blow, her movements were slower as she stayed on the defensive. A few stray dark hairs pulled loose from her usually well-kept braid, her eyes narrowed in concentration.

Ryker charged, and Captain Bennett sidestepped at the last second, but he was ready. He pulled up short and shoved her again with his shoulder, where, this time, she lost her balance and fell. Her eyes widened, but he moved before she could recover, pinning her to the ground with his sword. She grinned.

"It's good to see General Moreland isn't in the habit of tossing around the title of captain to just anyone." Her voice still held the cold steel that was always there, but her smile was the most genuine he had ever seen. Ryker smiled back—a true smile he hadn't felt for a long while. Captain Bennett's direct and harsh instructions made her fantastic at bossing him around, and she took no nonsense from her soldiers. Ryker knew a few of the other captains, but out of them all, he was pleased to have been placed with Captain Bennett; he appreciated this time with her.

"I would hope so since I was trained by two generals in my lifetime." Ryker offered her a hand, and she took it, her grip firm as he helped her to her feet. As had become their norm, the sky was beginning to lighten as they finished their training, having begun before the barracks awoke. They lit the torches around the training yard and battled with the descending moon overhead, finishing only when the sun peeked over the horizon.

Together, they returned their training swords, but before they went their separate ways, she raised a hand. "Come with me."

He fell into step beside her as the rest of the barracks came alive. None of the soldiers dared approach him while he was beside the captain, though a few gave him scathing looks he'd learned to ignore. Even at the end of his third week, he'd kept away from the rest of the soldiers. Now that he was no longer training with them, they'd stopped targeting him, but their continued disdain ensured he kept his distance.

He followed Captain Bennett past the dining hall, where soldiers began filing in, and took him back toward her quarters. It was fine if he missed breakfast—since he didn't bother anyway—but he hoped she wouldn't take too long. This was the one time of day when he could get a short, mostly dreamless nap.

Inside Captain Bennett's quarters, she picked up a piece of parchment from her desk but didn't hand it to him. Leaning her hip on the desk, she crossed her arms, her dark eyes seeming to stare right through him. Her scrutiny was another thing he'd gotten used to, but it almost seemed she'd forgotten he was there as the moment lengthened. He tilted his head. "Something wrong?"

She snapped out of her distraction and refocused on him. "I am sending you with the troops we have trained to join our forces in Ekrewell. However, I want you to deliver this message to General Averill and come back with his response."

His heart pounded, a mix of joy and dread. While it was exciting to know he'd proven himself enough to get this opportunity, he would be traveling with a bunch of soldiers who still held him in low regard. Artis would deter them from trying anything, but it meant he would keep to himself and his thoughts for the entire journey.

"Yes, Captain." None of his inner conflict was reflected in his response.

"You are not to open, read, or tell anyone on the patrol with you about the letter you carry. It is to go straight into the general's hands upon arriving; it's for *his* eyes only. Is that clear?" The edge to her voice was sharper than normal as she pierced him with her dark eyes.

Not sharing the mission with his fellow soldiers was an easy, but odd request, given that none of them spoke to him. It wasn't lost on Ryker this could all be a test of his loyalty to see if he would follow through with her orders. Even so, it did little to dampen the relief of being out on the field and doing more than weapons training every day. This could be his first step back to where he had been before. He would not let her down.

"Yes, Captain."

"Very good." She handed him the letter, and he placed it in the inner chest pocket of his tunic. Captain Bennett nodded, the hint of an approving smile on her lips.

He was ready to prove he was worth her trust.

～

AFTER THREE DAYS on the trail, Ryker felt like Captain Bennett was punishing him for something. After leaving Tourrenfield, the soldier in charge took them south along the main road past the Elmwoods, and once clear of the woods, they veered south-west out in the open plains, heading toward the South King's Road. They traveled at a grueling pace that would take them at least four more days to make it to Ekrewell. There was a pinch on the back of his neck, and he smacked the bug away. Artis growled and jerked back, biting at her rear leg. The heat was stifling, and the air sticky, though the sun remained low in the sky. He let out a string of coughs from the dirt billowing from the supply wagons. He'd been relegated to the back behind the carts, where the dirt shot out from the wagon wheels into his face and where no soldiers would have to interact with him.

A part of him had wanted to argue about his placement, but he wanted to be with the other soldiers as much as they wanted to be with him. Not at all. While most of the soldiers didn't believe him to be a traitor, they all held some level of distrust for him. Even if Ryker wasn't a traitor, he had still failed and lost them the princess. Instead of putting up a fight he would lose, he made sure to stay back far enough that the dust was bearable.

Ryker followed the wagons onto the South King's Road but kept his senses on high alert. He would not have chosen to take them on this path. Although they hadn't lost troops there in weeks, it did not make it a safe one. But Ryker wasn't in charge, so he kept his opinions to himself. He could only pray their lead soldier got lucky to ensure safe passage.

They trudged along until the sun reached the center of the sky, where they finally paused for a quick stretch to water and feed the animals. Archers stayed at the ready as everyone got to work. Ryker hopped off Artis's back and couldn't move for several moments. His rear was numb, and his legs wobbled as they struggled to support him. When he was finally secure on his feet, he gave Artis a drink, then let her bound around to release some of her energy while he paced back and forth to get the blood rushing through his lower half. He emptied the rest of his first flask of water and watched Artis prance around the wagons; she stayed clear of the other soldiers.

None of the other soldiers were of rank to own a lykos, so Artis was the only one. She had quickly sensed the others' dislike for Ryker and stayed close to him, growling if they so much as looked at him oddly. Artis only allowed one of the archers to approach them—a woman who gave him his rations for the day. While she was never friendly, she was not hostile either.

Ryker opened his mouth to call Artis back when six archers jerked back with a groan and fell to the dirt.

Arrows protruded from their throats.

Ryker's heart plummeted to his toes, and before he took his next breath, six more archers choked on arrows, collapsing with the others.

"Take cover! Archers shoot into the trees!" When the second set of soldiers hit the dirt, the commanding officer barked his orders while the soldiers ducked for cover. The few remaining archers tried to aim into the trees on the Gallerion side, but the attackers were invisible amongst the thick greenery.

Instinct kicked in, and Ryker jumped to where Artis had stalled behind one of the wagons. The troops recuperated from the shock and charged forward, drawing their shields and weapons, but they were still bowed down as the archers' targeted legs, forcing them to stumble while another arrow finished them off. Their numbers were dropping fast, and Ryker struggled to think of what to do.

"Artis, stay!"

Another archer fell not far from Ryker with an arrow

embedded in her stomach. It was the woman who brought him rations. She gasped and grabbed at the shaft with her hands, and he dove for cover behind the next wagon, pulling her with him. Tears trailed down the sides of her face, and blood dribbled from her mouth. The fear and pain swimming in her eyes pulled at his heart. Although he didn't know her name, she was a fellow soldier and deserved respect, surrendering her life in service of the Empire.

"Shh, it's gonna be alright. You're gonna be alright." Ryker lied, squeezing her hand. He held her close. The arrow was lodged deep into her stomach, and with too much blood pooling beneath her—and no proper mending equipment—all he could do was offer any comfort he could.

"I... Whhh...I." She tried to speak but blood spurted into her throat, her words garbled.

"Shh." Ryker quieted her again, wishing he could use her name. It was only a few moments before her eyes lost focus, and her breathing stopped. With great care, Ryker closed her eyes and rested her head in the dirt. He removed the quiver from her shoulders, wrapped it over his own, and took the bow from her hands.

"I'm sorry."

He left her there and peeked around the wagon toward the far side of the trees. Artis remained where he'd told her to, one wagon over. Soldiers still attempted to run into the trees with little success as bodies piled up along the road. He took a steady breath and loosened his grip on the bow before it splintered in his hands. He aimed into the trees. The bow wasn't his weapon of choice, but he waited and focused all the same. When another arrow shot out, Ryker let his fly. There was no indication he'd hit his target, but no more arrows flew from that spot. He prepared to nock another arrow when the deathly silence sunk in.

No more shouting.

No more arrows.

It was quiet, and he was alone.

No... Not again...

Leaves crunched in the woods across the road as several hooded figures appeared through the trees. They hadn't seen him behind the wagon, but it was only a matter of time as they drew nearer to the road. Ryker's hand flew to his chest pocket where Captain Bennett's letter was. There was a good chance it was nothing but a test to prove himself, but if there was a possibility it contained important information, he could not let them get their hands on it. From where he hid, he counted four archers, but there was more rustling in the trees behind them. There could be eight or ten in total.

Ryker couldn't shoot without them firing back, and the many arrows protruding from his fellow soldiers' throats made him question opening fire. A low growl drew his attention, and he spun to where Artis waited, bracing to pounce behind the other wagon. There were several paces of open space between the two carts. If Ryker was to run, the approaching archers would see them.

With trepidation, Ryker braced himself. Making eye contact with Artis, he nodded, and the two darted toward each other. She crouched low to the ground so he could leap on, but his heart plummeted as one of the figures let out a shout. Ryker didn't stop, but before he could pull himself up, Artis jerked away. One of the archers trained an arrow on Ryker, but Artis growled and lunged in front of him.

"NO!"

Her body lurched. She whimpered as the arrow lodged into her shoulder. Ryker tried to pull her away when she jerked again, collapsing. Ryker stumbled backward. Blood stained Artis's golden fur, her chest heaving as she struggled to rise.

When the archer drew his bow again, Ryker couldn't take it. He saw a flash of her intelligent eyes staring at him over a stall door and Keanon's grin as he presented the lykos to him until the memory twisted to them lying in a pool of blood.

Ryker could not watch her die.

He ran.

If he ran, maybe they would leave her alone. An arrow whizzed past his head, and he swerved to dodge it. He didn't pay attention to where he was going, ducking into the trees as one of the figures crashed through the underbrush behind him. His heart lurched when his foot snagged on a tree root, but he was grateful for it when an arrow flew overhead. He managed to catch himself and ducked between trees to keep the archer from targeting him again.

As Ryker ran, his grip tightened on the bow he'd managed to keep a hold of. It seemed he had a single pursuer, but he only had one shot to get this right. Clenching his jaw, Ryker ducked around another tree and plucked an arrow from the quiver. Right as he prepared to turn, his foot snagged on another root. He tried to catch himself, but the ground dipped. Ryker's stomach flipped as he flew forward, bringing his hands up to protect his face as his body rolled across the ground. Desperate, he tried to grab something to stop his fall. Dirt and pebbles dug inside his fingernails and cut into his palms as his hands slid over loose dirt, and he continued to tumble.

Air exploded from his lungs, and pain ricocheted along his spine when his back smacked flat against another large tree root. As he gasped for air, the world turned endlessly. Up was down, and down was up. Green leaves, brown dirt, and the blue sky swirled into one dizzying color in his eyes. He tried again to grab onto something—anything to stop the unending nightmare—but when his head struck a tree trunk, he got his wish as the world went dark.

CHAPTER 23
FREYA

"Stop!"

Freya raised her hand to halt Lanzo's arrow as Harper launched after the stray soldier. *So much for stopping...*

This set of troops was larger than what they were used to, so the team had spread apart, with Archer, Laia, and Cliff a little further south. They dealt with the front half of the Imperial fleet, while she, Harper, and Lanzo took the back. Now, only Freya and Lanzo were left.

The poor lykos tried but failed to pull itself to its feet as blood pooled in the surrounding dirt. The beast studied her through glazed, pain-filled eyes, softly crying as it struggled to stand. As dangerous as these animals were, Freya's heart tightened for the animal, abandoned by its owner to die.

Freya inched closer with her hands raised from her weapons. She knew Lanzo still had his bow ready if the creature decided to attack, but it continued to watch her cautiously. These animals were valuable, but they were also incredibly loyal to their owners, so much so that if their owners passed while they still lived, it was common for them to die of grief.

Convincing one to break their bond with their previous owner was difficult, but it could be done.

"It's alright." Freya soothed the lykos, who bared its teeth as she inched closer. It let out another whine and managed to push to its feet. It didn't appear Lanzo had struck anything vital. Its shoulder should be fine, and though the one in her side wasn't too deep, she was slowly losing blood. Without any care, the lykos would die.

Freya froze as the creature stood. Lanzo pulled back his bow behind her, but it didn't charge. Instead, the animal stumbled into the trees after its owner, leaving a trail of blood as it went. The swish of its gold and black tail urged Freya to follow. She took several involuntary steps toward it until a hand on her shoulder stopped her.

"Where are you going?"

"I'm going after Harper." It wasn't a complete lie. With the lykos out there, she would need to make sure Harper was alright. Lanzo raised a brow, so she added, "I know she can handle herself, but I want to make sure that thing doesn't sneak up on her."

Lanzo didn't argue further, though he looked amused. Freya called over her shoulder. "Gather the others and take the goods to Riverwood. We'll meet you on the way there." Lanzo simply grunted in response as Freya jogged into the trees after Harper.

The lone soldier had not been paying attention when he ran off, having crossed into Galleria instead of returning to the Empire. Their trail was easy enough to follow. Boot prints marked the dirt, and arrows embedded in the trees. A few drops of blood sprinkled along the ground. Freya didn't have to go far before catching up to her friend. Harper glanced over her shoulder as she approached.

The ground sloped down, and a pitiful sight was at the bottom of the hill. The soldier lay in a heap, unmoving. It was difficult to tell what shape he was in, but at least he would be easier to handle since he was unconscious. Freya was surprised Harper hadn't already taken the man out. Her team didn't take prisoners, especially not with the towns and cities as overpopulated as they were. They didn't need to take care of prisoners, too.

"You alright? I saw blood on my way here."

"It wasn't mine." Harper rolled her shoulders and eyed the fallen soldier. "Shame he didn't put up more of a fight."

Freya rolled her eyes but couldn't stop the smile tugging at her lips. "You're telling me what happened back there wasn't enough of a fight for you?" She gestured over her shoulder to the carnage they'd left behind.

"You call that a fight?"

A strong gust of wind blew into Freya's back like someone was pushing her forward; she stumbled a few paces to where the soldier lay. There was a familiar presence inside her head, one she hadn't felt since escaping from the Empire. It filled her with a powerful impulse to go and investigate the soldier herself. *No! Stop this.*

Harper raised a brow at Freya as she forced herself to step back. Her friend seemed unfazed by the wind.

Freya crossed her arms and feigned nonchalance despite the growing urge to inspect the fallen soldier. "Is he dead?"

Harper's eyes narrowed as she answered. "I'm not sure, but it's not that steep, so there's a fair chance he survived. Definitely banged up, though." She crossed her arms. "You alright?"

Before Freya could answer, a shout rang out through the woods, and they faced each other with wide eyes.

"That came from the team." Freya turned to look back the way they came, but her feet remained rooted in place. She thought the sensation would subside, but it was unceasing. Gritting her teeth, Freya could not resist the pull. "Go make sure they're alright." Freya told Harper. "I'll take care of this soldier quickly and catch up with you."

Harper glanced up at the sky and frowned. "What? There's no way I'm leaving without you." Her words were punctuated with a sudden gust of wind as the sky above grew dark. Another shout rang out from where they'd left their friends.

"We're wasting time! Go make sure they are safe and direct them to Riverwood; I am fully capable of taking care of one soldier," Freya argued, despite her conflicting feelings. A part of her wanted to sprint back to her friends, yet the other urged her toward the soldier. "I promise I will meet you guys there."

Harper hesitated a moment longer, clearly displeased, but her worry for their friends was strong. The forest darkened as dark clouds swirled overhead. Finally, Harper nodded, her jaw set. "Fine! But you have two days to meet us in Riverwood, or I will personally carry you back to your father."

"Good, now go!" Freya watched Harper sprint back into the trees before turning and making her way down the hill. *Alright, gods. This guy better be worth all this.* Branches swayed danger-ously overhead, and the wind blew leaves off the ground as the light faded to almost nothing.

At the bottom of the hill, Freya's trepidation rose as she took in the lone soldier. Blood stained a large tree root from where he must have bashed his head. He was face down, but there was a strange familiarity about him. It could have been his dark, wavy hair or tall, strong build. Freya's hands shook as she prepared to roll him over.

Without giving herself time to stall, Freya shoved him, and the soldier flopped onto his back, his handsome face exposed. Freya reeled and almost fell back as the first streak of lightning ripped across the sky, lighting up the man's face. Her heart hammered in her chest as if it wanted to beat out of her body.

"No, no, no, no. NO!"

This must be some cruel joke from the gods. Freya's punishment for disobeying her father. She swore at the sky right as the boom of thunder shook the ground, cloaking her words. She rested a hand on the hilt of her dagger as overwhelming sadness rushed through her again, clashing with her hatred. She dropped her arm.

"Keanon, you can't keep doing this! You aren't here anymore because of him!"

Freya gritted her teeth. What if she left him there? Animals could come by to finish the job. She wouldn't have to do it herself. Maybe he would even survive and stumble home.

"Please..."

Tears welled in her eyes. No matter how hard she tried, Freya couldn't get her body to obey her and leave; her legs wouldn't budge. When she peered back down, Ryker's banged-up, dirty face was still there. Twigs protruded from his hair, blood stained the side of his face, and the skin around his left eye purpled.

"Damn it, Keanon. Why do you keep doing this to me?"

Finally, Freya's body obeyed her, but only to relinquish him of weapons. The first cool drops of rain fell on her arm as she searched along his torso for any concealed daggers, trying not to remember how it felt to lay her head against a similar chest. Ryker was a bit thin, his ribs more pronounced, and his cheeks hollow. It twisted at her insides to remember another face so much like this one. It was harder to see him so peaceful as opposed to staring at her with hatred.

His weight loss made it easier to drag him to the nearest tree, and as the rain picked up, Freya pulled a rope from her packs and began tying him to it. She quickly tugged the knot, satisfied when it didn't pull loose. Then, the skies opened. She dove beneath a nearby tree for as much shelter as possible, but it was futile. Her clothes were soaked through in seconds. She pulled her knees to her chest as another flash lit up the sky, followed by a boom that rattled her teeth. Right before the light faded, a set of dark eyes locked with hers from the bushes; an icy chill ran through her body as darkness concealed whatever watched her. Freya was on her feet instantly, her back against the tree as she fixed her gaze on the spot in the darkness where the eyes had been. Cold seeped through her skin and cramped her tensed muscles, but she refused to budge.

Seconds ticked by, but nothing happened. The grooves on the hilt of her sword embedded into her palm as she waited, and she cursed the dark. As if on command, white light streaked across the sky. She gasped. On the ground between her and Ryker was a massive heap of golden fur with two arrows protruding from it.

The lykos watched her with pain-filled eyes, and Freya's heart hammered in her ears as the light faded and thunder reverberated through the air. Even in that state, if the lykos wanted to kill her, it could do so before she even drew her weapon.

When a whimper tickled her ears over the pouring rain, Freya moved. The poor creature had already lost a considerable amount of blood, but she would do what she could. Taking slow steps forwarded with her hands outstretched, Freya tried not to trip over the fallen animal. Roots and divots in the dirt unbalanced her steps, and muddy water sloshed over her boots as she approached. When her foot bumped into something large and solid, Freya slowly reached forward. The lykos could bite her hand off if it desired to, but something large, slobbery, and warm brushed her fingers instead. She took that as permission.

Kneeling, Freya brushed through its soaked, coarse fur. The lykos didn't move while she struggled to find the arrow, except for the occasional lick of her arm.

Finally, her fingers bumped against something hard. Gripping tight to the shaft of the arrow—as close to the wound as she dared—Freya hollered over the wind, "Please don't bite me!" and with all her strength, she pulled. A howl ripped through the air, but the lykos didn't attack as Freya pulled. Her hands slowly slid along the slippery surface, and she squeezed tighter until the shaft splintered in her palms.

The arrow popped free and sent her staggering back into the mud. She grimaced as mud splattered onto her face and mouth, yet there was little time to worry about her own discomfort. The creature's wound would continue to bleed if she didn't get it covered. Rifling through her bags, Freya yanked out some bandages. They were drenched, but it would have to be enough for now. She hoped the rain would wash the blood and dirt off the lykos to prevent infection.

A burst of light gave Freya enough time to locate the injury and press the bandage onto it. The lykos raised itself enough for Freya to wrap around its stomach. She ensured the knot was tight as another lightning strike revealed the second arrow. Bracing herself, Freya pulled again, her arms shaking from the effort. Her hands slipped until they reached the fletching, the wood digging into her palms.

Finally, it gave way. She lurched backward, sliding in the mud and landing flat on her back; air burst from her lungs, and pain shot down her spine. She gaped, desperate for air, but swallowed rainwater instead. Freya lay there, unable to move, until air crashed back into her lungs with a gasp. Coughs racked her body, and she pushed onto one elbow.

The woods flickered again, bright light revealing the lykos who eyed Freya wearily. With great effort, Freya crawled over and pulled out another ragged bandage. The shoulder was easier to deal with since she could wrap the gauze around its leg and head.

Spent but satisfied she had done enough for now, Freya

stretched her aching legs before her. The lykos laid its large head in her lap. Gently, she stroked its face to apologize and hoped she had done enough to ensure the creature survived till morning. Until then, they would both have to endure the pouring rain. Leaning on one arm to look at the dark sky, Freya watched lightning fork through the branches above. It was going to be a long night.

CHAPTER 24

VIVIAN

Vivian awoke, sprawled across her bed. She stared at a small crack in the ceiling with little motivation to get up. Parts of the palace had been neglected with everyone preparing for the festival. Not that she minded much, as it gave her something to trace with her eyes as she contemplated rising for the day.

It was the first day of the Winter's Light Festival. Across the room, her dress for the event hung by her changing screen. It was an elegant silk dress crafted of deep green with gold embroidery along the bodice and pink and purple flowers down one side of the skirt.

Prince Damian had asked to escort her throughout the festivities, and Vivian's heart raced at the prospect of spending an entire day with him. Whenever she closed her eyes, his piercing blue ones stared back, making her stomach flutter. It would be nice to get to know him more, given that she couldn't base her decision on his pretty eyes. Vivian huffed to the empty room. What *could* she base her decision on? The gods were not forthcoming in offering her more insight.

When the doors to her rooms burst open, Vivian was forced

out of bed with a tsk from her head maid, Marienn. The other maids flocked around to help her dress, seating her before a full-length mirror as they began working on her wild locks. Marienn, who had been with Vivian since she was little—and the only one who ever managed to tame Vivian's frizzy hair—gently pulled a smoothing cream through her curls until it was manageable before braiding it into two large plaits over either shoulder. Vivian thanked them as they ushered her into the hall.

The palace was in full preparation as servants rushed to finish last-minute tasks for the day's events. Vases filled with fresh blue and white flowers lined the corridors; windows were open, allowing in the last of the warmer weather before winter took hold, and everything had been polished to perfection.

As Vivian made her way down the hall, she frowned, remembering her conversation with her parents. In a few short days, she would travel across the kingdom to meet the emperor. What was he like? In the ten years since he'd been crowned king, she'd never met him. He had never traveled north, nor had her family gone south. She'd only heard bits about him, like his fair trades with the northern kingdoms. He'd been one of the old king's advisors for years before the family passed with no heir, and he was chosen. The emperor was closer to her father in age, a thought that made her stomach churn. Would he look old?

Vivian shoved her concerns to the back of her mind and stepped outside to the palace courtyard, where the chaos continued. Long tables were evenly spaced across the court-yard, arranged with white cloths, pale blue and white ribbons, and more wildflower centerpieces. On the left, outside the kitchens' doors, was the massive banquet table already filled with an assortment of pastries, fresh bread, fruit spreads, and a variety of cheeses.

She nabbed one of her favorites—a sweet cream-coated roll bursting with apricot jelly when she bit into it. The roll was fresh and warm, the dough melting in her mouth. She refrained from shoving the whole thing in her mouth to savor the sweetness instead, but when she popped the last bit in her mouth, the dough lodged in her throat just as Prince Damian stepped out of the stables. His bright blue eyes met hers across the way. He'd combed back his copper hair, but his bangs rested neatly across his forehead. She suppressed the desire to brush his hair aside, and the thought set her heart racing. He'd dressed up more like the prince he was and wore a dark green tunic with gold accented buttons down the front, perfectly matching the shades of her dress, and black trousers with black leather boots.

Tears burned as she fought to hold back a cough. Grabbing a goblet of water from the banquet table, she took a long drink to clear her throat and kept her eyes lowered, staring at the cobbled courtyard until a pair of well-kept leather boots came into view.

With a deep breath, she raised her watery eyes to meet the amused glint in the prince's. Vivian's face grew warm, and she took another sip from her cup to hide her embarrassment.

"Good morning," he said lightly. As soon as his gaze left hers to scan the busy courtyard, she breathed a little easier. Though his face appeared neutral, his eyes glittered with amusement, and she took a deep breath to compose herself. "Preparations are in full swing, I see." His voice barely concealed his mirth.

Vivian took a final sip of water before setting the cup on the table, relieved when her voice came out normal. "Yes, the grand feast will take place here later tonight, but there will be food offered throughout the day in the courtyard and along the main street. The day's festivities are in the square and outside the city walls."

"I noticed vendors preparing stalls along the road on my way back into the city today." Upon noticing her raised brow, he added, "I went on a morning ride with Tristain. He showed me around Calliva, the surrounding mountains, and some of the outposts. You have a beautiful kingdom."

Her heart warmed at Prince Damian's appreciation for her home, but then her stomach dropped. "What did you and Tristain talk about?"

The humorous glint returned to his eyes. "Why are you so concerned?"

"I—" She snapped her mouth shut when he laughed.

"Don't worry. We mostly talked about his upcoming wedding."

Vivian couldn't hide the way her body sagged in relief, knowing Tristain had refrained from mentioning their antics growing up, like Vivian's unprincess-like demeanor and their sneaking around. Prince Damian chuckled again, saving her from further embarrassment as he gestured to the gates. "Shall we join the festivities?"

He offered his arm, and her stomach fluttered as she took it. Together, they left the courtyard and made their way down to the already crowded streets. The boisterous conversation grew louder as they drew closer to the city center, where stalls lined either side of the main road. Mouthwatering, rich, and salty scents of roasted turkey legs and oxose skewers filled the air, mixed with sweet, fruity tarts and pies. The aroma made her stomach growl. She was grateful the commotion covered the sound.

First, Vivian guided the prince toward the stalls of crafted goods. Multicolored shards of glass hung off one stall, and when the wind blew, they clinked together, making a pretty tinkling sound and glittering when touched by sunlight. Young children ogled the carts displaying well-crafted wooden figurines and animals. Other stalls sold tapestries, wood carvings, vibrant clothing, and a variety of other wares.

Vivian laughed when the prince put on a bright red cap with a large, black chilver swan's feather sticking out of the side. The cap was too gaudy against his green tunic, and the bright red too much atop his copper hair.

"Not my color?"

"No, it looks great." Vivian tried to cover her laughter at his feigned seriousness, noting the glint of humor in his eyes.

"Maybe it will look better on you." He smirked before plopping it on her head. Her hair was too thick, and the hat barely settled on top of her braids. She crossed her arms, fighting back a smile. Prince Damian grinned with a teasing gleam in his eye. "Oh yeah, it's definitely more suited for you."

She laughed, but her eyes widened when he turned to the vendor to purchase it. "What are you doing?" she asked as someone bumped into her from behind. That was all it took for the precariously balanced cap to fall. Prince Damian snatched it before it hit the ground, grinning at her. Her breathing hitched as she stared into his face so close to hers.

"Careful, don't want to get your new hat dirty." His voice was low and soft.

No words came to her as she took the hat from him, her fingers brushing against his. Warmth coursed through her as her eyes latched onto his; she forgot how to breathe for several seconds. She didn't know how, but warmth glimmered in his cool blue eyes as he stared down at her.

After what seemed like an eternity, he stepped back. "Shall we continue?"

Vivian could only nod in response and continue down the street. Next, they focused on food as she led Prince Damian to the best food stalls. When they finally made it to the center plaza, the pair were stuffed with pastries and skewers.

The diamond-shaped plaza was cleared in the middle. The flow of traffic was pushed to the edges because a large stage was set in the center, with drums, harps, lutes, and even a grand organ. Blue and white ribbon decorated the tall pillars situated in the four corners of what would later be the dance floor.

The pair continued to move with the flow of traffic until they were outside the city gates, where the crowds dispersed into the open field. Most of the nobles from her father's court gathered on the edge of the woods with bows and spears as the men prepared to hunt a pronduo—a massive hooved, territorial creature with huge antlers—that roamed the woods around Brantyre. If they were successful today, the meat would be prepared for the wedding feast in a few days.

Most of the crowd situated themselves in groups on the outskirts of a grassy field right outside the palace walls. Four pillars, two with white ribbon and two with pale blue, created a perimeter for the large space. Within the field, the youth were gathered, splitting off into two teams. One of the young men in the center held a worn, tough leather ball under his arm, surveying the division of teams.

She would recognize those dark curls from anywhere, even from a distance. Tristain turned, his easy smile lighting his whole face as they approached. He called something to one of the others, tossing them the ball before jogging over.

"Hey, Vi. Prince Damian." He greeted the latter with a nod. "You come to watch the game?"

"I wouldn't miss it for anything." Vivian returned his grin, his easy joy infectious.

"You ever played, Your Highness?"

"Call me Damian," he corrected with a smile. He took in the field then shook his head. "I'm afraid I'm not familiar with this game."

With a mischievous grin, Tristain nudged Vivian's shoulder. "This one was so aggressive on the field when we were growing up."

"Hey!" She swatted him, and he burst into laughter. The damage was done, though.

"You played?" Prince Damian raised a brow.

Vivian's face grew warm from his scrutiny, and she tried to shrug it off. "Only when I was younger; I've not played in years."

Tristain opened his mouth to add more, but snapped it shut when another player called him back. She sighed with relief when he winked before jogging back to join the others. Over his shoulder, he called, "Be sure to cheer for us!"

Vivian was sure to find the perfect grassy spot for them to sit, so Prince Damian had a clear view of the game. A glimpse of lace caught her attention, and she met her sister's eyes, who sat across the field. Vivian's heart constricted at the cold look on Aida's face. They had not spoken since their argument in the hall, and their distance hurt. Over the years, they had bickered as siblings do, but never had an argument kept them apart for so long. The bitterness and hurt still lingering between them was eating at her, and they were running out of time to make things better. There were so many unknowns in their lives, yet one thing was for certain: Vivian would not be home for much longer.

Aida broke eye contact, and Vivian refocused as the game began. With Tristain playing, the rules would be stricter to avoid injuring the heir's betrothed, but the youth would be as merciless as they were allowed to be. The teams mostly guided the ball across the field with their feet, but there was shoving, kicking, hitting—and all other types of abuse between the teams—to get the ball in between the other teams' posts. On the far side of the field, General Johan barked reprimands whenever the players tried to break the rules. Both teams seemed evenly matched this year, and Vivian leaned in excitedly.

She burst out laughing when she glanced at the prince, whose mouth was ajar, his eyes wide in astonishment. She leaned closer to clarify, "We were never permitted to do half the things they are when we played growing up."

"Honestly." He turned and his gaze caught hers, making her heart beat faster. "This looks like a lot of fun." A big, genuine smile lit up his face as he turned back to the game. Vivian tried to stay focused as the game became more intense, but she couldn't fight how her eyes continued to stray to the prince's reaction. He cheered when points were scored and was indignant when the opposing team got away with something dirty. This was the first time she'd seen him fully relaxed, all stresses forgotten. It moved her so much that she couldn't help but jump to her feet to celebrate with him when Tristain scored the winning point.

Tristain pumped both fists in the air and charged to where Aida stood, clapping. Her eyes widened, and she placed both hands out in defense as he opened his muddy, sweaty arms to scoop her up.

"That was truly amazing to watch," said Prince Damian before Vivian's mood could sour with thoughts of her sister again.

"Maybe we could plan another game so you can play," she teased.

"Only if you play too."

She ducked her head, and he laughed before his smile faltered. "My sister would love to play this, too."

"Which sister?"

"My youngest, Freya. There's not a chance Kiarra would play, no matter the rules." A shadow of sadness and anxiety cast over his face, and though he tried to shake it, it didn't quite reach his eyes when he smiled again. "Shall we?" He offered his arm. The weight of his problems hit her anew, and her heart went out to him.

She took his arm, trying to shake the heaviness in her heart as he guided her back into the city. The day had shifted to early evening, the sun setting behind the mountains. Joyful music grew louder as they drew near the plaza, now filled with dancers. Lanterns had been tied up on strings, attached to the four pillars on each corner of the dance floor. They offered a soft glow for the many dancers twirling along in the center of the plaza. Many colored dresses swirled as the ladies spun, before their well-dressed partners met them in a waltz. When they reached the edge of the dance floor, the musicians switched to playing a soft, lilting melody, and all the dancers paired up.

Prince Damian glanced at her, extending his hand. "Would you care to dance?"

Stomach fluttering, Vivian placed her hand in his. It was stronger and calloused against her smoother skin. He led her into the swell of dancers and turned to place his other hand gently on her hip, while she laid hers on his shoulder. Her skin tingled from his touch as his blue eyes captured her. They glided through the steps of the dance, his moves graceful and precise as he took the lead. Lanterns illuminated his face as they spun. His copper hair settled lower across his forehead, framing his face, and the subtle signs of red lining his jaw appeared thicker than when he'd arrived. He twirled her to the dance, and she lost his gaze, catching it again the moment he brought her back to him.

"How do I know what to do?" Vivian asked, her question coming from her heart. His eyes softened, and his grip on her hand tightened.

"The gods don't always guide everyone the same way, but

when I feel they are leading me, I will have a strong pull towards something. I will constantly be thinking about it, and I won't be able to sleep. It's like a pulling in my heart I can't ignore." When she frowned, he added, "The day before my mother passed, I was seven. I had planned to spend the day with some friends, but something told me not to go. This time, I listened. My mother and I spent the next day together. We talked about my new sibling coming, my tutoring, everything. When I awoke the next day, I had a new baby sister, but my mother was gone." His eyes were distant and sad, but his smile was encouraging. "Because I listened to that strong feeling in my heart to spend time with my mother, I can now look back to that last day we had together and remember how much she loved me."

Vivian was silent as his story and the song came to an end. His story was so heartwarming. Vivian remembered moments in her life like that, yet they usually revolved around Aida. She would feel drawn to Aida's rooms at the exact moment Aida needed advice. So, if the gods were giving him such strong assurance that he was meant to be king, why couldn't she have that same assurance he was the one she was supposed to marry?

When they pulled apart, the distance between them seemed vaster than it had before. Leaving the dance behind, they made their way to the grand feast at the palace. As they walked, she considered everything. What was she feeling? What was her heart telling her was right? The problem was that all her feelings were mixed with the fear she would make the wrong decision and the confusion from everyone else around her.

They re-entered the palace courtyard, which slowly filled as people sat at the long tables. The table in front of the castle doors was reserved for the royal family, followed by tables for the nobles in her father's court. The rest of the seating was open for the people of the city, and anyone who couldn't fit inside the palace walls needn't worry, as there were many more tables along the main road for everyone else. Everyone would be served that evening from youngest to oldest, richest to poor. The royal cooks, along with the city's bakeries and taverns, helped prepare enough food to provide for the whole city. Every year, the servers took turns off so they, too, could join the feast.

Course upon course was served so everyone could have their fill: creamy carrot soup with fresh bread was followed by heaps of turkey and oxose steaks smothered in gravy with roasted potatoes and turnips. To finish, there were wedges of fresh cheese with spiced butternuts, cherry and apple tarts, spiced pears, and sugared apricots with fresh cream.

When everyone was bursting from all the amazing food, the sun finished its descent, and the city went dark. No one moved to light the sconces. Everyone sat on bated breath, a familiar bubbling of excitement palpable in the air. Natura did not disappoint. Lights of bright green, yellow, and blue ignited, shimmering and dancing across the sky. Everyone exclaimed in excitement and awe from the magical display, and though Vivian saw them every year, they never failed to take her breath away.

Prince Damian gasped, and she took in his wide-eyed wonder as the lights danced across his face. He whispered, "This is more beautiful than the Navean Sea at sunset."

Vivian's heart warmed as she watched him take it all in. At that moment, she wished life could be different. What would it be like to know him—possibly be betrothed to him—without this life-and-death decision looming over her shoulder? How could she sentence him to death? She couldn't. How could the gods expect her to?

CHAPTER 25
RYKER

owling winds and rain shook Ryker from his slumber. He winced at his pounding headache and the throbbing in his chest; he worried he'd bruised a couple of ribs. He pried his eyes open, greeted by total darkness. He tried to feel for further injuries, but he couldn't lift his arms. Confused, he squirmed against the bumpy, wet surface pressed against his back but could not pull away. Something chafed his arms and pulled tight against his middle when he moved.

A shiver raced down his spine. Cold rain pooled against his legs and soaked through his clothes. He squeezed his eyes shut, trying to remember what had happened for him to now be tied to a tree. Ryker's memory crashed into him. His fellow soldiers, the archers, rushing through the woods to escape... Whoever had ambushed them had caught him and kept him prisoner—but why? Why had they not killed him?

Why is this happening again?

Ryker didn't know if he was supposed to be grateful his life kept being spared. It seemed the gods were playing a sick joke.

Tempus allowed death to follow Ryker wherever he went yet refused to take him. Captain Bennett would be disappointed he hadn't been better prepared for this *unexpected event*. If General Moreland heard about this, would he remove Ryker from the army entirely? That was if he made it back to the Empire alive. Getting out of this would be hard without—

He leaned his head against the tree, squeezing his eyes closed as rain splattered on his face and dripped off his hair. *Artis...* He tried not to think about her, but her final moments played in his head. She had been alive when he ran but severely injured. The Gallerions had been ruthless.

Light flashed behind his eyelids, and he opened them in time to catch a glimpse of his captor. Piercing blue eyes locked onto his right before the forest went dark. A cold, creeping sensation crawled along his skin as the world faded into darkness again. Her hair was plastered to her face, darkened from the rain, but there was no mistaking those eyes. How was it possible? He ground his teeth as her image burned into his mind. The chilling feel of sharp steel against his throat made him shiver.

He dug his nails into his palms, the ropes biting into his arms.

The princess's ominous voice barely reached his ears over the storm. "Would you mind calming down? I put a lot of effort into saving your beast, but if it tries to attack me because of you, I'll not hesitate to kill it."

Before Ryker could ask what she was talking about, lightning flashed again in answer. Snuggled against the princess was Artis, who eyed him warily, her body tense as she sensed his mixed emotions. Pure relief and joy overshadowed his anger. Before the lightning faded, he noticed the princess had removed the arrows and dressed the wounds with bandages. However, his happiness was tainted by the person holding her.

Why had the princess put in the effort to save Artis? Why had she not killed him... again?

"What's going on?" He hollered over the storm right before thunder blasted through the air. Sopping mud sloshed against his legs whenever he moved. A small divot in the tree poked his back, but when he shifted, the ropes dug deeper into his arms.

Her hard, icy voice was tinged with humor. "We're stuck in a storm."

"I meant, why are you here?" He huffed.

"I could ask you the same thing," she snapped. "You ran into Galleria."

Clamping his jaw tight, he repressed all the vile things he wanted to say. Insults would not help him in this situation, and she had Artis's head in her lap. He internally cursed at the gods for their cruel sense of humor. Why did Tempus continue to take everything away from him except his life?

Had the princess found the letter he carried? Panic set in as he tried to shift around to feel for it, but his efforts were futile. The letter had been in the inner pocket of his tunic. She'd either found it disarming him, or it was soaked—and possibly ruined—from the rain. He hoped the letter had been a test and contained nothing important for General Averill. If it was simply a test of his loyalty, it wouldn't matter if the princess found it.

"You should try to rest. You weren't badly hurt, but sleep will do you good." The princess' voice was neither kind nor malicious, just factual and distant. It unnerved him. Another flash revealed she was still staring at him. Just like her voice, her face was not friendly. It was almost devoid of emotion. Only a slight glint of frustration in her eyes revealed any feelings at all, along with something else in her face he could not describe. But then the light faded, and she disappeared into the darkness.

There was little chance he would get any of his answers

tonight. He wasn't sure how to sleep with her so close, but he shifted to get as comfortable as possible against the tree trunk, grimacing as the ground squished beneath him.

The storm subsided to a steady rainfall, and Ryker leaned his head back, lulled by the sound. His eyes drifted closed and pulled his weary body into slumber.

～

"DON'T WORRY, girl, I'm almost done." A feminine voice and a small whimper woke him hours later. "You're so sweet. If only your rider was half as good as you."

Ryker's eyes felt crusted and heavy when he peeled them open. Confusion struck him. The rain had ceased, and the clouds were gone, and now stars glittered in the sky, the moon offering a soft glow as it rose in the sky. His clothes were brittle and dry except where he sat on the damp ground. Woods surrounded them, but there were no landmarks providing any indication of his whereabouts. But by the size of the trees, with their massive trunks and twining branches, he guessed he was in the northeastern half of Galleria.

Ryker felt more refreshed than he had in months. His slumber had been deep and uninterrupted by the horrors that normally haunted him.

They sat in a small clearing, a simple fire in the center to chase away the shadows. He was still tied tight to a tree like before while the princess knelt in front of Artis, tying a fresh bandage around her shoulder. Her face was softer than he'd ever seen, and she had a smile on her face as Artis licked her arm in appreciation.

She scratched behind Artis's ear. "What's her name?"

His mouth fell open, then snapped shut again. What was

this woman's game? Instead of answering, he asked his own question. "How long was I out?"

"All day."

"What?" It was the only explanation for their new surroundings, and the dryness of his clothes, but his mind still reeled. How had she managed to drag him for so long without waking him? That's when he noticed the rickety, wooden cart behind Artis. Even injured, she would be capable of pulling the cart without much strain—but he'd remained unconscious for all of it?

"Yep." The princess interrupted his whirling thoughts as she plopped herself on the ground across from him. "Heavy sleeper."

"I'm a soldier. We don't sleep heavy." He narrowed his eyes, studying her face for any clues as to what she'd done, but her expression was blank as she lifted a cup to her lips, unfazed.

The sight of the cup caused a sudden, painful feeling in his gut. "I uhh...need—" His face flamed, and his expression must have given away his intent because she frowned.

"I see."

Walking over, the princess crossed her arms and stared down at him. All the while, he held in the pain as much as he could. He was embarrassed enough as it was; he was not about to relieve himself in front of her.

"You have two choices here." The princess gestured with her hands as she spoke. "I can tie your hands behind your back, but then you would need my help to do much of anything."

He clamped his jaw, his face flaming from such a suggestion. "What is option two?"

"I can tie your hands in front; therefore, you will be able to do it all yourself. However, if you try anything, I will shoot the lykos." She frowned as she said it, but her gaze was unyielding.

Artis lifted her head at the princess's remark, yet even at the threat to her life, Artis didn't growl. Instead, she watched the princess with a curious tilt of her head. "I've grown fond of her," continued the princess, "so I would prefer not to, but I will not hesitate if you challenge me."

Ryker didn't exactly have much time to make his choice, and he didn't doubt she would follow through on her threat. He nodded his agreement, and she loosened his ties to the tree just enough to bind his hands in front and let the ropes fall away.

Before Ryker was on his feet, she raised daggers in each hand, ready to throw them in Artis's direction. "Go behind this tree. I'll be watching."

Wasting no time, Ryker ducked into the shadows before he burst. He took this small window of opportunity to think. He wasn't sure how many more days of travel they had, but if he proved he would follow her orders, she might slacken her vigilance. He would need to devise a plan of escape for when the opportunity arose, but for now, he swallowed his pride and returned to the princess. She nodded towards the tree.

"Where are you taking me?" He stepped to where she indicated but hesitated sitting on the uncomfortable ground.

"Riverwood."

He was surprised she answered. It may not have been an honest answer, but their surrounding terrain made sense if Riverwood was truly their destination. Considering where her team had ambushed his troops, they had at least a day or two of travel left.

Ryker pushed his luck one more time. "Why didn't you kill me?"

This time, she did not answer immediately, his question hanging in the air. The first flicker of emotion broke her stoic expression, and he noted the subtle shift in her eyes. It was the unreadable emotion he'd seen the night before during the storm. Was it uncertainty? Anger? Sadness? The moment passed, and he decided he didn't want to know her answer.

The princess stepped closer to him, preparing to tie him down, when a new voice broke through the night—a deep, familiar voice that sent a chill down his spine.

"Well, isn't this an interesting sight."

CHAPTER 26

FREYA

The hairs on the back of Freya's neck stood. She recognized the man's voice; it was one she'd heard before.

"I was told to be gentle with you... Of course, I was not instructed to be as careful with her."

His voice had left such an impression Freya's stomach clenched upon hearing it again. In one fluid motion, she pulled Ryker in front of her and brought a dagger to his throat as she faced the intruder. She was grateful she'd decided to draw the blade instead of her bow. Dark, cold eyes met hers, sending chills down her spine. Phantom chains rattled in her ears and pinched her wrists as she was taken back to their first encounter.

"Vaan?"

Freya ground her teeth when Ryker spoke but couldn't bring herself to tighten the blade. Imperial soldiers lurked in the trees around her camp. She counted at least ten but knew there were more. The nearest town was a day's journey away. *Thanks a lot, Keanon.*

"Ryker." Vaan shook his head with a wicked grin, his keen

eyes never leaving Freya's. "I tried to tell General Moreland you were untrustworthy."

She frowned at Vaan's words and scanned the woods as the soldiers closed in. What did he mean by that? What could Ryker have done to be on the Empire's bad side?

"What are you talking about?"

In answer, Vaan drew his blade and rolled his shoulders. "To catch you in the presence of the very princess you helped escape only a few weeks ago." He grinned with a dangerous gleam in his eye.

"You can't possibly count this as being with the princess," said Ryker.

Freya tightened her grip on the dagger, trying not to show her confusion. None of the surrounding soldiers had bows, but that didn't give her much advantage. With her back against the tree, she couldn't be grabbed from behind, but it also cut off any chance of retreat.

Vaan stalked into the clearing, the orange glow from the fire casting harsh shadows on his face. "You led another troop of soldiers into a trap to die, allowing Galleria to steal more of our army's much-needed supplies."

"Vaan, come on! I didn't lead those troops." Ryker's voice rose in panic, pulling tight against Freya's hold. She squeezed tighter, and Vaan was unmoved.

"Just another trait you and your brother share. I'm sure the emperor will be ecstatic when he hears I've recaptured the princess, as well as the traitor who let her escape."

Freya was about to be overwhelmed. There was no chance she could take them all on single-handedly. Yet Vaan's contempt for Ryker was clear, meaning she and Ryker shared a common enemy—if only for the moment. He was her only option to even the odds, albeit slightly. Making a quick, definitely stupid decision, Freya sliced the ropes tying Ryker's hands together and gave him her dagger.

"Take this."

His eyes were still frantic from Vaan's accusations, but he didn't drop the dagger as she placed it in his hands. The indecision on his face made her heart drop, but she had little time to stress about his allegiances. Past Ryker's shoulder, Artis growled and snapped at any soldiers that drew close. Freya cursed under her breath. She'd just given the girl her medicine, which not only numbed her injuries but lowered her energy. It was clear the lykos couldn't feel her legs as she remained on the ground.

Freya had no more time to contemplate her odds as the soldiers came at her fast. The moment they charged, Ryker disappeared from her side. Occasional flashes from the fire light let her know he'd made it over to Vaan, his dagger lowered. She was forced to focus as she took out one soldier, only for him to be replaced by two more. Cornered, Freya kept her back to the tree, making it easier to deflect blows to her arms and legs. None of the soldiers aimed to kill. They wanted to take her alive, which gave her an advantage. She didn't share the sentiment.

"NO!"

The chilling cry froze everyone mid-swing. Swords poised and chests heaving, everyone turned. Ryker was on the ground, blood dribbling from his mouth and nose. His horror-stricken face stared at Vaan standing over him, his hand still clenched from punching Ryker. Vaan was prepared for another attack, but it wasn't Ryker he was prepared to fight. A low growl filled the silence, making every soldier hold tighter to their swords. Despite the numbing medicine, the lykos stood, her hackles raised, prepared to pounce to protect her rider.

"Artis, DOWN!" Ryker commanded, but she wasn't listening.

Freya's stomach sank. Artis wasn't ready for this kind of fight. Even without the medicine slowing her movements, the hole in her shoulder was still prone to bleeding if the girl strained too much. The soldiers were changing targets, and Vaan was more than prepared for her to lunge. This was Freya's perfect opportunity to escape. She could disappear while they dealt with the lykos. If she left, Artis would die, and Ryker would too. Freya cursed, recalling how the sweet girl would lick her hand appreciatively whenever Freya tended to her and tilted her head while Freya talked. Then there was the ever-present pull Keanon had on her to protect his brother.

This fight was lost. There was only one thing she could do to ensure an escape later. Cursing under her breath, Freya barreled through everyone in her way until she stood in front of Artis. She swung her sword in a wide arc, pushing everyone back while pressing her other hand gently against Artis's forehead.

"Shh, down girl." She attempted to sway the lykos's bloodlust. "He's alright. Don't worry, he'll be alright." Freya stroked her face as she spoke, and though Artis's body remained tense, her stance eased, no longer prepared to attack. When Freya scanned the imperial soldiers around her, her gaze landed on Ryker's, his eyes wide with disbelief.

Vaan swung his sword towards Freya's, and she let it fly from her hand. With a final stroke before the soldiers grabbed her, Freya whispered softly so only Artis would hear. "We'll get them back for this soon." The lykos' ears perked from her words, and she narrowed her eyes as if in understanding.

When it was clear Freya and the lykos were no longer a threat, the soldiers apprehended her, took away her weapons, and bound her hands behind her back with her own ropes. Ryker's gaze remained locked with Freya's, disbelieving and confused.

"Well, that was fun." Contrary to his comment, Vaan

appeared bored. "Now, Ryker." Soldiers dragged Ryker to his feet before Vaan, who pulled something from Ryker's tunic pocket.

"Wait, that's—"

The soldiers holding Ryker yanked his arm behind his back as he tried to snatch the paper back from Vaan's hands.

With a sneer, Vaan opened it. After a quick scan, his eyes lit up with barely suppressed glee. "This is all the proof I needed of your disloyalty. Who gave this to you? Who were you delivering it to?" His piercing stare and frigid voice rippled through the clearing, and even the fire flickered when he spoke.

Why had Freya not searched him beyond removing his weapons? She wanted to kick herself for her lack of forethought, but when Vaan's words set in, she frowned. Ryker was disloyal? What was in the letter?

Ryker's mouth fell open and snapped closed, his expression filled with confusion and horror.

"I said, *who* gave this to you?" Vaan's voice was deadly as he slowly enunciated each word, leaning close to Ryker's face. She grew even more curious when Ryker's jaw clenched, defiance filling his eyes. Standing back, Vaan slid the paper into his chest pocket. "Fine. No matter. I'll get you to tell me soon enough, traitor."

Vaan turned, beckoning the soldiers to bring along his new prisoners. They shoved Freya onto the wagon she'd purchased to bring Ryker across Galleria. They tossed him in beside her. The torment on his face almost tugged at her heart. She wanted to ask him about the letter but bit her tongue. Soldiers surrounded their wagon; anything they said would be overheard. For now, she ignored Ryker and rolled awkwardly on her back, ignoring the discomfort as it pulled at her shoulders. Her fingers found what she was looking for as she wrapped them around a loose nail protruding from the worn wood. She twisted and pulled to free it but froze when Vaan loomed above her.

"Oh, princess," said Vaan. He sat atop an eldeer beside the wagon, staring down at her with cold eyes that made the hairs on her arms stand on end. Freya lay on bated breath as he studied her, praying he would not realize what she'd been doing. "If you attempt to call out, scream, or even raise your voice, it will be the last sound you ever make."

VIVIAN

Vivian stood before her full-length mirror as Marienn and her maids prepared her face and hair for the big day. On her bed was the dress Vivian was supposed to wear to the wedding ceremony. It was a deep blue satin dress with silver trim and white gemstones along the bodice; instead, Vivian wore her riding clothes and thick cloak. It was the last day of the festival, Aida's wedding day, and the day of Vivian's departure. Since she could not wear her dress, Vivian's maids spent more time on her hair. They pulled the front away from her face in several small braids, using heated flat rocks to smooth and straighten the remaining curls in the back.

Vivian's transformation was mind-blowing. She couldn't help wondering what Prince Damian would think, and her insides warmed as she pictured him. The past few days of festivities had been incredible. He'd proved to be an attentive, caring, and compassionate person. Even in her moments of doubt, he never once tried to force her into any decisions, and with every passing moment in his presence, she realized a betrothal to him could be quite pleasant. The more time they spent together, the more comfortable they became. While her heart still raced every time she prepared to see him, he showed how easy he was to talk to, and she really enjoyed his company. However, this choice wasn't fully up to her—no matter what her mother said. She couldn't let herself decide, not until she met the emperor.

When her maids were finished, Vivian made her way down the hall, halting at the top of the stairs. Below, the Gallerion retinue stood at the ready in the foyer, and Prince Damian nearly collided with her as he reached the landing. The prince was in his riding gear from the first day she'd met him, his expression earnest, almost frightening. The sharp downturn to his mouth and the frantic flare in his eyes immediately set her on edge.

"I was coming to see you before I departed." His voice was grim.

"What's happened?"

"I received word from home. The Empire is about to march on Blackstone. I've been requested to return home in haste." His expression softened, his eyes growing sorrowful as he finally took in her attire. Brushing a hand through his hair, he glanced back toward his waiting soldiers before surprising Vivian by taking her hand in his; his touch sent a shock of warmth through her. He gently pulled her back up the stairs and around the corner, away from all the prying eyes. When they had some privacy, he whispered, "I'm sorry to leave so suddenly. I was hoping to be here for your sister's wedding."

"I..." Words escaped her for a moment as she stood, momentarily stunned by his hands on hers and how closely they stood. His impending departure filled her with fear and sadness, and though this was always going to be their final day together, it was Prince Damian who was now departing first. The Empire was launching another attack on Galleria, and Prince Damian was returning to fight. Could he die in battle?

The prospect of his demise struck her stronger than she thought possible.

The only thing she could think to say was, "Please... promise you'll be careful. You'll stay safe."

His smile was sad, and though he obviously couldn't make such a promise, he nodded anyway.

"Don't you worry about the wedding, Your Highness." They both startled and turned to Vivian's mother, who appeared at the top of the stairs. "We appreciate you coming to stay and understand your need to return home."

Prince Damian bowed. "Galleria appreciates your hospitality, and I thank you for allowing me to participate in such an important time for your kingdom." Her mother smiled and nodded. As Prince Damian returned to the stairs, he gave Vivian one last regret-filled glance, which she returned with a wobbly smile. He bowed again to both of them, and the queen's smile grew. With that, he flew down the stairs, and Vivian rounded the corner to watch as the troops followed him out the doors. She watched the Gallarion's mount and ride out into the city from the large window revealing the palace courtyard.

Vivian would be leaving to see the emperor after the wedding ceremony. After meeting him, would they decide to side with the Empire? Vivian's heart hurt, and tears filled her throat. She couldn't explain why she felt so strongly for a man she'd known for only a few weeks.

A hand rested on her shoulder, and she met her mother's eyes.

"I know how all of this has weighed on you." Her mother smiled somberly as she guided her back up the hall, where they wouldn't be overheard. "When I said I wanted you to have a say in the choice we make, I never intended for you to feel like you had to make it all on your own. I only wanted to ensure your thoughts and opinions were considered as the priests, your father, and I figured out the right course to take. Whatever happens, we are all responsible to bear the weight of the consequences."

Vivian shook her head in frustration. "But I don't have any intuition here. Just too many questions."

Her mother gave a knowing look. "Are you so certain about that? The gods communicate their will in many ways. Have you been listening?"

Listening to what? Vivian was growing tired of her mother and Sasha's vague sentiments. *The gods don't speak with an audible voice* is what she wanted to snap back as her mother gave a final, encouraging smile before heading down to the foyer.

Vivian remained rooted in place, absently staring at a tapestry of the mountains. Her mother had meant to ease her burden, but Vivian couldn't shake the overwhelming pressure and fear remaining. Even if her parents made this choice without her input, the result would not only decide her future, but the future of Brantyre. No matter the outcome, their kingdom would go to war, and she would have to leave home.

Despite weeks of silence, there was one person she couldn't leave without speaking to. Heart heavy, Vivian returned the way she'd come and paused outside her sister's door. Since their argument, she had ignored and avoided Aida as much as her sister had avoided her. But it was Aida's wedding day and the day Vivian would depart to meet the emperor. With a deep breath, Vivian knocked, and Aida's soft voice welcomed her in. Her sister was a vision to behold. Her wedding dress was pale blue silk, with lace snowflakes embroidered along the bodice and full skirt. Her hair had been smoothed into soft curls about her face, tumbling down her back in waves. Her necklace was filled with countless blue gemstones that sparkled under the light.

Aida's expression hardened when she recognized who entered. She turned her back and crossed her arms. "What do you want?" Aida was good at hiding her emotions, but Vivian heard the wobble in her voice, and noted the stiffness in her posture—telltale signs of the hurt, fear, and anger she tried to hide.

Tears clogged Vivian's throat until she finally asked, "How are you?" Aida refused to turn or speak, but Vivian pushed forward. "I know you're upset. Everything happening is scary. I didn't want any of this either." She stepped into the room, pouring out everything in her heart. "All my life has been centered around you, Aida, but that was my choice. I love you, and all I ever wanted was to help you. Throughout your life, I could always see the burden of expectation placed on your shoulders—from the moment you were chosen at eight years old, too young to comprehend the weight of your responsibility. I chose to be the person you could come to, the one who could see through your mask to how you truly felt beneath the surface. When you needed me most, I was struggling with my own burdens and expectations; I was blind to how you were hurting, and it hurts so much to think I must leave you. You'll have Tristain by your side now, and I truly believe he loves you, but it is up to you to let him in."

Tears trailed down Vivian's cheeks, and though Aida didn't turn, her shoulders shook. Vivian took the final step, placing a hand on her sister's arm. "I feel this burden now, too. The one you have, the burden that says you cannot mess up—the pressure to always say or do the right thing. It's a scary feeling I could never truly share with you until now." Tentatively, Vivian turned Aida around, who didn't protest. For the first time in years, Aida cried. She wept fully, and Vivian pulled her into her arms. They stayed like that, crying in each other's arms until all their tears were spent.

Aida pulled her over to sit on her bed. Vivian picked at the plush purple comforter to keep her hand out of her carefully styled hair.

"I'm sorry, Vi." Aida's voice shook. "It was hard to watch everyone forget about me as they focused instead on what you should do. I was forgotten, and all the while, the questions plagued me. Who am I? Why did the gods choose and prepare me all those years ago to take it all away before I was even given a chance? What did I do to upset them? But I wasn't fair to you. I know all these changes scare you too. I was so self-absorbed that I failed to reciprocate all the ways you have been there for me through the years. When you came to me asking if I was alright, I knew you were being genuine, but I couldn't take anymore. I snapped."

Vivian gave her sister a wobbly smile and took her hand. Her sister's questions burned in her mind, though. What was wrong with Aida or their parents? Why were they being stripped of their responsibilities, and what was so special about Emperor Asher that he would be ordained to rule all seven king-doms? With a heavy heart, Vivian sighed. "I'm going to be leaving today."

"Mother told me. You both are going to meet the emperor in Lividia."

Vivian frowned and voiced her biggest fear. "What am I supposed to do?"

"What do you want to do?"

"It's not that simple. Nothing about our lives has been about what we want, Aida. Everything has been ordained for us, and I'm simply trying to follow what the gods want for me."

"That is a very harsh view of the gods."

The girls leaped from the bed at the intruding voice. High Priestess Sasha stood in the doorway, her discerning eyes contrasting her smile. Leaning both hands on her cane, she raised a brow, waiting.

Vivian's mouth dropped open, but no words came to her. Aida was quiet too.

"Come sit, dears." Sasha gestured to the couches, and the three of them sat: Vivian and Aida beside each other on one couch, and Sasha facing them on the other.

"Do you believe the gods want what is best for everyone?" When they both nodded, she continued. "Sometimes, what is best for us and the kingdom doesn't align with our own wants and desires, but that doesn't mean the gods never consider our hopes and dreams. If they didn't care, they wouldn't bother choosing an heir to rule; they wouldn't have bothered creating us at all. It can be harder for the royal family. Your responsibilities are much larger than most. However, that does not mean they do not wish good things for you two."

"What are you saying?"

"How do you think your father and mother chose Tristain to marry Aida?"

Vivian frowned, considering the question. While Tristain had grown up with the royal family, he hadn't been selected as Aida's betrothed until last year. She'd not thought much about the why, instead focusing on helping her sister sift through her feelings about the matter.

"Who an heir is married to is just as important as who the heir themselves is. Their spouse will rule alongside them and help create the next generation of potential heirs. The gods are equally as invested in guiding us to the correct spouse for their chosen king or queen, though they do not send this guidance through visions. Instead, the king and queen will pray often, searching for someone worthy of their child. When one has a strong inclination for someone in particular, they will consult the priests. If everyone agrees with the match, the steps are taken to announce the engagement. However, if even one priest or priestess has concerns, nothing is done until all worries are appeased or a better fit is found." Sasha leaned forward on her cane. "If you have strong feelings for Prince Damian, that holds a lot of weight in my mind. Yet you have not met the emperor. So, you must go; speak with him, ask your questions, and allow him to appease your worries. If he cannot, then you will have your answer."

CHAPTER 28

RYKER

Why did he go on? The question burned a hole in Ryker's heart as he stared at the night sky. After a long night traveling in the rickety wagon, Vaan had finally stopped for camp. They were at least another day's journey from the South King's Road, so the soldiers didn't light any fires but set up a few small tents. Ryker and Freya had been yanked from the wagon and tied to the same tree, but when anyone tried to approach Artis, she would growl and snap her teeth. When she curled up by Ryker's side, the soldiers left her alone.

Ryker had tried hard to prove himself, only to be labeled a traitor. What had he done for the gods to abandon him? He'd lost everything to help fulfill their will. He had nothing left to give to them.

"Hey." A whisper, so soft he thought he imagined it, pulled him from his thoughts. This was the princess's first address to him all night. Glancing at her blue eyes in the moonlight, he recalled how she'd stood between the soldiers and Artis.

"What was in that letter?" Her voice was low, which Ryker assumed was to keep the soldier on watch from hearing.

His mouth dropped open at the princess's boldness. He had no idea what was in Captain Bennett's note, and if he did, why would he tell her?

Unfazed by his continued silence, she shrugged. "Fine, don't tell me."

Before he could stop them, the words poured out. "I don't have a clue what it says." Her brows raised in question, and he sighed. "I was instructed not to read it, and now I know it was because the person who gave it to me was hiding something."

She seemed to ponder his response, the moon casting soft blue light across her face. "Why didn't you give Vaan the name of the person then? If you aren't working with them, why not save yourself and turn them in?" The bitter undercurrent in her voice was palpable. Ryker opened his mouth to shoot back, but she beat him to it. "You had no problems turning in your own brother."

It was like a slap to the face. He snapped his mouth shut. He could have turned her in when Vaan had asked for Captain Bennett's name. Ryker hadn't known the captain was a traitor, so there was no reason he couldn't have given her up. But if he had, it would have done little to help Ryker. Vaan would still take him back to the Empire as a traitor. After everything that had happened with Keanon and Ryker's demotion, there was nothing he could say or do to defend himself. He wondered if General Moreland would even believe him now.

When Vaan had demanded Captain Bennett's name, her words came back to haunt him.

"You need to learn to anticipate the unexpected better. Your life has been full of it recently; I should think you would have learned to stop assuming you know more than you do."

Her comment infuriated him because they were once again true. But as he'd stared into Vaan's cold, calculating eyes, the last part of her comment hit him anew. *Stop assuming you know more than you do...* Ryker had always trusted in the words of those stationed above him. Now, with Keanon's questions coming back to haunt him—and realizing Captain Bennett and others were working against the Empire—it smacked him like a blow to the gut that he may not understand anything at all.

"Why are the gods changing things? Is there a chance the priests misunderstood the vision?" Keanon's questions were another factor convincing Ryker not to give up Captain Bennett's name. It seemed like everyone Ryker got close to was hiding something, and he had to know what. What was Captain Bennett up to? What had Keanon learned or experienced that pushed him to such a drastic change? Ryker had to know what was happening, and he would start by shutting his mouth.

The princess seemed just as done talking to him as he was with her for the night. As exhausted as he was, his sleep was staggered throughout the night, interrupted by terrors that refused to leave. Artis laid her big head in his lap to offer comfort, licking his chin like always. He was sad he couldn't scratch her head with his arms clamped to his sides, yet nearness helped ease some of the tension in his body, and he fell back to sleep.

HE JERKED awake in the early morning light with tears in his eyes, and beside him, the princess watched him with a guarded expression. He turned away, hating that she could see him so vulnerable. He wondered if he'd had thrashed in his sleep when she had dragged him across Galleria too. Vaan's troops were packing up their minuscule camp, and Ryker braced himself for another agonizing day under the intense summer sun in the bumpy, old wagon.

"Let's get going! We have to make it to the border by the

end of the day." Vaan appeared among the soldiers, barking orders that they rushed to obey. "Get the prisoners in the wagon."

Four soldiers rushed over but froze when Artis growled.

"Down, Artis," Ryker commanded, and she reluctantly obeyed. Lying low on the ground, she watched through slitted eyes as the soldiers untied Ryker and the princess from the tree and then re-tied their hands behind their backs. Ryker grunted as his body crashed unceremoniously onto the rough wood, pain shooting up his arm and bursting in his shoulder from the impact. The princess landed beside him with a wince while Artis plodded silently alongside the wagon as they began their trek east.

Without a word, the princess rolled awkwardly as if searching for something. Concentration brewed in her eyes. He raised a questioning brow at her, but she ignored him. With the soldiers surrounding them, he refrained from speaking in case they overheard, but it was clear the princess was up to something.

If she had a way out of this, Ryker wanted to know what it was. Though the thought of working with the princess left a bitter taste in his mouth, he was determined to get out of there. Being dragged back to the Empire as a traitor—by Vaan, of all people—was not something he could allow to happen.

While he let the princess work on whatever she was doing, Ryker studied their surroundings. Vaan had shouted about making it to the border by nightfall and based on the massive trees on one side and the hills turning to mountains in the far distance on his other, they were in the northeastern tip of Galleria. The border for Brantyre was about a day and a half's journey north. The Empire would be within reach if they kept traveling east without stopping.

By midday, Ryker's throat was painfully dry. Overhead, the

sun beat down mercilessly. With no clouds in the sky, there was no shade to offer relief. Vaan didn't see fit to give the prisoners anything to drink either. Ryker could only imagine he was growing as red as the princess beside him, her face flushed, and jaw strained. Her body blocked his view, but he soon realized she was working on a loose nail. After searching with his own hands, he had not found one that protruded enough for him to get his slick, sweaty fingers around.

Finally, as the sun descended, they rolled onto the South King's Road. The relief from the soldiers was palpable as they conversed quietly amongst themselves for the first time on the journey. Ryker's heart jumped into his throat, and he barely kept himself from crying out when the princess flew into him suddenly, her head smacking into his chest. He suppressed a cough from the blow, taking in low, big gulps of air to ease the pain. When he glared down at the princess, the subtle upturn to her lips gave him pause. She'd freed the nail.

"Hold!" Vaan's voice called out, and everyone came to a halt. "I know you are all tired. We will set up a proper camp here for the night."

The soldiers' conversation became louder and easier as they dispersed to different tasks. Once again, Ryker and the princess were dragged out of the wagon and tied to a tree. He chanced a glance toward the princess, but her tight expression gave nothing away. Artis plopped herself on the ground beside them while the soldiers prepared camp. Ryker ground his teeth when Vaan sauntered over.

"So, Ryker." Vaan sneered as he knelt down. "Are you ready to share who gave you the letter?"

"I could tell you but seeing as I'm about to be executed as a traitor, I may as well do this one last thing to piss you off." Ryker flashed Vaan a smirk of his own. The blow was expected, but it still sent Ryker reeling. Vaan didn't hold back on the punch. Dark splotches filled Ryker's vision as his stomach swirled, his head swimming with a blend of green and brown. Slowly, his surroundings sharpened again.

Vaan had backed up a few paces, raising his hands in the air as Artis stepped between them, snapping her teeth in Vaan's direction. "Call off your mutt!" Vaan demanded, placing a hand on his sword.

"Artis, come." Ryker couldn't hide the smile on his face as Artis came and lay down beside him, teeth still bared.

"If you can't keep that mutt under control, I'm going to have my soldiers take her out." Vaan snarled, whirling away.

Ryker watched him go, knowing Vaan's threat wasn't worth much. Vaan had no archers among his soldiers, so as long as Ryker kept Artis under control, it was safer for his troops to leave her be. Her limp was almost gone, only returning at the end of the day after such a long journey. She would easily kill several of his soldiers before they could take her down.

Soon, the sun set behind the tree line in the distance, casting dark shadows along the woods. The soldiers lit two small campfires and began roasting meat, making Ryker's stomach groan. He couldn't remember the last time he'd eaten anything.

One of the soldiers came over with two cups in her hands. "Can't believe neither of you passed out in this heat," she mumbled, her face hard. She knelt and offered the cup to the princess first. Ryker was surprised when the princess hesitated, her face scrunched with distrust.

The soldier rolled her eyes. "I'm not about to poison you now." But to appease the princess, the soldier took the tiniest sip from the cup herself then offered it again. Still frowning, the princess drank the water. When it was finally Ryker's turn, he didn't hesitate. His lips were cracked, and mouth parched; the cool water offered short, but sweet relief as it washed down his throat.

The soldier left. It seemed they weren't going to be fed that night.

Leaning back against the tree, Ryker watched the sky darken and waited for the soldiers to retire. Beside him, the princess worked on the ropes binding them to the tree. He felt them pull as she hacked at them with the nail. He didn't complain.

Finally, when only two soldiers remained by the fire, their heads low in conversation, did Ryker speak. "So, what's your plan?"

The princess stiffened beside him but didn't respond.

"Do you have a plan?" he asked.

"Why should that concern you?" She bit back; her work on the ropes continued.

"I'm simply curious about what you're going to do when you get us out of these ropes." He glanced at the soldiers, who seemed oblivious to their conversation.

"Once I get us out of here, you can feel free to run off wherever you want." She flinched, possibly cutting herself with the nail. "I don't know what you're involved in now, and I don't care to know, but you and Artis can go wherever you want."

The princess's words struck him. He hadn't considered running away. It would be so easy. But what did he gain by running? His life? What was that worth at this point? He needed answers. There was a chance he could sneak his way back to Captain Bennett, but she could easily arrest him on the spot. As much as Ryker hated to admit it, staying with the princess could be his best chance at finding answers. Keanon had learned something while he was with her.

"Why did you turn in your brother?"

The question hit him like a sucker punch to the gut, and

tears burned in his throat. His lips moved before he could stop himself. "I didn't know what else to do."

"What does that mean?" Her accusation made his blood boil.

"What else was I supposed to do?" he hissed as loud as he dared, glancing at the soldiers nearby. "I thought he was compromised. I didn't know if you were manipulating and using him. I had to do something." He fought back hot tears and squeezed his hands so tight his nails dug painfully into his palms. "I went to someone I trusted. He was supposed to help. He was supposed to save Keanon, not sentence him to death."

"If you did all that to save him, why didn't you let us escape?" Her voice had lost some of its bite, but her anger lingered. "I had him free. We were going to get him to safety when you showed up with those soldiers."

Ryker shook his head, hating how his mind betrayed him as the memory he fought so hard to bury deep returned with a vengeance. He'd tried so hard to never relive that day, but now he couldn't stop it. "I knew something was wrong with how quickly that fire spread." His voice was monotone as the day played through his head; he recalled it vividly, even with his eyes open. "I had to see if my suspicions were true. When I found you three hiding in the shadows of the stables, I..." His heart squeezed, and he closed his eyes against the pain and tears. "I *was* going to let him escape."

As though watching it happen from outside his own body, Ryker saw himself begin to turn away when an old, familiar voice stopped him.

"Good work, Ryker. I see you found our escaped prisoner." General Moreland stood behind him with five soldiers. "I know this is hard, but let's go get him."

The princess's soft voice brought him back out of the

memory, but her next question shoved him back into the worst of it. "And what about what happened during the fight?"

Ryker had rushed to help General Moreland who had fallen. He moved to plunge his sword forward into the princess, but someone pushed her out of the way. The sword slid into solid flesh, but the eyes staring back at Ryker were not hers—they were his.

Keanon slid off the sword, the weight of his body nearly pulling it out of Ryker's hands. Blood trickled off the sharpened tip and dripped onto the dirt. A scream so shrill and agonizing pierced the air.

Ryker couldn't move.

Or breathe.

The princess cradled Keanon in her arms, and he stared up at her with love in his eyes. When he turned to look at Ryker, his eyes held no anger.

They held no hatred.

They held no regret.

CHAPTER 29
FREYA

Freya watched the assault of anguish on Ryker's face. She didn't know what to make of his confession; his sorrow and regret felt a little too late. The image of Keanon sliding off his brother's sword would haunt her dreams for eternity. Dragged away to prison, she'd watched helplessly as Ryker stood over Keanon's lifeless body. The familiar grief she'd worked so hard to avoid overwhelmed her again.

The ropes snapped and gave way. Their release was all she needed to suppress the memory. Her aching, bleeding hands from hours of working with the tiny nail made it hard to pry her fingers open. Slowly and silently, she shifted away from the tree and eyed the two guards still whispering by the fire.

"Well, you're free now." Glancing between the guards and Ryker, she said, "Do with that what you will, but I'm getting that letter and getting out of here." She picked up some of the rope and left before he could respond. The soldiers' backs were turned, so she took the chance to sneak toward them. She crouched low; every bit of ground she gained was agonizing. When one of them shifted in their seat, she froze on bated breath. She let it out when they didn't turn.

Freya wasn't sure how she would take out two soldiers by herself before they called for reinforcements, but she could at least get one. When she drew up behind one of them, movement caught the corner of her eye—a flash of golden fur. With a grin, Freya lunged. She wrapped the rope tight around the soldier's neck, who thrashed and gasped for breath. She pulled tighter, so they swallowed their words.

Slowly, the soldier's fighting slackened before they finally went limp. She lowered them to the ground. Artis had snuck up behind the other soldier, clamping down on their throat before they could call for help. Blood spurted from the wound, and Freya was, for once, glad her stomach was empty. She averted her eyes from the gash, and Artis left Freya, slinking back into the darkness toward her rider. The sweet girl got some of her own revenge.

Vaan's tent was two over from where she stood toward the center of the camp. Leaving the bodies, Freya slunk through the shadows, her heart pounding with every step. She searched her surroundings for any signs of movement, but the night sky offered little light.

Finally, she paused outside Vaan's tent. Holding her breath, she listened, but no sounds greeted her from inside. Swift and silent, she squeezed through the tent flaps, being sure to close it so the moonlight wouldn't illuminate inside. The darkness made sweat bead on her forehead. She stood, unable to move in the entryway. Soon, shapes formed throughout the tent, and she regained her composure, though the pounding in her ears didn't cease. Her panic worsened as she took in the empty bed in the far corner.

Wasting no more time, Freya launched herself first at the long table to her left, where they'd left her packs and weapons. Her ears strained for footsteps approaching as she hastily pulled on her gear. On impulse, she grabbed Ryker's too. Beside the bed was a small desk covered in papers, which she dove into next. Her heart beat a dangerous rhythm in her chest as she rifled through worthless maps and blank pages. Nothing appeared important; maps weren't labeled or marked, and she couldn't find the note. It wasn't there.

"What have we here?"

A jolt of ice sped down her spine as she whirled to the tent's entrance. The flap opened all the way, and moonlight cast the figure in the opening in shadows. Soft light turned his pale hair silver, yet his face was fully cast in darkness. She didn't need to see his face to know who stood before her. He moved like a hunter, watching his prey as he pulled something from his pocket.

"Were you, perhaps, looking for this?" Vaan gave her a wicked grin, holding the letter up into the moonlight.

When he stepped into the room, she lunged. Dagger in hand, Freya aimed for his smug face. He was ready, grabbing her wrist in an iron grip and keeping her blade inches from his face. She gritted her teeth as he squeezed, fearing her wrist would snap. He was pushing her hand back, so she sidestepped and yanked while he pushed, sending him flying forward. As he tipped over from the sudden force, she brought her knee into his stomach. Vaan gasped and loosened his hold enough for her to wrench free. Snatching the note from his grip, Freya bolted from the tent. The camp was still quiet as she sprinted the way she'd come. Vaan barreled behind her, but she dared not turn as he roared, "Stop her!"

At the command of their lead soldier, the camp came alive. She had just reached the edge of the next tent when a brute of a man stepped out and blocked her path, his barrel arms the size of tree trunks. He was quicker than his size would indicate as he swung his sword; she ducked just in time, narrowly avoiding being beheaded.

She pushed past him just as four soldiers rushed out of the tents, blocking either side of her. The troops were mobilizing fast. Freya pulled out her bow and knocked one of the soldiers to the ground with an arrow. She switched to her sword as the next soldier drew close. He blocked her first swing, and though she tried to sidestep, he predicted it, slicing the air and forcing her back.

Swinging again, he met her blade with his and shoved her back once more. A clink of metal behind her sent her spinning to meet another attack. The whole camp surrounded her, their swords drawn, yet nobody else moved. There was no need; she could not take them all by herself. Gritting her teeth, Freya did the one thing she could do. She only hoped he hadn't left her.

"RYKER!"

Silence lingered. The soldiers surrounding her parted for Vaan to step into the circle.

"Now I see how Ryker managed to lose you." He rolled his shoulders in an exaggerated stretch and flashed her a devious grin. "You're aggravatingly persistent and slippery, but your escape was flawed this time."

Freya glared at him, adjusting her grip on the sword. If they were going to take her again, she would take out as many as she could.

A howl pierced the night, and the soldiers cried out as a beast charged through the crowd, barreling through any that got in her way. A lone rider sat on her back and offered his hand as they drew near. Freya didn't hesitate. Clasping onto his outstretched arm, Ryker swung her up behind him onto Artis's back. Grabbing his shoulder with one hand, she slashed at the soldiers with the other.

Artis leaped out of the circle and ran back to Galleria.

CHAPTER 30

VIVIAN

Aida was a vision as she stood beside Tristain before the gates leading into Calliva City. Soft white snowflakes trailed from the bodice of her pale blue dress to the hem as if she wore the sky itself. Tristain was also quite handsome as he stood in all white beside her. Citizens gathered outside the gates to watch the ceremony while the palace residents were seated inside the courtyard. Aida and Tristain bowed their heads in prayer while High Priestess Sasha bestowed the blessings of the gods upon the couple's union. All in attendance sat in quiet reverence. The rest of the priests stood on either side of the couple.

Vivian fought the tears, torn between happiness at watching her sister's wedding but also fear and anxiety at the thought of her own. Who would be standing beside Vivian when her time came? She didn't know yet. Would they care about her like Tristain cared about Aida? Prince Damian seemed like the sort that would care, and perhaps their relationship could grow into love. But what about the emperor?

Aida and Tristain placed their hands beside each other's on

top of a large book labeled 'The Promises and Decrees of the Gods.' High Priestess Sasha spoke. "Tristain Ayton, you have been chosen to wed the gods' chosen heir. Do you accept the responsibility and take Aida as your wife? Will you support the chosen heir as her forever confidant and supportive figure? Will you cherish and care for her? Will you pray for her while leading alongside her? Will you follow the will of the gods in all things? Will you become Prince Tristain Ayton Leander?"

In a clear and concise voice, Tristain replied, "As the gods give me strength, I will."

Tears clogged Vivian's throat; Tristain's love for her sister was clear in his eyes, his care running deeper than obligation. He would stand by her side no matter what the future held for the kingdom of Brantyre.

"Aida Leander, you have been chosen by the gods to rule the kingdom of Brantyre. You were chosen to take on the responsibility of your father and mother before you and rule with grace, patience, and strength for the people of Brantyre."

Aida's chin rose as Priestess Sasha's words carried throughout the courtyard and down the streets of Calliva. Pride bubbled up inside Vivian at her sister's grace and confidence. A single tear trailed down Vivian's cheek. How she wished she could stay and support her sister through it all.

"However, you should not rule alone, and beside you is a man willing to take on the responsibility. The gods have deemed him fit to fill this role. Will you take him as your husband? Will you rule alongside him, support him, and care for him? Will you pray for him and lead alongside him? Will you follow the gods' will with him in all things?"

"As the gods give me strength, I will." Aida's response was just as strong as Tristain's and Priestess Sasha smiled.

"Then may the gods bless this union." Priestess Sasha lifted her hands as the first flecks of snow gently fell from the sky. One landed on Vivian's arm, and she watched it slowly dissolve into the dark fabric of her cloak. "Upon this day, I announce, for the first time: Prince Tristain and Princess Aida Leander. Husband and wife."

The crowd cheered as Aida and Tristain took each other's hands and bowed before their people. Everyone was on their feet as the new couple followed the priests back into the palace for one last prayer before joining the party. Vivian's heart hurt as she watched her sister leave. The crowd dispersed into the city to begin the festivities.

Vivian would miss these events. There would be dancing in the square and an open feast all day, but what she'd miss the most was skating on the frozen pond on the outskirts of Calliva. As the weather dropped throughout the week's festivities, the ice had thickened, and this day was the first it would be safe for skating. It had always been her favorite part of the Winter's Lights Festival.

"It's time to go." Her mother stood beside her, her eyes brimming with unshed tears. Fat snowflakes fell faster, forming a light coating of white along the walls and rooftops. Behind her mother, General Flynn stood with a large retinue of soldiers prepared to guide them to Lividia City. Leophinx stood in lines, ready in front of the stables; Talon was among them.

"Goodbye." Glenn wrapped his long arms around Vivian's stomach. She smiled down at him.

"Don't worry. I'm coming back." She reassured him as he gave her a wobbly smile. He nodded, clearly holding back tears. Before her own tears could fall, Vivian squeezed him and went to mount Talon. Priestess Sasha returned to the courtyard, and two soldiers assisted her into the carriage. Once the old priestess was seated, General Flynn gave the signal, and

Vivian's mother led the way down the streets of Calliva. The people watched them pass with a mix of curiosity and worry as they parted, allowing the royal entourage clear passage. Vivian's heart went out to them. As difficult as it was for Vivian to figure out what she should do, it must be so hard for the people to keep their faith and hopes high, especially with little information to go off. Soon, many of them could be forced to go to war. Vivian fought the welling of anxiety and despair before it overwhelmed her.

DESPITE ONLY ONE day on the road, Vivian was in tatters. Her stomach was churning, and she struggled not to grip too tightly to Talon's mane. She'd eaten very little before leaving Calliva and couldn't stomach much food on the road, overcome by her rising nerves. General Flynn kept them moving at a steady pace, ensuring they made great progress before the snowfall thickened. When they camped the first night, the snow was a mere coating on the ground, but when they rose the next day, a thick layer of snow blanketed the landscape. The leophinx picked their way through with little problem, their large paws distributing their weight across the snow so they wouldn't sink into it.

Vivian pulled her riding cloak tighter against the crisp mountain wind that blew in with more bite now the snow had come. Her breaths plumed and spiraled before floating away. While she loved the wildflowers and the warm tinge of the summer, the pure white snow on the trees and landscape had a beauty all its own. The day's stretched on with little consequence while her inner turmoil continued to mount.

On the final night of their journey, Vivian sat on the edge of her bed, wrapped in a bundle of blankets, stiff from the many days of riding. Her bed was firm and scratchy but she was too exhausted to care. Her vision blurred as she stared unseeing at the ground. By midday tomorrow, they would arrive at Lividia where the emperor waited. While she knew her mother and Sasha would be there, too, their presence was only a small comfort. As if her thoughts had manifested, Priestess Sasha came to sit beside her, leaning forward on her cane. Despite the long days of travel, the elderly woman still held herself with grace.

"You will do fine."

"I've never met Emperor Asher, not even when he was just a king."

"I know, but that's not important right now. Our time with the emperor will be much shorter than with Prince Damian. The snows have been rough, so we won't be able to spend more than one night in the city before returning home."

Vivian's face pinched. She hoped that, in such a short time, she would gain enough clarity to make her own choice.

"Remember, you are not the one making this decision." Priestess Sasha gave her a compassionate look, though her voice was firm. "Your mother has made it clear your thoughts will be considered, but in the end, your parents and I will consider all arguments as we make the final decision. Your voice will not be the only one that matters."

Vivian averted her gaze. After all the pain and indecision she'd been through since the emperor's proposal, Vivian wondered if she even wanted a say anymore. It was such a vital decision, and yet she'd had no strong inclinations one way or the other. But Priestess Sasha was right. She could rely on and trust her parents and Sasha to support her in helping make this decision.

Sasha placed a hand on her shoulder. "Keep your feelings and beliefs close to your heart in the next few days. When the time comes, you may even need to fight for what you believe, but I want you to know I have faith in your ability to make a good choice. I believe your mother does, too, which is why she has made it clear to everyone that your voice was to be respected and considered in the final decision. Just focus on where Ductu is directing you and remember: this will ultimately come down to what the priesthood decides."

RYKER

Pounding hooves quickly followed Ryker as he guided Artis into the trees. After the princess's accusations he'd sat in agony as the memories taunted him repeatedly, remembering his brother sliding off his sword. Emotions so overwhelming numbed him as seconds ticked into eternity. Ryker stared into nothing.

Artis butted her large head into his chest, yanking him out of the darkness. Tears he hadn't realized were falling stained his cheeks, and he whipped them away as he met Artis's urgent eyes. A ghost of a smile pulled at his lips as she licked his chin.

Ryker had forced himself to stand, with Artis pressing up against his side as though to offer support. Shouts rang out from the camp, and he ducked into the shadows behind the tree as soldiers poured out of their tents. Then, he heard the princess—a desperate, loud cry calling his name. It jolted him to hear the princess say his name for the first time. Artis whined and circled him, clearly wanting to go to her aid.

Staring into the camp, Ryker could see a large circle of soldiers forming. Then Vaan had appeared, his fists clenched. The princess had gone after the letter. If she got it, there was a chance he could find some answers. Artis whined louder and butted him again. The princess had spared his life twice and saved Artis too, though Ryker had no idea why. Why had she spared him and shown him grace? She clearly hated him yet continued to show him mercy. He couldn't make sense of it. If their roles had been reversed, he wouldn't have hesitated.

His decision would solidify his fate. He could never go back to the Empire. Gods forgive him.

The princess's shout tethered Ryker to the present. She clung to his shoulders as Artis flew. Under normal circumstances, she was faster than any horse, but with two riders and her recovering shoulder, they would need to find somewhere to hide or get help.

"Go left!"

The princess's voice finally registered, and he turned Artis to the left. They were too far from major cities, so he could only follow her directions. Despite her shouting, her words were barely audible over the rushing wind. Artis pushed herself to the limit, eating up the ground and leaving the soldiers far behind.

A river appeared through the trees, and the princess called for him to continue along it.

"There!" She pointed over his shoulder towards a large, gnarled tree growing on the side of a small drop in the ground. Roots twined around each other, a gap between them.

Ryker leaped off Artis with the princess right beside him. She plunged into the small alcove first, and he followed, his heart plummeting as he almost bowled her over. The roots tangled in his hair above his head, the dirt walls brushing against his shoulders.

"Artis won't fit."

The princess didn't respond as she knelt, brushing away loose dirt. It was too dark to see what she was doing, and he almost missed the soft click as the shouts from their pursuers grew closer.

She grabbed his arm, yanking him through an opening in the ground that wasn't there moments ago. Artis squeezed herself in behind them. They descended deeper into the darkness. His heart throbbed in his ears as the dark seemed to swallow them.

Finally, when they reached the last step, they collapsed to the ground, taking big gulps of air. After a few moments, the princess grabbed a torch off the wall and lit it, illuminating the space with warm light. Ryker took in his surroundings. Before them, a long corridor of stone stretched ahead, so deep that the light could not reach the end.

Without a word, the princess led the way down the tunnel. She took each turn without hesitation, even when it split in multiple directions while he followed behind.

His mind whirled over what he'd done. He'd ruined any chances of returning home. All he had now were questions and his desperate need for answers. Ryker had to figure out what was happening, and if it turned out he'd betrayed the gods will, all he could do was repent. Tempus hadn't deemed it fit to take him, despite Ryker's many occasions on the brink of death. He could only hope they would understand his plight when the Empire executed him for treason.

Needing an escape from his own mind, Ryker broke the unbearable silence. "Where are we?"

The torch twitched in her hand, her face pinching. She let his question linger.

"Well, I can deduce we are still under Galleria," continued Ryker. "Judging by the multiple paths from this one and your hesitance to share, it is clearly a tunnel system of some kind beneath the kingdom. There must be other openings throughout the kingdom in places people won't stumble upon them." Relief washed over him as he pulled his father's compass from around his neck. No one had taken it from him. He popped it open and continued."We appear to be heading northeast toward Riverwood where you wanted to take me before Vaan found us. So, I guess I can rephrase my question. How much further?" He smirked as she stalled, staring at him with her mouth open. "It's not hard to put together. Plus, this explains how your team has managed to sneak all along the border without our spies being able to find you."

"With this knowledge, you know I can't let you go back now?"

"Yeah, I sort of sealed that myself."

Her face twitched, and she frowned. After a moment, she said, "Thank you." Her voice was so soft he barely heard it.

Ryker chanced a longer look at her. She kept her gaze straight ahead, though he could still see her furrowed brow and the downturn of her lips. Stray hairs pulled from her braid, leaving copper strands across her tanned skin. With her dark clothes and cloak, she appeared all rogue—not how he imagined a princess to look or act, killing trained soldiers and sneaking through underground tunnels. Though, he supposed he knew little about princesses or royalty.

She stopped suddenly in the middle of a fork in the tunnels. "We should rest now." He didn't argue and found a place where the rocky ground was smooth to sit. She handed him a flask of water and some provisions from her bag, along with his weapons.

The water was gone in seconds, along with the food for which he hadn't even tasted. The small portion didn't make much of a dent in the chasm that was his stomach, but he wasn't going to complain, especially not when she offered one of her flasks to Artis and some rations.

When everyone was taken care of, the princess sat across

from him and pulled the letter out of her pocket. His eyes widened. After running from Vaan's soldiers, he'd forgotten all about the letter. His heart thudded with trepidation as she opened and read whatever was in the note. She scrunched her face in confusion and reread it again and again.

Apprehension filled him as he crossed over, holding out his hand. He was surprised when she handed it to him without resistance. When he scanned it, his heart sank. He scanned it again.

"It's coded." The princess sighed. "Our spies may be able to break it, but they may not be able to without the sender or receiver, and it appears you don't know what it says either."

Ryker frowned. He'd never seen an array of shapes like this anywhere before. Captain Bennett and General Averill had been careful with their communications should their letters fall into the wrong hands. Deciphering codes had not been something he'd trained in much, and he had no clue where to start with this one.

With a shake of his head, he told the princess, "No. I was not a part of whatever this person's doing. They used me because they knew I wasn't in a position to go against orders.

So, when they told me not to read or tell anybody about the letter, I didn't argue. If I was caught with the note by anyone, I couldn't be used to decode it either, so I was the perfect candidate. Their only risk was if I revealed who I got it from or who I was giving it to."

"Why didn't you tell Vaan?"

"I don't particularly like him."

She chuckled. "I can't imagine why."

He smiled at that. When the princess held out her hand for the letter, he hesitated a moment, his hand stilling in the air. Ryker's heart and mind rebelled against one another as every action he took led him further away from who he was—who he used to be... Everything around him had pushed him on a different course than the one he had wanted. Not even in his nightmares would he have imagined working with the princess, but he was tired of having everything decided for him. If he was going to start anticipating the unexpected, he at least wanted to make some of his own choices.

As the gods would have it, the princess was his best way to retrieve some of the answers he sought. He returned the letter to her, and she took it with a raised brow. Ryker sat back, staring at the ground.

"You may want some of this." The princess tossed a small cup, which Ryker narrowly caught before it hit him in the face. It was followed by a tiny vial.

"What is this?" He opened the vial and sniffed it while the princess grinned sheepishly.

"That's the stuff that kept you asleep when I was carting you to Riverwood."

He sniffed it again but still couldn't detect much about its contents.

"You only need a drop with a cup of water..." She lowered her voice. "It will make your sleep dreamless."

Ryker steeled his expression. It appeared his subconscious had given him away, yet her eyes held no judgment as she sipped on her own dose of the sleeping draft. Exhaustion catching up to him, he decided not to turn down the promise of a full night's sleep.

He poured water from his flask and a drop of the sleeping draft into the cup, and tossed it back. He was pleasantly surprised to discover it was as tasteless as it was odorless. Downing the rest, he adjusted himself against Artis's side and settled in.

When he woke, he groaned as his body protested. An irritating tingling, like pinpricks along his skin, raced along his arm from sleeping on it for too long. He shook vigorously to get the blood flowing again and cracked the kinks out of his neck.

Across from him, the princess was already awake. She sat cross-legged, resting her chin on her clasped hands. She had re-tied her hair into two thick braids down her back, washed her face, and wore a fresh set of clothes. The letter was on the floor in front of her, and he could almost see her mind racing with the changes in her expression, her eyes roving over the symbols.

"You break the code overnight?" Ryker stretched as he spoke. She barely glanced up at him.

"I want to know what these people are up to," she grumbled, "If there are people inside the Empire opposed to them, they could be key to ending the emperor's reign. We could...I... umm..." She snatched up the note and quickly stood, trying to disguise her discomfort.

"You need my help to get in contact with the person who wrote the note." He couldn't suppress his grin when she crossed her arms, disgruntled.

"Let's just go," she said, touching her wrists. The gesture was so subtle he almost missed it. Ryker stared closer at them, where a ring of red and wrinkled skin marked her arm. His heart sank as he realized how she'd acquired such scars. "If we move quickly, we might manage to meet up with my team and get proper treatment and food."

An image of the South King's Road littered with bodies and arrows protruding from throats made Ryker's stomach rebel against the food the princess offered him. The princess didn't notice his discomfort; she turned to pull her pack onto her shoulders, and grabbed a torch off the wall. Artis licked his hand as he scratched behind her ear, offering her this small comfort.

They traveled in silence for some time while Artis bounced between them, rushing ahead before bounding back to release some of her endless energy. The longer they traveled, the deeper the frown on the princess's face, and the greater his nerves got. All around them were endless rocks and winding tunnels. It made sense how her team had been impossible to track.

Their steps echoed softly across the walls. He wondered if Keanon had been in these tunnels; he had never mentioned them to the Empire. The tunnels would offer a huge advantage if the Empire were to ever find out about them, though how they would find their way around, he wasn't sure.

He broke the silence by asking, "How do you think your friends will react when they see me?"

The princess did not immediately answer, and her brows furrowed even more. With a sigh, she finally said, "It's going to be interesting, to say the least. Cliff will be furious with me; you'll know him when you see him. He's the tallest one with sandy brown hair. Harper and Laia will probably try to kill you. They both have blonde hair, but Harper is the shortest out of all of us. Lanzo will be concerned but shouldn't do anything rash. His family are from the north, and he has the dark skin to match his heritage." She gave him a concerned smile. "Archer is a mystery. He looks like a wild man with long dark hair and facial hair, but he's a kind soul. He's a mender and hates to leave anyone hurt or injured. But he is also very protective of us, so I'm not sure how he will react."

"Sounds like fun," he mumbled. Going through the names, Ryker shook his head in disbelief. Only six people took out entire Imperial fleets; the skill and abilities in these six people made his stomach clench again. It was clear the princess had real talent when it came to leading and fighting on her own.

"Why are you out doing the work of spies instead of staying with your father?"

Her smile was strained. "This is where I can help. The people of Galleria are suffering, and the longer this war goes on, the worse it will get. Innocent people have been killed or lost their homes and loved ones. If I can do something to ease any of their burdens, I will do it." Her conviction was moving, and he frowned at her words. They resonated with what that priest had said to him in Tourrenfield. How many more innocent people would die before this was over?

No more was said. They rounded the final corner to where the tunnel opened into a larger cave. In the center, several large, flattened boulders formed a circle, where the roughest, burliest man he'd ever seen—which must be Archer—sat with a young, blonde woman whom he recognized as the one who was captured with the princess. On the right, sleeping pallets were laid out. A lone figure lay across one, sleeping. He had sandy brown hair. Cliff. Two people were missing from the group.

"Freya!"

The blonde woman cried and rushed over along with the burly man. Ryker took a few steps back, but the movement caught their attention. They drew to a halt. The man gripped the hilt of his sword, his eyes flashing between Ryker, Freya, and Artis, who hunched low but didn't bare her teeth. The woman pulled out a dagger but Freya stepped in front of him before she could throw it.

"Wait!"

"What in the gods' glory is he doing here?" The next voice was cold and masculine, coming from Cliff who was pushing himself up from the pallets. He struggled to get to his feet with one arm in a sling. When he did, he loomed over Freya, his deep green eyes narrowed.

Freya didn't back down. She kept her arms out wide to keep anyone from getting to Ryker.

"It's a bit of a long story, but I will explain everything. I can't do that until you all back up." Freya spoke pointedly to the blonde woman, who still had her dagger poised to throw. Reluctantly, she lowered it.

Freya kept her eyes on her friends as she tilted her head to Ryker, silently urging him to sit by the wall. He kept his eyes on the room the whole time as he sat with Artis, who placed her head in his lap.

"Where's Harper and Lanzo?" Freya asked, still standing in front of Ryker as her three friends continued to keep their hands on their weapons.

"Right here!" A new voice shrieked.

A woman entered the cave. Her pale blonde hair fell just past her shoulders, her petite, round face was pinched with rage, and her dark brown eyes immediately narrowed on the princess. The massive broadsword strapped to her back didn't escape his notice, either.

Behind her, a northerner—judging by his dark skin— leaned against the wall and surveyed the cave. He had big shoulders and tiny braids pulled back by a single band down his back. The man, who he knew must be Lanzo, scanned the room until his dark eyes landed on Ryker. Lanzo held his gaze, and though he made no move toward him, Ryker's heart plummeted from the man's stare alone.

"We just got back from looking for you!" Harper said, pointing a finger in Freya's face.

"I'm sorry—"

"Where were you?" Harper cut off Freya's apology, continuing to stand over her. "What happened?"

"I—" Freya tried again but was interrupted.

"I told you I would drag your royal ass back home!"

"Hey!" The princess raised her voice, which held a certain authority he'd never heard her use before. Harper immediately backed off, though anger lingered on her face.

"If you would stop for a moment, I will explain everything."

Harper plopped herself on the ground and crossed her arms. The others did too, and Freya joined them.

"When I went after Harper to deal with the lone soldier, I had..." Freya's voice faltered as she glanced around the room, her eyes finding his for a moment. Ryker titled his head. The princess turned to the northerner as she continued. "You were calling for help, but I felt this powerful pull to check the fallen soldier. I sent Harper back to make sure you would be alright, but I had to go." Her eyes bored into Lanzo for a moment, and he nodded as though she had passed some secret information to him. Freya met Cliff's skeptical gaze.

What pull was she talking about? Lanzo glanced at Ryker, his eyes narrowed and curious as Freya continued about grabbing a cart and dragging him north. Ryker shifted under the northerner's scrutiny and tried to distract himself by focusing on Freya's story. During this part of the journey, he'd been asleep for the whole thing, but little had happened while he slept.

"I was nearly here when we were ambushed by Imperial soldiers." She glanced at the other blonde woman, Laia. "Vaan led the troops that got us."

"What was he doing in Galleria?" Laia asked tersely.

"And why are they up here when their army is down south?" Cliff remarked.

"I wasn't able to find out what they were doing, but it sounded like one of their reasons was to look for him." Freya gestured at Ryker.

When all six heads turned to him, he wanted to disappear into the ground. But by making eye contact with Freya, he found his voice, ignoring the judgmental glares from the others. "No, he wasn't there for me. I was a perk for sure, but I don't believe he knew what I was carrying. He got lucky with that." Up until that moment, Ryker hadn't even considered why Vaan was there.

Freya seemed to tuck away his answer, though everyone else sat rigid, eyeing him with suspicion. He pressed his hands into Artis's fur and held her close as she growled.

"I managed to cut the ropes and on my way out." The princess pulled out the note. "I grabbed this." She held it up for Cliff, who took it curiously. "The contents of that note had Vaan adamant Ryker was a traitor."

"It wouldn't have taken much to convince Vaan of my disloyalty, but the letter in my possession would have been enough to convince everyone else."

Cliff glared at Ryker before skimming the note.

"It's coded."

"Whoever is sharing these notes are inside the Empire but aren't their friends."

Cliff's brows furrowed as he read the letter again. "I can give this to General Rowe so he can send it to Blackstone."

"We should head back to Blackstone," Harper said, seeming to have forgotten her earlier anger.

"I agree," Cliff murmured, tucking the letter in his pocket. "Spies have informed us the Empire is about to march across the south."

At the mention of the impending attack, Ryker's stomach churned. General Moreland's words from weeks ago came back to him then. *We will win this war, Ryker. We've come to possess some new weaponry that could bring about King Alystaire's downfall by the end of the summer.*

"If we can get back at the same time, we could assist from the outside with supplies during the siege."

"Is that what you think is happening?" The words spilled out of Ryker before he could stop them, but if General Moreland's words were true, this was not a siege. Cliff, Harper and Laia glared at him, yet Lanzo studied him cautiously, while Archer watched, seeming almost indifferent.

"Why would the Empire try to assault the most defensible city in all of Eavdamos?"

Ryker ignored Cliff's condescending tone, meeting the princess's intense blue eyes instead as she considered his question. Ryker took the plunge. "After everything that happened with, umm... my brother." He glanced at his hands resting on Artis's head, the air around him seeming to crackle at the mention of Keanon. Ryker took a deep breath. He'd doomed himself to this life; he might as well go all the way. "I was no longer privy to any confidential information, but the general did tell me this. They've acquired something—a weapon of some kind." Everyone's hostile posture shifted. "They believe whatever they have will bring down Galleria before the end of the summer."

No one spoke. Trepidation was palpable throughout the

small cave as they all came to the same conclusion. This was not going to be a siege. It was an all-out assault.

"My father is not a fool. He has prepared for all possibilities, and Faulkner should have arrived to aid us as well." Freya stood, her voice filled with conviction, though her eyes betrayed her concern. "The Empire hasn't been sneaky in their approach, but I agree we should go back. Whatever the Empire thinks they have, we need to be there to help."

"We'll need to travel fast." Cliff raked a hand through his hair, face grim. "If the army is on the move, they should reach Blackstone in a week."

CHAPTER 32
VIVIAN

Vivian swallowed hard, trying to keep down the meager portion of food she'd eaten that morning. Talon crested the hill behind General Flynn, and the city of Lividia came into view. The city's stone walls rose tall against the snow-coated valley; buildings peeked over the top, smoke rising from their chimneys. On either side of the gates was a white Imperial flag depicting a bright red sun setting between two mountains. It flew in the wind.

Heart pounding and palms slick despite the cold, Vivian guided Talon to follow the soldiers inside. A stern-looking woman met them inside the gates, flanked by two soldiers. White flecks speckled her long brown hair; she studied them with narrowed dark eyes, scanning each person entering the gates until landing on Vivian and her mother.

"Greetings, Queen Renea. Princess Vivian." The older woman bowed low, and the soldiers behind her followed suit.

Her mother nodded respectfully. "General Quistis."

The serious looking woman nodded again and then indicated for them to follow. "Emperor Asher is waiting for you."

293

General Quistis led the way along, flanked by two shadows. Vivian's mother took the lead, directing Vivian and General Flynn to either side of her. High Priestess Sasha rode in her cart behind them, and their remaining soldiers surrounded the cart in a tight circle.

The city was reminiscent of Calliva, with tall buildings, winding cobbled streets, and a multitude of businesses on each road. Vivian's heart grew increasingly unsettled as they meandered toward the back of the city, where a tall spire temple stood above the rest of the buildings. Many Imperial soldiers made their way throughout the city, but where were the residents of Lividia? Vivian frowned, scanning the back roads, shops, and alleys, but couldn't make out any normal citizens among the troops. Unnerved, she gripped Talon's mane tighter. Something about the sea of gray uniforms marching along the streets set her on edge.

Finally, they were led into the temple courtyard, where her mother gave the command to dismount. General Flynn had their soldiers surround them as he went to assist Priestess Sasha from her cart, who came to stand beside Vivian, placing a hand on her arm with a reassuring squeeze. General Quistis watched them with narrowed eyes until her mother stepped forward, and the general opened the doors for them to enter.

The temple's stone walls rose tall toward a peaked roof with wooden spandrels, spanning the width of the temple. A large, brass candelabra hung from every other spandrel on a thick iron chain. Like the temple in Calliva, on the far wall above the altar, there was a polished, stained-glass window depicting the three gods. Standing before it was an imposing man.

He was regal in every sense of the word, dressed in rich purple robes accented with silver trim and a silver crown fully encrusted with multicolored gemstones. He had thick dark hair and a full beard peppered with gray. His amber eyes found Vivian's and followed her closely as they approached. The emperor's unwavering gaze made her stomach churn, but she kept her head high like her mother. While she had known he was close to her father's age, it appeared he could be a couple of years older. He could easily be thirty years older than Vivian, and the realization made her stomach churn.

When they finally stopped at the edge of the altar, the emperor turned his piercing gaze to her mother. Queen Renea gave a respectful bow reserved for visiting royalty in their lands. Vivian was quick to follow. Emperor Asher offered a slight nod to both in return.

"Welcome to Lividia, Queen Renea and Princess Vivian." The much older man—a priest, judging by his robes—stepped up beside the emperor. "It is an honor to have you with us, even in these troubled times."

"Likewise, it is an honor to be here. We are grateful for the opportunity to further discuss recent events." Though responding to the High Priest, Vivian's mother kept her eyes firmly on the emperor.

"If you would follow us." The High Priest waved his hand to a door on his right. "We have a meeting room prepared. I'm sure you are weary from your travels, but there is little time to rest with the snow coming down."

Her mother nodded, and they followed the two into a side room. It was a rather small room, filled mostly by a long table in the center and a small hearth on one wall that provided much needed warmth. They all sat, with Vivian positioned between her mother and Priestess Sasha. Their presence offered Vivian enough comfort to ease some of the tension in her body, though the emperor's intense gaze had her clamping her hands tightly in her lap.

Emperor Asher sat at the head of the table and spoke for the first time, his voice low and firm. "I want to get straight to the problem at hand. I know you worry about this prophecy and the war it has caused, and your concerns are valid and understandable. No one wants to take their people to war."

"Then why did you go straight to declaring war on Galleria?" Vivian startled herself as the words burst out of her. Heat worked its way up to her face, and she clasped her hands tighter. Both her mother and Priestess Sasha gave her a sideways glance, though there was a subtle upturn to her mother's lips.

Emperor Asher didn't seem offended by the question and gave her a sad smile. "When the priests first told me of the new prophecy they were receiving, I feared how the other kingdoms would respond. Such drastic changes and shifts in power would be met with repercussions. King Alystaire and King Therrowin proved my fears correct." As he spoke, he never took his eyes off Vivian's, as if he tried to pin her to the seat with his gaze. "King Alystaire had made his decision as soon as he sent me his refusal. Nothing I could have said or done would have swayed him, and going in person would have accomplished nothing. I was left with a choice to make. The gods had given me a great responsibility, and this was the first obstacle standing in my way. Would I bend the prophecy to keep the peace and avoid hardships? Or would I push forward with everything I had to ensure their will comes to pass?"

"It is a difficult balance to fulfill such a big responsibility and keep everyone happy," Priestess Sasha said, breaking the emperor's attention away from Vivian. She felt relieved to escape those piercing amber eyes.

"Yes, it is a heavy burden to be given such a position. It is why I have come to you to seek a wife." He addressed Queen Renea now. While Vivian was relieved not to have the emperor's eyes on her, it made her uncomfortable to be spoken about as if she wasn't there, especially while discussing her future. Prince Damian had sought Vivian out personally before going to meet her parents. She supposed that was abnormal. When he'd shown up, he caught her completely off guard.

The emperor continued, unaware of Vivian's discontent. "I wish to have an Empress by my side to rule together, and I assure you the gods' favor will shine on us all with this union. The Leander family will thrive, and all Eavdamos will prosper as one grand Empire."

His conviction was moving. He seemed genuine in his desire to achieve the best for all the people of Eavdamos, which Vivian could respect. After all, this was what she wanted, to ensure her family and the people of her kingdom were cared for, yet she couldn't shake the discomfort continuing to make her stomach churn. Was her nervousness simply because of his age? She couldn't allow herself to be so shallow and selfish.

"We are honored that you have selected our daughter to offer this esteemed proposal." Her mother straightened, her whole demeanor demanding attention and respect from everyone in the room. "I wish to discuss some of these matters with you personally if I may. High Priest Baralai, if you would be so kind as to give High Priestess Sasha some of your time as well."

Emperor Asher's expression was hard to read, but he gave Queen Renea a nod. She turned to Vivian. "Why don't you go rest for a bit?"

Vivian frowned. This was what she wanted, right? If her mother could ask questions to gain more insight, she would be able to better discuss with Vivian's father what they were meant to do. Sasha had reminded Vivian that the priests and her parents would make the final decision, but if Vivian was supposed to give her own input, it would help her to be privy to these discussions.

Without argument and with as much grace as she could muster, Vivian stood and walked out the side door back into the sanctuary, the emperor's eyes watching her every move. Two of General Flynn's soldiers followed her like shadows while the rest stayed in the room to watch over her mother and their High Priestess.

Vivian sat on a small bench in front of the pillar by the altar, staring up at the stained glass. It was an outline of what was once the Kingdom of Kovdoran, with the three gods blessing the land. It was a different yet familiar image, like the one in the palace temple in Calliva depicting her ancestors being crowned rulers of Brantyre.

Vivian's eyes threatened to pool with tears, plagued by her sister's questions and worries. Why would the gods choose and prepare Aida to rule only to take away the kingdom before she was given the chance? But how could this prophecy be false, like Galleria claimed? The implication of such a lie was too great. She dropped her head in her hands, her heart and mind warring.

"Mind if I sit?"

She bolted up at the sudden intrusion, and Emperor Asher chuckled lightly. "I apologize for startling you."

The glittering light through the stained-glass window had intensified since she first sat. So lost in her own thoughts, she had lost all sense of time as the sun now shone directly through the window. Her mother was nowhere in sight. Vivian assumed she must still be in the side room, possibly talking with the High Priest.

The emperor stood with the stained glass behind him. Sunlight streamed through, casting him in an array of colorful lights that sparkled when striking the gems in his crown. His amber eyes studied her with mild humor as Vivian regained her composure. She fought the desire to break eye contact as the intensity of his stare set her nerves on edge. Her heart rattled in her chest, and she clenched her hands so tightly in her lap they began to throb.

The emperor raised a brow, and she jolted when she realized she had not answered. "Oh, of course, you can sit." She inwardly cringed at her rushed words, louder than she'd intended. Either the emperor didn't notice or was kind enough to ignore it as he sat beside her on the bench.

"Do you have any more burning questions you wish to ask me?" he asked softly.

She was troubled by many questions and worries, but which ones could she ask? He hadn't seemed offended by her blunt question before, so not wishing to waste precious time, she asked the questions that bothered her most. "Why would the gods change the foundations *they* placed in Eavdamos for centuries?"

The emperor didn't immediately answer. His brows pinched as he gazed at each of the gods' altars. "I would be lying if I told you why the gods are doing this. We aren't always given the knowledge behind the gods' plans. All I can say is they have never led us astray yet, so I must believe they have only good things planned for us."

Vivian sighed but knew she shouldn't have expected another answer. How could he possibly know when the priesthood couldn't figure it out? Still, she pushed again, desperate to gain some sort of clarity. "What's wrong with my sister that the gods would take away her kingdom?" She threw Aida's question to her from days ago, and he offered a sympathetic smile.

"There's nothing wrong with your sister. If there was, she would not have been selected as your parents' heir. Maybe there is an upcoming ruler the gods are trying to avoid, or maybe they just wanted to unite all the lands into one. I will need your sister—as well as the other heirs from all the families—to help bring us all together and lead all the lands of Eavdamos. Galleria and Faulkern have made this harder, but I knew it would have challenges. We will overcome them and move forward with trust in the gods and hope for a united future."

LATER THAT NIGHT, Vivian tossed and turned on her rickety bed, her thoughts racing with the emperor's words. It all made sense. He made many compelling points, but it hurt to even consider siding against Prince Damian and, ultimately, sentencing him to death. The prince's nearness had begun to make her feel all warm and fluttery and secure, even in the short time they'd spent together. He was someone she could see herself living with for the rest of her life. While the emperor had been kind, his gaze unnerved her, and his age...

What about Aida? She was so sure about her role as queen. Aida's vehement disdain of the emperor's plans to make her governess was something Vivian couldn't ignore. How could Vivian live with herself if she forced that upon her sister? But the emperor had been understanding about that, too, and his reasons were valid.

After several more turns and squeezing her eyes shut to no avail, Vivian couldn't take it anymore. She tossed her blankets off. Prickles raced along her body as the cold night air seeped through a small slit in the tent's flaps. Her thick nightgown did little to keep it at bay, but her chest tightened. She needed to get out.

Desperate for fresh air, Vivian quickly pulled on her stockings and boots, then rushed to grab her heavy cloak off the rack. Careful not to let in too much moonlight or wake her sleeping mother, Vivian slid through the flap. Her breath puffed up in billows of fog as she picked her way through the camp toward Talon.

"It shouldn't be long."

Vivian jolted from the deep voice and ducked behind the nearest tent. She didn't know why she hid, but she held her breath and peeked around the corner. General Flynn walked with one of his soldiers. They must be switching with the current watch, but her heart wouldn't settle.

"Are you sure, Sir?" The young soldier's voice shook slightly.

General Flynn placed a hand on the young man's shoulder. "Don't worry; everything will be alright."

Vivian waited in the shadow of the tent as they continued past her toward the edge of camp. Neither of them noticed her in the dark, and she relaxed when they disappeared. The young soldier must be anxious about everything going on too. Crossing her arms against the cold, Vivian felt frustrated they still couldn't come to a decision for their people.

She went in the opposite direction the general had taken, where Talon and the rest of the mounts slept. When she drew closer, his big yellow eyes opened, and he lifted his head to greet her, emitting a contented purr as she scratched under his chin. He leaned his head into her hand.

"Why does this have to be so hard?"

With a heavy sigh, she forced herself to consider her options again.

"Help me, Ductu."

Leaning her forehead against Talon's thick fur, she thought of the emperor, who had alleviated and validated her concerns. But panic rose again as she envisioned his face and those amber eyes—and the responsibilities of becoming empress. Chills raked down her spine, though not from the cold. Squeezing her eyes shut and taking in slow breaths, Vivian managed to calm herself.

When she pictured the prince and how he hurt for his people, his bright blue eyes, and the way his copper hair fell across his forehead, it was almost thrilling to picture herself by his side as queen. The pressure and fears were still present, but how his hand held hers when they danced filled her with comfort and warmth. It did even now, with him miles away.

"Is this you, Wise One? Priestess Sasha said to listen to my feelings. Am I meant to side with Galleria? With Prince Damian?" Calm and peace washed over her heart for the first time since receiving his proposal. It was so relieving; tears trailed down her face.

A branch snapped somewhere in the trees, and Vivian's heart leaped into her throat. She spun, scanning the trees. Talon gave a low rumble, and Vivian pressed a hand to his head to keep him quiet. The moonlight reflected off the bright white snow, illuminating the woods while creating patches of dark shadows from the branches overhead. Another snap and Vivian ducked low, peeking over Talon's back. In the trees, a slight movement caught her eye, and she squinted through her leophinx's dark hairs. There was nothing. She slunk forward. No one came to view, and there were no signs in the fresh snow. Vivian almost turned back, convinced she'd imagined things, until a swaying branch caught her attention. After how powerfully she felt the gods had responded to her, Vivian knew she needed to trust her intuition. Her heart raced as she scanned the woods for any movement. Nothing appeared. Frowning, Vivian studied the ground. There were still bootprints leading in and out of camp from the soldiers that had yet to be covered with snow.

She should turn back. There was nothing she could note that was out of the ordinary, not that she was very knowledgeable in studying tracks. Before she could ponder what to do further, a shout rang out from the camp behind her. The shout was followed by more, and the whole camp turned to chaos.

Vivian rushed back. "What's happened?" she called over the noise when she neared the closest soldier.

His eyes were wide when they settled on her, and recognition made him quick to answer. "It's the queen, Princess. Someone has attacked the queen."

CHAPTER 33
FREYA

Over the next few days, Freya's team hastened for Blackstone. Under her careful eye, none of her friends attacked Ryker, while Artis quickly made friends with her whole team. She bounded happily between Harper and Laia for scratches, and Lanzo was caught sneaking her scraps of food several times when he cooked. Artis still showed her loyalty in the evening by snuggling up to Ryker.

Ryker was not finding the same ease with her team as Artis. She understood their distrust, though, and was proud of them for how well they held back from saying or doing anything cruel. He was allowed to eat with everyone, but he still chose to sit slightly apart from her friends, who tried their best to act normal. The tense atmosphere was outside their control, but their tolerance was all Freya could ask of them, especially since she hadn't fully come to terms with Ryker's presence herself.

One person she had known would be the first to warm to Ryker was Archer. They tried not to take many breaks as they traveled, but whenever they did, Archer would sit and talk with Ryker until it was time to go again. Artis would lay her large head in the burly man's lap while the two discussed weapons, medicine, maps, and geography. Freya would occasionally join them as well, and found herself admitting Ryker wasn't the worst person to converse with.

As they drew closer to Blackstone, a pit formed and grew in Freya's stomach. Every night, she took an extra drop of Archer's sleeping draft because the building dread would keep her awake. While she was anxious about what was coming and the Empire's new weapon, this nervous energy was something different. Something deep in her heart wouldn't let her relax and made her question every step she took.

On the final night of their travels, Freya sat with her legs crossed before the dying embers of Lanzo's fire. The rest of her team were asleep, but the mounting anxiety wouldn't allow Freya to rest. She'd already upped her dose to three drops, which dragged her body into exhaustion without enabling her mind to shut off the worry and fear. She contemplated the repercussions of taking a fourth drop when a soft voice interrupted her.

"Can't sleep?"

She jumped, heart leaping into her throat. Her insides were already weary and jittery, so Cliff appearing behind her sent her mind into a panic. Freya took a deep breath and closed her drooping eyes, trying to calm herself.

"Sorry." He gave her a gentle smile as he sat beside her.

She shook away his apology. "I can't shake this unnerving feeling. I'm already worried about this battle and what the Empire has planned, but this is different. It's driving me mad; it's like I know something big will happen tomorrow—more than just the impending battle."

Cliff rubbed a hand on the back of his neck. "Yeah, I've been feeling it, too... I'm worried about everyone." His eyes brimmed with concern as he took in the dark space where their friends slept. The silence lingered for several moments before he added, "I'm worried about you, too."

Freya's heart constricted as his eyes bored into hers. She didn't know how to respond, and he sighed as she kept quiet, combing his fingers through his hair. "A lot has happened recently, for you most of all." Cliff took her hand in his and squeezed. "Not everyone is worth saving."

She lowered her eyes to where their hands were joined. The sleeve of her tunic had rolled up, revealing the scars—forever a reminder of her loss. "Keanon would have disagreed."

"Please…" He shifted to face her. "Be more careful. There are too many people who love you for you to be reckless with your life."

Tears stung the corners of her eyes. She fought to keep them from falling and swallowed the lump in her throat. She felt like it was a lie the moment the words left her lips. "I'll be more careful."

Cliff smiled, though it didn't reach his eyes, and gave her hand a final squeeze before releasing it. "Try to get some sleep. We have some rough days ahead of us."

Sleep evaded her for most of the night, and Freya now moved forward on pure adrenaline and fear. Though her friends said nothing, she noticed their worried glances. The silence among the group was potent as they finally made the last turn. To the untrained eye, they hit a dead end, but a soft click followed when Freya pulled gently on the sconce on the wall. The men rushed to pull open the stone wall.

"Keep Artis reigned in," Laia called back, glancing at Ryker, who placed a hand on his lykos, commanding her to heel.

When the stone door stopped scraping across the ground,

pounding metal and frantic shouts greeted them on the other side. They filed through the door in a line, entering a tight storage space. Shelves lined either side of them, stacked with tools and stone working materials.

When Freya threw wide the storage door, she was greeted by a hammer slamming onto a blazing hot sword. The smithy they entered had tall ceilings and open space for the massive hearths on either side, with multiple weapons racks and workbenches housing smithing tools. She smiled at the blacksmith in greeting, who eyed them as they entered. Master Blacksmith Rémman was a barrel of a man, as big as Archer, with similar dark curly hair and a full beard; he was also Laia's uncle and guardian. His dark eyes were grim. "You're just in time, Your Highness. We need your help."

A ground-shattering boom accentuated his words, and her eyes widened. "What was that?"

"Empire's trying to take my damn city, that's what," he growled, slamming the hammer onto the sword as though it was an Imperial soldier.

"How are they getting past the walls?" A sinking sensation pulled her heart down to her toes as Ryker's warning hit her again.

Rémman shook his head. "Gods know how they did it. They got their hands on a large amount of blackstone boulders." The next swing of his hammer was followed by another boom that made Freya's teeth rattle.

The moment the ground stopped shaking beneath her, Freya darted for the side door to the ramparts. Her friends called after her, but their voices were distant from the pounding still ringing in her ears. When footfalls clipped on the stairs behind, she knew they followed.

Bursting through the door, chaos exploded. Soldiers lined up along the walls, ducking low for cover while they loaded arrows before launching them into the field below. The vast Imperial army marched in the valley at the base of the Blackstone Mountains. Thousands of soldiers filled the field. It was a sea of silver-plated armor glinting in the sunlight. Bowmen near the front shot up at the walls toward the Gallerion archers. On the bridge, the Imperial soldiers smashed a battering ram into the gates, using shields to stave off the arrows the Gallerions rained down from above.

Fear she'd only felt when Keanon had been arrested filled Freya's heart. There were only six catapults, but beside each one were carts full of large dark boulders. The soldiers loaded one of the catapults and launched a boulder into the wall.

Freya grabbed the wall as the ground shook so hard her knees buckled. Behind Freya, her team cried out as they grabbed onto whatever they could. Laia was at the top of the stairs, and the quake knocked her back before she could grab onto anything.

"I got you!" Ryker lunged, grabbing her before she fell.

When it was stable, everyone stood. Laia gave Ryker a subtle nod of gratitude as she stepped away while Freya peered over the edge at the horrifying sight below. It was difficult to make out with the dark black wall, but cracks had formed along the surface. One was so bad a small hole poked through to the city.

It couldn't be possible. It *shouldn't* be possible. Blackstone's mines were the sole source of blackstone in all Eavdamos.

Horns blasted over the shouts of battle, pulling Freya's gaze away from the horror. On the other side of the valley, the gold flags of Faulkern and the ocean blue of Galleria waved in the breeze, held by soldiers on horses. Two massive armies crested the hill and charged at the second blast into the valley below. The army was at least a thousand more than the Imperial army.

King Therrowin and Freya's father rode at the head of the charge.

"They won't make it," Lanzo said, appearing beside Freya. His expression was grim as he gauged the distance between her father's army and the catapults.

The wall was taking too much damage. There was no way the army could fight their way to the catapults before they plowed through the walls. There weren't enough soldiers inside the city to fight once the Empire broke through. They would be overwhelmed.

They would lose Blackstone.

"Princess!"

She spun at the commanding voice of General Vance, who raced down the rampart toward her. Even as a boulder crashed into the wall and Freya grabbed hold for support, the general kept moving, her gait unwavering. "I need you and your team to round up all unnecessary troops and any remaining civilians and get them out of here!"

"What about taking out the catapults?" Freya protested. "If we can destroy them before they break through the walls, we can save the city."

General Vance shook her head before Freya finished speaking. "We are about to lose the gates. Our soldiers are doing everything they can to keep it from falling until the king's army can fight their way through, but we must prepare for the possibility this city is lost. I don't want to risk any unnecessary casualties or innocent lives." Cracking stone from the gates beneath them accentuated General Vance's words, and the older woman placed a hand on Freya's shoulder, her expression firm. "We need to focus on saving lives right now."

Freya's jaw clenched, suppressing the overwhelming desire to argue. Already, her father's army was making strides through the Empire's, but the Imperial soldiers doubled their efforts with the catapults to burst through the gates faster. Three more boulders rocked the walls, and she gripped the side for support, her heart and mind warring with each other. General Vance was right, and Freya hated her for it. She couldn't be careless this time.

"What about you?" Harper asked her mother, stepping up beside Freya.

General Vance stood tall. "I will stay here with General Luarent and our soldiers until the walls fall."

Freya clamped her jaw shut as Harper tensed, her expression hardening at the softening in General Vance's face. Harper's dark eyes watered, but she said nothing.

Taking in all the faces of the archers on the walls and the soldiers rushing to hold the gates below, Freya's whole being hurt with the decision to leave them. But there were people in the city who still needed to get out, and the longer she waited, the more she put their lives at risk. With a pain that tore her heart into pieces, Freya gave General Vance one final nod and turned to go. Harper didn't move immediately; her eyes held her mother's for a heartbeat longer before she rushed back down the stairs to the blacksmiths.

At the bottom of the stairs, Freya took control. "Cliff, take Lanzo, Harper, and a couple soldiers through the city to find as many civilians as you can and get them out of here! Go out the back towards Verna, then take the coastline up to Seaymarr. I'll take Laia, Archer, and Ryker. We'll focus on the blacksmith's guild and injured soldiers." Everyone nodded, and Cliff led Lanzo and Harper out of the blacksmiths into the city.

Archer went to the mender's ward in the barracks to collect soldiers, while Freya took Ryker and Laia back into the smithy where Rémman worked. "General Vance has ordered all unnecessary people to evacuate the city."

"You expect us to leave all these precious blackstone

weapons and armor behind?" Master Rémman crossed his monstrous arms with a frown. "There's a reason we all stayed when they evacuated people the first time."

"Don't you dare argue your way out of this!" Laia pushed past Freya and stomped over until she stood right in front of him. While he was much bigger and taller than her, Laia was unfazed. "We are leaving, and you are coming with us."

His expression softened as it always did with Laia. He glanced back at the remaining smiths as another boom shook dust from the ceiling, cascading over their heads like rain. Sighing, he said, "Grab as much as you can carry without slowing us down and follow the Princess."

Freya joined the blacksmiths, grabbing three quivers of blackstone-tipped arrows and a pair of daggers, while Laia grabbed as many throwing knives as she could. Ryker hesitated, waiting by the door with Artis behind him. Freya grabbed a polished blackstone sword from the weapons rack and handed it to him just as Archer arrived with soldiers.

"We have an injured soldier who may have difficulty keeping up." He indicated the woman whose leg appeared crushed.

"Artis can carry her." Ryker offered before Freya said anything. Artis sprang forward, laying down so Archer could lift the woman onto her back. "She will only be able to carry up to three people before the weight will be too much. Only those who cannot walk can ride." Another soldier was lifted onto Artis's back.

When everyone was loaded with weapons, Freya led everyone back through the storage closet in a single line. Under one of the shelves in the back was the lever to release the door, and several soldiers gasped behind her when it opened. There would be time to explain and have everyone swear to secrecy.

Dirt and pebbles trickled onto their heads from the ceiling

as the ground shook from another boulder smashing into the walls above. Guilt hit Freya again for leaving so many people behind. She prayed Cliff had already made it out with the civilians.

"Watch out!"

Ryker yanked her arm back as the rocks above her head crashed to the ground. They fell back, and dust swirled around them, making her blink back the grit from her eyes. She shared a fearful glance with Ryker; coughing and spluttering, she called into the dirt cloud. "Is everyone alright?" The group gave her a chorus of affirmatives as Ryker helped Freya to her feet.

Her heart plummeted when the debris settled enough to reveal the sky peeking through the rocks above. Figures were shrouded in shadows from the sun glowing behind them as they descended the loose rocks into the tunnels. The pounding of her heart in her ears was so loud it drowned out the sounds of battle. Icy chills raced down her spine at the first glimpse of gray. Imperial soldiers had breached the tunnels.

"Laia, take the blacksmiths and Artis with all the injured to meet up with Cliff!" She launched an arrow into the first soldier, who hit the stone floor of the tunnel, but quickly switched to her sword as they descended with speed. Heart heavy, she made her next command, "Tell him to seal off all passages as you go! We'll hold them off until my father gets here!"

Laia hesitated a moment before tossing a knife into the throat of one of the soldiers; the soldier collapsed, rolling down the rock pile. Glancing at her uncle, Laia nodded and ran back down the tunnel with Artis on her heel. All able-bodied Galle-rion soldiers rallied around Freya as they created a barrier for the others to escape. Ryker and Archer drew their swords, but all fighting stalled as a familiar voice filled the tunnel.

Beside her, Ryker stiffened as an older man's face came into view. He stood on the rocks, staring down at them. His black uniform revealed he was a general, though his dark eyes were eerily familiar. Freya had fought with him the day she lost Keanon; he was the one who sentenced Keanon to death. His piercing gaze went straight past her and bore into the former Imperial captain beside her.

"Ryker?"

Freya didn't get to hear what they said next as more soldiers flooded the underground, and she was drawn into a fight. Working with her troops, she fought to keep the Imperial soldiers back, plunging her sword into a soldier who went after Archer and spinning before another came up behind her. The hole in the ceiling forced them to funnel through, but the sheer numbers flooding in were fast and overwhelming for their small troops.

Archer kept pace beside her while Ryker was locked in a fight with Vaan at the base of the rocky slope. Three soldiers dove toward her, forcing her to lose sight of him. Freya blocked a blow aimed at decapitating her while Archer took out one of the soldiers coming at her from the side. Blocking two more blows, she was able to push another soldier back, stabbing them through the exposed space in the armpit. He howled in pain, and she took the opportunity to go after the second one, slicing along the side of his leg. Archer finished the first soldier for her while Freya took out the second.

On the surface above, her father's war horns blasted. They were close, yet the realization spurred the Imperial soldiers to press forward. Sweat made the hilt of Freya's blade slick in her hands, and Gallerion soldiers dropped beside her. Despite how hard they pushed, they were losing ground. A distant blast shook the caves. Everyone wobbled on their feet, and more rocks from the ceiling collapsed onto soldiers.

"Get back!" She warned as more of the roof fell. They

jumped back just in time. Laia's crew must have blown the blacksmith's entrance to the city. Only one was left, and soon, the Empire couldn't use them to get in or out. However, that meant Freya and all the soldiers with her were stuck, with few options to retreat.

None of her soldiers had been crushed, but several Imperial soldiers were less lucky. Archer struggled to his feet beside her. Her heart sped when she caught sight of Ryker, his foot caught inside the pile of rocks. He fought to pull it loose, but the general was on top of him, hacking and slashing, keeping him pinned. Ryker could only block the blows, trying to shake his foot free with little success.

All the emotions Keanon had poured into Freya to intervene and keep from exacting revenge on Ryker struck her then. Whether it was his constant interference or divine intervention, she knew the impact Keanon could have had now rested on Ryker's shoulders. Freya saw an image of her brother with a crown on his head and a former Imperial captain standing at his side, pride and confidence in his eyes. Freya's friends and family were in this image, but she was not among them.

Wait!

Keanon's cry was so real in her mind that she could almost see him standing between her and Ryker. *You've been pushing me to keep him around, and now I know why.*

Stop! This isn't what I wanted!

Her grin wobbled as she sprinted forward.

I'll see you soon, Keanon.

CHAPTER 34

RYKER

"Ryker?"

Heart lodged in his throat, Ryker's body froze as he stared at the man who'd been his mentor and confidant through his deepest losses—the man who had loved him, advised him, demoted him, and sentenced his brother to death now stood before him, his dark eyes wide with surprise. Ryker's hands shook, nearly knocking the sword from his grasp as those familiar eyes turned from shock to disappointment and then rage.

"So, it's true?" General Moreland's question dripped with sad acceptance, like a sucker punch to Ryker's gut.

"Don't take it too personally, General."

The grating voice made Ryker cringe as Vaan appeared beside General Moreland. With a sneer, Vaan continued. "The apple never falls far from the tree. He was destined from birth to be a conniving, treacherous bastard."

Ryker clenched his sword tight, the blood rushing to his face. Vaan wasn't done.

"I suppose we should thank you for losing the princess all

those weeks ago. Her escape led us to the discovery of these tunnels. So, I guess you are good for something."

"Shut up, Vaan!" General Moreland snapped, but Ryker was done allowing Vaan to insult his family.

Ryker charged. A steady flow of Imperial soldiers held him back at first, but he slowly gained ground toward Vaan, who waited at the base of the rocky slope. Vaan drew his blade with a casual flair and grinned when Ryker's sword finally connected with his. Back and forth, they clashed, each vying for the upper hand. Vaan attacked with a swiftness and precision he'd only seen in one other sparring partner. Ryker smiled as he moved into a familiar dance, one he'd only had with a certain young, dark-haired Captain Bennett.

"You're going to die a traitor, Kessler." Vaan tried to taunt him, but Ryker ignored it, focusing on Vaan's string of powerful blows. Everything this man had said and done filtered through his mind, followed by everything that had led him to where he was now. Ryker had been pushed out and ostracized for the actions of others while everyone he'd ever cared about was stripped away from him.

He went on the offensive, pushing Vaan back with each swing. Channeling his rage, he changed the rhythm, watching when Vaan's face shifted from leisure to genuine worry.

Shouts of the surrounding battle encircled them as more Imperial soldiers flooded through the opening. Ryker knew the small troops Freya had brought with her would not be enough to hold them for long. Squaring his jaw, Ryker locked blades with Vaan and shoved with all his might. Vaan stumbled back a few steps, and as he reeled, Ryker lunged. Vaan met Ryker swing for swing, but he was off balance now. Ryker charged forward, smiling as Vaan tried to sidestep, just as Ryker predicted. Pulling up short, Ryker butted him in the face with his shoulder. Vaan teetered a moment, his eyes watering from the blow. Ryker knocked Vaan's sword from his hands as he fell to his knees; the weapon skittered across the cave.

"Wait." Vaan breathed, his plea barely audible as Ryker brought his sword to his chest. Finally, Vaan's eyes widened with fear.

"Go to Hell."

Ryker plunged, and Vaan gasped. Blood filled Vaan's mouth, and he choked, falling to the ground. Vaan's eyes locked with Ryker's, a last remnant of hate, pain, and fear lurking in their depths. Then, they dulled. Vaan's head tipped back, landing with a soft thud on the ground, his eyes staring lifelessly at the cave ceiling. A shockwave of emotion hit Ryker suddenly, and he staggered.

He'd killed an Imperial soldier.

A familiar voice shouted, pulling Ryker's attention toward the hole in the ceiling. General Moreland stood at the top, calling out orders to the soldiers still pouring into the tunnels. Through the distance, their eyes met, and Ryker's heart dropped from the fury in the general's gaze.

He lost sight of the general when a boom shook the ground. More rocks caved in from above, and Ryker clambered away as they plummeted toward him. Pain lanced up his leg when a boulder crashed onto his ankle. He bit down a scream and collapsed to one knee, trying to pry his leg free. The rock shifted on the uneven slope and pressed harder onto his foot. Hissing as a sharp piece of rock dug deep, Ryker switched to trying to lift the rock.

Pebbles cascading past him pulled his eyes up in time to grab for his sword. He raised it to meet General Moreland's blade.

"I expected better from you, Ryker." The words pierced him worse than the boulder crushing his ankle.

"I didn't—" Ryker tried, but his words were cut off as he blocked another stream of blows.

"I truly believed you could have been someone."

Ryker's arms shook from the power of General Moreland's attacks and the awkward angles he was forced to block with his leg still caught. The pain continued to grow up his leg each time he twisted to meet another swing, and nothing he did could dislodge his ankle. His sword felt heavier in his grasp, his hands slick with sweat. General Moreland's next swing almost knocked it from his grasp. Ryker tried to pull his leg free again, but General Moreland wouldn't relent. He brought his sword down onto Ryker's, whose legs gave out as he crumpled to the ground, his sword flying from his shaking, weary hands.

"This is not what I wanted for you, but you've given me no other choice."

Ryker couldn't reach for his sword as General Moreland advanced. He tried to pry his leg out, but his arms were weak, and he couldn't get away fast enough.

A flash of bright red hair blocked his view, and a clash of swords ricocheted off the stones. Freya shoved General Moreland, and he tumbled back a few paces, his face flushed with rage as he flew at her. The uneven rocks made each of their steps difficult as they tried to advance on each other.

"Free yourself!" Freya commanded, and Ryker put all his effort into shifting the boulder. It budged slightly, pinching his leg. He grit his teeth against the pain, his slick hands sliding along the rock's surface. He pressed harder against it, ignoring how the sharp edges bit into his hands.

Finally, there was a small space—just enough for him to pull his leg out. Ryker collapsed, crawling out of the way as the rock slid down the slope to the bottom of the pile. A horn blasted over the sounds of fighting. The Empire's horn to retreat.

General Moreland's cry of pain pulled Ryker's attention back. His heart stalled. Freya was on the ground, her sword gone; a gash in her shoulder soaked her tunic in blood. She'd plunged a dagger into General Moreland's calf, who pressed his foot down onto her stomach. Freya gasped and reached for another dagger at her hip as the general lowered his sword.

Ryker scrambled forward, pain flaring up his leg when he stood. Still, he pushed toward them. Freya managed to grab her second dagger and blocked the general's swipe. General Moreland lifted his foot from her stomach and kicked her hand, sending the dagger flying. He forced her back with his foot before she could crawl away.

"Stop!" Ryker called, hoping to regain the general's attention. It worked. General Moreland's dark eyes landed on Ryker, his stare filled with a powerful rage Ryker had never seen.

The horns blared again, and the Imperial soldiers turned, rushing out of the tunnels. General Moreland shook his head. With a final scalding look, he said, "Remember this moment, Ryker."

"No!" Ryker screamed as the general plunged his sword into Freya's stomach.

The world lost its sharp lines and structure. Blurred figures streaked past him. Shouts rang out somewhere in the distance. The general disappeared back out the tunnel as Ryker tumbled across the shifting stones to where Freya lay. Blood dripped down the rocks and pooled beneath her body, staining her mouth and cheeks red as her glassy eyes met his. Her breathless gasps made her stomach jerk, more blood gushing from the wound.

Ryker pressed his hands into the injury, blood soaking his hands and clothes in seconds. She gurgled as her mouth filled. Carefully, he removed one hand from her injury to gently turn her head, so the blood could pour out. He pressed back down hard but it refused to slow, and the puddle beneath them grew.

"No, no, no, no." Over and over, the word fell from his lips. Freya turned her head back, her eyes meeting his again. Tear streaks trailed beside the blood on her cheeks.

"Ryker?" Freya's voice was soft and hoarse. She coughed up more blood, and he shook his head.

"Stop speaking." Tears burned his eyes, making her face blur. Archer knelt on the other side, resting a soft hand on Freya's cheek. "Do something!" Ryker snapped at him.

"Here." With trembling fingers, Archer handed Ryker some bandages, and he used them to press down on the wound. The white cloth turned red the moment it touched the injury. Archer used a cloth, gently wiping the blood from her face as tears fell from his eyes.

"I'm sorry. I'm so sorry," Ryker whispered as Archer continued to hand him more bandages. Ryker was sorry for everything—for everything he'd done to Keanon, for the pain he'd caused Freya, for his miserable excuse of a life.

With another pain-filled gasp, Freya choked out, "I—I forgive—you—Ryker."

Sobs shook his shoulders as her words settled over him. Sunlight poked through the hole in the ceiling and glittered against her tear-filled eyes until her tears stopped flowing. Her haggard breathing stopped.

Ryker's mouth parted in a soundless cry. He lifted her head into his hands as sobs shook his shoulders. Fat tears fell from his eyes, and he couldn't breathe past the agony in his chest.

A flood of activity filled the tunnel again, but the soldiers that rushed inside had the emblem of Galleria on their chests. He hardly paid them any mind, not until one of them yanked him to his feet. Struggling against their hold, he watched

Archer gently pick up Freya's limp body. Ryker froze when the sharp edge of a sword pressed against his neck.

"Wait!"

Laia appeared in view, her face stricken as she took in Freya's lifeless form held tight in Archer's arms. Her eyes met Ryker's, brimming with tears. A flicker of compassion passed across her face so fast he was sure he'd imagined it.

"Who is this man?" asked the soldier holding him.

"He's, umm..." Laia's voice fumbled, trembling as she held back her sorrow. She stood taller, her face firm as she spoke again. "He's a friend."

Friend? The word shattered his heart. Ryker lowered his eyes as the sword dropped from his throat. He was not worthy of that title—not worthy of Freya's forgiveness.

But Laia persisted. "Yes, he's a friend. Bring him outside." She turned and led the way up the rocky slope with Archer beside her. The soldier behind Ryker still gripped his arm, pulling him along behind Laia. He blinked back the full brightness of the sun when he stepped outside, struck by the aftermath of the battle. The valley was littered with the bodies of Imperial, Gallerion, and Faulkern soldiers. All the catapults were burned to ash, but the damage was done. Though the cracks and holes in the wall were small, the Empire had blasted through the gates and taken Blackstone. Now, they were holed up inside while Galleria and Faulkern stationed themselves in the valley. With Freya's quick decision to seal off the tunnels, there would be no way for the Empire to sneak out.

Ryker flinched when the grip on his arm tightened, but he didn't resist as the troops parted before Laia. A tent was raised, where a protective ring of soldiers formed around it. They allowed Laia through, and Ryker was soon inside the tent. Six figures stood around a center table: five men and a woman, who watched them enter. Ryker guessed from their darker skin that three of them were from Faulkern. The woman was a general, and the two men were the spitting image of each other; with their heir of authority, they must be King Therrowin and his son, Prince Bastien. The other three men were Gallerions.

One of the men stepped forward when Archer laid Freya before them. He had dark hair peppered with gray. His blue eyes, brimming with tears, matched Freya's. A younger man, with the same copper hair as hers, fell to his knees beside her. Tears trailed down King Alystaire's face while Prince Damian wept openly, kneeling beside his sister's body.

King Alystaire's eyes found Ryker's across the room. "Who is this?" Despite the tears, his voice was powerful.

Laia opened her mouth to answer, but he spoke first. "My name is Ryker Kessler."

Immediate recognition entered the king's eyes, and they narrowed as he took him in.

"I—" He started to explain himself, but the king raised a hand, cutting him off.

"You cared about her." It wasn't a question. His words silenced everything Ryker had been prepared to say. Looking down at Freya's pale face, Ryker considered what the king said. He'd not known her long; in fact, he'd spent a good portion of the time hating her.

Friend. It was the word Laia had used earlier, and it hit him anew. He supposed he had grown to care about Freya in that sense. He hadn't been looking for it—hadn't asked for it—but after all the time they'd spent together, it had happened. He'd admired her strength and leadership. She had offered him comfort, kindness, and mercy despite every right to do otherwise. He'd found a friend in the most unlikely of people, yet had been unable to save her, unable to save any of the people he'd cared about in his life. Despair welled up inside him, making his eyes burn as he fought back tears.

He'd lost everyone. Sorrow bubbled with rage as he pictured the way General Moreland had stood on top of Freya. He heard the general's words ring in his ear as he sentenced his brother to death. General Moreland had told Ryker to fight.

Well, Ryker would.

"So, you will help us then?" The question pulled Ryker's gaze back to King Alystaire, who had been watching the emotions play across his face. His blue eyes pierced Ryker, and with the strength of a chosen king, he commanded, "Help us defeat the people who killed my daughter."

ACKNOWLEDGMENTS

This book started as one of those rare dreams I actually remembered when I woke up thirteen years ago. It was a story that persisted in my heart even when I tried to push it away. Now, I am so glad that I dove in and pursued this story, and I could never have completed it without the help of so many wonderful people!

First I want to bring appreciation to the One to bring me inspiration and give me the gift of storytelling. The ultimate Creator and Creative whom I could only hope but replicate. My Savior and King forevermore.

I have to thank my entire family that supported me through the whole journey. Thank you to my parents for believing in me and supporting this crazy dream of mine. To my brother, Justin, for being a creative bouncing board of ideas and willing to listen to me rant when the story wasn't coming together as I thought it would. Huge thanks to my sisters, Sarah and Rachel for their willingness to be first, second, and third readers, to offer their critiques and suggestions turning the story into what it is today. And a final thanks to my younger brother, Chris, for also pursuing a daring dream that encouraged me to go after mine no matter what.

Thank you Eden Northover, my amazing editor for the hours listening and editing, and all the encouragement. For helping through the whole process, and helping me see my obsessive use of commas. Thank you to my cover artist, Paul at trif book design for his ability to create an amazing cover when

I couldn't even visualize it. Rik Similä at Kellerika Maps for the gorgeous map work of Eavdamos.

I also want to thank those that listened with excitement to all my writer/author talks. Emily, Selinam, and Rebecca for their constant words of encouragement and excitement during this whole journey.

Finally, I must thank you, the readers for picking up this book. For joining me and these characters on this crazy adventure to this new world.

ABOUT THE AUTHOR

Brooke Lesniak was raised in Richmond Virginia in a boisterous family of five. When she graduated high school, she decided to explore the world. By twenty-five she traveled to five different countries, falling in love with the beautiful rocky shores of New Zealand and the vast deserts of Niger. Combined with her love for storytelling she decided to create her own worlds and settled back into her hometown to start working on Division.